J

THE FAMILY WHO MADE HIM WHOLE

BY
JENNIFER TAYLOR

D1418986

MILLS &
BOON

For Max, my gorgeous little grandson.
The best Christmas present I've ever had.

First published in Great Britain 2012
by Mills & Boon, an imprint of Harlequin (UK) Limited.
Harlequin (UK) Limited, Eton House, 18-24 Paradise Road,
Richmond, Surrey TW9 1SR

© Jennifer Taylor 2012

ISBN: 978 0 263 89201 7

Harlequin (UK) policy is to use papers that are natural, renewable and recyclable products and made from wood grown in sustainable forests. The logging and manufacturing process conform to the legal environmental regulations of the country of origin.

Printed and bound in Spain
by Blackprint CPI, Barcelona

Dear Reader

Single mums seem to get a lot of bad press these days, yet in my experience they do a fantastic job of raising their children under very difficult circumstances. My own mother became a single parent after my father died, and I know how hard she worked to give me a happy home life. My latest trilogy, *Bride's Bay Surgery*, focuses on three single mums, Hannah, Emily and Becky, who are committed to do their very best for their children.

In the first book of the series Hannah is determined that she will do all she can for her little boy. She doesn't have time for a relationship, so when she meets Tom Bradbury she is determined to keep him at arm's length. Tom is equally determined not to get involved. His family has a poor track record when it comes to love and marriage, so he has made up his mind to remain single. However, that was before he met Hannah. Meeting her makes him reassess his whole attitude to life!

I hope you enjoy reading Tom and Hannah's story as much as I enjoyed writing it. If you would like to contact me then please e-mail me at the following address: Jennifertaylor01@aol.com I would love to hear from you.

Best wishes

Jennifer

CHAPTER ONE

'AND this is my godson, Tom Bradbury. Tom has very kindly been helping out until you arrived. Tom, this is Hannah Morris, my new colleague. I'm sure you must be almost as delighted to see her as I am!'

'Nice to meet you, Dr Bradbury.' Hannah pinned a polite smile to her lips when the younger man laughed. She wasn't going to be drawn into asking why he should be so pleased to see her because she wasn't interested. She'd had her fair share of tall, dark, handsome men and intended to steer well clear of anyone who fitted that description in the future.

'It's good to meet you too, Hannah. But, please, forget the title and call me Tom.' He held out his hand, leaving her with no option other than to take it.

Hannah felt a quiver of awareness run through her when their palms touched and tensed. She didn't want to feel anything for this man, yet there was no denying the surge of electricity that was racing along her veins. It was a relief when he released her and turned to Simon Harper, the senior partner in the practice.

'We don't stand on ceremony around here, do we, Simon?'

'Certainly not.' Simon smiled at her. 'Most of our

patients call us by our first names, so I hope that won't bother you, my dear. The days when the local GP was considered only second to God in the pecking order are long gone, I'm pleased to say.'

'Of course not.' Hannah summoned another smile although she had to admit that the idea of being on such familiar terms with her patients would take some getting used to. She had always preferred to maintain a professional distance and hadn't encouraged that kind of familiarity, but if that was the way things were done at Bride's Bay Surgery then she would have to get used to it.

'I'd stop right there if I were you, Simon. You don't want to scare her off!'

Hannah stiffened when Tom Bradbury laughed again. He really did have the most attractive laugh, she thought, the richly mellow tones making goose-bumps break out all over her body. She cleared her throat, refusing to dwell on the reason why it'd had such a strange effect on her. 'There's no danger of that. Although, admittedly, I'm more used to my patients calling me Dr Morris, I'm sure I shall adapt.'

'That's the spirit.' Simon gave her an approving smile. 'I knew I was right to pick you for this post, Hannah. You're going to fit in *perfectly* around here.'

Hannah murmured something although she couldn't deny that Simon's unwitting choice of words had touched a nerve. She had always tried to be perfect in everything she did. Right from the time she had been a child, lining up her dolls in perfectly straight rows, she'd had a compulsion to make her life as flawless as possible. She knew what it stemmed from, of course. When she was seven her father had been involved in a serious road accident. She could still remember the horror of wondering if he would survive. The only way she'd been able to cope was by making everything else in her life as perfect as possible. To her mind, if everything was in its proper order then things would turn out right.

Thankfully, her father had recovered; however, the need for order had remained with her as she'd grown up. When she'd met Andrew, and discovered that he had felt the same, it had seemed as though they had been meant to be together. They could each strive for perfection, knowing the other would understand. It was only in this last year that she had realised what a terrible mistake she had made.

'Hannah?'

Someone touched her on the arm and she jumped, feeling the colour rush to her cheeks when she found Tom Bradbury staring down at her. At over six feet in height he was a lot taller than her and she was suddenly struck by the difference in their stature. He looked so big and solid as he stood there with a frown drawing his black brows together that she had the craziest urge to lean on him. The past twelve months had been hard and it would be wonderful if someone could take the burden off her for a little while…

'Are you all right?' He stepped closer, his blue eyes filled with concern as he peered into her face, and Hannah realised with a start that she had to pull herself together. Tom Bradbury wouldn't be interested in her problems, neither did she want him to be.

'I'm fine, thank you.' She looked around the room. 'Where's Simon?'

'He's gone through to the house to make some coffee, or, hopefully, he's gone to ask Ros to make it for us.' Tom smiled and she was relieved to see that his face held nothing more than the sort of polite interest one showed to a stranger. 'A word of advice here from one who knows: if Simon offers to make you a cup of coffee, refuse. His coffee is enough to make strong men weep!'

An unwilling smile curved Hannah's mouth. 'It can't be that bad, surely?'

'Oh, it is. Trust me.' Tom chuckled. 'Simon may be a brilliant doctor, adored by all his patients, but his coffee is in a league of its own. If you value your health then make sure you get to the kettle before him!'

His blue eyes held hers fast for a moment before he turned and headed towards the door and it was only then that Hannah realised she had stopped breathing. She took a quick breath and then a second for good measure before she followed him. It was the newness of it all, she assured herself as he led the way along the corridor towards the house. The fact that this was her first day in a new job, the first day of her new life, in fact. She was bound to feel on edge and keyed up....

He pushed open a door, waiting politely for her to precede him, and Hannah sucked in her breath when her shoulder brushed his chest as she passed. Maybe it was understandable that she should feel nervous when she had needed to make so many changes to her life of late, but did that really explain why her blood pressure had shot up several degrees and her pulse was racing?

She sighed as she stepped into an attractive country-style kitchen because she knew what the answer was even if she didn't like it. The reason her heart was racing and her blood pressure was soaring was standing right behind her. Tom Bradbury was to blame. He and he alone had made her feel all those things. Admittedly, it was a surprise to find herself responding this way, but she mustn't let it throw her. Maybe she *did* find him attractive but that was all it was—pure physical attraction, nothing more. After all, she had just escaped from one disastrous relationship and she certainly didn't intend to find herself caught up in another one!

Tom took the cup of coffee Ros offered him and walked over to the window. It was the middle of May and the sun was glinting off the sea. It was the kind of glorious Devon day that always made him glad to be alive but for some reason he was less aware of his surroundings at that moment than he was of the woman behind him.

He took a sip of his coffee and turned, letting his gaze rest on the figure seated at the table. Hannah Morris was pretty in a restrained kind of way with that pale, fine skin and that rich auburn hair that fell softly to her shoulders. Her eyes were green, a deep sea green— he'd noticed that before—framed by thick black lashes that he would swear hadn't been enhanced by even a trace of mascara. In fact, now that he thought about it, she was wearing very little make-up, just a touch of gloss on her lips and maybe, although he couldn't be sure, a hint of blusher on her cheeks.

Tom took a larger swallow of his coffee, somewhat surprised that he had taken such an interest in Simon's new colleague. Although his godfather had told him about Hannah Morris when he had decided to offer her the job, Tom was aware that he hadn't really been listening. All he could recall was that she was thirty-one years old and had worked at a large practice on the outskirts of London for the past few years. What else Simon had divulged had gone in one ear and out of the other and all of a sudden he wished that he'd paid more attention. There was something about Dr Morris that intrigued him, and it wasn't just the fact that it had been a long time since he'd reacted *that* strongly when he had touched a woman's hand!

The thought caused him more than a little discomfort so it was a relief when Ros appeared at his side. 'Penny for them.' She smiled up at him, her face breaking into the warmly caring smile that had made Tom wish on more than one occasion when he'd been growing up that she had been his mother instead of the more glamorous Tessa.

'I'm not sure they're worth a penny even with the current rate of inflation,' he observed dryly, then changed the subject. 'Glad to see you got to the coffee pot before Simon.'

'Oh, no fear of that. I had the coffee on the go by the time he appeared.' Ros laughed but he could tell that she wasn't fooled by his airy dismissal of her question. Ros knew him far too well, a fact he must bear in mind when his thoughts were tempted to wander again.

As though unable to resist, his gaze moved back to Hannah and he felt a shudder run through him when he discovered that she was watching him. Just for a moment their eyes met before she looked away but it was long enough. Tom took another gulp of coffee, hoping it would quell the tremor that had been triggered inside him, but no such luck. He could feel it working its way down his body and inwardly groaned.

He didn't do this kind of thing! He didn't respond so instantly to a woman, certainly never felt as though he had suddenly found himself with one foot on an emotional roller-coaster that was about to speed off. He liked women, enjoyed their company, but the key word in that statement was *women*.

He liked them in the plural. When he dated he always made it clear that he was happy for his date to see other men, as he would be seeing other women. However, he knew without the shadow of a doubt that Hannah Morris wasn't a plural type of woman. She would expect any man she dated to be strictly faithful and if there was one thing he couldn't guarantee it was that kind of commitment.

'So what do you think of Simon's new protégé?'

Tom dragged his thoughts back into line as he turned to Ros, although he had to admit that he was more than a little stunned by the way he was behaving. He had known Hannah Morris for less than ten minutes and yet here he was, pondering the weighty matter of his own shortcomings. 'She seems very nice.'

'Nice!' Ros hooted. 'Is that the best you can come up with, Tom? She's *nice*?'

'Well, I've hardly had a chance to get to know her,' he countered, a shade defensively.

'Maybe not, but it's not like you to be so slow.' Ros's eyes were filled with laughter as she looked at him. 'Usually, you have a woman summed up and categorised in less time than this.'

'Categorised? I'm not sure I know what you mean,' he said stiffly.

'Oh, come on! Of course you do. I've watched you growing up, don't forget. I've seen the effect you have on the female half of the population and watched you in action, too.' Ross chuckled. 'I'm not sure if you use some sort of scoring system but women seem to fall into one of two categories where you're concerned. They're either fair game or strictly off limits. What I can't work out is which category Hannah comes into.'

'So what are you two muttering about?' Simon came over to refill his cup and smiled at them. 'You look as though you're plotting some sort of mischief.'

'Mischief?' Ros took the cup off him. 'It's a long time since I could be accused of causing any mischief!'

Tom moved away while Ros topped up her husband's cup, relieved to have been let off the hook. He frowned as he turned to stare out of the window again. Was Ros right? Did he view women in such a calculating way? He hated to think that he did, yet he knew in his heart it was true.

Since his first—and only!—ill-fated foray into love, he had been determined not to leave behind a trail of destruction like his parents had done. Although he enjoyed dating, definitely enjoyed sex, he didn't do the rest and he never would. There would be no happily-ever-after for him. No wife and family gathered around the hearth waiting for his return. He preferred his life to be free of such complications and that way nobody would get hurt, neither him nor some poor unsuspecting woman who'd had the misfortune to fall in love with him.

He glanced round when someone laughed, felt the hair on the back of his neck lift when he realised it was Hannah. In that second he knew that although he may have managed to avoid commitment in the past, he might find it harder to do so in the future. There was just something about Hannah Morris that drew him, something he could neither explain nor reason away. He could only thank his lucky stars that he was leaving. By this time next week, he would be on his way to Paris and he would make sure it was a long time before he came back!

Hannah spooned a little more sugar into her cup as she listened to the affectionate banter between Simon and his wife. It was obvious how fond they were of each other and she couldn't prevent the sudden pang of envy that rose up inside her. She had hoped that she and Andrew would have that kind of a relationship, but it hadn't happened. There had always been a certain distance between them even though they had appeared to have had so much in common. It was funny how you could think you knew someone and be proved so wrong.

'More coffee, my dear?'

Simon reached across the table for her cup but she shook her head. 'No, thank you.' She turned and smiled at Ros. 'It was delicious but I'll be buzzing if I have any more.'

'I know what you mean.' Ros smiled back. A pretty woman in her fifties with light brown hair that curled around her face, she exuded an air of calm that was very soothing. 'I have to limit myself to no more than three cups a day otherwise I'm high as a kite on all the caffeine!'

Hannah laughed when Ros pulled a rueful face. She glanced round when a movement caught her eye and felt herself tense when she realised that Tom Bradbury was watching her again. It had happened several times now; she had glanced up and found him staring at her and she wasn't sure what to make of it. Was it just the fact that she was new or was there something more behind his interest?

She hurriedly dismissed the thought, refusing to go down that route. She wasn't looking for romance. She just wanted to be left alone to create a new life for herself and her son. Charlie was all that mattered, his happiness was her main concern. Everything else was inconsequential.

'Simon told me that you have a little boy, Hannah. What's his name and how old is he?'

Hannah roused herself when Ros spoke. 'His name's Charlie and he's nine months old.'

'And into everything, I bet!' Ros laughed as she turned to her husband. 'Remember when our two were that age? You needed eyes in the back of your head. They're twins and that made it worse, of course, but I wouldn't have believed the havoc they could cause if I hadn't seen it for myself.'

Hannah smiled, trying not to let Ros see that the remark had hit a nerve. Sadly, Charlie couldn't get up to very much mischief. He had been born with talipes— club feet—and at the moment his legs were encased in casts, which severely restricted his movement. Although he was a happy, intelligent little boy, he wasn't able to do a lot of the things a child his age normally did. Still, she consoled herself, once the casts came off the situation should improve, and if they hadn't worked there was a good chance that a second operation would solve the problem.

'Do your children still live in Bride's Bay?' she asked, changing the subject because the thought of her son needing further surgery made her feel a little panicky.

'I wish!' Ros sighed. 'Daniel is a research botanist. He's in Borneo at the moment, tracking down a plant which the locals claim has healing powers. And Becky moved to New Zealand with her husband a couple of years ago. She's just had a baby, a little girl called Millie, and as you can imagine we're dying to see her.'

'We'll get over there as soon as we can,' Simon assured her, patting her hand.

'I know, darling, but I don't want to wait, that's the problem. Babies grow so quickly and I just feel that we're missing out on so much...' Ros stopped and gasped. 'Why didn't I think of it before! I mean, this would be the ideal time, wouldn't it? Tom knows the ins and outs of running the practice almost as well as you do, and now that Hannah is here, we're fully staffed.'

She turned beseechingly to Hannah. 'If you and Tom would hold the fort, it means that Simon and I can go and visit our first grandchild!'

CHAPTER TWO

'PLEASE take a seat, Mrs Granger.'

Hannah waited while the woman made herself comfortable. It was almost lunchtime and Barbara Granger was her last patient. The morning had been surprisingly busy. She'd not had a minute to herself, in fact, and suddenly found herself wondering if she should have accepted Tom Bradbury's offer to split her list. It would have made far more sense to ease herself in gently, yet she'd felt strangely reluctant to accept his help. Something had warned her that once she did, it might be difficult to stop.

The thought was so ridiculous that she was hard pressed not to show her disgust. Tom Bradbury meant nothing to her. He was just someone she would be working with for a short while, although, if Ros had her way, it might be longer than either of them had anticipated. The idea was disquieting and she had to make a conscious effort not to dwell on it as she smiled at the woman seated across the desk.

'I'm Hannah Morris, the new doctor.'

'Nice to meet you, dear.' Barbara Granger smiled back. 'I'm sure you'll be very happy here. Bride's Bay is such a lovely little town—everyone is very friendly, as you'll soon discover. Margery worked here for over ten years and we were all very sorry when she decided to leave.'

'I'm sure she will be missed,' Hannah agreed. Every patient she had seen had commented on how sad they'd been when Simon's previous partner had left. It had made her realise what an integral part of the town the practice was. After working in London, where patients rarely formed a close attachment to their doctor, it was good to know that she was now a valued part of the community.

'Yes, she will. But folk have to do what's best for them, don't they.' Barbara settled her handbag on her knees. 'I know how much Margery missed her family. Her two sisters live in Edinburgh and it will be lovely for her to be able to spend more time with them.'

'It will indeed. Now, what was it you wanted to see me about, Mrs Granger?' Hannah gently steered the conversation back to the reason for the visit. 'Is something worrying you?'

'Yes, although it's not about me. It's my Peter, you see. He's going into hospital soon and he's in a right state about it.'

'Is Peter your husband?' Hannah asked gently, wondering about the ethics of discussing the matter. Patient confidentiality was a key issue and she wouldn't want to cross any boundaries.

'No, my son.' Barbara sighed. 'Peter has Down's syndrome. I should have explained that to you before I began.'

'It's quite all right,' Hannah assured her. 'I take it that you are his main carer?'

'I was until last year when he got a place in an assisted living facility in the centre of town.' Barbara pulled a face. 'Such a horrible name. Calling it a facility makes it sound like some sort of institution but it's nothing like that. The local council converted one of the houses near the post office so it could be used by people with disabilities like my Peter's, and it's very homely. He loves it there.'

'That sounds like a wonderful idea,' Hannah said enthusiastically. 'Your son has his independence, yet there are people around who can offer support if he needs it.'

'Exactly. Oh, I wasn't sure if he should go when Simon first suggested it. His dad left soon after Peter was born. He couldn't handle the thought of having a handicapped child, you see, so I've looked after Peter by myself. It's always been just the two of us and I was worried in case it was too much for him, but he's come on in leaps and bounds, as it turns out.'

'You must be so relieved,' Hannah agreed quietly. As the single mother of a child who needed extra care, she understood how difficult it must have been for Barbara. Maybe it was different when both parents were involved; at least they could discuss any issues and reach a decision together. However, it was much harder when you were solely responsible for your child's welfare, as she'd discovered.

She knew how she'd agonised over Charlie's treatment, spending many a sleepless night worrying about what it entailed. It would have helped enormously if she'd had someone to talk it over with but, like Barbara Granger, she'd been on her own. It must have taken a lot of courage to allow her son to leave home, Hannah thought admiringly as she smiled at her.

'So why is Peter going into hospital?'

'He needs an operation on one of the valves in his heart. As I'm sure you know, dear, a lot of people with Down's have heart problems, so it isn't the first time Peter has needed treatment. It was fine while he was a child—I was able to stay in the hospital with him. But now he's nineteen and classed as an adult that isn't possible. He's getting very anxious about it, which is why I thought I'd have a word with you.'

Hannah frowned. 'I understand your concerns, Mrs Granger, although I'm not sure what I can do to help. Can you leave it with me? I'll speak to Simon and see what he suggests.'

'Of course.' Barbara stood up. 'Just give me a call when you've worked something out or, better still, pop in for a coffee if you're passing. I live right next door to the nursery and you can always call in after you've dropped off your little boy. Lovely little chap. Let's hope they can sort out that problem with his feet, eh?'

Barbara bade her a cheery goodbye, obviously finding nothing unusual about the fact that she knew so much about Hannah's private life. Hannah shook her head as she gathered up the notes she had used. She had been in the town for just two days and already it seemed that everyone knew all about her!

'Was that Barbara Granger I saw leaving?'

Hannah jumped when a deep voice addressed her from the doorway. She looked up, trying to quell the racing of her heart when she saw Tom standing there. He had shed his jacket and rolled up the sleeves of his pale blue shirt so that his tanned forearms were bare. He looked so big and overwhelmingly male that her mouth went dry. She may not be in the market for another relationship but she would need to be dead from the neck up *and* down not to be aware of him! It was only when she saw one dark brow lift that she realised he was waiting for her to answer.

'It was. Apparently, her son is going into hospital soon and he's getting very stressed about it,' she said, shuffling the notes into a pile.

'Something to do with Peter's heart, I take it?' Tom came into the room and stopped beside the desk. Hannah continued her shuffling, although for some reason her normally deft fingers seemed to have all turned to thumbs.

'Mmm. He needs an operation to repair one of the valves.' The pile of notes suddenly disintegrated into an untidy heap and she clamped her lips together in annoyance. Picking up the top few folders, she tried again then jumped when a large hand appeared in front of her.

'Here, give me half and I'll help you carry them through to the office.'

Tom didn't wait for her to comply with his offer as he scooped up half of the buff envelopes and Hannah had to bite down even harder to stem the retort that was trying to escape. She didn't need his help, but short of making a scene there was little she could do.

She trailed after him, aware that she was in danger of making a mountain out of the proverbial molehill. Tom was just trying to be helpful and it was stupid to see it as a threat. She knew it was true yet it was difficult to accept it. She really didn't want to be beholden to him for anything.

He plonked the notes into a tray then stood aside while she deposited hers on top. 'Lizzie will sort them out when she gets back from lunch,' he assured her, resting one lean hip against the edge of the desk.

'It might help if I put them into some kind of order,' Hannah murmured, taking a couple of folders off the pile.

'There's no need. Lizzie is a whiz with the filing. She'll have them sorted in no time.' He took the folders off her and dropped them back into the tray, leaving her gasping at his high-handedness. However, he seemed oblivious as he returned the conversation to what they had been discussing.

'Peter is a lovely fellow. Although he has Down's, he's quite a high achiever. He works at The Ship Inn, collecting the empty glasses and, occasionally, waiting on in the dining room if it's busy.'

'Really!' Hannah exclaimed in surprise.

'Yes. That's the joy of a place like Bride's Bay. Folk look out for one another and do all they can to help. Mitch Johnson, who runs the pub, took Peter on last winter and it's worked out really well for everyone.'

'That's wonderful. I had no idea people were so supportive. Where I worked before, there were plans to build a unit for people with disabilities like Peter's but the local residents objected and it didn't go ahead.'

'Sadly, that happens all too often. I'd put it down to ignorance if I didn't have a nasty suspicion that it was more a fear of it having an impact on property prices than anything else.' Tom shrugged when she looked at him. 'If you live next to one of those units, you could find that the value of your home drops.'

'I'm sure you're right.' Hannah was surprised by how disgusted he sounded. She wouldn't have summed him up as someone with strong altruistic leanings, although why she should have made that assumption it was impossible to say. She hurried on, not wanting to dwell on the thought that she might have been unfair to him. 'Anyway, I was going to have a word with Simon to see what he could suggest. It sounds as though Peter needs some reassurance.'

'The hospital has just instigated a scheme whereby vulnerable adults are given a tour of the areas they'll be using during their stay.' Tom straightened and went over to the filing cabinet. 'They sent us a leaflet only last week if I can find it… Ah! Here it is.'

He handed her the leaflet and Hannah sucked in her breath when their hands brushed. She murmured her thanks as she took it over to the window to read, although for a few seconds the words seemed to dance before her eyes. She had to stop this nonsense, had to stop reacting whenever Tom touched her. It was ridiculous to be this responsive to a man she barely knew.

The thought steadied her. She skimmed through the leaflet and nodded. 'This sounds ideal. I'm sure Peter will feel a lot happier if he knows exactly where he's going.'

'Precisely.' Tom followed her across the room, bending so that he could point out a paragraph that was particularly relevant. 'They will even introduce him to the members of staff who'll be looking after him. That's probably more important than anything else. If Peter knows the nurses and doctors, etcetera, he'll be less likely to worry.'

'I'm sure you're right,' Hannah agreed tersely, anxious to put a little distance between them. She went to step back then realised that Tom had beaten her to it and already moved away. He smiled at her but she couldn't fail to see the wariness in his eyes.

'If I were you, I'd give them a call right away, Hannah. The sooner you get it organised the better.'

'Of course,' she murmured, wondering why he appeared so on edge. He'd probably realised that he'd been crowding her, she decided, impinging on her personal space. However, logical though it sounded, she wasn't convinced it was the answer and it bothered her. 'I'll do it now, so long as you don't think Simon will mind.'

'Of course he won't mind. He's gone out on a call but, believe me, he would never have taken you on if he didn't have faith in your judgement.'

'That's good to know.'

Hannah headed for the door, relieved to make her escape. Being around Tom seemed to confuse her for some reason and she didn't appreciate feeling this way. She liked order in her life, not uncertainty, although she was trying not to be as rigid in her outlook as she'd used to be. As she had discovered when she'd been expecting Charlie, not everything went according to plan.

The thought still had the power to hurt. She couldn't help feeling guilty about the way she had tried so hard to structure every aspect of her life. If *she'd* been more flexible then Andrew might not have been so uncompromising too, she thought for the umpteenth time, then sighed when she realised how unlikely that was.

'So how do you feel about us holding the fort while Simon and Ros visit their daughter?'

'I suppose it would make sense,' Hannah said, pausing reluctantly.

'But?' He gave a short laugh. 'There was a definite "but" in there if I'm not mistaken.'

'Was there?' He was far too astute, she realised with a sinking heart. She summoned a smile, keen to convince him that she wasn't the least bit worried by the thought of them working together. 'I suppose I'm a little concerned at the thought of being so new to the practice. It takes a while to find your feet and I wouldn't like to make any major blunders.'

'I'm sure you're far too professional to commit any blunders.'

He returned her smile but once again she could see the wariness in his eyes. It struck her all of a sudden that if she had a problem with Tom then he had a problem with her too. The thought was unsettling because she didn't want there to be *any* issues between them, nothing to make either of them more aware of the other, and she hurried on. 'Let's hope so. Anyway, what about you? Would you be able to delay taking up your new job?'

'Yes, I expect so.' He shrugged. 'Benedict—he's the director of the clinic I'm going to work at—is a friend from way back. I'm sure he would agree to let me start a few weeks later if I explained the situation to him.'

'In that case, there doesn't appear to be a problem.' She gave a light laugh, determined to nip things in the bud. Maybe she *did* find him attractive but so what? She was a grown woman, a mother as well, and she wasn't going to allow herself to get carried away! 'If Ros and Simon do decide to go, I'm sure we'll cope.'

'I'm sure we will too,' Tom murmured. He glanced round when the phone rang, hating the fact that he felt so relieved to be interrupted. He knew it was ridiculous to be so aware of her, but he couldn't seem to stop. Even learning that she was a mother—a definite no-no in his book—hadn't dampened his interest. As soon as he was near her, common sense flew right out of the window.

It was a worrying thought and Tom knew that he

needed to take it on board. Normally, he was the one who called the shots, the one who was always in control, but not this time, it seemed. He needed to get himself back on track and there was no time like the present. He smiled coolly at her, hoping that she couldn't tell how on edge he felt. 'I'd better get that.'

'Of course.'

She didn't say anything else before she left the room so there was no basis for thinking that she was as relieved as he was to put an end to the conversation. Tom lifted the receiver to his ear and listened while the caller explained that the dog had eaten his prescription. It was the sort of anecdote he normally relished, but he found it difficult to concentrate that day. Was Hannah as confused by her feelings as he was by his?

'Are you still there, Doctor?'

'I...um...yes.'

Tom dragged his mind back to the missing prescription and told the caller to come into the surgery and collect another one. He printed it out and left it in the tray then headed out to the corridor. He had to stop thinking about Hannah all the time. If it did turn out that they would be working together for longer than expected then he needed to put things into perspective. It shouldn't be difficult. He just had to remember that he was incapable of being faithful to *any* woman. He was genetically programmed to play the field like generations of his family had done before him. So long as he remembered that, everything would be fine, but if he ever imagined that he could break the cycle...

He cut off that thought. He couldn't change who he was, couldn't erase his heritage, the bad bits or the good. He had tried to do so once before and had failed miserably, and he certainly wasn't going to try it again. No matter how tempted he was, he wouldn't get involved with Hannah, especially when there was a child on the scene.

Children needed stability more than anything else. They needed people who would stay around while they were growing up and he couldn't promise to do that. Oh, he might *think* he could but, if push came to shove, would he? Could he? Or would the family genes rise to the fore and he'd turn out exactly like the rest of them— incapable of making a commitment and sticking to it?

Tom squared his shoulders. It was a risk he wasn't prepared to take. No matter how attracted he was to Hannah, she was off limits.

CHAPTER THREE

I<small>T WAS</small> just gone six when Hannah arrived at the nursery to collect Charlie. Simon had insisted that she and Tom should split her evening list, which meant she had managed to get away earlier than expected. Now, as she rang the bell, she found herself wondering why she had been so reluctant to let Tom help her. After all, the world hadn't come to an end because he had seen some patients for her!

'Oh, hi, Hannah. Come on in. Charlie's in the playroom—we can't get him out of the sand tray. He loves it!'

Lucy Burrows, one of the nursery nurses, laughed as she opened the door. Hannah briskly dismissed the thought that she had overreacted as she followed Lucy inside. The sooner she accepted that Tom was just someone she worked with the better. Now, as she paused in the doorway and watched Charlie giggling happily, she was overwhelmed with relief.

Taking Charlie away from everything he knew had been a gamble. Children thrived on stability and she'd been afraid that the move would unsettle him, but so far everything seemed to be working out surprisingly well. He seemed to have settled into the tiny cottage she had rented down by the harbour and he seemed equally happy here at the nursery. After what they had been through in the past year, it was hard to believe that their lives might be changing for the better. If only Andrew had stuck around, surely he would have realised that having a child with talipes wasn't the disaster he imagined?

Hannah's mouth compressed as she went over to her son. The likelihood of her ex altering his views was zero. From the moment they had discovered during her pregnancy that there was a problem with Charlie's feet, Andrew hadn't wanted anything to do with him. He had wanted a perfect child and he had made that clear.

'Hello, darling. Are you having a lovely time?' Hannah crouched down beside the little boy. With his dark brown curls and deep blue eyes, Charlie looked a lot like Andrew. It had hurt at first to see the resemblance, but she had learned to harden her heart. It took more than shared genes to be a *real* father.

Charlie gurgled in delight when he saw her. Hannah picked him up, inhaling his lovely warm baby smell. Even though she needed to work to support them, she missed him so much whenever they were apart.

'He's been as good as gold,' Lucy told her. 'You'd think he'd been coming here for ages, not that it was his first day.'

'That's a good boy.'

Hannah gave Charlie a kiss as she hitched him more securely onto her hip. Although the casts on his legs were lightweight ones, they were still cumbersome and made carrying him rather awkward. She collected his bag and took him out to the car. Digging into her pocket, she tried to ease out the keys but, with Charlie straddling her hip, it wasn't easy. She groaned when she ended up dropping them on the ground.

'Here, let me get them for you.'

All of a sudden Tom was there and she jumped. He smiled as he picked up the bunch of keys. 'I'll get the door for you as well.'

He unlocked the car and opened the rear door, standing back while she strapped Charlie into his seat. She straightened up, forcing herself to smile when he dropped the keys into her hand. Maybe it was the shock of seeing him when she'd least expected it, but her heart was racing again.

'Thanks. You could do with an extra pair of hands when you have a baby,' she said, lightly.

'So I can see.' He smiled back, his deep blue eyes crinkling attractively at the corners. With his tanned skin and athletic build, not to mention that air of confidence he exuded, he must have women fighting to go out with him, she thought, then wondered why the idea made her feel so dejected.

'Well, I'd better get off,' she said, opening the driver's door before any more foolish thoughts could infiltrate her mind. She didn't *want* to go out with him— it was the last thing she wanted! 'Charlie will want his tea.'

'Of course.' He glanced at his watch and grimaced. 'I'd better get my skates on too. I was supposed to be at the lifeboat station for six and it's five past already.'

Hannah paused. 'Are you part of the lifeboat crew?'

'No. I'd love to be, but the fact that I spend most of my time working abroad means it isn't possible.' He shrugged. 'I'm filling in for Simon tonight. He teaches first aid to the crew. There's a couple of new guys who've just started and they need to complete the course as part of their training.'

'Oh, I see.' Hannah hesitated but there was no way she could avoid offering him a lift when she was heading that way. 'I'm going that way so why don't you hop in? It'll save you some time.'

'Oh, I wouldn't want to take you out of your way…'

'You aren't.' She summoned a smile when she realised how sharp she'd sounded. However, his reluctance to get into the car had stung. 'I'm renting a cottage down by the harbour so I'm going that way.'

'Oh! Right. Then thank you.'

He strode around the car and slid into the passenger seat. Hannah started the engine and pulled out into the traffic. Although the roads were nowhere near as busy as they were in London, she was surprised by the number of vehicles there were about.

'It's a lot busier than I expected,' she observed, easing round a car and caravan combination that was partially blocking the road.

'We're coming into the holiday season. By the middle of July, you won't be able to move in the town centre—it'll be one big traffic jam.'

'Really?' She frowned. 'I had no idea that Bride's Bay was so popular with the tourists.'

'All the towns along this stretch of coast are tourist magnets.' Tom smiled at her. 'You'll learn to live with it, as everyone does. Yes, it does get hectic at times, but the plus side is that the holidaymakers bring a lot of money into the town.'

'Which can only be a good thing,' she concluded. 'Without the extra income then people would need to move away to find work.'

'Exactly. As it is, most of the folk in Bride's Bay have lived here all their lives. That's what makes it so special.'

His tone was warm and she glanced curiously at him. 'You obviously love the town.'

'I do. I've been coming here since I was a child and I can honestly say that it's my favourite place to be.'

'So why didn't you opt to become Simon's partner?' She slowed to let an elderly couple cross the road and glanced at him. 'I'm sure he would have been delighted.'

'I like variety, which is why I prefer to take short-term contracts.'

It was a reasonable answer yet Hannah doubted it was the whole truth. If Tom loved the town so much then the logical step would be for him to settle down here. She was about to point that out when a loud bang made her jump.

'What on earth was that!' she exclaimed, drawing the car to a halt.

'A maroon. They let them off from the lifeboat station to alert the crew when there's a boat in trouble.' Tom leant forward and pointed through the windscreen. 'Look! You can see the trail of smoke it's left behind.'

Hannah leant forward to look then felt her breath catch when she realised how close they were. There was just the tiniest space separating them and it shrank even more when Tom suddenly turned and she found herself staring into his eyes. She felt a shiver run through her when she saw his eyes darken, turning from sapphire blue to midnight in the space of a heartbeat. When he bent towards her she didn't move, couldn't have done so when it felt as though she was drowning in their indigo depths…

Charlie started to cry when a second rocket exploded and the spell was broken. Hannah took a quick breath as she turned to reassure him, but her heart was racing out of control. If they hadn't been interrupted would she have let Tom kiss her? Because that was where they'd been heading.

Her heart sank as she realised that she would have done. She would have let Tom kiss her, kissed him back, and there was no point denying it. On the contrary, she needed to face the truth, admit that she was deeply attracted to him, and do something about it.

She couldn't get involved with Tom. It was far too soon after what had happened between her and Andrew. Discovering that the one person she should have been able to rely on had let her down had knocked her for six and it would be a long time before she could trust anyone again. Then there was Charlie. She intended to focus all her time and energy on making sure that everything possible was done for him. The child may have been let down by his father but he wasn't going to be let down by her too.

Hannah took a deep breath. Nothing was going to happen between her and Tom, not now. *Not ever.*

Tom could feel the heat that had been pooling in the pit of his stomach turning to ice. He couldn't believe what had happened. One minute he'd been looking through the windscreen and the next...

He swore under his breath as he reached for the door handle. He had come within a hair's breadth of kissing Hannah. That was bad enough, but the fact that he appeared to have so little self-control where she was concerned was far more worrying. He *knew* that she wasn't right for him but it hadn't stopped him. He would have kissed her and to hell with the consequences because kissing her had seemed more important than anything else. It made him see how dangerous the situation was. Hannah could turn his world upside down, if he let her.

'I'll walk from here. It's not far now and it'll be quicker than waiting for the traffic to clear.' He opened the car door, using that as an excuse not to look at her. He didn't appreciate feeling so vulnerable. He had always been in control before, of himself and his relationships, but it appeared that he was putty in her hands.

The thought of her hands being anywhere near him was too much. Tom shot out of the car, pausing briefly, as politeness dictated, to thank her. Maybe he should have simply cut and run but he needed to take charge of what was happening, be proactive rather than reactive. 'Thanks for the lift, Hannah. I appreciate it.'

'It was nothing.'

Her voice was husky and he felt the hair all over his body stand to attention. Even though he really didn't want to have to look at her, he couldn't resist. The lump of ice rapidly melted again when he saw the stunned expression on her face. In that second he knew that if he *had* kissed her, she wouldn't have stopped him!

Quite frankly, it was the last thing he needed to know. Tom slammed the door and headed off down the hill as though the hounds of hell were snapping at his heels. In a way they were, because it would be his own version of hell if he allowed the situation to gather momentum. He took a deep breath as he weaved his way through the crowd that had gathered to watch the lifeboat being launched. He was attracted to Hannah, more attracted to her than he'd been to any woman. She seemed to push all the right buttons, or maybe that should be all the *wrong* ones because he certainly didn't want to feel this way. He was happy with his lot, enjoyed his life free from complications...

Didn't he?

Tom's mouth thinned. He wasn't going down that route. He had to do what was right and for him that meant living his life unencumbered by a wife and a family. It was the only way he could guarantee that he wouldn't turn out like the rest of the Bradburys.

He didn't intend to leave behind a string of broken marriages and tawdry affairs. *He* didn't plan to break any hearts or ruin any lives. So maybe he'd thought he could buck the trend once, be the one member of his family who could make a marriage work, but he'd soon discovered he was mistaken. How long had his engagement lasted? Two months? Three? Definitely no longer. As soon as he'd realised he was losing interest, he had broken it off.

It had been a salutary lesson, however, and one he needed to remember. Attraction could and did wane. Maybe he was attracted to Hannah at this very moment, but in a week or so's time it could be a different story. It wasn't fair to Hannah to start something that was doomed to failure. It wasn't fair to him either! He didn't need this kind of pressure. He didn't need the worry of constantly wondering if he would hurt her. He wanted to get on with his life and enjoy it, and if that meant staying single then so be it.

Hannah gave Charlie his tea then knelt on the rug and played a noisy game of cars with him. Charlie loved it when they crashed into one another, laughing loudly when his red plastic fire-engine sent her little white ambulance skittering across the floor.

'You're going to be a demon driver when you grow up, my boy,' she smilingly admonished him as she retrieved both vehicles.

Charlie gurgled happily as he sent the toy fire-engine spinning across the room closely followed by the ambulance. Although the casts on his legs meant he couldn't crawl, he had developed his own technique for getting about which involved shuffling on his bottom. Hannah chuckled as she watched him make his way towards the toys.

'You're a determined little chap. I'll say that for you.' She went to help him get the ambulance, which had rolled under a chair, then paused when someone knocked on the front door. 'I won't be a second, darling,' she said, veering off to answer it. There was a young man outside wearing bright yellow oilskins and he smiled uncertainly at her.

'Are you Dr Morris?'

'Yes, that's right. What can I do for you?'

'I'm Billy Robinson, one of the lifeboat crew. Tom asked me to fetch you. We've got two casualties at the station and he needs a hand.' He looked past her and grinned when he saw Charlie. 'Tom said you had a little 'un and to bring him along. There's plenty of folk there who'll be more than happy to look after him for you.'

'In that case, of course I'll come,' Hannah agreed immediately. 'I just need to fetch my bag from the kitchen.'

She hurried back through the tiny sitting-room into the equally compact kitchen. Her medical bag was on the table and she quickly checked that she had everything she needed. When she went back, Billy was holding Charlie, who was laughing happily up at him.

'He seems to have taken to you,' Hannah observed as she shut the front door.

'Oh, I'm well used to kids,' Billy told her cheerfully. 'There's seven of us at home and I'm the oldest, so I've done my share of babysitting.'

Hannah laughed at the rueful note in his voice. He seemed a pleasant young man and she didn't have any qualms about letting him carry Charlie the short distance to the lifeboat station. The doors were open and she hurried inside, taking in the scene that met her. Tom was kneeling beside a middle-aged man, setting up a portable defibrillator, whilst two of the lifeboat's crew were performing artificial respiration on him. It was obvious they had everything under control so she hurried over to the second casualty, a woman. There was another crew member with her and Hannah knelt down beside him.

'I'm Dr...' She paused and corrected herself. 'I'm Hannah Morris. Can you give me some idea what's happened to her?'

'Nice to meet you, Hannah. I'm Jim Cairns and this here is Marilyn Baines. She and her husband were out on their yacht when the rudder broke and they ran aground on some rocks. From what I can gather, the main mast broke and hit her on the head.'

'Right.' Hannah bent over the woman. 'My name's Hannah and I'm a doctor. I need to examine you, Marilyn, if that's all right?'

'Ye...' Marilyn tried to speak but it was obvious that she was still very woozy from the blow to her head.

'Just relax.' Hannah smiled reassuringly as she set

about examining her, starting with the injury to her head. It was obviously tender because Marilyn winced when she gently probed it. 'Sorry. It's a nasty blow and you'll need a CT scan at the hospital.'

'Clive...how is he?' the woman managed to ask.

Hannah gently eased her back down when she tried to sit up. 'Dr Bradbury is with him. Let's concentrate on you for now.'

She carried on, noting down a broken left wrist and dislocated left shoulder. There could be damage to the left humerus as well but that would need to be confirmed when an X-ray was done. There was no doubt that the poor woman was in a great deal of pain so Hannah drew up 10 mg of morphine.

'I'm going to give you something for the pain, Marilyn. Have you had morphine before?'

'No,' Marilyn whispered.

'Sometimes it can make you feel a bit queasy but it's nothing to worry about.' She swabbed the woman's good arm and slid in the needle. The drug took effect almost immediately, although she waited a couple of minutes to see how Marilyn had tolerated it before she set about strapping her wrist and stabilising her shoulder ready for transfer to the hospital.

'How long before the ambulance gets here?' she asked, glancing at Jim.

'The helicopter is on its way,' a familiar voice answered from behind her.

Hannah took a deep breath before she turned, determined that she wasn't going to allow Tom to upset her equilibrium again. He's just a colleague, she reminded herself. Just someone you work with. However, as her gaze skimmed up the long legs and narrow hips before coming to rest on a firmly muscled chest, she realised with a sinking heart that Tom could never be *just* anyone.

She had tried to tell herself that it was purely physical attraction she felt, but it wasn't true. Tom appealed to her on many different levels, ranging from his innate warmth to the consideration he showed to other people. She only had to remember how concerned he'd been about Peter Granger to know that it wasn't an act either. He genuinely wanted to do his best for people, wanted to help them, and that was very appealing.

It was also in marked contrast to Andrew's attitude. Her ex had always put himself and his needs first, as she knew to her cost. However, she sensed that Tom didn't do that, that, despite his playboy lifestyle, he cared about other people. It all added up to one seriously attractive package and the thought scared her.

She might not like the idea, certainly hadn't wished for it to happen, but she had a feeling that Tom was about to take on a far more important role in her life than that of colleague.

CHAPTER FOUR

'IT WILL be faster if the transfer is made by helicopter.' Tom fixed a smile to his mouth. He had made his decision to keep Hannah at arm's length and he intended to stick to it. He blanked out the thought that the length of his arm wasn't *that* far and carried on. 'It'll cut almost half an hour off the journey time.'

'I see.'

Hannah stood up, making it clear that she wanted to speak to him in private, and he reluctantly followed her. He made a rapid calculation, stopping when he judged himself to be just beyond touching range. There was no point taking *any* chances.

'How bad is he?' she asked, glancing over to where one of the crew was keeping watch over his patient.

'Not good. He's had an infarc—a bad one too— and he needs to be in the coronary care unit ASAP. Although we managed to get his heart started again, there's definite signs of arrhythmia.'

'As you say, he needs urgent treatment.'

'He does. How about your patient?' Tom kept his tone light but even then he feared it wasn't anywhere near as bland as Hannah's as she outlined the woman's injuries. Was she merely better at hiding her feelings or was the explanation far more simple? Had he made a mistake about her being interested in him?

The thought should have reassured him. It didn't. In fact, it felt like a kick in the guts to wonder if he had misinterpreted her response to that near-miss kiss. He'd thought that she had welcomed his advances, whereas she had probably been so shocked that she hadn't resisted! The thought made him wince and he saw her look at him in concern.

'Are you all right?'

'Fine. Just my stomach rumbling.' He gave her a tight smile, cursing his own stupidity. He should be rejoicing because he'd been let off the hook, not feeling down in the dumps because she wasn't interested! 'I skipped lunch and haven't made it as far as supper.'

'Me too. Well, I did sneak a piece of toast off Charlie's plate so I've fared a little better than you.'

She smiled back and this time Tom could see a hint of something in her eyes. What it was he had no idea and didn't investigate. However, his spirits rose a fraction and he grinned at her.

'We're a right pair, aren't we?'

'I…um… If you say so.'

Thankfully, the roar of an engine announced the arrival of the helicopter so he was spared having to reply. He went back to his patient and got him ready for the transfer. Hannah was doing the same, getting her patient ready to be transferred to hospital. She worked quickly and methodically, sorting everything out with the minimum of fuss. As well as being both beautiful and sexy, she was a damn fine doctor, Tom thought, and sighed. What a beguiling combination. No wonder he was having such a hard time keeping his distance.

Hannah handed over her patient, briefly reporting her findings to the crew: head injury, which would need a CT scan doing; fractured left wrist; forward dislocation to the left shoulder; and possible fracture to the left humerus. Then it was Tom's turn.

She stepped aside as he succinctly explained what had happened to Clives Baines and what treatment the man had received. His voice was as confident as ever. When it came to medical matters, he obviously knew his stuff; however, when it came to anything else, she could only speculate.

What was he like as a lover? she wondered. Would he be tender, caring and patient? Or would he be eager, greedy and determined to satisfy his own needs? Maybe he would be a mixture of both—tender and giving but also eager and demanding as he drew a response from his partner.

Hannah shivered. She didn't want to think about such things but now that she'd started it was difficult to stop. A picture of Tom, lying naked in bed, sprang into her mind, but the picture wasn't complete. There was no one lying beside him and she didn't dare fill in the gap when she knew whose face she would see. That would be a step too far, picturing herself lying beside him.

'Right. That's all sorted. Do you want to take Charlie outside so he can watch the helicopter taking off?'

All of a sudden Tom was standing beside her and she hurriedly applied a mental eraser to the images in her head. 'Good idea. I'm sure he'll love it.'

She felt quite proud of herself when she heard how calm she sounded. If she could maintain this kind of balance then everything would be fine, she assured herself as she went to collect her son, who was playing a noisy game of pat-a-cake with Billy. Maybe she was attracted to Tom but so long as she recognised the fact, she could deal with it.

'Thanks for looking after him,' she said, scooping a reluctant Charlie into her arms. 'I hope he's not been too much trouble.'

'He's been as good as gold,' Billy assured her. 'Pity about those casts on his legs. They must be a real nuisance for him.'

'They'll be coming off soon,' Hannah explained, and Billy's face brightened.

'That's good to hear. He'll have to come round to our house then and play with my little brother. He's just turned one so they're much of an age.'

Billy said goodbye and left. Hannah frowned when she heard him asking one of the other men if he fancied a pint.

'Something wrong?'

She glanced round when Tom joined her. 'Not really. I was just a bit surprised when Billy mentioned he had a little brother a few months older than Charlie.'

'His mum was more than a bit surprised when she found out she was pregnant again!' Tom laughed. 'There's a ten-year gap between the baby and the next child so it came as a bolt out of the blue.'

'It must have done,' Hannah replied, smiling as she followed him outside. The helicopter had landed in a nearby field and they were just in time to watch it taking off.

'Look,' Tom said, lifting Charlie out of her arms so he could see over the top of the crowd. 'Helicopter. Whee!'

Hannah wasn't sure how to react. Tom hadn't asked

her permission to hold Charlie yet it seemed churlish to complain when it was obvious that her son was enjoying himself. She stood silently beside them, thinking how wonderful it would have been if it had been Andrew holding him, Andrew playing the doting father; Andrew accepting him for what he was, not what he'd wanted him to be.

'That was fun, wasn't it, tiger?' Tom swung Charlie round to face him, laughing when the little boy grabbed his nose. 'Hey, that's quite a grip you've got, young man. Can I have my nose back, please?'

He gently released the baby's fingers then balanced him on his hip as he forged a way through the crowd. Hannah shrugged off the moment of introspection as she hurried after them.

'I'll take him now, thanks. He's rather heavy.'

'All the more reason for me to carry him when you've got your bag to lug home.' Tom paused and glanced at her empty hands. 'You are taking it home, I suppose?'

'Oh, er, yes, of course.' Hannah felt herself blush when she realised that she hadn't given a thought to her medical bag. Bearing in mind that it contained a variety of drugs and expensive equipment, she should have been more careful.

'We'll wait here while you fetch it,' Tom told her. 'I'll show Charlie the fishing boats. He'll love them.'

He went over to the harbour wall, leaving her hovering in a sort of no-man's land. She wanted to go after him and insist he give back her son, while on the other hand she needed to fetch her bag. In the end duty won and she hurried back inside the lifeboat station. Jim Cairns was standing guard over her case and he smiled at her.

'Here it is, Hannah. No one's touched anything.'

'Thanks, Jim. I'd forget my head if it wasn't screwed on tight.'

It was obviously the right thing to say because he laughed. Hannah had a feeling that her lapse had created a bond between them and it was something she would take on board. It didn't always need perfection to make a situation turn out right.

Tom placed Charlie on his knee as he sat down on the harbour wall. The baby seemed entranced by the scene, waving his chubby little fists as he watched the boats set off for an evening's fishing, and Tom smiled. He'd had very little to do with any children outside his work and it was fascinating to observe Charlie's reaction. Even at such a tender age, Charlie was taking everything in, his head turning this way and that as he watched the boats leave the harbour. It was growing dusk and when some of the boats turned on their lights, Charlie gave a little squeal of excitement.

Tom laughed. 'You like this, don't you, tiger?' He buzzed the top of the baby's head with a kiss, surprised by the sudden rush of longing that assailed him. He had long since ruled out the possibility having children yet all of a sudden he found himself thinking how wonderful it would be to watch his child discovering the world. There must be a special kind of magic seeing everything through a child's eyes and he couldn't help wishing that he could experience it for himself. Maybe he shouldn't rule out the possibility of him having a family at some point?

The thought was contrary to everything he had always believed. Tom pushed it aside when Hannah came to join them. He patted the wall, doing his best to behave as though nothing had happened even though it had. Could he really see himself as a father? It was the ultimate commitment, after all, and normally he would have shied away from the idea. However, he couldn't deny that for the first time ever it held a definite appeal.

'Sit yourself down while we finish watching the boats.' He summoned a smile, determined that he wasn't going to get carried away. Maybe the idea did appeal at the moment but he could very easily change his mind.

The thought should have set him back on course faster than anything else could have done but Tom found it lingering at the back of his mind as they watched the last few boats set sail. Charlie gave a little sigh, obviously worn out by all the excitement, and Tom took it as his cue that they should leave. Standing up, he swung the baby into his arms, somewhat surprised by how natural it felt to carry him.

'Shall I take him now?' Hannah suggested, but he shook his head.

'No, we're fine, aren't we, tiger?' He dropped another kiss on the baby's head and heard her sigh softly.

'Thank you.'

'What for?' he asked in surprise.

'For looking after him.' She paused then hurried on. 'For accepting him for who he is.'

Tom frowned, unsure what she meant. 'Who he is?'

'Yes. Some people see the casts and can't see past them.' She shrugged. 'They treat him differently.'

'More fool them.' He settled the little boy more comfortably in his arms, surprised by how protective he felt. 'Anyone would be proud to have a lovely little fellow like this.'

'Anyone except his father.'

Tom could hear the pain in her voice and for the first time in his life he had no idea what to say. He, Tom Bradbury, master of the glib response, the bon mot, the pithy retort, was struck dumb. Charlie's father wasn't proud to have a beautiful little boy like this?

'It's time I went home. Charlie's usually in bed by now.'

Hannah swept the child out of his arms and started up the hill, her head held high, her back rigid, and Tom's heart began to ache. Although he had no idea what had happened between her and the baby's father, it didn't take a genius to work out that whatever it was still hurt her. The thought unlocked his tongue and he hurried after her.

'At least let me carry your bag.' He whipped it out of her hand, not giving her time to object, as he knew she would. Hannah was hurting and hurting badly and whilst he didn't mind being the whipping boy for her anger, he refused to stand aside and watch her struggle.

They walked back from the harbour in silence. Tom guessed that she was not only upset about what Charlie's father had done but about the way she had reacted. She was a very private person and the last thing she must want was to have to explain the situation to him.

For some reason the thought made him even more determined to draw her out and that surprised him. Normally, he didn't involve himself in other people's affairs. However, discovering what had happened to Hannah and—possibly—doing something to help her seemed far more important than maintaining his neutrality. He cared that she was upset. He cared that she'd been hurt. And it was a strange experience to feel this way.

They reached her house and stopped. Hitching Charlie more securely onto her hip she went to bend down but Tom stopped her.

'I take it the key is hidden under that plant pot?' He didn't wait for her to reply as he picked up the key. He shook his head as he slid it into the lock. 'That would be the first place any burglar worth his salt would look.'

'I'll find somewhere else if it bothers you so much,' she retorted.

Tom didn't take offence. If she needed to vent some of her anger, his shoulders were broad enough to take it. Pushing open the door, he stepped aside with a bow. 'After you, madam.'

Hannah stopped dead, her green eyes glittering as she stared back at him. 'I can manage from here, thank you. You don't need to come in.'

She held out her hand for her bag only just then Charlie started to wriggle and almost slipped from her grasp. Tom raised a brow and saw her flush. Swinging round, she stomped inside, leaving him to follow if he chose, which he did. Dropping her case onto a chair, he looked around. Honey-coloured walls and an eclectic mix of furniture gave the room a wonderfully cosy feel. He found himself suddenly filled with envy. It must be marvellous to have a home like this, a place you would look forward to coming back to.

'I like what you've done to the place,' he said simply, because it would be wrong to tell her that. It hinted at a loneliness he refused to admit to. 'I've been in this cottage before, when the previous tenant fell down the stairs, and it certainly didn't look like this then.'

'I had a local firm in to decorate before I moved in. It needed updating.'

'It certainly did.'

Tom laughed as he took another look around the room. There were windows at both ends and he could imagine how the sunlight would reflect off those honey-coloured walls during the day. It struck him all of a sudden that not one of the expensive apartments he'd lived in over the past few years could hold a candle to this tiny cottage. It took love and commitment to turn a place into a home, and Hannah was blessed with both.

'I'm sorry but I need to get Charlie settled for the night.'

Her voice held just enough of an edge to remind him that he was persona non grata, and Tom swiftly returned his thoughts to what really mattered—Hannah herself. Maybe she didn't want him there but something told him that she needed to talk.

'Fine. You go ahead.' He sat down on the sofa and smiled innocently up at her. 'If there's anything I can do, give me a shout.'

She hesitated, obviously torn between ordering him to leave and behaving with at least a modicum of good manners. In the end manners won. Swinging round, she marched up the stairs, the sound of her footsteps making her true feelings abundantly clear, and Tom grimaced. He didn't usually force himself on people so maybe he should leave?

He stood up abruptly, refusing to allow himself an escape clause. Hannah needed to talk and in the absence of anyone else, he would have to do. He made his way into the kitchen, pausing once again to admire the room. Gleaming white walls, pale blue painted cupboards and an array of colourful china had lifted the place out of its former doldrums. It all looked very inviting and he wasn't someone who was slow to accept an invitation.

Opening the fridge, he rooted through the contents: an onion, some tomatoes, a head of garlic and—wonder of wonders!—a lump of Parmesan cheese. Without pausing to wonder if Hannah would object, he set about making her some supper, frying the onions and garlic in olive oil before chopping the tomatoes and adding them to the pan. He turned down the heat and opened the cupboards, thanking his stars when he discovered a packet of linguini as well as some dried oregano.

'What are you doing?'

The question brought him spinning round and his heart sank when he saw Hannah in the doorway. She had her hands on her hips and her lips pressed tightly together and if that wasn't enough to warn him she was none too pleased, her expression certainly would have done. Tom opted for the conciliatory approach—the gentle smile and soothing voice. Maybe he had overstepped the mark but he didn't want her to throw him out. Not yet. Not until they'd talked and he, hopefully, had found something to say that would help her.

'I thought I'd make you some supper.' He directed her gaze to the pan, wondering why it was so important that she bare her soul to him. Normally, he'd have run a mile to avoid this very situation but this was different.

This was Hannah and she needed him despite what she believed. Growing up in such a dysfunctional family as his, he knew how it felt to have no one to talk to. His parents had been far too busy with their own lives to bother with him so he had learned to keep his counsel. It wasn't that they were deliberately cruel, just self-centred, but he knew how it felt to bottle things up and he didn't want Hannah to do that if he could help her. From what little he'd gleaned so far, she'd been through enough. The thought spurred him on.

'It seems the least I can do bearing in mind that it's my fault you've had nothing to eat tonight.'

'Oh!'

She walked over to the stove and he saw her swallow as she inhaled the rich aroma of tomato sauce. Was her mouth watering? He hoped so. Maybe she wouldn't open up about Charlie's father. After all, he couldn't make her tell him if it wasn't what she wanted, but at least he would have the satisfaction of knowing that she'd had a decent meal.

'It's very kind of you,' she began, but he cut her off.

'It's no big deal. Honestly.' He went over to the stove and stirred the sauce, trying not to let her see that it was a big deal, for him at least. He'd never felt this way before, never felt this need to protect someone. Was it the emotional fragility he sensed in her that made him want to take care of her? He wasn't sure. All he knew was that he wanted to look after her and if the only way he could do that was by feeding her then so be it.

'This'll be ready soon,' he said neutrally, glancing up. 'Is Charlie all settled for the night?'

'Nearly.' She stepped back, making it plain that she didn't want to be too close to him. 'He just needs his bedtime bottle.'

'Why don't you get it ready while I keep an eye on the sauce?' he suggested, refusing to feel hurt. On the contrary, he should be glad that one of them was behaving sensibly.

'All right.' She opened the fridge and took out a carton of formula, pouring it into a baby's bottle and zapping it in the microwave for a couple of seconds. She headed for the door then paused and he could almost feel the reluctance oozing out of her. 'Would you like to stay for supper?'

Tom knew he should refuse. It obviously wasn't what she wanted but he wasn't going to let that deter him. 'That would be great. Thank you.' He smiled reassuringly. 'There's no rush. I'll put the pasta on when you've finished feeding Charlie.'

'Right.'

Tom turned his attention to the pan as she left the room, determined that his mind wasn't going to wander. They would have supper and if Hannah wanted to talk about her ex then she could. However, he wouldn't press her, not for anything, not to talk or to kiss him or to let him make love to her...

He groaned. How long had he held out? One second? Two? He would have to do better than that if he was to get through the evening without making a fool of himself!

CHAPTER FIVE

HANNAH took a deep breath as she closed the bedroom door. She still wasn't convinced this was a good idea but what else could she have done? Inviting Tom to stay for supper had been the right thing to do, the *natural* thing, in fact. However, she couldn't deny that her nerves were jangling at the thought of them spending any more time together. She was far too aware of him as it was and it certainly wouldn't help to sit across the table from him while they shared the supper he had cooked. It hinted at an intimacy she wasn't ready for... Correction: an intimacy that was never going to happen!

Tom was humming to himself when she went back to the kitchen. He hadn't heard her coming in and it gave her a few seconds to take stock. He'd obviously been busy while she was upstairs, she realised, taking note of the neatly laid table. He'd even found the Parmesan in the fridge and filled an earthenware bowl with shavings. The nutty scent of the cheese mingled with the rich aroma of the sauce made her realise how hungry she was and her stomach rumbled. He looked up and grinned.

'It sounds as though you need feeding. I just have to cook the pasta and it'll be ready.'

'Lovely.' Hannah summoned a smile. Maybe this wasn't how she had envisaged spending the evening but there was no need to worry. She had shared meals with colleagues in the past and nothing had happened, so why should this be any different? 'Is there anything I can do to help?'

'I don't think so... Oh, maybe put out some glasses of water?'

'Actually, I think I've got a bottle of wine somewhere.' She closed her mind to the insidious little voice that was bent on making mischief as she went to find the wine. So maybe it *was* a bit different, having supper with Tom, but she could handle it. 'Ah, yes, here it is.'

She placed the bottle on the counter and fetched the corkscrew. Peeling off the foil, she set to work but the cork refused to budge.

'Let me try. Some of these corks can be the very devil to shift.'

Tom held out his hand and she sighed as she passed the bottle to him. To her mind, he had done enough by making their supper and she didn't want him taking over.

'Damn!' The irritation in his voice brought her eyes to his face and he grimaced. 'I've only managed to break the wretched cork and push it down inside the bottle.'

'Don't worry. It's not a major disaster.' Hannah took the bottle over to the sink, feeling happier now that she had something to do. She found a jug then hunted a tea-strainer out of the drawer and decanted the wine through it. 'I've got most of the bits out so it should be drinkable,' she told him.

'Good.' Tom strained the pasta and added the sauce

then tipped it into a dish. He brought it over to the table, using a couple of big spoons to serve out two generous portions. 'I hope it's all right. I've not made it for ages so there's no guarantee as to how it's turned out.'

Hannah forked up a mouthful, nodding enthusiastically by way of reply, and he laughed. 'I'll take that as a good sign, shall I?'

'Uh-huh.' She managed to swallow and smiled at him. 'My compliments to the chef. This sauce is delicious.'

'That's a relief.' He scattered Parmesan shavings over his pasta and dug in. They ate in silence for several minutes before Hannah picked up the jug.

'Will you have some wine?'

'Please.' He moved his glass closer so she could fill it, grinning as he scooped out a stray bit of cork with his finger. 'I won't bother with the chewy bits.' Raising it to his lips, he took a sip. 'Hmm. Very nice, despite its inauspicious start. You obviously know your wine, Hannah.'

'Oh, I can't take any credit for it. Andrew's the wine buff, not me.'

Her response was automatic and as soon as the words were out of her mouth, she regretted them. She bent over her plate, willing him not to ask any questions. She didn't want to talk about Andrew and what had happened; it was still too raw. She had told nobody the real reason for their break-up; neither her family nor her friends knew the truth. However, she knew that she wouldn't be able to lie to Tom and it was too much, too soon; too dangerous to open up to him. She bit her lip. The fact was that she was far too vulnerable around him.

Tom counted to fifty. Slowly. It was an old ploy, one he'd used to great effect many times. Instead of jumping in and thereby running the risk of regretting it, he gave himself a breathing space to take stock. If he said this or that, how would it impact on him? Would he find himself more involved than he wanted to be? It was a way of separating his emotions and normally it worked like a dream but not tonight. Not with Hannah.

He placed his fork on his plate, seeing the way she avoided his eyes. 'What happened between you and Charlie's father?' Maybe he should have tried a less direct approach but there seemed no point beating around the bush. He wanted to know, she needed to tell him, so it was simpler to leap straight in. 'You said something earlier that implied his relationship with Charlie isn't what it should be. What happened, Hannah? What did he do?'

'It's none of your business.' She started to rise but he reached across the table and captured her hand.

'Probably not.' He looked steadily back at her. 'But I'd still like to know.'

'Why?'

The question was as bald as his had been and he flinched. Did he really want to admit that he cared? Of course not, but now that he'd started this he couldn't stop.

'Because you're hurting. Because you're angry and upset. Because you need to talk to someone.' He paused but he'd already burned his bridges. 'Because I'd like to be that someone, if you'll let me, Hannah.'

Her eyes misted with tears. 'Talking won't change anything. It certainly won't make Andrew change his mind.'

'I disagree. Oh, not about your ex—as I have no idea what he did, I'm not qualified to comment. However, it could help you and that's the most important thing.' He gave her fingers a gentle squeeze then let her go, knowing that he would find it impossible to do so if he held onto her any longer. 'Has it something to do with the fact that Charlie has talipes?'

'How did you guess?' Her tone was bitter, laced with a pain that cut him to the quick. 'Andrew wanted a perfect baby, you see, a child he could show off to his friends. What he didn't want was a son who had a handicap.'

'But talipes can be corrected! Manipulation, casts, even an operation to sever the ligaments and tendons if those don't work. It's treatable.'

'Yes, it is. But that wasn't good enough for Andrew. He didn't want a child who would need to be *repaired*, as he put it. He wanted one who was perfect from the moment he was born.' She bit her lip and he could see the pain in her eyes. 'When we were told at my twenty-week scan that Charlie would be born with the condition, Andrew wanted me to have a termination.'

It was worse than he'd expected, far, far worse. Tom struggled to find something to say but he knew that whatever he came up with would fall far short of what was needed. In the end he settled on something non-judgmental, even though it stuck in his throat to offer an excuse for the other man's behaviour.

'Was it the shock? I mean, it's a lot for any prospective parent to take in. Everyone hopes for a healthy baby so that even something like this can seem like a major issue.'

'If that had been the case we could have worked

through it. In fact, I thought that was what it was at first—Andrew was simply so shocked that he had no idea what he was saying.' She laughed harshly. 'I was wrong. He didn't change his mind no matter how hard I tried to convince him that it was something we could deal with. He wanted me to get rid of the baby because he wasn't perfect. And I refused.'

'So what happened?' he asked slowly, wondering how she had coped. Not only had she needed to deal with her own shock but she'd lost the support of the one person she should have been able to rely on. Anger rose inside him at the thought of how she'd been let down. If he could have ten minutes alone with her ex... He shoved that thought to the back of his mind. 'Was that why you split up?'

'Yes. Oh, it wasn't the reason Andrew gave, not what he told his friends and colleagues. It wouldn't have made him look good, would it? He chose something a little more palatable...that we'd drifted apart. Obviously, he would help to support the baby financially—if it was his.'

'What! He actually implied that Charlie wasn't his son?'

'Oh, yes.' She smiled tightly. 'Andrew's a barrister and he's very keen on facts. He came up with all sorts of information about how talipes often runs in families. As he was keen to point out, there'd been no child in his family born with the condition.'

'But that's crazy! All right, so there's a greater chance of a child being born with the condition if there's a family history of it, but that isn't always the case.'

'You know that and I know that. Andrew knew it too but it was the perfect excuse. Oh, he was very careful. He just dropped the odd hint, here and there.' She laughed. 'I didn't find out what he was up to until I bumped into one of his colleagues and she let it slip. Suffice to say that he won't be making any more claims like that in the future.'

'And was this before or after Charlie was born?'

'Before. Charlie was born a month later. Andrew still hasn't seen him. So far as he's concerned, Charlie doesn't exist.'

The tears she'd been holding in check suddenly spilled over. Tom got up and came around the table. Kneeling down, he drew her into his arms. 'Shh. It's all right, Hannah. Everything is going to be fine, you'll see.'

She buried her face in his shoulder. Tom guessed that she was embarrassed about breaking down but he knew it would help. Nobody should have to shoulder a burden like this on their own—it wasn't right. He ran his hand over her hair, feeling the silky tendrils clinging to his fingers. He could smell the lemon scent of her shampoo, nothing exotic, just a clean, fresh fragrance that stirred his senses in a way he wouldn't have expected, and suppressed a shudder. He didn't want to alarm her. He wanted to comfort her, make her feel a little bit better. If he could.

She raised her head at last and looked wonderingly at him. 'That's the first time I've cried.'

'Is it?' He smoothed his thumbs over her cheeks, using his own skin to soak up her tears. The shudder he'd been holding back tried again to surface but he stamped on it. No pressure. Nothing to make her feel uncomfortable. And definitely nothing that would hint at the way he would really like to comfort her.

A picture of him pressing his lips to her wet face suddenly filled his head. He would kiss away her tears, soothe her pain with his mouth, comfort her with his hands. He knew he could do all that, but it wouldn't be right. She was at her most vulnerable and he refused to take advantage. He wanted to protect her, cherish her, and the fact that he felt this strongly shocked him. He had always avoided emotional involvement. Not even his erstwhile fiancée had touched him on a deeper level if he was honest. And yet just holding Hannah in his arms filled him with a whole range of emotions.

He let her go and stood up, his heart hammering. He felt both elated and terrified. It was good to know that he wasn't emotionally bankrupt after all, yet he was scared witless at the thought of the damage he could cause. The truth was that he didn't trust himself, couldn't put his hand on his heart and swear that he would feel this way in a year's time. Hell, if his first and only attempt at love was anything to go by, he could forget measuring the time in years and resort to months! So how would he feel in a month's time? Still keen to protect her? Still longing to cherish her and make her happy? He had no idea and that was why this had to stop now.

'You needed to get it out of your system so you can move on,' he said flatly, sitting down. He went to fork up another mouthful of linguine but the pasta had gone cold and was stuck together in an unappetising lump. He put down the fork, wondering if it was an omen. His interest could turn as cold and as stolid as this food.

'I know that. And I will...I am.' She got up and ripped off a piece of kitchen roll. She blew her nose then sat down and picked up her glass, taking a sip of the wine before continuing. 'Moving here was the first step. It was a big decision to leave London but it was the right thing to do. Charlie and I need a fresh start and living here will give us that.'

'Bride's Bay is a good place to live,' he agreed, wanting to add his own endorsement to her plans. Maybe he couldn't offer her the kind of support he yearned to but he could provide encouragement. 'It's a great place to raise a child. I have many happy memories of the times I stayed here when I was growing up.'

'Simon said that he's your godfather?'

He heard the curiosity in her voice and breathed a sigh of relief. It would be easier to turn the conversation away from what she had been through, easier for him. 'That's right. He and my father were at Cambridge together.'

'So your families are friends? That must be nice.'

Tom shrugged. 'Simon and my father have remained friends but my mother was never part of the scene. She works abroad a lot of the time and that's not really conducive to forging close friendships.'

'Oh. I see. What does she do?'

He wasn't sure if he wanted to go into the ins and outs of his family history but he could hardly refuse to answer. 'She's an opera singer. Tessa Wylde...you may have heard of her.'

'Of course I've heard of her!' Hannah looked at him in amazement. 'I can't believe that your mother is Tessa Wylde.' She frowned. 'But I thought she was married to a peer, Lord Something or other?'

'That's right. My father is Lord Bradbury.' He hated this bit, hated the fact that it altered people's view of him to learn that he was part of the so-called aristocracy. However, apart from an understandable surprise, she didn't seem impressed.

'Fancy that. And do you have a title too?' She grinned. 'Should I address you as sir or my lord?'

'No way!' He laughed. 'Oh, there's probably some archaic form of address if you dig deep enough, but it's not something I ever use. I prefer Tom or Dr Bradbury at a push. My half-brother, Joseph, will inherit the title and he's welcome to it.'

'Half-brother? So your father was married before he met your mother?'

She was obviously keen to learn more and Tom knew that he couldn't fudge the issue even though he would have loved to do so. 'Yes. In fact, my mother is his fourth wife.'

'Good heavens!' She clapped her hand over her mouth. 'Sorry. That wasn't very tactful.'

'Don't worry about it.' He summoned a smile. 'Mother's own track record isn't much better. She was married twice before she met my father. And both of them have had umpteen affairs, both before and after the nuptials. As for Joseph, well, it looks as though he's heading the same way. He's in the process of getting divorced, in fact.'

He shrugged, trying to make light of his family's chequered marital history. 'It's a family tradition. We Bradburys get married, divorced and have affairs at a rate of knots. We're genetically programmed to be unfaithful!'

CHAPTER SIX

HANNAH wasn't sure what to say. Although Tom was smiling, she sensed it was merely a cover. Was he embarrassed by the thought of his family's behaviour?

She frowned. He didn't strike her as the sort of person who would feel ashamed of other people's actions yet there was definitely something troubling him. It was on the tip of her tongue to ask him when she thought better of it. She didn't want to become involved in his affairs. It was too dangerous.

'They say that you can choose your friends but not your family,' she observed lightly.

'And very true it is too.' He gave her a wide smile but she could tell how false it was. She realised all of a sudden that the charm that was so much in evidence was merely a front to hide his true feelings. Tom kept his emotions strictly to himself. He didn't share them.

It was an intriguing thought, one that might have made her dig deeper if she hadn't decided not to get involved. At the present time she had enough to contend with. She needed to concentrate on making a life for herself and Charlie. Getting inside Tom's skin and discovering what made him tick wasn't an option.

'So what about your family, Hannah? Do you have sisters or brothers?'

'One of each. Sarah is a nurse and Dominic's an engineer,' she told him, relieved to get back onto safer ground.

'I see. And how about your parents—are they still alive?' He prompted her to tell him more, mainly, she suspected, so he wouldn't have to tell *her* anything else, but that was fine.

'Yes, they're both fit and well, I'm happy to say. Dad was in the police. He retired last year and spends as much time as possible fishing. Mum's still working— she's a dinner lady at the local high school and she loves her job. She's planning to stay there as long as she can.'

'It's great if you do a job you enjoy.'

'It is.'

'Do they live in London?'

'No, Liverpool.'

'Really?' His brows rose. 'Weren't you tempted to move back there when you decided to leave London?'

'Not really.' She shrugged. 'It's a long time since I lived there so the ties have been well and truly cut. I wanted to move to the coast for Charlie's sake so that's why I applied for this job.'

'And your family can always come and visit you.'

She nodded, not wanting to explain that she rarely saw them these days. Andrew had always found an excuse whenever she had wanted to visit her parents so that trips home had become increasingly rare in the last few years. She sighed. She'd often wondered if he'd thought that her parents' neat little semi wasn't grand enough but had managed to dismiss the idea. Now it seemed more likely. For Andrew, a visit to her family's modest home would have fallen far short of his ideas of perfection.

It was another black mark against him, a minor one compared to what he had done to Charlie, granted, but something else she should never have allowed to happen. Once again Hannah was struck with guilt for the way she had behaved. She had been so driven by her own need to create a perfect life that she had allowed Andrew to influence her to such an extent that she'd lost touch with her family. She would have to do something to rectify the situation, she decided, always assuming that her parents would forgive her for the way she had behaved.

The conversation seemed to run out of steam after that. When she suggested making coffee, Tom shook his head. 'Thanks but I'll pass on the coffee, if you don't mind.' He pushed back his chair. 'I've a few things to sort out if I'm to start that job in Paris next week.'

'You're still planning to go?' she queried, getting up.

'It all depends on what Simon and Ros decide to do. If they're set on visiting Becky then I'll have to wait until they get back.'

He picked up his plate and took it over to the sink then went back for the bowl but she took it off him. 'Leave that. I'll clear up later.'

'Sure?'

He didn't insist, making her realise that he was keen to leave. Why wouldn't he be? she thought as she led the way through the sitting room. He'd prepared her supper, listened to her tale of woe and offered his support; he'd done more than enough for one evening and far more than she should have let him. She opened the front door, suddenly as eager as he was to bring the evening to an end.

'Well, thanks again for making supper,' she said brightly.

'It was my pleasure.'

He paused in the doorway, the light from the street casting a shadow over his face so that it was hard to see what he was thinking. Hannah stepped closer and maybe he interpreted her action in a way she'd not intended because he suddenly bent and dropped a kiss on her cheek. He drew back and she shivered when she was deprived of the warmth of his mouth.

'It really was a pleasure, too, Hannah.'

He gave her a last smile then stepped out of the door. Hannah hastily closed it, not trusting herself stand there and watch him leave. She had a feeling that she might do something really stupid, like call him back...

She put her hand to her cheek, pressing her fingertips against the spot where his lips had touched, but the heat had gone now. There was just the memory of it in her mind, an echo of sensation, but even that was enough to make her shiver. It had been a typical social kiss to all intents, the sort of kiss people bestowed on friends and acquaintances every day of the week, yet it seemed to have taken on a far greater significance in her mind. Maybe Tom had kissed her as a friend but she knew that even a simple kiss could lead to something more. The scariest thing was admitting that she wouldn't mind if it did.

'Thanks for the update... Yes, it is a shame, but you win some and you lose some.'

Tom ended the call. It was just gone eight and he'd

been getting ready to see his first patient when Jim Cairns had phoned to tell him that Clive Baines, the man who'd been rescued from the yacht, had died during the night. Although Tom wasn't entirely surprised by the news, he found it dispiriting. *Was* there anything else he could have done to help him?

He shrugged off the thought and buzzed for his first patient. Giving in to self-doubt was non-productive and normally not one of his failings. However, he'd felt unsettled ever since he'd left Hannah's house the previous night. Learning what she had been through had affected him more than he had imagined it would do and he was having the devil of a job getting back on even keel. Maybe he *did* want to help her but he was very aware that it could cause more harm than good if he tried.

'Morning, Tom, and how are you today?'

'Still here so that's one for the plus column,' Tom replied as cheerfully as he could when Mitch Johnson came bustling into the room. At a little over six feet in height and almost as round as he was tall, the landlord of The Ship Inn cut an unmistakable figure in the town. Now he plonked himself down on a chair and grinned at the younger man.

'I know what you mean. It's always a good day when I wake up in the morning.' Mitch laughed loudly, enjoying his own joke, and Tom smiled.

'Too right it is. Anyway, what can I do for you today?'

'Simon told me to pop in so you could review my medication. I happened to mention that I've been having a few funny turns of late when he called in for a drink and he was concerned in case it's these new pills I'm taking.'

'What do you mean by funny turns?' Tom asked, bringing up the patient's file on the computer. Mitch had a history of hypertension—high blood pressure—and had been treated with a range of medication over the years. As high blood pressure increased the chances of him having a stroke or developing heart disease, he had regular check-ups both at the surgery and at the hospital. Tom noted that Mitch been seen at the hospital the previous month and that his medication had been changed then.

'I've been finding that everything looks fuzzy, sort of out of focus, if you know what I mean,' Mitch explained. 'I went and had my eyes tested but according to the optician there's nothing wrong with them. Then last week I started with a blinding headache which lasted a whole day. I've not had anything like it before either.'

'Hmm. It sounds as though the new medication could be to blame.' Tom frowned as he checked the name of the tablets. 'I've not come across these before. Let me have a look and see what it says about them.'

He picked up his copy of *MIMS*, which listed all the medications they prescribed, but the one Mitch was taking wasn't included. 'No, they're not in here. They must be very new.' He picked up the phone. 'I'll have a word with the doctor you saw last time you visited the hospital and ask him what he knows about them.'

He put through the call but the doctor in question was in the clinic. Tom asked to speak to the consultant but she was on maternity leave. He hung up. 'Dr Latimer's in clinic so I'll have to phone back later and speak to him. He must be new because I've not come across him before either.'

'That's right. He told me he'd only been working

there for just over a month,' Mitch confirmed. 'Usually I see Dr Fairburn but she's on maternity leave.'

'So I believe. Not to worry. We'll soon get it sorted out. In the meantime, I suggest you go back on your old medication. Do you know why Dr Latimer changed it?'

'Not really.' Mitch shrugged. 'To be honest, I felt fine taking the others. I don't know why he decided to change them because my blood pressure's been stable for months.'

'Hopefully, he'll explain his reasons when I speak to him,' Tom said, although he, too, thought it odd that Dr Latimer had prescribed something different. He printed out a script and handed it to Mitch. 'I'll check your BP while you're here. Can you roll up your sleeve?'

He checked Mitch's BP, frowning when he saw the reading. 'It's on the high side, which would explain the headaches you've been having as well as the blurred vision. We need to keep an eye on it so I want you to pop in next week and let Emily check it again.'

'Hopefully, it will have settled down by then.' Mitch rolled down his sleeve and stood up. 'Thanks, Tom. Oh, I heard about that chap you helped last night. Shame he didn't make it.'

'It is.' Tom managed to smile but he could feel the gloom descending on him again and it was very odd. He had long since accepted that he couldn't save everyone; nobody could. He did his best and that was all he could do so why had he taken this case so much to heart? Was it the fact that he hadn't been able to help Hannah either that made him feel so useless?

He sighed as Mitch bade him a cheery goodbye. Hannah had been constantly on his mind. It wasn't just the fact that he felt so useless but everything else, like that kiss, for instance. Why in heaven's name had he kissed her? It had been a crazy thing to do. He had tried to dismiss it as nothing more than a token but in the depths of the night he had woken more than once recalling how soft and smooth her skin had felt, how warm and tempting when he had pressed his lips against it.

A shudder ran through him and he groaned. He had to stop this, had to stop thinking about her. With a bit of luck he would be leaving at the end of the week and that would be the end of the matter. Once he'd put some distance between them he could forget how she made him feel. She would be out of his life for good and that was the best thing that could happen for him and for her.

Hannah worked straight through till lunch then went to the office where Lizzie, the receptionist, was sorting the morning's post. A pretty woman in her thirties with bright red hair and freckles, Lizzie had worked at the practice since she had left school. Now she looked up and smiled.

'How's it going?'

'Fine. I think!' Hannah laughed as she placed the files she had used in the tray.

'Well, from what I've heard you're a big hit. Joyce Cairns was in earlier and she was saying that her Jim had spoken very highly of you,' Lizzie told her.

'That's good to hear.' Hannah smiled back, feeling her pulse leap when she heard footsteps coming along the corridor. She didn't need to check who they belonged to because she recognised Tom's firm tread.

She sighed as she separated a couple of letters that needed posting and placed them in the box. Tom had been on her mind far too much since last night. Even this morning she had found herself thinking about that kiss and how it had made her feel, and it was the last thing she needed. Her emotions had been through the wringer recently and she needed time to recover.

Then there was the fact that Charlie needed so much care and would continue to need it for the foreseeable future. One of the most hurtful things Andrew had said was that he wasn't prepared to give up his life for a child and it was something she had taken to heart. If her son's own father wasn't prepared to devote any time to him, why should another man wish to do so? She had seen couples go through similar experiences in the course of her work and knew that having a child who needed extra care put a strain on a relationship. She wasn't prepared to subject herself and Charlie to that kind of pressure so that was another reason why she had ruled out having a relationship. However, as Tom came into the room, she found herself thinking that it was a good job he was leaving otherwise she could have had a real problem on her hands.

'Right, that's the morning over so onto round two. I'm down for the house calls this afternoon, I believe.'

Tom dropped his files into the tray and turned. Hannah saw him start when he spotted her and summoned a smile. The last thing she needed was him realising that she'd been standing there, thinking about him.

'Busy, busy, busy. The life of a GP is all go,' she said lightly.

'It is indeed.'

He returned her smile with one that was as bland as hers had been and yet there was something in his eyes that told her he was as aware of her as she was of him. Heat flowed through her and she turned away, afraid that he would notice her reaction too.

'That's right, you're down for the calls today. There's quite a long list, too.' Lizzie picked up a sheet of paper and handed it to him. 'I've put Susan Allsop at the top. She didn't sound at all well when she phoned. Her hubby's away, so I thought it might be best if you made her your first call.'

'Will do.' Tom skimmed through the list. 'This should keep me busy. See you later, folks. Have fun.'

Hannah breathed a sigh of relief when he left. The less time she spent around him the better. She was just about to check the roster to see what she was scheduled for when Simon came bustling into the room.

'I'm glad I caught you before you went for lunch, Hannah. I've just had a word with Tom and asked him to take you with him.'

'Oh, right. I see.' Hannah couldn't keep the anxiety out of her voice and she saw Simon frown.

'It isn't a problem, is it?'

'Of course not.' She dredged up a smile, hating the fact that she was allowing this awareness of Tom to get in the way of doing her job. 'So long as Tom doesn't mind me tagging along, I'm happy to go with him.'

'Good.' Simon smiled at her. 'It'll be easier for you if you have some idea of where everything is.'

'Of course.' Hannah took a deep breath, determined that she wasn't going to let this new development throw her. She would be spending the afternoon with Tom; so what? She was a grown woman and she could handle a couple of hours in his company without doing something she would regret. She closed her mind to what could happen as she smiled at Simon. There was no point thinking about that kiss when there wasn't going to be a repeat! 'It'll be a big help when I have to do the calls by myself.'

'Exactly.' Simon beamed at her. 'Sat nav is all well and good but nothing beats first-hand knowledge. Tom knows the countryside around here almost as well as I do. He'll be the perfect teacher.'

'I'm sure he will.'

Hannah shivered as she made her way to the door. The thought of Tom teaching her anything made her go hot and cold. She collected her case then made her way to the car park. Tom was waiting for her with the engine running. He looked round when she opened the car door and she could tell at once that he, too, had reservations. Tom was as keen to maintain his distance as she was, it seemed.

The thought should have reassured her but it didn't. The fact that he had as big a problem with her as she had with him merely highlighted the danger of them spending time together. However, short of refusing to accompany him, there was nothing she could do.

Hannah took a deep breath and slid into the passenger seat.

CHAPTER SEVEN

Tom could feel his heart thumping as he put the car into gear and silently cursed himself. He and Hannah weren't going on a date—they were working! The sooner he got that straight in his head, the better.

'Where to first?'

He jumped when she spoke, feeling his heart increase its tempo until it felt as though it was trying to leap right out of his chest. It took every scrap of willpower he possessed to reply calm. 'Susan Allsop's home at Dentons Cove. It's some distance from here, a good fifteen miles, I'd reckon.'

'I hadn't realised the practice's catchment area was so extensive.'

Tom breathed a sigh of relief when Hannah responded in the same no-nonsense tone. So long as they stuck to practicalities, they would be fine. 'It's a lot bigger than you'd get in a city. Obviously there's a higher concentration of people in a city and that determines how big an area each practice covers.'

'Where's the nearest practice to Bride's Bay?'

'Westcombe.'

'Really? That's a long way away,' she said in surprise, twisting round so she could look at him.

'It is.' Tom kept his eyes on the road. Talking he could handle but if he had to spend too much time looking at her... He cut short that thought. He refused to go down the route of speculating what might happen. One, very *chaste,* kiss didn't make a romance. And it certainly didn't mark the beginning of an affair! 'There was another practice further along the coast but it closed last year when the GP who ran it retired.'

'I'm surprised that nobody wanted to take it over.'

He shrugged. 'So many people had moved away to find work that there weren't enough patients to make it a viable proposition.'

'It must have put extra pressure on Simon,' she suggested, and he nodded.

'It did. Most of the remaining patients transferred to his list. That's why Simon was so keen to find a replacement when Margery announced she was leaving. He knew he wouldn't be able to manage with just locum cover.'

'Lucky for me. The job came up at just the right time.'

She gave a little laugh and Tom couldn't resist any longer. He glanced sideways, feeling his pulse leap when she smiled at him. He'd met women who were far more beautiful than her, he thought wonderingly, met, dated *and* slept with them. However, he could honestly say that not one of them had had this effect on him.

'Mmm.' He cleared his throat, determined that he wasn't going to give in to this attraction he felt. Hannah didn't need him messing up her life. He didn't need his life messed up either. He had to fight his feelings no matter how difficult it was. 'Odd how things work out, isn't it?'

'It is.'

There was a strange note in her voice that piqued his interest but he refused to allow himself even the tiniest leeway. So what if she was thinking that if she hadn't taken this job they would never have met? He knew what he had to do and he would stick to it. He wouldn't be responsible for breaking her heart.

They drove in silence after that. Tom knew that he should have spent the time pointing out the various landmarks along the way. However, he didn't trust himself to engage her in conversation. Even the most innocent comment could turn into something far more engaging and he couldn't take that risk. It was a relief when they reached the road leading down to Dentons Cove.

'Susan's house is down here,' he explained as he turned off the main road. 'She and her husband, Brian, bought a couple of old fishermen's cottages a few years ago and turned them into a guest house. They're both artists and they run courses for people interested in painting.'

'I'm sure the courses must be very popular. The view is fabulous,' she said, taking in the vista of sea and sky that greeted them as they drove down the narrow lane.

'It is. It's a favourite spot of mine. No matter what time of the year you come here, the scenery is spectacular.'

'But not spectacular enough to tempt you to move here permanently?'

'No.'

Tom didn't say anything else as he drew up outside the row of cottages. There was no point explaining why he couldn't put down roots. Although he had told her a little about his dysfunctional family, he wasn't prepared to admit how big an influence their behaviour had had on him. Thrusting open the car door, he got out, wishing not for the first time that he'd been born into a normal family. Then he could have been like everyone else. He could have fallen in love, got married, had kids...

He made himself stop right there. He was who he was and that was the end of the matter. He had been perfectly happy with his life, too, until he'd met Hannah. He glanced at her as she got out of the car and felt his heart ache with a sudden sense of loss that shocked him. Having Hannah in his life had never been an option so why did he feel so bereft?

Hannah closed the car door, using the few seconds it took to calm her nerves. Sitting so close to Tom on the drive to the cove had been even more of an ordeal than she had imagined. She was so aware of him that each time he'd moved her pulse had raced. She couldn't recall reacting like this around anyone before, not even Andrew, and the thought made her feel even more rattled. Somehow she had to slot Tom into his rightful place as a colleague. Once she'd done that, everything would be fine.

'Did Lizzie give you a print-out of Susan Allsop's recent notes?' she asked, adopting her most professional tone.

'She did. Sorry. I should have let you take a look at them.' He handed her the sheet, waiting patiently while she acquainted herself with the patient's medical history. She nodded when she came to the end.

'A history of diabetes, which seems to be under control.'

'Yes. Susan was diagnosed shortly after she moved

here and has been very good about monitoring her blood glucose levels. She also sticks to the diet the diabetes team at the hospital recommended and so far has had no real problems.'

'It says here that she had an appointment at the surgery last week to check her blood pressure.'

'That's right. Emily, our practice nurse, saw her. She deals with all the routine checks. Susan comes into the surgery every three months to have her BP checked as diabetics have a higher-than-average risk of developing hypertension, as you know.'

Tom took the print-out off her and Hannah sucked in her breath when their hands brushed. It took her all her time to concentrate as he continued when she could feel her fingers tingling from the contact.

'Everything was fine according to Emily's notes so I'm not sure what's happened since then. We'd better go and find out.'

He slid the sheet into his case and knocked on the cottage door. Hannah stood to one side, distracting herself from any more such nonsense by admiring the colourful window boxes. Tom knocked again, louder this time, looking puzzled when nobody answered his summons.

'That's strange. I'm sure Susan wouldn't have gone out when she'd requested a home visit.'

'Maybe she's at the back of the house and hasn't heard you.'

'Could be.' Tom knocked a third time, but still failed to get a response. He looked concerned when he turned to her. 'I don't like this one little bit. I'll try going round to the back of the house and see if I have more success there.'

'I'll come with you,' Hannah offered immediately, following him as he walked briskly to the end of the row of cottages and turned down a narrow path. It led to the rear gardens, each one neatly fenced off from its neighbour with latticework panels. Tom counted the gates as they passed them.

'This should be it.' He undid the latch and let himself into the garden. Like the window boxes, it was a riot of colour and she sighed wistfully as she followed him to the back door.

'I wish my garden looked like this. The only thing growing there at the moment is weeds.'

'You can't hope to make everything perfect all at once,' he said lightly. 'You've done wonders with the inside of the house, don't forget.'

'You're right.' Hannah smiled, appreciating the timely reminder not to set her sights too high. She was done with aiming for perfection all the time and would be content that she had achieved so much. 'Thank you for reminding me.'

'My pleasure.' He gave her a crooked grin then turned to the door, rapping loudly with his knuckles on the lavender-painted wood. He seemed completely focussed on the reason for their visit but she had seen the awareness in his eyes and knew that he was having as hard a time as she was keeping his feelings in check. Maybe they did both know it would be a mistake to get involved but knowing a thing didn't always rule out it happening.

Hannah shivered. All it would take was a moment of weakness and they could find themselves in a situation they would both regret.

Tom kept his attention on the door. He knew that

he had given himself away and hated to think that he might have made Hannah feel uncomfortable. If only he could press a button and erase his feelings, he thought as he knocked again. Then life could return to normal.

The thought was less appealing than it should have been. However, he really didn't want to dwell on the idea that being fancy-free wasn't all it was cracked up to be. He turned to Hannah, determined that he wasn't going to make a difficult situation worse. 'I'm going to try one the neighbours and check if they've seen Susan today. There's no way that she would have gone out when she knew we were coming.'

'I agree.' Hannah stepped around him and peered through the window. 'There's no sign of her but there's a cup of tea and a plate of sandwiches on the table. It looks as though she never got round to eating her lunch.'

'Not a good sign,' Tom said grimly. He headed down the path and went to the cottage next door. An elderly man answered his knock and Tom smiled at him. 'I'm sorry to bother you but have you seen Mrs Allsop today? I'm Tom Bradbury. I'm a doctor at Bride's Bay Surgery.'

'I know who you are, son. You saw my wife last year, Edith Harris, remember? You sorted out her arthritis for her.'

'Of course I remember Mrs Harris,' Tom confirmed. 'How is she doing?'

'Fine. She says she's not felt so well for years.' The old man frowned as he peered over the fence. 'You're looking for Susan, are you?'

'That's right. I've tried the front door and the back but there's no reply. Do you know if she's gone out?' Tom queried.

'I doubt it. Edith was speaking to her yesterday and Susan told her that she wasn't feeling too well—sort of light-headed and dizzy.' The old man reached back inside the house and produced a key. 'We have a key to her house. It's handy if she's out and the meter needs to be read. Why don't we let ourselves in and check that everything's all right, Doctor?'

'That's a great idea, Mr Harris,' Tom said in relief. He moved aside so the old man could lead the way, quickly introducing him to Hannah in passing.

'Nice to meet you,' Mr Harris said politely as they made their way to Susan's door. He inserted the key into the lock but when he tried to open the door it wouldn't budge. 'Something's stopping it,' he said, glancing at Tom.

'Here, let me see if I can open it.' Tom positioned himself in front of the door and pushed as hard as he could. It opened a couple of inches, just enough for him to see a foot through the gap. He turned urgently to Hannah. 'It looks as though Susan has collapsed. We need to get in there, pronto.'

'Let's see if we can open the door a bit more then maybe I can slide inside.'

Hannah hurried to his side, placing her shoulder next to his. Tom sucked in his breath when he felt her breasts brush his back as she moved closer. 'On three,' he said through gritted teeth because this wasn't the time for thoughts like the ones that were dancing around his head. 'One. Two. Three!'

They both pushed as hard as they could and succeeded in opening the door another couple of inches. Hannah slipped off her jacket and handed it to him.

'I should be able to get through there now.' She

inched her way through the gap and a moment later he heard the sound of furniture scraping across the floor.

'Are you OK?' he called, wishing that he hadn't let her go first. What if Susan hadn't collapsed? What if she'd been attacked, struck down by someone out to harm her, someone who even now could be lurking in the house? Fear rose inside him and he put his shoulder to the door once more. 'I'm coming in, Hannah. Stand clear!'

This time the door bounced back on its hinges, catapulting him inside. Hannah looked up from where she was kneeling next to Susan and he saw the amusement in her eyes. 'You certainly know how to make an entrance, Dr Bradbury.'

Tom grinned self-consciously as he went to join her. 'I was worried in case there was someone lurking in the shadows.'

'Lurking?'

'Uh-huh. A burglar or someone of that ilk,' he said, dropping to his knees. He checked Susan's pulse, nodding when he felt it beating away, then curled back her eyelids and checked her response to light. Although she was unconscious, her vital signs were good and that was reassuring. Opening his case, he took out a device for testing blood glucose levels. If, as he suspected, there was too little glucose in her blood it could have caused her to collapse and it needed to be checked straight away.

'Ah, I see.' Hannah took an alcohol wipe out of the bag and cleaned Susan's finger so he could take a sample of her blood. 'Well there don't appear to be any bogeymen in here, although rest assured that you'll be the first person I call if I do come across any.'

She was openly laughing now and Tom was assailed by a rush of pleasure at the thought that it was all his doing. He had a feeling that there'd been far too little laughter in her life of late. He grinned back as he spread the blood on a chemically coated strip and popped it into the machine to obtain a reading. He knew that she would see how he felt, yet suddenly he didn't care. He liked her. A lot. And for the first time in his life perhaps he was going to allow his heart to rule his head.

'Fine by me, so long as you promise to return the favour.' His eyes held hers fast for a moment. 'When I wake up in the middle of the night thinking there's a bogeyman under the bed, I hope you'll be there to chase him away, Hannah.'

CHAPTER EIGHT

'You've had a hypoglycaemic attack, Susan. In other words, there was too little glucose in your blood and that's why you passed out.'

Tom's voice was gently reassuring as he helped Susan Allsop onto a chair and Hannah sighed. She could do with some reassurance herself. The whole time that she and Tom had been working together to help Susan—administering an injection of glucagon, checking her BP and heart rate—the same disturbing thought had been humming away inside her head: her relationship with Tom had moved onto a whole new level.

'But I've done everything I usually do, taken my insulin and stuck to my diet,' Susan protested. 'I don't understand why this has happened if I've done everything I'm supposed to do.'

Hannah forced herself to focus on what was happening. There would be time to think about the rest later, although how it would help was open to question. She was attracted to Tom, he was attracted to her—the situation was pretty clear from what she could see. It was how she intended to handle it that needed sorting out.

She pushed that thought to the back of her mind as Tom explained that sometimes glitches occurred.

Whilst in no way playing down the seriousness of what had happened, he was obviously trying not to frighten the woman and Hannah found herself thinking what a good doctor he was. A frightened patient didn't respond nearly as well as one who had confidence in the advice they were being given.

'Have your glucose levels fluctuated recently?' he asked finally.

'Not really,' Susan replied hesitantly.

'But your readings have altered?'

'I suppose so.' Susan bit her lip then hurried on. 'I'm afraid I didn't really take that much notice. I've been so busy with Brian being away, you see. We have guests arriving next week and all the bedrooms need repainting. I haven't had time to think about anything else.'

'Which could explain why this has happened,' Hannah put in gently. She smiled when Susan glanced uncertainly at her. 'The extra work you've been doing has affected the balance between the amount of insulin you need and the food you eat. You'd suffer the same effect if you skipped a meal or didn't eat enough carbohydrates.'

'Really?' Susan looked surprised. 'I had no idea. I mean, I know that I have to eat at set times and that I need to be careful about how much carbohydrate I have but I didn't realise that being extra busy could cause a problem.'

'I'm afraid it does have an effect,' Tom agreed. 'That's why it's so important to take note of any changes in your glucose levels. It's the indicator that things aren't as they should be.'

He gave Susan a moment to absorb that then stood

up. Hannah stepped aside to let him pass, refusing to let herself dwell on the thought of how good he smelled. She had enough to contend with without that as well. She went and stood by the open door, not sure she could trust herself where he was concerned. Everything about him seemed to be a turn-on, from the way he smiled to the fact that his skin smelled so clean and fresh.

What was it about him that made her aware of things she would never have noticed normally? she wondered as she watched him pack everything back into his case. She had no idea but there was no use pretending that she was indifferent to him when every cell in her body was repudiating the idea. The fact was that Tom affected her more than any man had ever done.

It was a sobering thought. Hannah let it settle in her mind while he explained to Susan that he would make an appointment for her to see the diabetic care team. Even though the current crisis had been dealt with, he felt it would be best if she was given a thorough check-up at the hospital. Susan obviously wasn't happy about the idea but she saw the sense in what he was saying and agreed. He made a quick call to the hospital and fixed up an appointment for her to be seen the following day. Mr Harris had gone to fetch his wife and they insisted that Susan should go back to their house and spend the afternoon with them. Tom had a word with the elderly couple, asking them to phone the surgery if they were at all worried. Although he didn't anticipate any problems, he wanted to be sure that every eventuality was covered. Once they had assured him that they would phone immediately if Susan didn't seem herself, they left.

Hannah followed him back to the car, steeling herself to get through the rest of the afternoon without making a fool of herself. Maybe they were attracted to one another but they were working and that had to take precedence over everything else.

'Where to next?' she asked, determined to set the tone for the rest of the day.

'I'm not sure. Let me take a look at that list and work out which is the best route to take from here.'

He reached over the back of the seat and snared the print-out, frowning as he glanced down the list. Hannah looked away when she felt her stomach muscles quiver. The situation must be serious if she found even a frown arousing!

'The rest of the calls are all in or around Bride's Bay.' Tom glanced up and she hurriedly smoothed her face into a suitably noncommittal expression. Thankfully, he seemed oblivious to what had been going through her mind as he continued. 'We'll head back, do a couple calls on the way, and maybe stop for lunch before we do the rest, if that suits you?'

'I'm happy to work straight through,' she said quickly, not sure if it was wise to risk having lunch together. 'In fact, I'd prefer to get the calls out of the way. There's a few things I need to sort out before evening surgery and it would be a help if we got back early.'

'Fine by me,' Tom agreed.

He started the engine and turned the car around, pointing out the various landmarks along the way, and Hannah breathed a sigh of relief. If they could continue behaving like this then there was no reason to worry. Tom would be leaving at the end of the week so all she had to do was get through the next few days and that would be it. He would be out of her life for good, which was what she wanted…

Wasn't it?

Tom was relieved when the day came to an end. Although he enjoyed working at the surgery because it was such a change of pace from his usual hectic schedule, today had turned into something of an ordeal. He bade Lizzie a brisk goodnight and just as briskly headed out to his car. Maybe it was cowardly but he wanted to avoid running into Hannah if he could.

He sighed as he drove out of the car park. He had never, ever taken evasive action like this before. The women he dated came and went without creating the tiniest ripple in his life. Not even his ex-fiancée had made much impression on him, if he was truthful. But Hannah was different. He would remember her for the rest of his life.

It was a sobering thought. He deliberately expunged it from his mind as he headed into the town centre. Although he usually ate with Simon and Ros, he felt the need to be on his own tonight so he would have supper at The Ship then take in a movie at the cinema. A nice, gory action film would fill in a couple of hours and stop him brooding.

He was almost in the town centre when he saw Hannah's car drawn up by the side of the road. The bonnet was up and clouds of steam were issuing from it. He hesitated a moment, debating the wisdom of playing the good Samaritan, but no matter how much sense it made to drive past, there was no way that his conscience would allow him to leave her stranded.

He drew up behind her car and got out. Walking

round to the front of the vehicle, he found Hannah peering under the bonnet. 'Looks like your radiator has blown.'

'So the man from the roadside rescue service informed me,' she said tartly, glaring at him.

Tom held up his hands. 'Hey, don't shoot the messenger.'

'Sorry.' She dredged up a smile but he could tell that she was feeling very stressed.

'Don't worry about it.' He glanced into the car but there was no sign of Charlie. 'You've obviously not made it to the nursery yet. Have you phoned them?'

'Yes. I explained that I'd be late but the problem is that I have no idea how long it will take for the breakdown truck to get here.' She checked her watch. 'I can't wait any longer. I'll have to leave the car here and call a taxi.'

'No need for that. You can take my car.' He handed her the keys, shaking his head when she started to protest. 'No, you need to fetch Charlie, that's the most important thing. Let's transfer his seat into the back of my car then you can get him while I wait here for the breakdown truck.'

He opened her car, quickly unclipping the seat belt so that he could remove the child seat. Hannah hurried ahead of him, opening the door so he could place it in the back of his car. 'I'll let you do the seat belt so you're sure it's fastened properly,' he explained, stepping aside.

Hannah fastened the seat into place then closed the door. She looked uncertainly up at him. 'Are you sure you don't mind, Tom? I mean, it's an expensive car and....'

'And nothing.' He placed his finger against her lips, feeling the tiny shudder that rippled along his veins when he felt the moistness of her breath on his skin. 'I wouldn't have offered if I hadn't wanted to. And a car is just a means of getting from A to B at the end of the day.'

She laughed softly, moving her head so that his hand fell to his side. 'Most men wouldn't agree with you about that. They see their car as an extension of themselves.'

'Everyone's different.' He shrugged, curbing the urge to find some other way to touch her. Even if he held her hand, it would be too much. 'Anyway, off you go and fetch the little chap. Don't bother coming back for me. Charlie's probably ready for his supper so I'll get the driver to drop me off at your house while I pick up my car.'

'But you could be here for ages,' she protested worriedly. 'I'll come back after I've fed Charlie.'

'No. You just worry about getting him settled. I'll be fine.' He smiled at her, loving the way her eyes had darkened with concern at the thought of him having to wait around. He couldn't remember the last time anyone had worried about him like this.

He blanked out the thought and shooed her into his car. The seat was too far back for her to reach the pedals so he showed her how to adjust it then closed the door. She waved as she drove away and he waved back, surprised at how lost he felt when the car disappeared round a bend. How would he feel when he left for Paris? he wondered as he settled down to wait for the breakdown truck. Bereft? Lost? Lonely?

He sighed. He would feel all those things and it just proved that the sooner he was gone the better.

It was almost eight p.m. by the time Hannah heard a vehicle pull up outside. She rushed to the window in time to see Tom climb out of the cab of the tow truck. Hurrying to the door, she swung it open, apology written all over her face.

'I am *so* sorry!' she exclaimed, ushering him inside. 'I had no idea it would take the driver so long to get to you.'

'No worries.' Tom smiled at her as he stepped into the hallway. 'Apparently, it's been their busiest day this year. For some reason umpteen cars chose today to break down.'

'Typical,' Hannah snorted. She closed the front door and led the way into the sitting room. Picking up his keys from the old wooden trunk that doubled as both a toy box and a coffee table, she handed them to him. 'Anyway, I can't tell you how grateful I am for the loan of your car. It really was kind of you, Tom.'

'It was my pleasure.' He slid the keys into his pocket and looked around. 'I take it that Charlie's tucked up in bed?'

'He is. He wolfed down his supper, had his bath and that was it. I won't hear a peep out of him until the morning, I expect.'

'Obviously, you're a first-rate mum,' he said, laughing.

'Hmm, I don't think so. It's more a case of being lucky enough to have a child who sleeps.' She shrugged. 'I'm still very much at the trial and error stage of motherhood, believe me.'

'I don't suppose anyone knows it all at first. It's a learning process, isn't it? That's what must make being a parent such a special experience.'

'You're right. It is special. I wouldn't swop being a mother for anything,' she admitted.

'I can see that.'

His eyes were tender as they rested on her and Hannah felt a rush of warmth pour through her veins. It had been a long time since she'd been on the receiving end of so much caring and it felt good. She turned away, not wanting to dwell on the thought that it was all the more special because it was Tom doing the caring. 'Can I get you a drink? Or some supper? You've been hanging around for hours waiting for that wretched truck—you must be starving.'

'No. It's fine. I'll get something at The Ship.' He glanced at his watch and grimaced. 'Although I'm cutting it rather fine. They stop serving at nine.'

'In that case, I insist. It's the least I can do after everything you've done for me.' She didn't give him time to protest any more as she hurried into the kitchen and opened the fridge. Taking out a packet of bacon and some plump local sausages, she placed them on the worktop. 'How about a fry-up? Sausage, bacon, eggs, mushrooms.'

'Sounds delicious. My mouth's watering already.'

He followed her into the room, sitting down at the table while she set to work. Hannah took her largest frying pan out of the cupboard and soon had the bacon and sausages sizzling away. She cracked a couple of eggs into the pan, scooping the hot fat over them to set the yolks before glancing up.

'A slice of fried bread to go with it? Or would that be overkill?'

'My cholesterol levels can stand it,' he assured her, taking off his jacket and draping it over the back of the chair. 'Just!'

'Good.' Hannah laughed as she placed everything onto kitchen paper to drain while she fried the bread. She added a slice for herself, unable to resist the delicious aroma wafting from the pan. Tom groaned when she placed the loaded plate in front of him.

'If this tastes even half as good as it smells I shall be a very happy chappie.'

He dug in, wasting no time as he forked up a mouthful of food. Hannah put the kettle on then sat down opposite him and tucked into her fried bread with relish. 'I've no excuse for eating this,' she mumbled around a mouthful of the savoury concoction. 'I had supper with Charlie. *This* is pure greed!'

'A little of what you fancy does you good,' Tom teased her as he speared a mushroom with his fork.

'And puts inches on your hips,' she countered wryly.

'Rubbish! You certainly don't need to have any concerns on that score. You have a great figure, Hannah.'

She hadn't been fishing for compliments but that was how it must have sounded, she realised, and gave a little shrug. 'I've still got some of my baby weight to lose.'

'Well, you look great to me.' Tom picked up a piece of crispy bacon and offered it to her. 'How about some of this bacon? It really is delicious.'

'No, thanks. I refuse to let you lead me any further astray,' she retorted, then realised how that comment could be interpreted. Thankfully, either he didn't see it that way or judiciously chose to ignore the implication because he merely smiled as he bit the end off the bacon. He finished his supper in record time, leaning back in the chair with a sigh of contentment.

'That was great. It definitely made up for hanging around, waiting for that truck to arrive.'

'I'm glad. I don't feel quite so guilty now.' She removed their plates and took them over to the sink. 'What do you want to drink? Tea or coffee?'

'Oh, tea, please.' He stretched out his legs, trying to make himself comfortable on the hard-backed chair, and she frowned.

'Go on into the sitting room and I'll bring it through.'

'Thanks.'

He headed into the other room, opting for one end of the sofa. Hannah made a pot of tea and loaded everything onto a tray, feeling a sudden attack of nerves assail her. It had been fine while she'd been busy cooking but all of a sudden she was acutely aware of the intimacy of the situation. After all, she and Tom were alone in the house apart from Charlie and she wasn't sure if that was a wise thing or not. Picking up the tray, she headed into the sitting room, determined that she wasn't going to be carried away by such foolish notions. Maybe they were alone but it didn't mean that anything was going to happen.

'How do you take your tea?' she asked, placing the tray on the trunk and kneeling on the floor next to it.

'Milk and two sugars, please.' He watched her pour the tea, nodding his head when she placed the mug in front of him. 'Thanks.'

Hannah poured some tea for herself, just adding milk. 'Obviously you're sweet enough,' he observed, and she grimaced.

'That's so old it's sprouted whiskers!'

He chuckled. 'Sorry. Obviously, I need to work on my chat-up lines.'

It was a throw-away comment and she knew that he hadn't intended it any other way; however, it had an effect all the same. Her hand was shaking as she picked up her mug and sat down.

'That was a slip of the tongue, Hannah,' he said quietly. 'I didn't mean to make you feel uncomfortable.'

'Of course not!' She gave a tinkly laugh as she lifted the mug to her mouth but the tea was too hot to drink so she put it down. 'Did the mechanic say how long it would be before my car's fixed?' she asked to change the subject.

'The garage will give you a call tomorrow and let you know. They may need to order a new radiator if they haven't got one in stock.'

'Let's hope they've got one in otherwise I'll have to hire a car. Is there anywhere local that hires out cars?'

'Jim Cairns will sort you out. He owns the garage and has a couple of vehicles that he hires out.'

'Oh, right. That's good to know.' She took a sip of her tea, wondering what else to say to keep the conversation flowing. It was easier while they were talking— there was less time to think. She searched her mind, finally settling on what had happened that afternoon. 'I hope the diabetic care team get Susan Allsop sorted out. She seems like a really nice person.'

'She is. Her husband is just the same, very easy to get on with,' Tom assured her.

'That's probably why they've made such a success of running their guest house.'

'I'm sure you're right.'

He picked up his cup, staring down at the tea with a concentration it didn't merit. Hannah bit her lip as she reached for her own cup. It was obvious that he was finding it as much of a strain as she was and just knowing that sent alarm scudding through her. She didn't want Tom to feel like she did. It was too dangerous.

She put down the cup, determined that she was going to keep control of the situation. 'I really appreciated you taking me with you today. It's given me a much better idea of where everything is.'

'Good.' His tone was flat. 'The worst part of starting a new job is finding your way around, I always find.'

'It is.' She summoned a smile. 'At least I won't get lost if I need to visit Dentons Cove again.'

'I hope not.' He took a swallow of his tea then put down the mug. 'That was great but it's time I was off.'

'Of course,' she concurred, hoping her relief wasn't too obvious. She jumped to her feet, only realising at the last second that Tom had done the same thing. They collided with a thud that knocked her off balance.

'Careful!' Tom caught her arm when she reeled back. He hauled her upright, his eyes very dark as he stared into her face. 'Are you OK?'

'I…um… Fine.'

Hannah heard the breathless note in her voice but there was nothing she could do about it. They were so close that she could feel the hardness of his chest against her breasts. Heat rushed through her when she felt her nipples tauten and realised that he must have felt what was happening to her too. There was a moment when he continued to stare into her eyes and then slowly, so very slowly that she wasn't sure if it was really happening, he bent and pressed his mouth to hers.

That was when she knew it was real, when she felt his lips close over hers. Tom was kissing her, *really* kissing her, and although she knew it was foolish, she was kissing him back!

She heard him groan deep in his throat, heard him murmur her name in a tone that hinted at all the things he was feeling, from longing to despair, but it didn't surprise her. She knew how he felt because she felt the same way. She wanted this kiss and yet she knew in her heart it was wrong. It was just a question of which emotion would be the stronger, desire or common sense.

'This is crazy!' He tore his mouth away, cupping her face between his hands, and his eyes were filled with remorse as well as desire. 'I shouldn't be doing this. *You* shouldn't let me!'

'I know.' She met his eyes, knowing that he would see the same conflict of emotions on her face. 'I know it's crazy. And I know that I'll regret it...'

'But?' he put in urgently.

'But I can't help myself,' she whispered. She raised her hands, holding his face between them as he held hers because she needed him to understand how powerless she was to stop what was happening. She wanted him and, despite all her reservations, nothing seemed to matter more than that. 'I want you, Tom. I want us to make love even though I know we shouldn't.'

'So do I!'

He pulled her back into his arms, holding her so close that she couldn't fail to feel the urgent power of his arousal pressing into her. His mouth was hot and hungry when it found hers again and she responded instantly to its demands. She kissed him with all the pent-up emotion that had been building inside her ever since they had met and felt the shudder that ran through him. That he should be so vulnerable shocked her because she hadn't expected that, hadn't expected a kiss to make him tremble like this.

A wave of tenderness rose up inside her as she pressed herself against him, letting him feel the effect he had on her. It was only fair that he should know how much the kiss had aroused her too. His arms tightened around her, moulding her against him in a way that left little to either of their imaginations. He could feel the hardness of her nipples pressing against his chest, she could feel his arousal...

He suddenly bent and swung her off her feet, lifting her in his arms as he walked towards the stairs. His face was set, his eyes dark pools of desire as he looked down into her face. 'Are you sure this is what you want, Hannah? Absolutely certain?'

'Yes,' she told him, because it would be a lie to say anything else. 'I want us to make love, Tom, even if we only do it this one time.'

She saw by his expression that he understood. This wasn't the start of something more. This was one night of passion, one night they could share; one night out of their lives that maybe...hopefully...they would look back on in the future with pleasure.

'It will be good,' he whispered as he kissed her hungrily. 'I'll make sure it is, Hannah, for both of us.'

'I know.'

She smiled up at him, not having any doubts about that. It would be good, better than that, it would wonderful because it was all they would have. One night out of all the thousands of nights to come. One night to enjoy each other's bodies, to let their passion soar, to feel things they would never feel again, at least not for each other. This one night was going to be so very special. It was going to be theirs.

CHAPTER NINE

Tom didn't switch on the light as he carried Hannah into her bedroom. He didn't need to. He could enjoy her beautiful body just as much by touch and taste and feel.

A shiver ran through him as he laid her down on the bed. He had never envisaged this happening, actively tried to prevent it, but now they had reached this point he knew that he wouldn't regret it. No matter how hard it was in the future or how much he missed her, he would never wish that this night had never happened.

The thought filled him with tenderness as he bent and brushed her mouth with his. Her lips were so soft and sweet that he couldn't seem to get enough of them so the kiss ran on and on until they were both breathless. Drawing back, he stared into her face, loving the way that she didn't try to hide her feelings from him. Hannah had enjoyed the kiss as much as he had done and she was willing to own up to it too.

He sat down on the edge of the bed and gathered her into his arms, loving the feel of her body nestled against him. Sex for him in the past had always been a far more mechanical experience. He did this or that and achieved the desired results. However, he realised all of a sudden that this approach wasn't good enough

tonight. He didn't want to add A to B and end up at C—
no way! He wanted to be involved all the way through,
wanted Hannah to be involved too. They weren't just
having sex. They were making love.

The thought was so mind-blowing that he couldn't
handle it. It opened up a whole host of possibilities he
simply couldn't face. Dipping his head, he kissed her
again, slowly and with a passion that seemed to spring
from the very core of him, a place that had never been
visited before. It was as though the feel of her mouth
under his had opened up all the secret places inside
him and the emotions he'd kept hidden there had come
pouring out. If this was the difference between making love and having sex then it struck him how much
he'd been missing.

His hand smoothed down her body, faithfully following the swell of her breasts, the dip of her waist,
the curve of her hips. Although she was slender, she
had curves in all the right places and he gloried in the
feel and shape of her. His hand glided on, reached her
thighs and lingered while he took a moment to breathe.
It sounded crazy but his lungs didn't seem able to draw
in enough oxygen any longer.

He breathed in greedily then groaned when he felt
her nipples pressing against his chest. It would have
taken a lot more willpower than he possessed to ignore
their demand. His hand swept back up her body until it
was cupping her left breast, the pad of his thumb sensu-
ally rubbing the hard, tight bud, and she sighed softly
and with unconcealed pleasure. She turned slightly so
that the full weight of her breast fell into his palm and
he groaned again, unable to believe how good it felt to
touch her. All his previous experiences suddenly paled

into nothing and he realised with a jolt how ill equipped he was to handle this situation. Although he'd enjoyed his share of sex over the years and developed his skills as a lover, *making love* was very different. Although he knew that he could satisfy her physically, he wasn't sure that he could fulfil her emotional needs. Bearing in mind his earlier claims that this night was going to be special, he could only pray that he was up to it.

The thought made him tense and Hannah looked at him in concern. 'Tom? Is something wrong?'

'No,' he began, then realised that he couldn't lie. What if he failed to make this night as wonderful as he'd promised her it would be? He couldn't bear to think that he might disappoint her, that tomorrow morning she would regret what they'd done because it hadn't lived up to her expectations.

'I think I've got a bad case of cold feet,' he said, struggling to inject a little levity into his voice. It sounded closer to panic to his ears but he dredged up a smile in the hope that it would convince her.

'Cold feet?' She frowned. 'You mean that you don't want to go through with this...'

'No!'

The word shot out of his mouth and she jumped. She drew back, the frown that had been wrinkling her brow a moment earlier deepening. 'Then what do you mean?'

'That I'm scared stiff I'll disappoint you.' His voice was louder than he'd intended and he saw her glance towards the door. He moderated his tone, knowing that she was worried about him waking Charlie. 'Sex has always been just that in the past, Hannah, but this is different. I...well, I'm afraid that I won't be able to meet your expectations as I promised to do.'

'Oh, that's so silly!' The frown melted away as she leant forward and brushed her lips over his. 'You won't disappoint me, Tom. You'll see.'

He wasn't sure he shared her confidence but he wasn't going to labour the point. Not when she'd been so understanding. The tension oozed out of him, and he laughed softly as he gathered her into his arms. 'I hope you're right, sweetheart.'

'I know I am.'

Her lips found his, warm and soft and so achingly tender that his insides melted. However, when he tried to take charge of the kiss, she moved away, her mouth skimming across his cheek and along his jaw, her sharp little teeth nibbling the cord in his neck as it slid down his throat, and he shuddered. Never had he experienced anything quite so erotic as these hot, sweet kisses!

Her lips found the pulse at the base of his throat and stopped, the tip of her tongue snaking out to taste his skin, and he couldn't stand it any more. He needed to take a much more active role in the proceedings and to hell with worrying if he had the wherewithal to deliver on his promise! With one quick movement, he rolled her onto her back, using his forearms to support his weight as he loomed over her. Her eyes were huge, her lips parted, her breathing rapid, and his desire for her ran riot.

He kissed her hard and hungrily, not letting her go until the need to breathe became too urgent to ignore. They were both panting when he pulled back, both trembling, both filled with need, and his heart overflowed with all kinds of emotions when he realised it. Hannah wanted him just as much and in just as many ways as he wanted her!

The thought was all he needed. Dragging his shirt over his head, he tossed it onto the floor. Hannah was unfastening her blouse, murmuring in frustration when one of the tiny pearl buttons snagged on a loose thread. She undid it at last and tossed it aside, and he gulped. Although he hadn't switched on a lamp there was enough light filtering in from the landing to see by. The sight of her full breasts encased in that lacy white bra would have been temptation enough for any man. And it was way too much for him.

He slid the bra straps down her arms so that her breasts spilled out of their lacy covering. Her nipples were already dark and taut yet they tightened even more when he ran the palms of his hands over them. Hannah moaned softly and closed her eyes so he did it again, slowly and with exquisite care, feeling his own body respond in the most blatant way. Quite frankly, if he didn't get out his trousers soon he was in danger of doing himself permanent damage!

He shed his trousers and underwear then stripped off Hannah's skirt and panties. Her skin was smooth and warm to the touch when he ran his hands over it, flowing beneath his fingers like silk. He reached the very source of her heat and paused, wanting to be sure, one hundred per cent certain, that it was what she wanted. Even though it would be agony to stop now, he would do if it was what she wanted.

'Hannah?'

He didn't put the question into words, didn't need to because she understood. Opening her eyes, she looked at him and he felt a rush of relief run through him when he realised that there wasn't a trace of doubt in her gaze. Bending, he kissed her slowly and passionately, parting her lips as his fingers sought out her most secret place, and felt her shudder.

When he entered her a few moments later, Tom realised that nothing he'd experienced in the past had prepared him for this. This was what love-making was all about. This was how sex was meant to be. Here and now, with Hannah in his arms and their bodies joined in the most intimate way possible, he finally understood what he had been missing for all these years.

It was still dark when Hannah awoke, the sun not even peeping over the horizon. She lay quite still, listening to the sound of Tom's breathing while she tried to work out how she felt. Oh, she knew how she *should* feel—that was a given bearing in mind what had happened. But did she honestly regret making love with him? Did she wish it hadn't happened and feel angry with herself for giving in to temptation when she'd sworn she wouldn't?

A tiny sighed escaped her as she was forced to admit that she felt none of those things. She didn't regret their love-making, neither did she wish it hadn't happened. As for feeling angry with herself, well, quite frankly, she felt more like leaping up and punching the air than anything else! Making love with Tom had been fantastic, better than that, it had been life-affirmingly wonderful from start to finish. The only thing she regretted was that she hadn't met him before she'd met Andrew and then the past miserable twelve months might never have happened.

A wave of euphoria washed over her and she wriggled a little, savouring the feeling, and heard Tom's breathing change. She forced herself to lie still in the hope that he would drop off back to sleep but it appeared the damage had been done. He rolled onto his side, pushing his hair out of his eyes as he peered at the dial of his watch.

'Five-fifteen? Do you always wake at this unearthly hour?' he murmured, his sleep-laden voice sounding sexier than ever, and Hannah couldn't stop herself. She wriggled again.

'Not normally,' she murmured, struggling to get a grip. So she and Tom had had great sex. Fine. Now it was the morning after the night before and although she'd be the first to admit that she wasn't an expert on the protocol of this kind of situation, she suspected that she shouldn't make it quite so clear that she'd be happy if there was a repeat!

'So what woke you?' He lifted a strand of hair off her cheek and tucked it behind her ear and she did her best not to wriggle or tremble or anything else.

'I'm not sure. Maybe Charlie made a noise and it woke me,' she muttered, although it was an out-and-out lie.

'Hmm. Possibly.' His fingers traced the shell of her ear, following the curve until they reached her jaw where they lingered, warm and oddly reassuring, and she felt herself relax a little.

'Mother's instinct,' she claimed, happily perpetuating the small untruth because she enjoyed the feel of his fingers on her skin. 'We're programmed to wake at even the slightest noise our child makes.'

'So long as it was that and not the fact that you were worrying about what happened last night,' he murmured in a deceptively mild tone.

Hannah flushed, knowing that she'd been found out. 'That may have had something to do with it.'

'I'm sorry if you're upset, Hannah. It's the very last thing I wanted.' His tone was harsher now but it didn't disguise the underlying pain, and she knew that she couldn't allow him to jump to the wrong conclusions.

'I'm not upset.' She turned to face him. 'Last night was wonderful, Tom, and I enjoyed every second.'

'So did I.' He smiled but she could see the doubt in his eyes and knew that he still didn't understand. How could he when she'd had to work it out for herself?

'Good. It would be awful if you hadn't enjoyed it as much as me. And even worse if you regretted it.' Her eyes held his fast because she didn't want there to be any mistake about what she was saying. 'I don't regret what happened. Maybe I should, I don't know. After all, I don't make a habit of having one-night stands. But all I can say is that I enjoyed making love with you and that this morning I feel better than I've felt for a very long time.'

'Hannah! Sweetheart, I don't know what to say...'

He broke off, closing his eyes, and she guessed that he was struggling to get a grip on his emotions. The thought touched her deeply and she reached out and laid her hand on his cheek.

'You don't have to say anything. That's the beauty of this situation, isn't it? We spent the night together and enjoyed it. It's as simple as that.'

'Is it?' His eyes opened and she shivered when she found herself staring into their azure depths. 'Is it really that simple, Hannah?'

'It has to be. You're leaving in a few days' time and I'm staying here to build a new life for myself and Charlie. Last night was a one-off—we both knew that.'

'You're right. Of course you are.' He pulled her to

him and kissed her lightly on the lips. 'I'm just glad that you're happy with the situation. I would have hated it if you'd been hurt or upset.'

He obviously meant that and her eyes filled with tears but she blinked them away. She wouldn't allow anything to spoil what they'd had, not when it had given her so much that she hadn't even realised she had lost. After they had found out that Charlie wouldn't be perfect when he was born, Andrew had become very distant. He had made no attempt to sleep with her, hadn't even shown any inclination to kiss or cuddle her. Although it had hurt to be rejected so thoroughly, she hadn't realised how much she had missed the physical contact until last night. Making love with Tom hadn't been merely a matter of them having great sex; it had been so much more than that.

The thought made her feel a little on edge but there was no time to worry about it when Tom's hands were stroking her body, bringing it to life once more. Maybe she should have stopped him by insisting that they had only agreed to the one night but it seemed churlish to do so, especially when she was enjoying his touch so much.

Hannah closed her eyes and gave herself up to the magic, feeling the hot waves of desire chase away all the hurt and loneliness she'd endured during the past year. When she was in Tom's arms, when his mouth was on hers and his hands were reminding her of how it felt to be a woman, she couldn't think about anything else. She didn't want to. She just wanted to enjoy what was happening and savour the time they had together.

One night may have turned into one night plus a morning but that was it. There wouldn't be any more. This was the last time they would make love, at least to each other, and she intended to appreciate every second, relish every minute. This was their time, hers and Tom's. A wonderful memory to look back on with pleasure.

'Ah, Tom. There you are. What happened to you last night, or shouldn't I ask?'

Tom felt a rush of heat invade him when he turned to find Simon standing behind him. Just for a moment his mind went blank, which was a miracle considering the thoughts that had been filling it on the drive to the surgery.

'Hmm. Obviously I shouldn't ask leading questions like that.' Simon laughed as he clapped him on the shoulder. 'Sorry. I didn't mean to pry. It's just that Ros mentioned your bed hadn't been slept in and we were worried in case something had happened to you.'

'I stayed with a friend,' Tom said, praying that his godfather wouldn't ask which friend. Out of the corner of his eye he saw the surgery door open and tensed when he saw Hannah coming in. She was wearing her usual working attire—a neat black skirt teamed with a crisp white blouse—but it was just the tiniest step back in time to picture what she'd been wearing the last time he'd seen her...

He blanked out the thought. Picturing Hannah naked in her bed wasn't going to help one little bit! Fortunately, Simon seemed to have been distracted by her arrival. He smiled jovially at her.

'Good morning, my dear. You're bright and early. I hope it isn't because you didn't sleep last night.'

'I...um...no, not at all.'

Tom saw the rush of colour run up her cheeks and hastily intervened. Bearing in mind that it was his fault that she'd woken at such an unearthly hour, it seemed the least he could do. 'Did I tell you that I've managed to book myself on a flight to Paris leaving on Monday morning?'

'Good. Well, not good that you're leaving, of course, but I'm glad that you managed to get things sorted after all the recent shenanigans.' Simon sighed. 'Ros is still rather miffed because I said we couldn't go to see Becky but I really don't think it's fair to ask you to change your plans so late in the day. And it certainly isn't fair to Hannah to abandon her when she's only been here a week.'

Was that all it was? Tom thought wonderingly. They'd known each other not quite a week and yet it felt as though she'd been part of his life for ever.

'Maybe you can go later in the year,' Hannah suggested, and Tom knew—he just *knew*—that the same thought had flown through her head too.

He turned away, murmuring something about a patient needing an early blood test. It wasn't a lie. One of his patients was booked in for a fasting cholesterol test but Emily was doing it, not him. He made his way to the treatment room where he found Barry Rogers already waiting. He took the bloods, brushing aside Emily's apologies when she arrived a few minutes later and discovered it had been done. As he told her truthfully, she wasn't late, he was early and there was nothing to apologise for.

Tom made his way to his consulting room and busied himself with setting up for the day. It was a task that demanded minimal concentration but he focussed all his energy on getting ready. It was easier that way. Safer. He couldn't afford to let his mind wander, wouldn't allow himself to wish that he wasn't leaving. He had to leave to protect Hannah. Last night had proved that it would take very little for him to fall in love with her and that was something he couldn't countenance. Maybe he would love her for a short while but how long would his feelings last?

He'd thought he'd been in love with his ex-fiancée, hadn't he? After all, she had ticked all the boxes, at least on paper. She'd been beautiful, witty, clever and sophisticated. He had enjoyed spending time with her and had convinced himself that his feelings would last. He'd been determined to buck the trend and prove that he could do what no one else in his family had done. He was going to marry her and they would live happily ever after...only it hadn't worked out that way. Just a few weeks after they'd announced their engagement he'd started to have second thoughts, and a couple of months further down the line, he'd realised that he had made a huge mistake.

Their break-up had been less than amicable, not that he blamed her for that. After all, he was the one who had changed his mind and she'd had every right to be angry. But what if it happened again? What if his feelings for Hannah melted away as they had done before? She deserved so much more after what had happened to her recently. She deserved to find happiness with a man who would look after her for ever more. What she didn't deserve was someone like him, someone who couldn't promise to love and honour her, and stick to it.

Tom stabbed his finger on the button to summon his first patient. He knew what he had to do and if it hurt then it was his hard luck. Far better to live with an aching heart than a guilty conscience.

CHAPTER TEN

THE day proved to be less stressful than Hannah might have expected, given the circumstances. She spoke to Tom several times and there was no trace of awkwardness between them. Maybe it was the fact that they had set out clear boundaries before they had slept together but it was a relief, all the same. It made her feel very positive about what had happened. One of the worst things about her break-up with Andrew was the effect it had had on her confidence. However, last night had changed all that and she felt far more in control of her life.

She was on her way to the office after evening surgery finished when Simon waylaid her. 'I'm glad I caught you, my dear. I won't keep you because I know you must be anxious to collect your little boy from the nursery, but I just wanted to know if you're free on Saturday night. Ros is organising a bit of a "do" for Tom before he leaves. Everyone's coming—it's a proper staff outing, in fact, so naturally we're hoping you'll come along too.'

'I'm not sure if I can,' Hannah said slowly, wondering about the wisdom of what was being suggested. Last night may not have caused any major repercussions but would it be pushing it to spend another night in Tom's company? She hurried on, deciding that it would be silly to push her luck. 'I don't have a babysitter for Charlie, I'm afraid.'

'Oh, that's not a problem,' Simon assured her. 'Emily's in much the same boat as you. Her parents are away at the moment and she's not got a babysitter, so she's bringing her little boy along. There's no reason why you can't bring Charlie. I'm sure he'll enjoy it.'

'I'm sure he will,' Hannah murmured, realising that she couldn't refuse now. After all, she didn't want everyone to think that she was being stand-offish. And what on earth could happen, anyway? She and Tom were hardly going to be overcome by a fit of passion surrounded by their colleagues! She summoned a smile. 'In that case, I'd love to come. Thank you.'

'Wonderful! Ros will be delighted.'

Simon patted her on the shoulder then carried on. Hannah deposited her files in the tray then said goodnight to Lizzie and their part-time receptionist, Alison Blake. Emily came in as she was leaving and smiled at her.

'Simon just told me that you're going to bring Charlie on Saturday night.'

'That's right. I was a bit dubious at first but he told me you were bringing your son along too. How old is he?'

'Theo is two and a holy terror.' Emily laughed, her pretty face lighting up in a way that told how much she adored the little boy. 'He's into *everything*. Simon and Ros don't know what they're letting themselves in for!'

Hannah chuckled. 'From what Ros was telling me

about their twins when they were small, I doubt they'll turn a hair.'

'Fingers crossed.' Emily grimaced. 'Anyway, it will be nice to meet your little one. Hopefully he'll provide a distraction when my Theo gets into his stride!'

They both laughed before they parted company. Hannah got into the hire car that Jim Cairns had delivered to the surgery for her and drove to the nursery, thinking how good it was to have another woman in a similar situation to hers to talk to. She knew from various comments that had been made that Emily was a single mother too and it would be great to compare notes. The fact that Emily's son was not that much older than Charlie was an added bonus. It would be wonderful if the two boys grew up to be friends.

It was yet another positive thought and it helped to boost the feeling that her life was on the up at last. Maybe she hadn't envisaged sleeping with Tom but it hadn't had a detrimental effect, had it? And after the weekend it wouldn't be an issue. Tom would be on his way to Paris and that would be the end of the matter.

The thought should have buoyed her up even more but as she parked outside the nursery, she couldn't quell a pang of regret at the thought of not seeing him again. Maybe she had known him only for a week but there was no denying that he had made a big impression on her.

Tom spent the best part of Saturday packing. Although he travelled light there were always things that he accumulated along the way. He stored some of the books he'd bought in Simon's attic then put the remainder in a local charity's collection bag. Although his official home was the family's estate in Shropshire, he rarely went back there, so most of his belongings were scattered around the globe at the various places where he'd worked. At some point he would have to retrieve them, he thought as he added a couple of sweaters to the bag. However, before he did that he would need to have a place to take them. And having a home of his own wasn't something he had thought about. Until recently.

He sighed as he carried the bag out to his car. Getting hung up on the idea of setting down roots would be a mistake. Oh, he knew why he was thinking along those lines, of course. It was all down to Hannah. However, nothing was going to happen between them, at least, nothing more than already had.

Once again his thoughts flew back to that night they had spent together and he slammed the boot lid. He had to stop thinking about it! He had to stop torturing himself by wishing it would happen again. They had both agreed that it must be a one-off and he wasn't going to sink so low as to try to change her mind. When he left Bride's Bay, he intended to leave with a clear conscience.

Hannah put Charlie down for a nap at four o'clock then took advantage of the free time and had a bath. She washed her hair, wrapping it in a towel while she gave herself a much-needed pedicure. Looking after a baby as well as working left little time to pamper herself and it was a treat to indulge herself for once. She applied a coat of pale pink varnish to her toenails then blow-dried her hair, leaving it to fall around her face in loose chestnut waves. By the time Charlie woke up an hour later, she was ready. Putting an apron over the pretty floral dress she had decided to wear, she changed him into a clean blue T-shirt and matching shorts. With his dark curls all brushed and shining, he looked so adorable that her heart melted. How could anyone think that this gorgeous little boy was less than perfect?

She decided to walk to The Ship as it was such a lovely evening so popped Charlie in his pushchair and set off. She had just got there when Tom pulled into the car park so she waited for him because it would have been silly not to. He got out of the car, looking so big and handsome in a pair of well-washed jeans and a deep blue polo shirt that her heart melted a second time. If only Tom had been Charlie's father, she thought wistfully, then realised how foolish it was to think such a thing.

'Hi! That was good timing.' Tom came over to join them, stooping down so he could say hello to Charlie, who responded by holding up his arms to be picked up. Tom laughed as he lifted him out of the pram. 'Tired of being strapped in, are you, tiger? I don't blame you.'

He balanced the baby on his hip, making it look so natural that Hannah couldn't stop the previous thought resurfacing. Tom would make a wonderful father, a father who would love and care for his child no matter what. A lump came to her throat and she cleared her throat, afraid that her emotions would get the better of her.

'He hates being fastened in for long, which doesn't bode well for the evening. I only hope he doesn't disturb everyone when they're trying to enjoy their meal.'

'Nobody will mind,' Tom assured her. His eyes skimmed over her and he smiled. 'You look really lovely tonight, Hannah. That dress suits you.'

'Oh. Thank you.' She felt the heat rush up her face and turned away. He probably says that to all the women he's slept with, she told herself bluntly, but it had little effect. Maybe he did dish out compliments readily enough but there was no doubt that he had been sincere.

The thought was a boost to her ego. As she led the way into the pub, she couldn't help thinking how good it felt to be appreciated. Although Andrew had taken a keen interest in her appearance, he'd been more concerned that she should look the part than anything else. He had wanted her to fit into the perfect life he'd been so eager to create for them and had expected her to dress accordingly. It struck her all of a sudden how empowering it was to be able to choose what *she* wanted to wear.

'Penny for them.'

Tom jogged her elbow and she jumped. She gave him a quick smile, unwilling to confess how influenced she'd been by her ex. She had been so eager to create that perfect life too that she had stopped being herself, and it was galling to admit it. 'Sorry, I was miles away. Shall I take Charlie?'

She held out her arms but Tom shook his head. 'No, he's fine with me, aren't you, sunshine?'

He brushed the baby's head with a kiss and once again Hannah was struck by how natural it looked. The fact that there was a definite similarity between him and Charlie also helped. As she followed him across the dining room, she couldn't help wondering how many people thought that they were a real family.

It was an unsettling thought mainly because she knew it would be too easy to get hung up on it. When they reached their party, she lifted Charlie out of Tom's arms and popped him in the high-chair that Ros had thoughtfully placed beside the table. Tom wasn't Charlie's dad and he never would be. There was no point fantasising.

'We're just waiting for Emily now and then we're all here,' Ros announced, beaming at them. 'Did you and Tom drive down together?'

'No. I walked,' Hannah explained, making sure the straps on the baby's harness were secure. She looked up and flushed when she saw the speculative look on Ros's face. It was obvious what the other woman was thinking and she hurried on. 'I bumped into Tom on the way in and he offered to carry Charlie.'

'It was perfect timing,' Tom said easily, pulling out a chair and sitting down next to the high-chair. He laughed when Charlie immediately made a grab for his nose. 'Oh, no, not the nose again, young man. If you keep on pulling it I'll end up like Cyrano de Bergerac!'

Everyone laughed. 'I take it that it's a favourite trick of his?' Ros said archly, and Tom grinned.

'Seems to be, doesn't it, Hannah? Every time I see this little chap, he makes a grab for my poor old nose.'

Hannah smiled, deeming it safer not to say anything. However, from the look on Ros's face, she was already adding two and two and coming up with her own answer! She busied herself with finding a bib for Charlie along with all the other paraphernalia he might need during the meal—wet wipes and a drinking cup, a plastic spoon and a dish. Tom studied the items she'd amassed with open amusement.

'It's like a military operation taking him out. You must have to be very organised.'

'You get used to it,' she assured him. She handed Charlie his cup of juice, her hand at the ready to catch it when he dropped it over the side of the chair, which he did.

Tom laughed out loud. 'You'd go down a storm on the local cricket team with reactions like that!'

'I get plenty of practice.' She smiled back, loving the way his eyes lit up when he looked at her. Maybe he was an accomplished flirt, but there was no point pretending that it didn't make her feel good to know that he found her attractive.

There was no time to dwell on that thought, thankfully, as Emily arrived just then. Once Emily and little Theo were settled, they decided to order. Hannah opted for chicken in lemon sauce, one of her favourite dishes. She'd brought a jar of baby food for Charlie and the waitress offered to warm it for her. It was brought back a few minutes later by a young man whom Tom introduced as Peter Granger, Barbara's son. Hannah smiled at him. 'It's nice to meet you, Peter.'

'You too, Dr Hannah,' he said shyly as he handed her the dish.

'Did your mum manage to arrange for you to visit the hospital?'

'Yes. I'm going next week to meet the doctors and nurses who'll be looking after me.' He gave her a quick smile. 'Mum says I won't feel so worried if I meet everyone before I have my operation.'

'It will be much nicer for you,' Hannah assured him.

'That was a good idea on your part, my dear,' Simon told her after Peter hurried away. 'Well done for thinking of it.'

'I can't take all the credit,' Hannah protested. 'It was Tom's idea. He'd seen the leaflet the hospital sent out and he showed it to me.'

'Excellent teamwork, then, wouldn't you say?'

Simon turned to Lizzie's husband and the subject was dropped. However, Hannah found herself thinking about the comment. She and Tom did work well together and there was no denying it. They seemed to be in accord when it came to their patients and there was no doubt at all that they were in even more accord in other areas.

Heat rushed through her and she busied herself spooning dinner into Charlie's mouth. She didn't want to think about how good it had been when she and Tom had made love. Maybe she would meet someone in the future who would make her feel just as good, but she would have to wait and see. She certainly wasn't going to rush into anything and end up regretting it.

If…and it was a very big *if*…she reached a point where she was ready to form another relationship then she would need to be sure it was not only right for her but right for Charlie too. Charlie had been let down once and she would never risk it happening again. *If* she did decide to spend her life with someone then he would have to accept Charlie for who he was. He would also need to love and care for Charlie as though he was his own flesh and blood because anything less wasn't acceptable.

It was a lot to ask of any man, Hannah thought, glancing at Tom. And especially of a man like Tom who'd admitted that he had problems with commitment. It made her see that wishing Tom could play a role in her and Charlie's future would be a mistake.

Tom had to admit that he had mixed feelings about the evening. Whilst he enjoyed being with everyone, it proved to be rather a strain to sit beside Hannah and pretend that they were nothing more than colleagues. Even though he knew it was how he must think of her, it was difficult after what had happened the other night. He kept getting flashbacks to the time they'd spent together, vividly erotic images of her laughing up at him, her lips swollen from his kisses, her eyes heavy with passion. And each time it happened, his nerves tightened that bit more and his body grew hot and hungry.

He wanted her again, wanted to make love to her, wanted to take her back to her house and do everything they'd done the other night, then wake up in the morning and do it all over again. It was like a hunger inside him, one he couldn't sate no matter how hard he tried to distract himself. It was a relief when everyone started to make a move. Emily was obviously eager to get Theo home, and Lizzie and her husband wanted to watch the latest episode of some reality show on TV. Tom smiled around the table, appreciating the fact that everyone had turned out to wish him well.

'I'd just like to thank you all for coming tonight. It's been a great evening and a great couple of months at the surgery too. I can honestly say that I've enjoyed every moment of my time here.'

'And we've enjoyed having you, Tom,' Simon assured him. He glanced at Ros and Tom frowned when he saw the look that passed between them. They were obviously up to something, although he had no idea what.

'I may as well cut to the chase, Tom. I've just received word that the primary care trust has decided to back plans to extend Bride's Bay Surgery. With several practices closing recently, they are concerned that there isn't sufficient provision for the number of patients in the area. Consequently Bride's Bay Surgery will be extended and given health-centre status. We'll have a full complement of staff—physios, midwives, community care nurses, etcetera. It also means that we'll need at least two more doctors.'

'I see,' Tom said slowly, suddenly realising where this was leading. He cleared his throat. 'It all sounds very exciting.'

'It is.' Simon leant across the table. 'It's a wonderful opportunity not only for the patients but for the staff. That's why I want you to consider being part of it.'

'I don't know what to say,' Tom said truthfully. He glanced around the table, seeking inspiration. He didn't want to hurt Simon after everything his godfather had done for him but he knew that he had to turn down the offer. It went against his strictest rule to remain in one place for too long.

His gaze alighted on Hannah and he felt a rush of emotions hit him. Maybe it did go against everything he believed but surely rules could be broken if there was a good enough reason. If he stayed in Bride's Bay then he could get to know her better, allow these feelings he had to develop into something deeper. He could lie to himself all he liked but the truth was that she affected him in ways he had never imagined any woman could do. She made him long for a life he had always believed was beyond his reach. When he was with her he wanted it all—a wife, a family, a home of his own. But could he do it? Could he promise to be faithful and stick to it? Because one thing was certain: Hannah deserved nothing less than a lifetime's commitment.

CHAPTER ELEVEN

THE party broke up a short time later. Hannah lifted Charlie out of the high chair and attempted to strap him into his pram but he was having none of it. He let out a loud wail, making it clear what he thought of the idea.

'It's all right, darling,' she said, soothingly. 'It'll only be for a few minutes so be a good boy for Mummy.'

She tried to settle him in his pushchair, no easy feat at the best of times thanks to the casts on his legs, but he resisted her efforts. She could see people turning to look and decided to give it up rather than disturb everyone. Hitching him onto her hip, she attempted to steer the pushchair towards the door, one-handed.

'Here. Let me take him.' Tom deftly lifted Charlie out of her arms and swung him into the air. He grinned when the little boy immediately stopped screaming. 'Hmm, it doesn't take much to cheer you up, does it?'

Hannah followed them across the restaurant, too relieved to have averted a scene to feel affronted that her son had responded better to Tom than he had to her. This wasn't the time to start having doubts about her ability as a mother!

Tom reached the door and waited for her, holding it open while she manoeuvred the pushchair outside.

Lizzie and her husband Frank waved as they hurried over to their car. They were giving Alison a lift and the three of them soon disappeared. Emily and Theo had already left, and Simon and Ros had stopped to speak to Mitch Johnson. It meant that she and Tom were alone except for Charlie.

'Thanks.' Hannah summoned a smile, praying that Tom couldn't tell how on edge she felt. Simon's proposal that Tom should consider working at the surgery on a permanent basis had come like a bolt from the blue and she wasn't sure how she felt about it. Scared was probably the truthful answer, although there were other emotions trying to surface. Would she have slept with him if she'd had any idea this would happen? she wondered as they crossed the car park. Probably not, she decided, not when it could lead to all sorts of complications.

'Charlie's usually very good,' she said quickly, refusing to dwell on it. If Tom did decide to accept Simon's offer then she would have to deal with it. However, there was no point worrying unnecessarily, was there? 'But when he decides he doesn't want to do a thing then he really lets you know.'

'He's probably tired of sitting still, aren't you, sunshine?' Tom chucked the little boy under the chin, earning himself a sleepy smile. He settled him more comfortably against his chest then glanced at her. 'Shall I carry him home for you? There doesn't seem any point upsetting him again, does there?'

Hannah hesitated but she had to admit that it made sense. 'If you're sure you don't mind...'

'Of course I don't.'

There was a hint of impatience in his voice that surprised her, although she didn't say anything. It took them just a few minutes to walk back up the road from the harbour. It was still light, the sun riding low in the sky and casting a thick band of gold along the horizon. The fishermen were getting ready to set sail and the sound of their voices carried on the breeze. Hannah sighed as she reached for her key and unlocked the front door.

'It's so beautiful and peaceful here. I'd forgotten that places like this still exist.'

'Bride's Bay is very special,' Tom agreed, following her inside. He glanced at Charlie, frowning when he saw that the child's eyes were closed. 'I think he's asleep. Shall I carry him upstairs?'

'Please.'

Hannah moved aside, feeling her pulse leap when his shoulder brushed hers as he passed. She followed him up the stairs, reaching past him to open the door to Charlie's bedroom. It was little more than a box room, in all honesty, with a sloping ceiling at one end and a tiny window set in the eaves. However, the bright blue curtains and bedding printed with yellow diggers she'd chosen made it look very cheerful. Tom obviously thought so because he smiled as he looked around.

'I love this room. It's a real little boy's room. I wish I'd had a bedroom like this when I was growing up.'

'I had a lot of fun choosing everything,' she assured him. She took Charlie from him and laid him on the changing table, quickly changing his nappy and popping on a cotton sleepsuit. He didn't wake up as she gently placed him in his cot after she'd finished.

'Is that it?' Tom sounded so surprised that she laughed.

'Hopefully. I expect he's exhausted after all the excitement of being out tonight. With a bit of luck he'll sleep straight through till the morning.'

'You make it look so easy,' Tom said admiringly, following her from the room. 'So many people bang on and on about how hard it is looking after a baby, but you don't seem to have any problems.'

'Oh, I do, believe me. There've been days when I've been tearing my hair out. You just have to ride them out and hope things improve.'

'It can't be easy when you're on your own,' he said quietly, and she shrugged.

'It's just the way things are.'

She led the way down the stairs, not sure that she wanted to be drawn into a discussion about the difficulties of being a single parent. After all, it wasn't Tom's problem and it never would be. The thought was dispiriting and she hurried on. 'Well, thanks for walking us home. I really appreciate it.'

'Not a problem.' He gave her a quick smile. 'I'd better be off. There's still a few things I need to sort out ready for Monday.'

'Are you all packed?'

'More or less. I only ever travel light and that helps.'

'You can be up and off in a matter of hours,' she suggested, and he grimaced.

'Something like that.' He reached for the door latch then paused. 'I don't suppose I'll see you again before I leave, Hannah, so take care of yourself, won't you?'

'And you,' she murmured, feeling a sudden rush of tears spring to her eyes. She blinked them away but not fast enough obviously because he sighed.

'I hope those tears aren't for me, Hannah, because I

don't deserve them. Whilst I don't regret the other night, I do know that I should never have allowed it to happen.'

'It wasn't down to you, though. It was what we both wanted.'

'Yes. And that means an awful lot to me, too.' He bent and kissed her on the cheek, his lips lingering in a way that told her how much he needed the contact. Maybe it was that thought or maybe it was the fact that all of a sudden she needed to touch him too but the next second her arms were around his neck. She heard him breathe in sharply and held on, sensing that he was about to pull away.

'Hannah, no. We mustn't. We agreed that the other night should be a one-off.'

The words should have brought her back down to earth with a bump. After all, what he said was perfectly true. However, no matter how sensible he was trying to be, it couldn't disguise the hunger in his voice.

'I know what we agreed, Tom. But can you put your hand on your heart and swear that you aren't tempted to spend one more night together?'

'I... No!'

He dragged her into his arms, holding her so tight that she was crushed against the wall of his chest. When he bent and kissed her with a hunger that he didn't attempt to disguise, she kissed him back, just as hungrily. Maybe they had planned on having only the one night but she needed this night too, needed Tom to hold her, love her, to turn her life into all positives.

He lifted her into his arms and carried her into the sitting room, laying her down on the sofa before kneeling down beside her. His eyes were tender as they skimmed her face, filled with a range of emotions that touched something deep inside her. Maybe he hadn't planned on this happening but it was what he wanted. She could tell that from looking at him and that was all she needed to know. He wouldn't regret them breaking the rules any more than she would!

'I've never met anyone like you, Hannah,' he said softly, cupping her cheek with his big warm hand.

'Haven't you?'

'No.' He pressed a kiss to her lips, drawing back so he could look into her eyes. 'Women have come and gone in my life and, if I'm honest, they've caused barely a ripple. But you're different.'

'There must have been someone special,' she suggested, wondering if he was spinning her a line.

'I thought there was once.' He sighed. 'I was engaged at one point but it didn't work out and we spilt up.'

'Is that why you avoid getting involved these days?' she asked, feeling a small stab of pain pierce her heart at the thought.

'No.' He smiled as he brushed her mouth with a kiss. 'So if you think I'm suffering from a broken heart, forget it. I was the one who called things off. I realised that I'd lost interest and that going ahead with the marriage would be a huge mistake.'

'I see. And there's been nobody else since then?'

'Nobody important. Apart from you. I shall never forget you, Hannah.'

'I'm glad.' She kissed him on the mouth, more touched by the admission than she could say. Knowing that she meant something to him made what they had shared all the more special. 'I'll never forget you, either, Tom. You may not believe this but you've given me so much. And I don't just mean great sex!'

He laughed, his eyes filling with amusement. 'Is that a fact?'

'Hmm.' She smiled back, loving the fact that even in the throes of passion they could find something to laugh about. 'I'd lost a lot of my confidence in the past year but you've made me see that I can take charge of my life. I'll always be grateful to you for that.'

'And for the sex?' he suggested, leering comically at her.

'And for the sex,' she repeated, chuckling.

'Good.'

He dropped a kiss on her lips then let his mouth glide across her cheek and Hannah closed her eyes. She wanted to savour every second because this really would be the last time. His mouth glided on—along her jaw, down her throat, pausing when it came to the tiny pulse that was beating in such a frenzy of excitement.

'I love the way your pulse races when I do this,' he murmured. He pressed his mouth against the spot, the tip of his tongue tasting her flesh, and she shivered. Love-making, *Tom's way*, was so different from what she had experienced before. Even the smallest touch, the lightest caress, seemed to be so much more erotic. It felt as though she had never really made love properly before she'd made love with him and the thought was a revelation.

She twined her fingers through his hair, holding his head against her while he lavished more kisses on her throat. When his mouth moved on, she almost protested but there were more delights to come. His lips glided back and forth over the swell of her breasts, scattering kisses at random before finding her nipples and she gasped at the hot rush of sensation that rose inside her as he suckled her through the thin cotton fabric of her dress.

Her hands went to his back, stroking the long, strong line of his spine as she urged him to continue and he did. He drew back at last but only long enough to unzip her dress. He drew the bodice down, exposing her breasts in their lacy covering to his gaze, and she felt the shudder that passed through him and understood. If this felt like a first for her then it felt like that to him too.

'You're so beautiful, Hannah. So very, very beautiful.'

His voice was filled with awe as he ran his palms over her throbbing nipples and she sighed. Like any woman who'd had a child, she was aware that her body had changed; however, any doubts she may have had about how she looked faded into nothing. Tom obviously liked what he saw and that was all she needed to know.

Closing her eyes, she gave herself up to the moment, letting the exquisite sensations grow and build inside her. When he eased the straps of her bra down her arms and took her nipples into his mouth one after the other, she cried out, unable to hold back the outpouring of emotion. Not even what had happened the first time they'd made love had prepared her for this!

Her hands went to the front of his shirt, wanting—*needing*—to feel him, skin on skin. Tom murmured something as he eased himself away and dragged his shirt over his head. He tossed it on the floor then lay down beside her, drawing her into his arms so their two bodies seemed to merge into one. Hannah bit her lip when she felt the warm, hair roughened skin on his chest brush against her aching nipples. Her senses seemed to be heightened to such a degree that it seemed almost too much to bear. It was the sweetest kind of torment to have to wait until their bodies were joined even more intimately.

'You make me wish things could be different, Hannah.' His voice was low, grating in a way that told her how much it cost him to make the admission.

'Maybe they can,' she said quietly, but he shook his head.

'No. No matter how much I may want to change, I daren't take that risk.' He took her face between his hands. 'I can't make you any promises when it could turn out that I'm incapable of keeping my word, like the rest of the Bradburys. All I can give you is this.'

He kissed her hungrily, his tongue mating with hers in a ritual as old as time. Hannah clung to him as she kissed him back, feeling the sharp sting of tears burning her eyes. Maybe it wasn't her place, but she wished with all her heart that she could make him see that he had the power to change if it was what he truly wanted. So what if he had called off his engagement because he'd lost interest in his fiancée? It didn't mean it would happen again. He set far too much store by his family's failings and failed to see that *he* could do whatever *he* wanted, but how could she make him understand that? Should she even try when it went way beyond what they had agreed?

Another night of passion was all this was. It wasn't the precursor to an affair, certainly wasn't the lead-up to anything more. It couldn't be. She needed to concentrate on building a new life for herself and Charlie. She didn't have the time for a relationship and all that it entailed. Maybe she would like to get to know Tom better. And maybe she would love to have the time to allow these feelings she had for him to develop but it wasn't going to happen.

It was the wrong time and the wrong place, and she knew that. As Tom drew her into his arms, Hannah realised that this was all she could ever have, these few hours in Tom's arms. It was up to her to make sure they were special for both of them.

Charles de Gaulle Airport was bustling when he arrived. Tom snaked his way between the crowds, thankful that he only had a carry-on bag and didn't need to wait for any luggage. The sooner he got to the clinic, the happier he'd be.

He sighed as he made his way to the car-hire desk. Leaving Bride's Bay that morning had been the hardest thing he had ever done. Right up until the moment his plane had taken off he had been tempted not to go through with it. He'd kept thinking about everything he was giving up—thinking about Hannah—and it had proved almost too much. It was only the thought of the harm it could cause if he stayed that had made him get on the plane.

Sadness washed over him as he realised that he could never go back. What had happened on Saturday night had proved beyond any doubt how vulnerable he was. Oh, he could try to justify his actions any way he chose but the truth was that he had wanted Hannah so much that he hadn't been able to stop himself making love to her. If he went back, it would happen again and again until he was completely under her spell... For however long it lasted.

It all came back to the same thing, he thought dully. He couldn't promise that his feelings would last. He could end up hurting her and he knew that he couldn't live with himself if he did that. No matter how painful it was, he had to make the break. The truth was that Hannah would be better off without him.

He handed the clerk his driving licence, waiting impatiently while she filled in the paperwork. She finally handed him the keys and he hurried outside to find the car. Five minutes later he was on his way to the start of a new episode in his life. That was how he must think of it, as a new beginning rather than the end of something special. He would focus on the future and whenever his mind tried to sneak in thoughts of Hannah he would stamp them out.

He took a deep breath. Give it a couple of weeks and he wouldn't remember what she looked like.

CHAPTER TWELVE

THE days flew past and Hannah found herself increasingly busy. A steady influx of tourists into the town meant that their lists grew longer by the day. Both morning and evening surgeries were packed and usually overran. Although she worried about the amount of time she was away from Charlie, she was glad that there wasn't a minute to spare. At least while she was working, she wasn't thinking about Tom and that was something to be grateful for.

It was much harder when she was at home. Then her thoughts constantly returned to Tom. She kept wondering how he was and if he was enjoying his new job or if he missed Bride's Bay. Maybe he missed her too, missed the daily contact they'd had, missed hearing her voice as she missed hearing his. Even though she knew how silly it was, she hoped he did. Maybe Tom didn't *do* commitment, but she would hate to think that he had forgotten her. What they'd had together had been too special. It should be remembered.

She was in the office one lunchtime about three weeks after Tom had left, getting ready for the afternoon's anti-smoking clinic, when the phone rang. Lizzie had gone to the post office and Alison was tidying the waiting room so she picked up the receiver. 'Bride's Bay Surgery. Dr Morris speaking.'

She frowned when an unfamiliar voice asked to speak to Simon. Lizzie normally dealt with any phone calls, weeding out the ones from the various pharmaceutical companies that were keen to promote their products. She certainly didn't want to pass this on to Simon if it was yet another sales pitch.

'Who's calling, please?' she asked, deciding it would be simpler if she screened the call. Her frown deepened when the caller identified herself as the sister in charge of the IC unit at Christ Church hospital in New Zealand. She knew from what Simon and Ros had told her that that was where their daughter lived.

Hannah put through the call but she had a bad feeling about it. When Lizzie came back she quickly explained what had happened and could tell that she was concerned too. Abandoning her preparations, she went and knocked on the door of Simon's consulting room. He was sitting at his desk when she went in and she could tell at once that something awful had happened.

'What is it?' she demanded, hurrying into the room.

'That phone call. It was about Becky...' He broke off and she could tell that he was close to tears.

'Is she all right?'

'I don't know. There's been an accident. Becky and Steve were in their car when they were hit by a lorry. Steve...well, Steve's dead and Becky's in ICU.'

'How dreadful!' Hannah exclaimed. 'What about the baby?'

'She wasn't with them, mercifully. They'd left her with a babysitter while they went out for dinner.' Simon stumbled to his feet. 'I'll have to tell Ros. Then we need to sort out what to do.'

He hurried out of the room, leaving Hannah at a loss to know what to do. Although she wanted to help, she knew that the couple needed time on their own to come to terms with what had happened. She went back to the office and told Lizzie what had gone on. Once Lizzie had recovered from her shock, Hannah asked her if she would contact everyone who was booked in for the clinic and explain that it had been cancelled. Simon was in no fit state to worry about work, so she would do the house calls then take over his list for evening surgery.

The sheer logistics of covering everything herself was mind-boggling but she refused to dwell on it. She collected the list of calls and set off. Thankfully, there weren't too many and she was back at the surgery shortly before three p.m. Simon came out to meet her as she drew up.

'Have you heard anything more about your daughter?' she asked as she got out of the car.

'She's been taken off life support and is breathing for herself,' he told her, his relief evident.

'That's good news.' Hannah followed him into the surgery. 'Have they said what injuries she's sustained?'

'A lot of internal damage, apparently.' He rubbed a hand over his eyes. 'I can't believe this has happened. As for Steve…well, what can I say? Becky's going to be devastated when she finds out.'

'She doesn't know yet?' Hannah said quietly.

'Not yet. In fact, they're thinking about holding off telling her until Ros and I get there in case the shock proves too much.'

'Have you managed to book your flight?'

'Yes. We leave tomorrow morning.' Simon sighed. 'Ros is packing. At least it's given her something to focus on. She was very fond of Steve—we both were. It's such a tragedy.' He made a valiant effort to rally himself. 'Anyway, about the surgery, I'm sorry to leave you in the lurch like this, Hannah.'

'Don't be silly. Nobody could have foretold something like this would happen. I'll be fine. Really.'

'I know you will, especially now that I've arranged for Tom to give you a hand.' Simon smiled, mercifully missing the start she gave. 'I feel much happier now that he's agreed to cover for me. At least I won't feel that I have to rush back if he's here.'

'I...um...of course not.' Hannah managed a shaky smile, although she had never felt less like smiling. She quickly excused herself and went to her room, sitting down at her desk while she tried to deal with this new bombshell.

She had never imagined that she would see Tom again so soon. Whenever she'd pictured them meeting it had been at some point in the future. She'd assured herself that several months down the line she would be able to handle the encounter with equanimity. She would be polite but distant. And there certainly wouldn't be a repeat of what had happened the last time she'd seen him.

The pictures that were constantly hovering at the back of her mind came flooding back and she groaned. Would she be able to stick to that, though? Or would the temptation to spend another night with him prove too much? Tom had made it clear that he wasn't looking for commitment so could she handle a relationship that was based purely on physical attraction? She had no idea and that was the most worrying thought of all. She hated to think that the time might come when she wanted more than he could give her.

Tom pulled up in the surgery car park and switched off the engine. It was well past seven p.m. but the lights were still on. Leaving his bag in the car, he made his way inside, smiling at Lizzie who was looking uncharacteristically harassed.

'You're working late tonight. On overtime, are you?'

'Tom! Oh, it's so good to see you.' Lizzie rushed around the desk and hugged him.

Tom laughed as he hugged her back. 'I should go away more often if that's the sort of reception I get.'

'Don't joke about it.' Lizzie resumed her seat, grimacing as she glanced towards waiting room. Tom could see at least a dozen people still waiting and frowned.

'You are running late.'

'Tell me about it.' Lizzie rolled her eyes. 'It's been a madhouse here today. You wouldn't believe the number of folk who wanted an appointment. Poor Hannah has been run off her feet trying to deal with everything all on her own.'

'It can't have been easy for her,' Tom agreed, trying to control the flutter his stomach gave at the mention of Hannah's name. The butterflies that were flapping around inside him refused to settle down, however, and he gave up. He would save his energy until it was really needed, like when he actually saw her.

The thought sent a rush of blood to his head as well as to other parts of his body and he cleared his throat. 'I may as well see some patients while I'm here. Give

me a couple of minutes to get set up then send the next
one through, will you?'

'It'll be a pleasure!' Lizzie grinned as she handed
him a buff folder. 'Mrs Price has been moaning on and
on about the length of time she's had to wait so I'll let
you deal with her. A dose of the legendary Bradbury
charm should work wonders!'

'Thanks. I think!' Tom replied drolly, although the
comment had touched a nerve. Even Lizzie saw him as
somewhat lightweight, the sort of man who charmed
his way out of awkward situations.

The idea wouldn't have fazed him normally. However, as he made his way to the consulting room, he
found himself regretting the fact that he had earned
himself that kind of a reputation. He didn't want to be
thought of merely as a charmer but as someone who
could be relied on and it wasn't the first time he had
thought that either if he was honest. In the past few
weeks, he'd realised that his attitude to life had changed.
Although he had always given one hundred per cent
when it came to his work, it no longer seemed enough
that he should deal with a patient and send them on
their way. He wanted to be involved, long term, to see
their treatment through to its conclusion, and that was
something that had never bothered him before.

Was it meeting Hannah that had made the difference? he wondered as he switched on the lights. His
outlook on life had altered because he felt so differently about her? He guessed it was true and it was worrying to know how big an influence she'd had on him.
Although he hadn't hesitated when Simon had asked
for his help, he had realised what a risk he was taking
by returning to Bride's Bay.

He had tried his best not to think about Hannah in the past few weeks, but he hadn't succeeded. She'd got so far under his skin that he could no more forget about her than he could forget about breathing. It made him see how careful he would have to be. It would be far too easy to allow his feelings to dictate his actions and that was something he couldn't afford to do. Maybe he had changed in a lot of ways but it didn't mean that he was capable of making a commitment and sticking to it.

Hannah checked her watch. Although she had phoned the nursery to warn them she would be late, she'd never imagined it would take this long to get through the list. She got up and hurried out to the corridor. Hopefully, Lizzie could reschedule some appointments for the morning. Even though it would mean her coming in extra early, it would be better than leaving Charlie any longer.

'Hello, Hannah. How are you?'

The sound of Tom's voice brought her to a halt. Hannah turned round, feeling her pulse leap when she saw him. He gave her a tight smile and she could see the wariness in his eyes. Was he thinking about that last night they'd spent together, regretting the fact that it had happened? It was impossible to tell so she could only speculate, based on her own feelings. Whilst she didn't regret sleeping with him, she did regret the fact that she'd not been able to put him out of her mind ever since.

'Tom. I wasn't expecting you till tomorrow.'

'I noticed that the lights were on when I arrived so I called in.' He shrugged. 'I thought I'd give you a hand, seeing as I was here.'

'That was good of you,' she said stiffly.

'Not at all. I'm happy to help.' He glanced at his watch and frowned. 'What's happening about Charlie? You normally pick him up before now.'

'I phoned the nursery and warned them I'd be late, although I didn't expect to be this late,' Hannah admitted, worriedly. 'I'm hoping that Lizzie might be able to persuade a few people to rebook their appointments for the morning.'

'Don't worry about that. I'll see them.' He shook his head when she started to protest. 'No, I mean it, Hannah. You get yourself off and collect Charlie. That's far more important.'

'Well, if you're sure…'

'I'm sure.' He smiled at her and she couldn't stop her heart leaping when she saw the warmth in his eyes. 'Go on—off you go. Charlie must be wondering where you've got to.'

'I'm sure he is.' Hannah smiled back, unable to keep the warmth out of her eyes too. 'It's good to have you back, Tom.'

'It's good to be back,' he said softly, and she could tell that he meant it.

Hannah hurriedly fetched her bag, trying not to speculate about what it could mean. Tom had stressed how reluctant he was to remain in one place for any length of time, yet he seemed to be genuinely pleased to be back in Bride's Bay. Had he had a change of heart? Was he now prepared to consider settling down? She had no idea but the thought buoyed her up. The idea of Tom becoming a permanent fixture in her life was far more attractive than it should have been.

* * *

Tom saw the rest of the patients then sent Lizzie home and locked up. He set the alarm then made his way through to the house. It felt odd not to have Ros there to greet him, he thought as he switched on the lights. Normally she would have supper ready and they would eat it sitting around the kitchen table while they swapped stories about their day.

It was one of the things he enjoyed most about being in Bride's Bay, in fact. Normally he ate out, dining at various expensive restaurants wherever he happened to be living at the time. Although the food was always excellent, he much preferred the casual intimacy that came from sharing a meal with people he liked. He couldn't help thinking how good it would be if he had someone to go home to on a permanent basis, someone like Hannah, for instance. He could imagine how much better his evenings would be if he could spend them with her.

He sighed as he filled the kettle and switched it on. He mustn't think like that, mustn't let himself be seduced by the thought of a life with Hannah. The idea of domestic bliss might seem attractive at the moment but would it still appear so in a few months' time? It wasn't fair to Hannah to start something he might not be able to continue, neither was it fair to Charlie. He had to stop daydreaming and accept his life for what it was. He had a lot to be grateful for, after all. He was single, healthy and unencumbered by responsibilities. He could go wherever he chose and do whatever he wanted. A lot of men would give their right arms to be in his position.

Tom made himself a cup of coffee and took it through to the sitting room. He switched on the television because it seemed far too quiet with only himself for company. And if his thoughts wandered more than once to Hannah, he told himself it was only to be expected. After all, he cared about her and Charlie, and hoped they could be friends, although he understood if she preferred to keep her distance. He'd only be in Bride's Bay until Simon got back and then he'd move on, maybe return to Paris or go somewhere else. The world was his oyster, as the saying went. He could go wherever he wanted…

Except the only place he *really* wanted to be was right here.

In Bride's Bay.

And with Hannah and little Charlie by his side.

Oh, hell!

CHAPTER THIRTEEN

HANNAH felt exhausted when she arrived at the surgery the following morning. Unusually for him, Charlie had been difficult to settle the previous night, clinging to her and sobbing when she had tried to put him in his cot. She'd ended up sitting in the rocking chair with him until he had dropped off to sleep. He'd woken several times during the night too and each time she'd had to go through the same routine. She guessed that it might have had something to do with her having been so late collecting him from the nursery and could only hope it wouldn't happen again. She'd be in no fit state to work if she lost another night's sleep.

'Good morning. How are you today?'

'Tired.' Hannah summoned a smile as she turned to greet Tom. She felt a shiver run through her when she saw that his hair was still damp from his morning shower. She knew from experience that it would feel cool and silky to the touch and swallowed a groan. She really didn't need this today of all days!

'Rough night?' he asked, frowning.

'You could say that. Charlie woke up several times and I couldn't settle him.'

'That's not like him. Is he sickening for something?'

He sounded so concerned that her heart melted and she smiled at him. 'I think it had more to do with the fact that his routine had been disturbed.'

'Because you were late collecting him from the nursery?' Tom sighed. 'It's not fair to you or Charlie, Hannah. We'll have to make sure you leave on time from now on.'

'Easier said than done,' she said lightly, because it would be far too easy to wallow in his solicitude. 'If it continues to be as busy as it's been lately then we'll need to extend our opening hours, not reduce them.'

'It certainly proves that Simon's right about this new health centre. Obviously, there's an urgent need for it.'

'There is. Even without the addition of any visitors to the town, we're hard pressed to cope.' She paused, wondering if she should ask the question, but in the end it was too tempting to resist. 'Have you thought any more about what Simon suggested?'

'That I should consider joining the team?' He shrugged. 'I don't think so. I can't really see myself spending the next twenty-odd years working here.'

Lizzie popped her head round the office door just then to say there was a phone call for him so Hannah was spared having to find anything to say. However, as she made her way to her room, she could feel her spirits sinking. Nothing was going to induce Tom to stay in Bride's Bay. It made her see how foolish it would be to harbour any hope that he might have changed his mind. He was a free agent and he obviously had every intention of staying that way.

The morning flew past. With appointments scheduled every six minutes, Tom was hard pressed to keep up. Six minutes wasn't long enough to take a history and make a diagnosis and he refused to cut corners. By the time he came to his last patient, he had given up all hope of sticking to the schedule.

The sooner this new health centre was built the better, he thought as he pressed the buzzer. There was obviously a need for it plus it would give the community access to a lot more facilities. It was an exciting prospect, in fact, and he found himself wishing all of a sudden that he could be part of it, before common sense reasserted itself. He wasn't going to stay around long enough to play a role in the new centre's inception.

The thought was more dispiriting than it should have been. He pushed it aside as Mitch Johnson entered the room. 'Morning, Mitch. What can I do for you today? It's not your blood pressure, is it?'

'No, no, that's fine. I saw Emily last week and she was quite happy with the reading,' the landlord of The Ship informed him. 'Going back onto my usual medication has settled things down nicely.'

'Good. I'm glad to hear it.'

'Did you ever manage to speak to that locum at the hospital who changed my tablets?' Mitch asked as he sat down.

'Yes, I did. He said that he'd prescribed them for other patients and they'd had a beneficial effect.' Tom shrugged. 'What suits one person doesn't always suit another is all I can say.'

'I suppose so. Anyway, I'm here about this cough I have. It's been going on for weeks now and it's driving me mad. I've tried all sorts of cough medicines from the chemist's but they've not done any good.'

'What sort of a cough is it? Dry or chesty?'

'A really dry one, and it's worse at night, too. Marie

said that if I don't do something about it, she's going to divorce me. She's fed up with me waking her up every night, coughing!'

Tom laughed. 'Well, we can't have that. Let me listen to your chest and see if we can find out what's causing it.'

He picked up his stethoscope and listened to Mitch's chest, back and front. 'Your chest's clear, which is what I expected. The kind of dry cough you described is usually associated with asthma, an infection or even an allergic reaction.'

'I've never suffered from asthma,' Mitch protested.

'No, I know that. You'd have other symptoms if you did, like breathlessness and wheezing. It could be that you've picked up a bug. Have you had a temperature or felt under the weather?'

'No. Apart from this cough I feel fine.' Mitch rolled his eyes. 'I was coughing so much this morning that the blasted parrot started copying me!'

'Parrot? I didn't know you had a parrot,' Tom said, frowning.

'It was Marie's idea. She had one when she was a child and decided that we should have one at the pub. I wasn't keen but you know what she's like when she gets an idea in her head—there's no stopping her.'

'So when did you get it?'

'Oh, it must be almost a month ago now.'

'And how long after it arrived did this cough start?'

'A week, maybe a bit less…' Mitch broke off and stared at him. 'You think Polly could be the cause of me coughing?'

'I think it's a distinct possibility. A lot of people are allergic to birds' feathers. You could be one of them.'

Tom grinned. 'It could come down to a straight choice if I'm right—you or Polly. One of you may have to go.'

'And I know which one Marie will choose in her present state of mind,' Mitch replied gloomily.

He took the script Tom handed him and left, promising to come back if the cough hadn't cleared up in a week's time. Tom was still smiling as he gathered up the notes and took them through to the office. He could just imagine feisty Marie's reaction if Mitch suggested her beloved bird would have to go!

'Good morning?'

He glanced round when Hannah came in, trying to quell the lurch his heart gave. It didn't matter that it was only a couple of hours since he'd seen her, he still found himself reacting to the sight of her. 'A busy one. I'm way behind schedule.'

'Me too.' She sighed. 'Six minutes for each appointment isn't long enough, is it?'

'No, it isn't. Simon used to allow at least ten minutes for each patient, and even then some needed a lot longer than that.'

'I know. The trouble is that there's so many people wanting appointments these days that we'd never get through the list. Reducing the time allocated to each patient is the only way we can fit everyone in.'

'But it doesn't work,' he pointed out. 'We've both run over time this morning and no doubt we'll do the same again tonight. The only way to solve the problem is by hiring another doctor.'

'That's not something we can do, though. Simon's the only one who can make a decision like that.'

'Unfortunately, he is.' Tom shook his head. 'And he's got enough on his plate without having to worry about taking on additional staff. But once he gets back, I'm definitely going to suggest it to him.'

'It's not really your problem, though, is it? Or it won't be once Simon gets back.'

'Because I'll be leaving?' He shrugged. 'Maybe not, but I don't like to think of you two struggling even if it doesn't directly affect me.'

Hannah didn't say anything, leaving him with the impression that she didn't believe his concern was genuine and it was galling to know she thought that. As he made his way through to the house to make himself some lunch, Tom found himself wondering how he could convince her that he really did care...

He sighed when it struck him that it was the last thing he should do. Letting Hannah know how important she was to him would be a mistake. He needed to keep his distance, for her sake as well as his.

The week came to an end much to Hannah's relief. Whether it was the fact that they had continued to be so busy at the surgery or because Charlie had kept waking up at night, she didn't know, but she felt worn out. She got up on Saturday morning, gave Charlie his breakfast and dressed him. Leaving him playing with some building blocks, she had a shower and got dressed, opting for a pair of white linen trousers and a sleeveless cotton top. It was a glorious day, the sun beating down from a cloudless blue sky. She was sorely tempted to spend the day in the garden but there were jobs that needed doing, the first one being a long overdue trip to the supermarket.

She carried Charlie out to the car and strapped him in his seat. It was already hot outside and she turned on the air conditioning. There was a queue of traffic heading for the retail park so it was slow going and Charlie was grumbling by the time they arrived. Hannah carried him over to where the trolleys were parked, but the moment she tried to put him into the baby seat, he started squirming around.

'Come on, darling, be a good boy,' she said persuasively. 'Once we've done the shopping, we'll go home and play.'

She managed to settle him in the seat and fastened the harness. The supermarket was packed and it seemed to take twice as long as normal to get round all the aisles. By the time she joined the queue for the checkout, Charlie had had enough and started wailing loudly.

Hannah found his cup of juice in her bag and tried to pacify him with that but he refused to drink it and cried all the harder. He was making such a racket that people were turning to see what was going on. She was just about to abandon her trolley and leave when Tom appeared.

'Hey, what's all that noise about, young man?' He bent and blew a raspberry on the back of Charlie's hand. The little boy immediately stopped crying and looked at him in surprise. Tom grinned as he blew a second raspberry on the baby's cheek and was rewarded by a chuckle. 'That's better.' He straightened up, the smile still lingering as he turned to her. 'I take it that he's tired of being in the trolley.'

'That, plus the fact that he's due for his morning nap,' Hannah explained. She took a quick breath, determined that Tom's unexpected appearance wasn't going to throw her. 'I didn't expect it to be so busy.'

'There's a sailing regatta on today so I expect a lot

of people have come to watch that.' He held up his basket. 'I'm going to watch it myself and came to buy a few bits and pieces to make a picnic.'

Hannah's brows rose as she studied the contents of his basket. 'Smoked salmon, pâté, oysters, Champagne... not quite your usual picnic fare.'

'You mean it should have been curling cheese sandwiches and stewed tea out of a flask?' He grinned at her. 'Pass! I think I can do a bit better than that.'

'It looks like it, too.' Hannah laughed, appreciating the fact that he'd taken her teasing in good part. She glanced round in relief when the queue started to move. 'Thank heavens. We might get out of here before teatime.'

'With a bit of luck.' Tom bent and tickled Charlie under the chin when the little boy began to fuss again. 'You can't wait to get out of that trolley, can you, tiger?'

'He hates being fastened in,' Hannah explained. She broke off a grape and popped it in the baby's mouth in the hope it would distract him but he spat it out.

'Why don't you take him outside while I pay for your shopping?' Tom suggested.

'Oh, I can't let you do that!'

'Why not? I need to pay for my shopping, so it's not a big deal to pay for yours as well. And surely it's easier if I queue up instead of keeping poor Charlie here any longer.'

'But I don't have enough cash on me to pay for all this,' Hannah pointed out. 'I was going to use my debit card.'

'You can pay me back next week. I'll trust you not to flee the country,' he told her, grinning.

Hannah laughed. 'OK. You've talked me into it, not

that I took much persuading.' She lifted Charlie out of the seat. 'I'm parked over on the far side of the car park, near the railings.'

'I know. I parked next to you,' he informed her, taking charge of her trolley. The queue moved forward again and he sketched her a wave. 'See you later.'

'Thanks, Tom,' she said quietly, and he turned and smiled at her.

'You're welcome. I'm happy to help any way I can.'

He pushed the trolley towards the checkout as she made her way from the queue. Charlie was gurgling happily now that he'd been freed from the seat, bouncing up and down as he pointed to things that caught his eye. Hannah responded automatically as they made their way out of the store. There'd been something in Tom's voice when he'd said that he was happy to help, which told her it hadn't been just the usual sort of meaningless remark people made. He'd genuinely meant it and it was good to know that he cared enough to want to make her life easier.

She sighed as she carried Charlie over to a patch of grass near to where she'd parked and put him down. She was looking for signs that Tom felt something for her and it was pointless. Maybe he *did* care and maybe he *did* want to help, but he wasn't about to change his whole way of life for her, and why should he? She was a single mum with a small child who would need a great deal of care in the coming years. Maybe they were compatible, sexually, but that wasn't enough to make him want to spend his life with her, was it? The most they could ever be was friends and she should be happy with that.

Hannah knelt down on the grass, trying not to think

about what she really wanted. She had to focus on what really mattered, on making sure that Charlie was healthy and happy. If she achieved that aim then she would be perfectly content.

Tom paid for the groceries and wheeled the trolley out of the store. He crossed the car park and stopped beside Hannah's car. There was no sign of her and Charlie and he looked around, quickly spotting them sitting on the grass.

His heart lifted as he saw little Charlie laugh when Hannah tickled him. It was lovely to see them having so much fun together, he thought. It struck him all of a sudden how much he had missed being part of both their lives while he'd been in Paris. He had missed Hannah, of course, but he had also missed Charlie too, and that surprised him. He hadn't realised how fond he'd grown of the little boy or how much he'd enjoyed being around him. It made him reassess his ideas on fatherhood. Maybe he shouldn't rule out the idea of having a family of his own one day?

It was something Tom knew he needed to think about but not right now. Leaving the trolley next to the car, he went over to them. 'If you let me have your keys, I'll load your shopping into the boot.'

'Are you sure you don't mind?' Hannah said, hunting her keys out of her bag.

'Of course not.' Tom took the keys off her. 'I won't be long.'

He went back to the cars and sorted out the groceries, putting his shopping into his car once he'd dealt with hers. Hannah smiled when he went back a few minutes later.

'That was quick. It takes me a lot longer than that to sort everything out.'

'What can I say?' He blew on his knuckles and polished them on the front of his T-shirt. 'Talent will out.'

'So they say.' She laughed as she attempted to stand up, no easy feat with Charlie in her arms.

Tom put his hand under her elbow to help her, feeling the hot surge of blood that scorched his veins when his fingers encountered warm, bare flesh. Although her outfit was in no way revealing, it was very different from her usual attire, and he found his senses suddenly going into overdrive as he took stock of the way the cotton top clung to the lush curve of her breasts.

'Thanks.'

Hannah hastily stepped away and he realised that he wasn't the only one who'd been affected by his touch. Had she felt it too, he wondered, felt the blood rush through her veins, leaving her feeling breathless and giddy like he was?

'Well, I suppose I'd better get off home before the fish fingers start to defrost.' She gave him a quick smile but he could see the awareness in her eyes and had his answer. She was as receptive to his touch as he was to touching her and the realisation drove every sensible thought from his head.

'What are you doing this afternoon?' he said hurriedly as she started to move away.

She stopped and glanced back. 'This afternoon?'

'Yes. Have you anything planned?'

'Oh, just the usual.' She shrugged when he looked at her. 'You know—washing, ironing, cleaning—all the jobs I don't seem to have time for during the week.'

'But there's nothing really urgent on the agenda, though?'

'No, I suppose not,' she conceded.

'In that case, can I persuade you to put off doing them for a while longer?'

'Why?' she demanded bluntly.

'Because I'm hoping that you'll agree to spend the afternoon with me, you and Charlie, I mean.' He took a deep breath, wondering if he was mad to suggest it. 'We can go to Dentons Cove and watch the regatta. Charlie will love seeing all the yachts. And when he gets tired of that, I can show him how to make sand pies...' He tailed off when she shook her head.

'I don't think it's a good idea, Tom.'

'Why not?' he demanded belligerently, because he really, really wanted her to agree.

'You know why.' She tipped back her head and looked him in the eyes. 'I have no intention of sleeping with you again.'

'I never asked you to!'

'No, you didn't. But we both know it will happen if we spend any time together. It's happened twice already and I don't intend for it to happen a third time.' She gave a little sigh. 'I'm sorry, Tom, but I think it would be better if we stuck to being colleagues. It's simpler that way.'

'If that's what you want,' he said, shocked by how shattered he felt. Even though he knew it made sense, it hurt to be rejected.

'It is.'

She gave him a quick smile then walked over to her car. Tom stayed where he was and watched as she strapped Charlie into his seat and drove away. He was tempted to go after her but what was the point? She wouldn't change her mind and why should she? All he'd ever offered her was sex and although it may have been the best sex he'd ever had, it wasn't enough for someone like Hannah. She deserved so much more, a lifetime's worth of commitment at the very least, and he couldn't give her that.

Could he?

The question seemed to sear itself into his brain. As he got in his car, Tom could feel it burning deeper and deeper into his psyche. Could he commit himself to Hannah and mean it? Could he promise to love her for ever and stick to it? A couple of months ago he would have scoffed at the idea of him remaining true to any woman, but now it didn't seem such an alien concept. Not if that woman was Hannah.

CHAPTER FOURTEEN

THE next couple of weeks passed in a blur. Hannah felt as though time was moving at twice its normal speed. The fact that it continued to be so busy at the surgery didn't help either. Both morning and evening surgeries were packed and finishing on time was a pipe dream. Although Tom offered several times to see some of her patients so she could go and collect Charlie, she always refused. It just seemed better that she maintain her independence.

As for Charlie, he was still waking up at night. His casts had been removed and he'd been given special boots to wear. Made from a soft material, with a metal bar to keep his feet at shoulder width apart, he had quickly learned to cope with them during the day. However, they needed to be worn at night too and he hated having them put on after his bath. Hannah tried everything she could think of to distract him, playing umpteen games of peek-a-boo and singing to him, but as soon as he saw her pick up the boots, he started screaming and it took her ages to calm him down. Between the stress of that and the situation with Tom, it was little wonder her nerves felt as though they were in shreds.

On a more positive note, Simon's daughter was

making excellent progress. She had been discharged from hospital and Ros was looking after her. Simon phoned several times to update them on her progress and Hannah wasn't surprised when he started talking about coming back to England. The plan was that Ros would stay in New Zealand to look after Becky and the baby while he returned. Although she would be glad to have him back, it meant the time was fast approaching when Tom would leave. Even though she knew it was for the best, she couldn't help feeling lost at the thought of never seeing him again. Several times she even found herself wishing that she'd agreed to go on that picnic with him. At least it would have been another memory, something else to look back on in the future.

She had just finished the weekly antenatal clinic when Lizzie popped her head round the door. Tom was doing the house calls and she assumed he'd phoned to warn them he would be late for evening surgery. It had happened a couple of times and she sighed at the thought of yet another late finish.

'Has Tom phoned to say he's going to be late?' she asked, piling some leaflets on healthy eating into a cardboard box.

'No. Jim Cairns is on the phone,' Lizzie explained. 'A man has fallen down the cliffs roughly halfway between here and Dentons Cove. The lifeboat's on standby in case he goes into the sea but, apparently, he's stuck on a ledge. The search and rescue team are on their way but they don't have a doctor with them. Jim wants to know if you or Tom can help.'

'Of course,' Hannah agreed immediately. Leaving the rest of the leaflets on the desk, she picked up her bag and checked the contents. 'I could do with some more saline... Oh, and some morphine as well.'

'I'll ask Emily if she can get them for you,' Lizzie offered.

Emily arrived a few minutes later and handed Hannah the items she'd requested. 'Lizzie said that someone has fallen off the cliff.'

'That's right.' Hannah frowned as she mentally ran through a list of what she would need. 'Will the search and rescue team have things like splints and bandages?'

'Oh, yes. They're very well equipped,' Emily assured her, following her from the room. 'These things can take quite a bit of time so if you get stuck, call me. I can pick Charlie up from nursery when I collect Theo. He knows me quite well now so he should be all right about it, especially as Theo will be with me. They play together, I believe.'

'Would you?' Hannah smiled in relief. 'Thanks, Emily. I'll phone the nursery and let them know what's happening if it looks like things are going to drag on.'

She got the directions off Lizzie and hurried out to her car. The schools were just finishing for the day and it took some time to get through the town centre traffic. She took the road to Dentons Cove, relieved that she'd been that way before when Tom had taken her to Susan Allsop's home. At least she had an idea where she was going, even though she hadn't been paying very much attention on the journey.

She sighed. She'd been more concerned about what had been happening between her and Tom to take notice of the scenery. Even though she'd only known him for a short time, she'd been aware of the attraction between them. Right from the beginning, Tom had made her feel things she had never felt before and it made her realise that she had never really loved Andrew. He had merely conformed to her view of the perfect mate but he had never aroused her passion, certainly never made her want him the way she wanted Tom. Tom might not be perfection, but he was perfect for *her*.

The thought was the last thing she needed. Hannah forced it from her mind as she drove along the road. She came to a bend and slowed down because from what Lizzie had told her, she must be nearing her destination. She rounded the bend and spotted several cars drawn up at the side of the road. There was a police car there and the officer came over when she pulled up.

'I'm Hannah Morris, one of the doctors from Bride's Bay Surgery.'

'Good to meet you, Doc. If you could park over there in that field, I'll take you across to meet the team.'

Hannah parked her car and followed him to where a group of people was gathered near the edge of the cliff. Susan Allsop was one of them and she came hurrying over to her.

'I'm so glad you're here, Hannah! It's one of our guests who's fallen, a man called Ian Lawson. I don't know how it happened. We always make it clear that everyone must stay away from the edge, don't we, Brian?'

'We do, but some folk won't be told,' Brian Allsop replied philosophically. A tall man with a bushy grey beard, he smiled at Hannah. 'The chap who's fallen doesn't take kindly to being given advice. He seems to think he knows better than everyone else does.'

'Oh, dear. That doesn't bode well,' Hannah replied, grimacing.

She looked round when a small man with bright red

hair came over and introduce himself as Alan Parker, the leader of the search and rescue team. They shook hands before he led her to the cliff edge.

'He's stuck about halfway down on a ledge. One of our guys has been down to take a look at him and he's in a pretty bad way. His leg's busted and he's probably got concussion as well. To be frank, Hannah, we're not happy about moving him until you've seen him. We don't want to cause any more damage.'

'Of course,' Hannah agreed, her heart sinking at the thought of having to climb down the cliff. 'What do you want me to do?'

'If you're happy with the idea then we'll lower you down to the ledge. You'll be wearing a rope and a harness so you'll be quite safe. One of the team's down there, John Banks, and he'll help you.' Alan glanced at her shoes. 'I don't suppose you have anything else to wear apart from those heels, do you?'

'I'm afraid not.'

'I can lend you a pair of flat shoes,' Susan offered, overhearing what had been said. 'I keep a spare pair in the car in case we go somewhere muddy. We're about the same size, I imagine.'

'Thank you.' Hannah smiled at her. 'Obviously, I need to be better prepared in the future.'

Susan hurried off to fetch the shoes while Alan and one of the other men sorted out the harness. Fortunately, Hannah was wearing trousers so it was a simple matter to slip it on. Once the clasps had been fastened and checked, a rope was attached to the metal loop at the front. Susan had come back with the shoes by then and Hannah put them on. Then she was led to the edge of the cliff.

'It'll be easier if you go down backwards,' Alan explained. 'I don't know what you're like with heights but most folk find it a bit daunting to see nothing but sky in front of them.'

Hannah nodded, saving her breath for the descent. She knelt down and inched her way over the edge of the cliff, her heart pounding as she tried to find a foothold. She managed to jam her toe into a crack in the rocks and heaved a sigh of relief. At least she'd overcome the first hurdle!

It took her a good five minutes to reach the ledge and she was trembling by the time she got there. The injured man was lying on his side with John Banks crouched beside him. Hannah knelt down next to them, very conscious of the fact that inches away from them the land fell away in a sheer drop. It would be straight down into the sea if they weren't careful.

'How's he doing?' she asked, trying not to think about that.

'Not too good. His leg's in a right state and I've no idea what the rest of him's like.'

Hannah checked the man's leg, frowning when she discovered a nasty open fracture of the tibia. 'I see what you mean. That needs covering before infection sets in.'

She carried on with her examination, gently rotating the man's hips as a fall like this could result in a fracture to the pelvis. She grimaced when she found definite signs of instability. 'He's got a fractured pelvis. The main problem when that happens is the damage it can cause to the underlying organs, particularly the bladder. He'll need immediate surgery so getting him out of here is a priority. Is the helicopter on standby, do you know?'

'I'll check.'

Hannah continued her examination while the information was relayed. Although the patient was unconscious, it was impossible to say how serious his head injury was. A CT scan would reveal any underlying damage so that was another reason for getting him to hospital as quickly as possible.

'Alan's put in a request for the helicopter but they've been called to another incident,' John informed her finally. 'If they finish there before we're done, they'll fly over. Otherwise I'm afraid it's a trip by ambulance for him.'

'That's a shame but there's nothing we can do,' Hannah agreed. She set to work, covering the open fracture with a dressing before helping John fit an inflatable splint to the leg. Her next task was to stabilise his pelvis, which took rather longer. By the time she'd finished, the patient was coming round. Not surprisingly he seemed groggy and disorientated.

'I'm Hannah Morris and I'm a doctor,' she told him, laying a hand on his shoulder when he tried to sit up. 'You've had a nasty fall and you need to lie still.'

'I want to get up!' he exclaimed, giving her a hefty push.

Hannah reeled backwards, gasping when she felt herself tipping over the edge of the ledge. Fortunately, John managed to grab her harness and haul her back but she was shaking by the time she was upright again.

'Are you all right?' John asked in concern, and she drummed up a smile.

'Just about.' She turned to the injured man. 'I'm going to give you something for the pain. Then we'll see about getting you out of here. It will be easier for all of us if you do as you're told. Understand?'

He didn't reply, muttering something under his breath that she couldn't hear. Hannah ignored him as she drew up a shot of morphine and administered it. The sooner they were back at the top of the cliff the better.

It all took some time. Hannah offered to stay while a second member of the team was lowered down to help get the injured man onto a stretcher. Although the morphine had helped, it could need a second dose to deaden the pain and she wanted to be on hand. There was very little room with four of them crammed into such a small space but they finally got the patient secured and the order was given to raise him. Hannah kept close to the cliff face as bits of rock and other debris that had been dislodged by the stretcher began to tumble down. The stretcher was finally hauled over the top and she breathed a sigh of relief. Another couple of minutes and she'd be back on terra firma.

The thought had barely crossed her mind when she felt the ground beneath her start to sway. She let out a yelp of fear as she realised that the ledge itself was starting to give way. She scrabbled at the cliff face, trying to find hand—and foot-holes, but it was hopeless; a second later she was hanging, suspended in mid-air, with only the rope saving her from a long drop into the sea. She closed her eyes, feeling the fear rise up inside her, fear not for herself but for Charlie. Who would look after Charlie if anything happened to her?

Unbidden a picture came to mind and she bit her lip. Tom wouldn't do it. Why should he? And yet the thought lingered, a thought so ridiculous that she shouldn't have given it a moment's consideration: if she had to choose someone to look after her beloved son, she couldn't think of anyone better than Tom.

Tom arrived back at the surgery on time by the skin of his teeth. Only by rushing through the last couple of calls had he managed not to be late, and it wasn't a situation he enjoyed. It wasn't fair not to give every patient his full attention but he'd had no choice. He didn't want Hannah having to work late again tonight if he could help it.

He sighed as pushed open the door. Worrying about Hannah was becoming a habit. He hated to see her looking so tired and drawn. He'd overheard her telling Emily that Charlie wasn't sleeping and could imagine how exhausted she must be. Lack of sleep on top of the pressure of work was enough to wear anyone out and he knew that he had to do something about it. The problem was what could he do when she kept refusing his help?

'Made it,' he declared, forcing himself not to go down the same old route. The reason why Hannah wouldn't allow him to help her was because he was leaving. She didn't want to rely on him when there was no point. It would be different if he stayed, though, wouldn't it? Then he could persuade her to accept his help…and a whole lot more.

Heat poured through his veins and he breathed in sharply to control the rush of desire that made him go weak. It was a moment before he realised that he'd missed what Lizzie had said. 'Sorry, what was that?'

'I said it's a good job you're back because Hannah's not here.'

'Where's she gone? I thought she was covering the antenatal clinic this afternoon,' Tom said, puzzled.

'She was. She did. But Jim Cairns phoned not long after it finished to say that someone had fallen off the cliffs between here and Dentons Cove,' Lizzie explained. 'The S and R team didn't have a doctor so they asked if you or Hannah could attend. I've no idea what time she'll be back.'

'I see.' Tom felt unease hit him as he glanced at his watch. Although Hannah hadn't been gone that long, he would feel better if he spoke to her. He came to a swift decision. 'I'll give her a call and see how it's going.'

'Would you? Thanks. I'd do it myself but people are already starting to arrive.'

Tom went out to the porch and called Hannah's mobile but there was no reply. That didn't mean much, of course; she could be too busy to answer or in a place where there was poor reception. There were areas all around Bride's Bay where it was impossible to make or receive mobile phone calls. He put his phone away and went to get ready for surgery, but all the time he was sorting things out he couldn't stop worrying about Hannah. The thought that she might be in danger wouldn't go away. He couldn't bear to think that something bad might happen to her. He couldn't bear it for any number of reasons, the main one being that imagining a world without Hannah in it was *impossible*.

Tom had just seen his last patient out when Lizzie came rushing into the room. By some minor miracle, it hadn't been as busy that night and he'd been able to cover Hannah's list as well as his own. He rose to his feet, his heart pounding because he could tell that something had happened.

'What is it? Is it Hannah?'

'Yes! Alan Parker's just phoned to say that she's been

taken to hospital.' Lizzie's voice caught. 'Apparently, the ledge she was on gave way.'

'What! Did she fall? Is she badly injured?' Tom demanded.

'I don't know. The reception was so bad that I could barely hear what Alan was trying to tell me. All I know is that she's been taken to the hospital,' Lizzie explained.

'I'll get onto ED and find out what's going on,' Tom told her, reaching for the phone. He paused. 'What about Charlie? He needs to be picked up from nursery.'

'Emily had already offered to collect him if Hannah wasn't back so she's going to take him home with her.'

'Good. That's one less thing to worry about.'

Tom didn't waste any more time as he put through the call. He quickly explained who he was and why he was calling but was met with the usual stone wall: it was hospital policy not to give out information about a patient to anyone who wasn't a relative. He slammed down the phone and stormed towards the door. They'd have a far harder job telling him that to his face.

The drive to the hospital seemed to take forever. By the time he found somewhere to park his nerves were at breaking point. It didn't help that he kept picturing Hannah lying like a broken doll at the bottom of the cliff. Fear rose up inside him but he forced it down. Now wasn't the time to lose control, not when he needed to get past all the usual bureaucracy. He made his way to the reception desk.

'You have a patient here by the name of Hannah Morris. I'd like to see her.'

'And you are?'

This was the tricky bit. Tom knew that if he said he was a colleague he hadn't a hope of getting in to see her.

He took a deep breath but the words seemed to flow so easily off his tongue that they didn't sound like a lie. Maybe that was because he wanted them to be true more than he'd ever wanted anything.

'I'm her partner, Tom Bradbury.'

CHAPTER FIFTEEN

HANNAH was just leaving the treatment room when she saw Tom standing by the reception desk. She stopped dead, shocked to see him there where she'd least expected it.

'I'm her partner, Tom Bradbury.'

Her breath caught when she heard the emotion in his voice. No one hearing it could have misunderstood what he meant but it didn't make sense. Tom wasn't her partner, not in that sense...not in any sense. He was a free agent, a man who avoided commitment like the plague.

'Oh, right. I see. If you'd care to wait a moment, Mr Bradbury, I'll see what I can find out for you.'

The receptionist had obviously heard the same thing that she had done, Hannah realised giddily. She put her hand on the wall to steady herself as the room began to swim. What was going on? Why was Tom claiming to be something he wasn't? She had no idea and before she could work it out he glanced round and saw her.

'Hannah!'

There it was again, that wealth of emotions that ranged from fear to something she was afraid to put a name to. That couldn't be love she could hear in his voice; it simply couldn't! Her head was reeling as he hurried over to her so that she could only stand there and stare at him in silence.

'Are you all right? I couldn't believe it when Lizzie told me you'd been brought here...' He tailed off, his face chalk white, his eyes haunted. He looked like a man who had suffered some sort of terrible shock and Hannah did the only thing she could think of, the only thing that made any kind of sense. Opening her arms, she wrapped them around him and held him, feeling the shudder that passed through him as his arms closed around her.

'I was so scared,' he said hoarsely. 'So afraid that I might never see you again.'

'And that would have mattered to you?' she said softly.

'Yes.' He took her face between his hands. 'I can't bear to think of a world without you in it, Hannah. I don't even want to try.'

He kissed her then, his lips saying everything he couldn't bring himself to say, and Hannah felt a wave of happiness rise up inside her. Tom *loved* her. Maybe he hadn't said the actual words but she knew it was true, knew that it was time *she* admitted the truth. She smiled up at him with her heart in her eyes. 'You don't need to imagine it, Tom, because I'm not going anywhere...'

'Hannah! Thank heavens you're still here.'

Hannah swung round when she recognised Emily's voice. Fear rose up inside her when she saw that her friend was carrying Charlie. 'What's happened?' she demanded, hurrying over to them.

'Theo tried to carry Charlie upstairs and dropped him,' Emily explained. 'He fell down about three steps and banged his head on the newel post at the bottom.'

She turned Charlie round so that Hannah could see the huge bruise on the his forehead. Hannah gasped in dismay as she lifted him out of Emily's arms. 'Oh, you poor little thing!'

'I am *so* sorry. I'd only gone to make them a drink and then I heard Charlie scream…'

Emily broke off and shuddered. Hannah could tell how awful she felt and despite her concern for her son knew that she couldn't let Emily torture herself this way.

'It was an accident,' she said firmly, rocking Charlie to and fro when he started to whimper. 'It wasn't your fault, Emily. It was just one of those things that happen.'

'But it was my fault! I know what a little monkey Theo can be and I should never have left him alone with Charlie,' Emily protested.

'You can't watch kids every second of the day. As Hannah said, it was an accident, Emily, and you aren't to blame.'

Tom added his own reassurances and Hannah felt a shiver run through her. If Emily had arrived a few seconds later she would have admitted to Tom how she felt but would it have been the right thing to do?

Maybe it had been an accident but if she'd been taking care of Charlie herself, it might never have happened. Guilt filled her at the thought that she had failed her son. How could she think of telling Tom that she loved him, with all that it entailed, when she should be concentrating on making sure that Charlie was safe?

Thoughts rushed through her head. She was barely aware of Emily leaving or the fact that Tom had gone to the desk and demanded that Charlie be seen immediately. She carried the baby into a cubicle, sitting down on the couch with him on her knee while the registrar checked him over. Although Charlie seemed alert and responsive, the registrar decided that he should have a CT scan. They were ushered to the radiology unit by one of the nursing staff and left there.

Charlie took a very dim view of all the machinery and kicked up a fuss but in the end the scan was done and they returned to A and E. The registrar was with another patient so they had to wait. Hannah turned to Tom, hoping that she could persuade him to leave. Quite frankly, she needed time on her own to come to terms with what had happened, not only to Charlie but between them.

'There's no knowing how long this will take so why don't you go on home? It seems pointless you hanging around here.'

'I'd like to make sure that Charlie's OK,' he said flatly, and she could tell from his tone that he'd seen through her ruse. Colour ran up her face but she met his gaze.

'It will be easier if you leave, Tom. I need to focus on Charlie, and I don't intend to let anything or anyone distract me.'

An expression of pain crossed his face as he stood up. 'If that's how you feel then of course I'll leave. Have you enough money for a taxi?'

She hadn't thought about that and bit her lip. A fine mother she was when she didn't even have the means to get her child home. Tom handed her some notes and she murmured her thanks, avoiding his eyes in case she weakened. She didn't want him to leave but what choice did she have? Charlie came first—he had to.

'If you need me then phone, Hannah. Promise?'

Tom bent and looked into her eyes and it was all she could do not to beg him to put his arms around her. The temptation to lean on him was so strong that she wasn't sure how she managed to resist but she did.

'Don't worry about us. We'll be fine, won't we, sweetheart?' She dropped a kiss on Charlie's cheek because it was easier to look at him than at Tom.

'Fine.' Tom straightened abruptly and she could tell from his stance that he was both physically and mentally drawing away from her. Her heart ached at the thought even though it was what she wanted. There wasn't room in her life for him and Charlie.

Tears welled to her eyes as she watched him leave. Whatever they could have had together was over. Tom wouldn't try to win her round and why should he now that he understood the situation? Few men would wish to play second fiddle to another man's child and Tom was no different from anyone else.

Tom felt completely numb as he got into his car. It was as though every scrap of emotion had drained from his body, leaving him feeling like an empty shell. He drove out of the car park, automatically taking the road that led to Bride's Bay. Hannah didn't want him—that was what it boiled down to. She didn't want him in her life and he couldn't blame her in a way. He'd hardly set himself up as the perfect catch, had he? He'd banged on and on about not doing commitment, about not wanting to settle down; what sane woman would want him in her life, especially when she had a child to consider? Hannah had done the only thing she could do, the only *sensible* thing—she'd sent him packing and he should accept that and write it off to experience...

Only he couldn't! He couldn't just walk away and leave her to get on with her life when he loved her. He couldn't turn his back on Charlie either. Somehow the little tyke had wormed his way into his heart and he couldn't bear to think that he wouldn't be around to watch him growing up. He should never have allowed her to push him away!

Tom cursed roundly as he turned the car around and headed back to the hospital. He knew that Hannah wouldn't welcome him but hard luck. Maybe he wouldn't be able to talk her round but by heaven he was going to give it his best shot! He made his way into A and E, heading straight for the cubicles. Hannah gasped when he pushed aside the curtain and he could tell that she was nonplussed by his arrival. Good. Maybe he'd have the chance to state his side of the argument this time.

'I know what you're going to say, Hannah, so don't bother. Every word you uttered before is etched on my heart.' He pressed his hand to his chest in a gesture that would have seemed melodramatic any other time but now merely reflected how deeply he felt.

'In that case, why are you here?' she said acerbically, but he heard the quaver in her voice and knew that it was no easier for her than it was for him. The thought spurred him on.

'Because you're making a mistake. Oh, not about taking care of Charlie, obviously. He has to come first and I wouldn't want it any other way. But cutting me out of your life isn't what you really want, is it?' He smiled at her, hoping he looked more confident than he felt. Everything hinged on his ability to convince her that his feelings were genuine, that they would last a lifetime and beyond.

Once again the old doubts surfaced but he thrust them aside. This wasn't the time to waver; this was the time for action! 'You're doing it because you think it's the right thing to do, because you're afraid that I won't be able to handle the situation.'

'Charlie's father couldn't,' she shot back, but he saw the pain in her eyes and knew how much she was hurting so didn't take offence.

'I know he couldn't. More fool him for letting go of something so precious, is all I can say.'

He went over to the couch and knelt in front of her, placing his hand on Charlie's head. The baby was half-asleep but he smiled gummily at him and Tom felt his heart overflow with love. He could hear the emotion in his voice when he continued but he didn't care. He loved this child as much as he would love his own children if he was lucky enough to have some one day.

'More fool him for letting go of you too, Hannah.' He lent forward and kissed her, his lips lingering for a single heartbeat before he drew back. He didn't intend to push his luck by being too forward. 'That's something I'll never do.'

'I thought you didn't do commitment? How did you put it? Ah, yes, you're genetically programmed to be unfaithful. Not exactly confidence inspiring, is it, Tom?' She stared back at him and he could tell that she was determined to hold out. He smiled inwardly. That was all right because he was just as determined.

'No, it isn't. It's not the least bit inspiring so I don't blame you if you're sceptical about my sincerity. What I will say is that I've never felt this way about anyone before. I want to be with you, Hannah, not just for today or for the next month or the next year even but forever. I want to share your life, yours and Charlie's lives, and I want you both to share mine.'

'It's easy to say that now but you could change your mind. Looking after a baby isn't easy and when you factor in the other problems...'

'I understand all that.' He could tell she was working herself up into an outright rebuttal and headed her off, afraid that if he didn't do so they'd be back to square one, with him out in the cold both physically and metaphorically speaking. 'I understand that Charlie will need treatment for his talipes and that it could be intensive at times too.' He shrugged. 'I'll cope. We'll cope. Together.' He cracked a smile, hoping to lighten the mood. 'Don't they say that things are better done in pairs? Tea for two. It takes two to tango...'

'We'd be three, though. You, me and *Charlie*. How does that support your theory?'

She was as sharp as a tack and she'd drawn blood but he'd be damned if he'd be put off. 'Three it is, then. The Three Musketeers against the world. Sounds good to me.'

'I know you mean well, Tom...'

'I do.' He cut her off, not giving a fig about politeness. 'I want what's best for you and Charlie, Hannah.'

'And what if I think it's better if you stay out of our lives?'

'Then I'll have to do what you want. If I can't persuade you to see sense then I'll abide by your wishes.' He stood up, his heart breaking because not even his best efforts were having an effect. 'I won't try to badger you into doing something you don't want to do. I love you too much for that. If you can't imagine a future with me, I'll have to accept it, no matter how hard it is.'

He turned to leave, defeat weighing him down. He

had failed spectacularly, failed to win her back, and now he would have to suffer the consequences.

'Tom, wait.'

He stopped abruptly, praying that she wasn't going to apologise. He couldn't bear that, couldn't stand to hear her say she was sorry because she could never love him. Pain ripped through his guts so that it took every scrap of willpower to stand there like a condemned man waiting to hear his fate. 'Yes?'

'I can imagine a future with you. That's what scares me.'

It was the last thing he'd expected her to say. He spun round, his heart pounding as he stared at her. 'I don't understand.'

'It's simple. I can picture us growing old together and imagine the life we could have raising Charlie and any other children that may come along. But is it a pipe dream? Can it really happen or am I fooling myself into thinking that it can?' She sighed as she glanced at the baby. 'Charlie was rejected by his own father and I can't and won't take the chance of him being rejected again.'

'I would never, *ever* reject him.' He strode back into the cubicle and knelt in front of her. 'I'd never do that to any child and certainly not to this little fellow.' His voice broke because he wasn't used to dealing with all this emotion. 'I'd never do it to you, either, Hannah, because I love you too much.'

'Are you sure? Absolutely certain that you know what you're saying? It's a big commitment, Tom. It's not like buying a new car or changing jobs. It's for ever and ever and you need to be sure that you can handle that kind of scenario.' She bit her lip. 'I'd hate it if one day you came to regret it. I don't want us to become a burden to you.'

'You could never be that.'

He drew her into his arms, her and Charlie, and held them close, held them to his heart where they would always remain. All of a sudden all his doubts melted away and he knew—he just knew!—that he could do it. He could offer Hannah the happy-ever-after she deserved and mean it. Mean it with every fibre of his being, every tiny molecule that made him who he was. There wasn't a gene in his body that could make him change his mind about this.

He kissed her tenderly, hungrily, loving the way she kissed him back without reservation. That more than anything told him that she believed him and he made himself a promise right there and then that he would never do anything to betray her trust. It was only when the registrar appeared that they broke apart but even then he kept hold of her hand, needing the contact as much as he sensed she needed it too. They were in this together and would face whatever life threw at them side by side.

'It's good news,' the registrar informed them cheerfully. 'The scan's clear so you can take this little fellow home. If I were you I'd get a gate for the stairs until he's mastered the art of getting up and down them.'

'We'll do that.' Tom stood up, overwhelmed with relief as he shook the other man's hand. 'Thank you.'

'My pleasure.' The registrar smiled. 'I've not got kids myself but I can imagine that they must put you through the mill at times.'

'I expect they do,' Tom concurred, glancing at Hannah. 'But it's worth it.'

Hannah smiled, feeling her heart overflow with happiness. No matter how hard it was, Tom was going to stick around. He helped her to her feet after the registrar left, putting his arms around her and holding her so tightly that she couldn't contain the groan that slid from her lips.

'Darling, what is it?' he demanded in concern.

'A couple of badly bruised ribs, I'm afraid. You need to treat me like the most delicate china,' she told him with a grin.

'That won't be difficult.' He dropped a kiss on her nose then gently put his arm around her waist. 'Is that better?'

'Much. Thank you.' She smiled into his eyes, loving the way they darkened with desire. Her heart was racing as he led her and Charlie from the cubicle. He stopped when they reached the main doors.

'You two wait here while I fetch the car.'

'I can manage to walk to the car,' she protested, laughing at him.

'I'm sure you can, but I don't want you pushing yourself. Apart from those bruised ribs, you've had a couple of nasty shocks today and you need to take things easy.'

Hannah nodded. Just thinking about those terrible minutes when she'd been left dangling at the end of that rope made her feel sick, and then there was Charlie's accident... She shuddered and Tom's face darkened as he led her over to a chair and sat her down.

'Stay here. I just need to pop over to Jim Cairns's garage to borrow a baby seat for Charlie. It'll only take me a couple of minutes. OK?'

'Fine. We'll be right here, Tom, waiting for you.'

An expression of joy crossed his face as he bent and kissed her. 'I love you, Hannah. So much.'

'I love you too,' she whispered, meaning it with all her heart.

Tom kissed her again then hurried out of the door. Charlie was fast asleep, worn out by the events of the day, so she closed her eyes, letting the emotions wash over her. Happiness was the main one, of course, although she had to admit that there was uncertainty too. Was she being overly optimistic by thinking that Tom had conquered his fears about commitment? Oh, she didn't doubt that he loved her—she could tell that he did from the way he looked at her. But would the time ever come when he'd feel ready for marriage? She had no idea but she needed to face the fact that Tom might never be ready to take that final step.

Tom parked outside the main doors and took a deep breath. Everything had happened so fast that his head was spinning. Hannah loved him—he could barely take it in. And yet in a funny way it didn't seem strange that she should. After all, he loved her, didn't he?

His heart sang with happiness at the thought. He felt like leaping out of the car and shouting it out loud so everyone could hear but he didn't think it would go down too well with the security guard who was heading towards him to tell him to move his car. Not even a declaration of love would permit him to park illegally!

He jumped out of the car, ignoring the man's shout as he hurried inside. Hannah was sitting where he'd left her and his heart swelled that bit more. She was so precious to him that he wanted to sweep her into his arms and never let her go. This time it was forever.

He helped her to her feet, his arm snaking around her

waist as they went out to the car. There was an envelope under the wiper—undoubtedly a parking ticket—but he tossed it into the back with barely a glance. He couldn't care less if he was given a dozen tickets so long as Hannah wasn't inconvenienced!

The drove back to Bride's Bay in silence. Tom guessed that she had a lot to think about, as he did. He drew up outside her house, wondering where they went from here. It had been different at the hospital. He'd been propelled by a sense of urgency then, but now that it had passed he wasn't sure what happened next. Should he ask her if he could come in so they could talk or would it be better if he left it until tomorrow?

'I need to get Charlie to bed,' she said, glancing at him.

'Do you want me to go?' he asked, not wanting to push her any more than he already had.

'No. Unless you want to, of course.'

'I don't.' He kissed her on the cheek then opened the car door. 'I'll get Charlie out for you.'

He opened the rear door and lifted Charlie out of his seat, thinking how right it felt to do such a thing. This was where he belonged. 'How about I take Charlie up and give him his bath?'

'You don't have to do that, Tom,' she protested, and he smiled.

'I know, but I'd really like to—if you trust me enough, of course.'

'Of course I trust you,' she said immediately, and his smile widened. Hannah trusted him with her precious child and that meant the world to him. He bent and kissed her on the cheek.

'Thank you. It's good to hear you say that.' He stood

up and turned the baby round to face him. 'OK, it's you and me from here on, tiger. Be gentle with me, won't you? I'm a complete novice at this!'

Charlie chuckled as he made a grab for his nose and Tom laughed. He carried the baby inside and up to the bathroom and turned on the taps, feeling a sense of peace fill him. Maybe there were still some issues that he and Hannah needed to sort out, but there was nothing they couldn't deal with so long as they did it together. They loved each other and nothing was going to keep them apart from now on.

Hannah stripped off her filthy clothes and tossed them into the hamper. Taking her dressing gown out of the wardrobe, she pulled it on and stepped in front of the mirror. She looked a mess, she decided. Her hair was in tangles and there was a smudge of dirt on her cheek, but it seemed too much of an effort to take a shower. She wiped off the worst of the dirt then ran a brush through her hair and headed downstairs. Tom would have finished bathing Charlie soon and she would need to get him ready for bed, or rather ready to begin their nightly routine. She sighed. Please heaven Charlie wouldn't kick up his usual fuss tonight of all nights.

She went into the sitting room and sat down on the sofa, closing her eyes as she rested her head against the cushions. It had been a long day and she was worn out after everything that had happened. She must have drifted off to sleep because the next thing she knew Tom was gently waking her.

'I've made you some tea and sandwiches,' he told her, pointing to the tray.

'What about Charlie?' she said, quickly rousing herself.

'Fast asleep. I just popped him in his cot and that was it.'

'I should have told you that he needed his boots back on,' she said worriedly, scrambling to her feet.

'It's all sorted.' Tom gently pushed her back down onto the cushions. 'I popped them back on before I put him in his cot.'

'Really?' Hannah gasped. 'And he didn't object?'

'I think he was too tired to bother.' He sat down and grinned at her. 'We played a rather soggy game of submarines while he was in the bath and I think that wore him out. I'm afraid the floor's a bit of a mess, although it should dry eventually.'

'Don't worry about the floor! The fact that you managed to settle him at all is a minor miracle. He hates having his boots back on after I've bathed him. You'll have to give me a few tips.'

'It was probably the novelty factor. Being bathed by me distracted him.'

'Well, whatever it was I owe you a vote of thanks. There's nothing more stressful than having to do something that you know is going to upset your child.'

Tears sprang to her eyes and she heard Tom sigh. 'You've had a lot to contend with recently, Hannah.'

'It's no worse for me than it is for any other working mum,' she countered, not wanting him to think that she was looking for sympathy.

'I'd dispute that if I didn't suspect it could start us arguing,' he teased, and she laughed.

'We won't argue.'

'No?'

'No.' She took a quick breath. 'I don't want to argue with you, Tom. It's the last thing I want to do.'

'Me too. Or should that be neither?' He took hold of her hands. 'I love you, Hannah.'

'And I love you too.' She smiled at him. 'See? We're in total agreement.'

He laughed and pulled Hannah closer. 'So it appears.'

'And you're sure about what you're doing?' She bit her lip when she heard the uncertainty in her voice. Tom obviously heard it too because he gripped her hands even tighter.

'I am sure. One hundred per cent certain, in fact. I love you, Hannah, and I want to spend my life with you. I want to be there whenever you need me and be a father to Charlie, too.'

'And you don't think you'll change your mind?' she said, needing all the reassurance he could give her.

'I know I won't. This is it. You are what's been missing from my life.' He kissed her on the mouth then drew back. 'Please believe me. I don't want you torturing yourself with doubts and spoiling what we have. I'm in this for the long haul. For ever.'

'Oh, Tom!'

Hannah put her arms around him and hugged him. There wasn't a doubt in her mind that he was sincere. Tom loved her and he would be there for her every single day and every night too. Maybe he hadn't mentioned marriage but it no longer seemed important. They didn't need a piece of paper to confirm their love; they just needed each other. And Charlie, of course, because he was part of this too.

They made love right there on the sofa and it was even more wonderful than before. Maybe it was the fact that they had admitted their feelings at last but they seemed to reach new heights. Hannah gave herself up to the glory of their love-making, sure that she had made the right decision. Maybe she hadn't planned on falling in love so soon but it didn't matter. Tom loved her and she loved him, and they were going to spend their lives together. Everything had worked out perfectly.

* * * * *

THE DOCTOR
MEETS HER MATCH

BY
ANNIE CLAYDON

MILLS &
BOON

To Kath. For the past, the present and the future.

First published in Great Britain 2012
by Mills & Boon, an imprint of Harlequin (UK) Limited.
Harlequin (UK) Limited, Eton House, 18-24 Paradise Road,
Richmond, Surrey TW9 1SR

© Annie Claydon 2012

ISBN: 978 0 263 89201 7

Harlequin (UK) policy is to use papers that are natural, renewable and recyclable products and made from wood grown in sustainable forests. The logging and manufacturing process conform to the legal environmental regulations of the country of origin.

Printed and bound in Spain
by Blackprint CPI, Barcelona

Dear Reader

I like a peaceful life. Although I'm prepared to argue for things I feel strongly about, I won't go out to pick a fight with anyone. So in many ways it went against the grain to write about Nick and Abby, who don't seem to agree on anything and have little hesitation in telling each other so.

As they battled their way through the pages, though, I grew to love them. Their passion. Their refusal to give up when many would have just shrugged and walked away. They're both fighters and, although they can't see it, that's one of the many reasons they should be together.

Thank you for reading Nick and Abby's story. I hope you enjoy it. I'm always delighted to hear from readers, and you can e-mail me via my website, which is at: www.annieclaydon.com

Annie

CHAPTER ONE

ABBY had five seconds to recover from the shock of seeing Nick again. Five heartbeats before his heavy eyelids fluttered open and he focussed on her. She could have done with ten at the very least.

The working clamour of the A and E department receded to the very edge of her consciousness. There was only Nick now, propped up on a trolley, one leg free of the cellular blanket that covered him, and his eyes dull with pain.

Somehow she got her legs to work and she took two steps forward into the cubicle and pulled the curtain shut behind her. Glancing at the A and E notes in the vain hope that somewhere there was another fireman with trauma to the knee who she was really supposed to be examining, she saw his name printed at the top. Nick Hunter. How on earth could she have missed that?

'Abby?'

'Nick.' This was no good. She should be calm, in control, not red faced and staring at him as if she'd just seen a ghost. She wrenched her gaze from his dark, suede-soft eyes. 'I've been called down from Orthopaedics to see you. I gather you've been waiting a while.'

'They're pretty busy with the guy I pulled out of that car. How is he? He didn't look good...'

'They're working on him.' Abby almost snapped at him, and she took a deep breath and started again. 'I'll see if I can find out for you. But first we need to get you sorted out.'

'Okay. Thanks.' He was watching her intently. Waiting for her next move.

What on earth *was* her next move? Nick wasn't just a patient, he was a...what? Not a friend any more. He'd seen to that when he'd cut off all contact with her six months ago, not returning her calls and disappearing out of her life like a puff of smoke. He wasn't a lover. He'd never been that, even if at one time Abby had wanted it, more than she now cared to admit.

He was a guy that she'd met at the swimming pool, got to know, along with the group he swam with, and then gone on a couple of casual dates with. That was all. Hardly a close personal relationship, although at the time it had felt a lot like it.

All the same, she had to put this onto a professional footing. Keep it there. 'Right, then. A and E is very busy tonight and I've been called to see you as my speciality is orthopaedics...' She licked her lips. He knew all that. 'So, are you happy for me to examine you?'

He shrugged and Abby's stomach twisted. She'd obviously made a lot more of this than it actually was. 'Of course...'

'Because I can get another doctor...' Easier said than done at seven o' clock on a Friday evening, when everyone else was either busy or had gone home, but she'd deal with that if she came to it. 'We know each other, Nick. If you have any objection to me examining and treating you then you should say so now. It's quite okay…'

'I'd rather it was you, Abby.' His gaze seemed to soften. 'You're better qualified than anyone here to treat a knee injury, and from the looks of it I'll have to wait a while to see anyone else. I'm fine with it…as long as you are?'

He shot her a look that made her heart hurt. But she'd been down that road before and Abby wasn't going to be seduced by his smile again. If he could get past what had happened, so should she. It had probably meant nothing to him anyway.

She concentrated on the facts. Act always in the patient's best interests. Right now, it was clearly not in Nick's best interests to wait another three hours for treatment, just because of what had gone on in her head six months ago. Nothing even remotely inappropriate had happened. She had to pull herself together and get on with her job. 'So it's just your knee, then. Nothing else?'

'Just my knee. I think I've twisted it badly.'

'How did it happen? You were underneath the car when you did it or did you fall?'

'No, the frame of the car buckled as I was crawling back out from underneath it. Caught my knee here.' He indicated an angry red haematoma.

'Did you twist the leg at all?' Keep it on this level. Details of his injury. His medical condition. They were a welcome barrier, standing between a woman and the man who had hurt her.

He grinned. 'Probably. I was concentrating on moving as fast as I could at that point.'

Unwanted respect flared in Abby's chest. Crawling

into the tangled remains of a car to get someone out of the wreckage took a special kind of courage. 'Okay, let me take a look at it. Tell me if I'm hurting you.'

Pulling a pair of surgical gloves from the dispenser, she gently probed the swelling around the knee, lifting it slightly to check the movement of the joint. His sharp intake of breath stopped her, and when she swung round she could see his fingers gripped tightly around the bars at the side of the bed.

'I said tell me if it hurts, Nick. I'm not a mind reader.'

'Right. Yeah, it hurts.'

'And this?'

'Yes.'

'Okay. What's this scar, here? It looks as if you've had some surgery.'

'I had an operation on the knee four years ago to repair torn cartilage.'

'How did you do that?'

He managed to muster a grin and the temperature in the cubicle shot back up suddenly. 'Put my foot through a floorboard in a burnt out building. I twisted the knee as I fell.' Even here, even now, he was the best-looking man Abby had ever seen. Dark brown hair, cut short so that it spiked haphazardly when he ran his hand through it. A short, deep scar, running through his eyebrow, which was the one asymmetric feature of an otherwise stunningly handsome face.

'I'll see if I can find a record of that on our system. The operation was done here?'

He nodded, his lips quirking downwards then pressing together in a thin line.

'Right, then.' She scanned the notes quickly. 'It says here that you were offered pain control in the ambulance and you turned it down. Would you like something now?'

'No. I'm fine, thanks.'

He didn't need to pretend he wasn't in pain. She was a doctor, not a woman he needed to impress. 'On a scale of one to ten...'

'About one and a quarter.' He didn't even let her finish.

'Really?' She raised an eyebrow to make it clear that she didn't believe him for a minute, and he ignored her. Abby had seen that kind of flat-out denial before but it was puzzling coming from Nick. She'd get back to that one later.

'Okay, let me know if you change your mind and I can give you something that will make you much more comfortable.' He nodded almost imperceptibly. 'I'm going to send you for some X-rays, and I'll come back and see you again when I've reviewed them.' That would give Abby at least half an hour to gather her wits. Maybe more. Perhaps the next time she laid eyes on him, she'd be able to retain her composure a little better.

'Thanks.' He hesitated, as if something was bothering him. 'I hope I'm not keeping you from going home. It must be gone seven o'clock.'

Twenty past. The charge nurse from A and E had called her just as she'd finished catching up on the week's paperwork and had been about to leave. 'Not a problem. That's what I'm here for.' It seemed that finally, despite all Abby's promises to herself, she was going to be spending one more evening in Nick's company.

By the time Nick's X-rays were back, Abby had already found his notes on the computer and read them.

And it gave her no pleasure whatsoever to find he was wrong. She took a deep breath before she made her way back to his bedside to deliver the bad news.

'Hey, there.' His smile was too broad. Slightly brittle. 'How are you doing?'

'Thought you might be able to tell me.' He nodded at the large manila folder she carried.

'Yeah.' Abby sat down by his bedside. Whatever she felt about his behaviour towards her, she had to give him credit for his resilience. She knew how much pain he must be in, and it was searing through her. That trick of being able to insulate yourself from a patient's pain didn't seem to be working so well for her at the moment.

'What's the verdict, then?'

'The X-rays show a hairline crack on your patella.'

He stared at her as if he didn't understand, or perhaps he just wasn't taking her word for it. Abby drew one of the X-rays out of the folder, holding it up to the strip light above his head. 'Here, can you see?'

He shifted closer to her to look, and reached up, steadying her hand with his. His touch was still electric. The soft brush of his fingers against her wrist made the hairs on the back of her neck stand up. 'I can't see anything.'

'Right there.' She indicated the line of the fracture, trying to ignore the fact that she was leaning over him. That she would be able to hear his heartbeat if she got any closer. 'The good news is that it's not displaced, so it should heal relatively quickly.'

'I see.' He squinted at the area she had indicated. 'It doesn't look too bad, then?'

Abby bit her tongue. Asking him whether that statement was based on medical knowledge or wishful thinking probably wasn't appropriate. Neither was enjoying leaning over him. At the swimming pool it had been pretty much impossible not to notice Nick's beautiful physique. Here it was irrelevant.

She straightened quickly. 'Well, a fractured patella is never good. But it could have been a lot worse. From the looks of your knee there may well be some other damage, though, and I'm ordering an MRI scan to see what's happening with the cartilage and to get a better view of the fracture.'

'But if that's okay...?' He sat up straight on the trolley, as if their business was now finished and he could go. Abby fixed him with the sternest glare she could muster. This was her territory and she was in charge.

'There's still the matter of the crack on your patella. You're going to need to rest it and wear a brace for four to six weeks.'

He ran his hand back through his hair in a gesture of frustration. 'Four weeks?'

'Four to six weeks. That's pretty much how long a bone takes to mend.' Abby bit her lip. Enough sarcasm. He was in pain here, and she knew how much Nick loved his job. The least she could do was show him a bit of understanding. 'I'm sorry, but you won't be fit enough to go back to work for a while.'

'How long?'

'I can't tell for sure at this point. I'm going to refer you on for an early appointment with a colleague who specialises in injuries of this kind. By the time you see him, we should have managed to get some of this swelling down and the MRI results will be available. He'll be able to tell you much more.'

'Yes. Of course.' He took a deep breath. 'Thanks for everything, Abby. Can I go now?'

He really didn't want to be around her. She could tell from the way he was focussing past her, on something just over her right shoulder. He'd do anything but look her in the eye.

That was fine. Abby didn't much want to be around Nick either but that wasn't the point of this particular exercise. She was a doctor and he was a patient. If she reminded herself of that enough times, she'd get it in the end. 'Not yet. I need to sort out a suitable knee brace for you, along with some painkillers and anti-inflammatory drugs.' She fixed him with a stern look. 'Stay there, I'll be back shortly.'

Abby didn't wait for his answer. Making for the curtain, which covered the entrance to the cubicle, she yanked it firmly closed and caught the charge nurse's eye. If he attempted to run out on her this time, he'd find that the A and E staff were more than a match for him.

Abby was in a class all of her own when she did stern. Nick tried not to think about that, and concentrated on all the reasons why continuing their relationship had been a seriously bad idea. Why he'd been right to walk away before the shimmer in her light blue eyes, the little quirk of her mouth when she'd smiled, had pulled him spiralling out of control. Even now it was tough work to resist her.

Not that she was doing a great deal of smiling this evening. She didn't seem to be having much trouble with resisting him either. She'd drawn back so quickly when he'd touched her that he'd wondered whether an apology was in order. Common sense was yet another thing he had to award her ten out of ten for.

He pulled himself up into a sitting position and swung his good leg over the edge of the trolley. So far so good. Kind of. He gripped his injured leg and tried to move it and pain seared from his calf to his thigh. Not such a good idea. Nick reached for his jacket, which was over the back of the chair where his clothes were folded, managing to pull his phone from the pocket with the tips of his fingers.

When he switched it on, there were two missed calls, and a text. *Off duty in ten. Be there in half an hour.* Nick looked at his watch. Sam would be arriving in fifteen minutes and, with any luck, by that time Nick would be dressed and ready to go.

'It'll be a lot easier with this. And you're supposed to keep that switched off.'

Nick's gaze jerked upwards from the small screen on his phone and found Abby's half-amused grimace. 'What will?'

'Your escape.' She shrugged, walking to his bedside and propping the pair of elbow crutches she carried against the chair. 'Swing your leg back onto the bed while I sort this knee brace out.'

She fiddled for a while with the ugly-looking contraption, rolling her eyes and grinning when the Velcro straps tangled themselves together and stuck fast. Nick added *kindness* to the list of her virtues. Even though he'd treated her badly, there was no trace of reproach in her attitude towards him.

'Just relax and let me move your leg. I'll try not to hurt you too much.' She gently took hold of his leg and Nick braced himself for the pain, letting out an involuntary breath when it wasn't half as bad as when he'd tried to move it himself.

'There.' She carefully fastened the brace and stood back, reviewing her handiwork. 'How does that feel?'

'Better. Thanks, it feels much better with the support.' Nick had been concentrating on the gentle warmth of her fingers, the way her corn-coloured plait of hair threatened to slip forward over her shoulder when she bent forward. Her scent, which seemed to be more than just the astringent, soapy smell of the other doctors and nurses here. They were far more potent than the drugs he'd refused.

'Good. I've set it at an angle to keep your knee bent, and you should leave it like that until you see my colleague. Don't put any weight on the leg for the time being, and it'll help if you use cushions to support it when you're sitting or lying down.' She paused, seemingly deep in thought. 'Let's see if we can't get you back onto your feet.'

At last! Nick sat up and she helped him swing his leg over the side of the trolley. 'Lean on my shoulder if you need to.'

He couldn't think of anything more comforting at that moment than to take advantage of her offer. 'Thanks, but I'm okay.' Levering himself upwards with his arms, he put one foot to the floor and stood up slowly.

'Good. That's good.' She reached for the crutches, extending one to almost its full height, and gave it to him. 'Yes, that looks about right.' She adjusted the other and suddenly Nick was free. Able to move around again.

'Walk up and down a bit.' She watched carefully as he took a few tentative steps, leaning on the crutches, and nodded in approval. 'That looks fine. Is it comfortable?'

'Yes. The brace is a little tight.'

'It needs to be. As the swelling goes down, you should tighten it a little so it feels snug. Without cutting off the circulation to your foot, that is.' A sudden grin, which was quashed almost immediately, made Nick's head swim slightly. His own body was producing powerful endorphins in response to that lopsided, shining smile of hers, and he could do nothing to stop it.

'Thanks. Can I get dressed now?'

The words had an almost instant effect on her. She backed away. 'Do you need someone to help you? I can send someone in.'

'I'm fine.' Nick grinned to himself as she disappeared out of the cubicle. Maybe he should have thought of that one sooner.

The A and E nurse had cut the leg of his trousers to get them off and it was easy enough to slip them back on again. Discarding the flimsy hospital gown and pulling on his shirt, Nick struggled with getting his sock onto his injured leg and decided to carry his boot. A quick phone call elicited the information that Sam was outside, trying to find a parking space.

'Right.' The curtain had twitched slightly, indicating that she'd checked first to make sure he was dressed, before she breezed back into his cubicle. 'I've got a leaflet here, to give you some guidelines on how to manage the leg.' She proffered a printed sheet and Nick took it. Next to one of the items she had drawn a star and written a few notes. Even her handwriting was bewitching. Nick wondered briefly whether it was possible to be seduced by someone's handwriting, before folding the sheet and putting it into his jacket pocket.

'Thanks. I appreciate all you've done, Abby.' It was

time for him to leave. Before she got around to the prescription she held in her hand. Before he got too used to the light that seemed to shine from her and gravitated towards it, like a moth whose wings had already been burned by the flame.

'Oh, no, you don't.' She was quicker than he was at the moment, and blocked his path. 'Sit down for a moment. I've had a colleague write you a prescription for something to control your pain.'

She was keeping him well and truly at arm's length. Somehow the fact that she'd got someone else to write the prescription rankled more than anything. As if she was trying to wipe him from every corner of her life. Nick wondered if she'd been hurt as badly as he had by what had happened between them.

'I don't need it.' The words sounded harsh and ungrateful. 'Thanks, Abby, but I don't want it. Sam'll be here to pick me up any minute.'

'Sam!' She jumped like a startled fawn, flushing slightly. She did remember, then. The leisurely Sunday morning breakfasts after training when Sam and the half-dozen others at the table had faded into blurred insignificance, and there had only been Nick and Abby. The reckless slide into dinner and the cinema. He'd fallen for her hard and fast, before sanity had taken hold and convinced him to draw back.

She pulled herself together with impressive speed. 'He'll have to wait, then, we're not finished yet. You should have something to control the pain and bring the inflammation down. I really can't recommend that you be discharged without it…'

'Then I'll discharge myself.'

The conversation had finally degenerated into a

game of chicken. Whose nerve was going to break first. In the end, no one broke. Sam's light touch on Abby's shoulder made her jump again and she whirled round to face him.

'Abby. Where have you been? Long time no see…' Nick directed his most ferocious glare in Sam's direction and Sam got the message. 'So how's he doing, then?'

She pursed her lips as if she was considering the question and Nick broke in. 'We're done here.'

'Really?' Sam gave Abby a quizzical look and she frowned.

'No. Not really. Nick…'

In between him and Sam, she suddenly looked small. Vulnerable. Staring up at them with what looked like frightened defiance in her eyes. The urge to protect her leaked into Nick's aching bones, almost before he realised that the only thing Abby needed protecting from was him.

He slid past her, brushing against her as he went. 'I'm sorry.' He was sorry for everything. The way he'd left her without a word of explanation six months ago. How he was leaving things between them now. But if she knew his reasons she'd be the first to want him gone. 'Thanks for all you've done.'

The words stuck in his throat because he knew they weren't enough. But they were all he could give her and he lunged forward on his crutches. He heard her exclamation of frustration behind him and Nick made for the exit doors without looking back.

CHAPTER TWO

SAM had given her a grinning shrug and followed Nick, jogging to catch up with him. Abby didn't stop to watch them go. She did what she had schooled herself to do as a teenager and which now came as second nature to her. If someone hurts you, don't go running after them. Turn away. Be strong.

'How did that go?' She was concentrating hard on Not Caring and the voice at her elbow made her jump.

'Michael. I didn't see you there.'

'Penny for them?' Michael Gibson, the A and E doctor who would have seen Nick had he not been with a more urgent patient, was standing beside her.

'Not worth it.' She held the prescription form up for Michael to see. 'He didn't take it.'

'No? Why not?'

'I don't know. He just said that he didn't need it. Stayed long enough for an X-ray and for me to give him a diagnosis and then as soon as I let him get his hands on a pair of crutches he was off. I couldn't stop him.'

'What were you thinking of doing? Handcuffing him to the bed?'

Don't say things like that, Michael. You'll give a girl

ideas. 'I…I just can't help thinking that he would have taken it from someone else.'

Michael sighed. 'Look, Abs. You asked him if he was okay with you treating him, you ran everything past me. Aren't you overthinking this a bit? People make decisions about what level of treatment they're going to take from us all the time.'

'I guess so.' Abby wasn't convinced. She wouldn't lay the blame on Nick when she should be shouldering it herself. His decision must have been something to do with her.

Michael looked at his watch. 'Can you do me a favour and write up the notes, then sort out a referral?'

'Of course. You get on. I'll put him on the list for an early MRI scan and get him an appointment up in Orthopaedics.' Abby grinned. 'With someone else, who might be able to talk some sense into him.'

'Don't sweat it so much, Abby.' The charge nurse had caught Michael's eye and he was already turning to see his next patient for the evening. 'All we can do is our best.'

She'd spent half the night considering that rationally, and the other half beating her head against an imaginary brick wall, which might just as well have been real from the way her head was throbbing this morning. The only thing that Abby was sure of was that she'd messed up somehow and that she had to put it right.

Something had made him act that way. He was perfectly at liberty to walk out on her as a woman and she was at liberty to hate him for it. But if a little of the past had leaked through into her attitude towards Nick last night and made him refuse medical treatment he needed, that was unforgivable. Whatever Michael had said, she had to put it right.

Not giving herself time to change her mind, Abby got out of the car, marched quickly up the front path and pressed the doorbell. No one answered. She was about to turn and walk away when a bump from inside the house told her that Nick hadn't gone out. She thumbed the doorbell again, this time letting it ring insistently.

'Okay! Give me a minute…' The door was flung open and Nick froze.

'Hello.' She was expecting to see him this time, but that didn't seem to lessen the shock all that much.

'Hi…Abby.' He had the presence of mind not to say it, but his eyes demanded an answer. *What are you doing here?*

'I came to see how you were.' Her hands were shaking but her lips were smiling. Not too much. Professional.

'You didn't need to. I'm fine. Thanks.' Nick was leaning on the crutches she'd given him, his loose sweatpants stretched over the bulky brace. That was something. At least he hadn't taken it off and thrown it away as soon as he'd got home.

'I think we have a little unfinished business, Nick.'

He pressed his lips together. 'I know. I should have called you, it was unforgivable…'

'Not that.' Abby had spent some time convincing herself that the events of six months ago were all water under the bridge, and she wasn't going to let Nick bring it up now. 'I mean from last night. You left before I had a chance to finish…' She stopped, flushing. Her voice sounded like a pathetic, childish whine, as if she was begging for his attention.

Understanding flickered in his eyes. His warmth curled around her senses and just as Abby's knees began to liquefy her defences clicked in. This man was not going to see her vulnerable. Not again.

'I left because I was done. It was nothing to do with you.'

Abby straightened herself. 'What was it to do with?'

'It's none of your business, Abby...' He seemed to be about to say more but stopped himself. 'Look, as I said, it's really good of you to come here and I want to thank you for everything you've done. But you'll have to excuse me.'

She wasn't giving up without a fight. The door was closing, and there were only two things that Abby could think of to do. She wasn't quite angry enough to punch him—not yet, anyway—so she stuck her foot in the doorway, bracing herself for the blow of the door as he tried to close it.

It didn't come. There was nothing wrong with Nick's reflexes and he whipped the door back open before it hit her foot. 'Abby...' His gaze met hers, dark and full of pain, and concern for him grated across her nerve endings. There was no point in that. Nick wasn't the type to accept sympathy. She faced him down, and saw a flare of what might have been tenderness.

Wordlessly he stepped back from the doorway, turned, and made his way back along the hall, leaving the door open behind him. It wasn't the most cordial of invitations she'd ever received but Abby followed him, closing the door behind her.

'Can I get you some coffee?' He had led her through to the kitchen, a large, bright room where the house had been extended at the back. Indicating that she should sit down at the sturdy wooden table, he swung across to the counter and reached up into a cupboard for a tin of coffee beans.

'Thanks.' Abby sat down. Making coffee and drinking it would take at least ten minutes. She could use that time.

'Toast?' The room smelled of fresh bread and there was a loaf, just out of the breadmaker, on the countertop.

'Thanks. I didn't have breakfast this morning.' Fifteen minutes. Even better. Time enough to sort this out and then get out of there.

Nick didn't turn to face her and Abby sat down. Without a word, he ground the coffee beans and switched the coffee machine on, then shifted awkwardly across to cut the bread, leaning one of his crutches against the sink.

'Here, let me help you.'

'I can manage.'

She dropped back down into her chair. He seemed to be managing not to look at her as well. It occurred to Abby that the offer of coffee hadn't been intended as hospitality as much as an excuse not to sit down and talk to her.

Finally he was done. He'd made tea for himself, and Abby jumped up to ferry the cups and plates to the table, while Nick lowered himself into a chair.

'We don't need to argue about this.' He gave her a persuasive grin. 'We could just agree to differ and enjoy our breakfast.'

Nick's charm didn't work on her any more. Much. 'Or we could talk about why I think it's important that you take the medication you've been offered. I'm here to help you. As a friend, Nick.' 'Friends' was dangerous territory. But being his doctor was becoming more inappropriate by the minute, and that was the only other excuse she had to be there.

His lips twitched. 'And you think that I'm not helping myself?'

'From where I'm sitting, that's how it looks.' Abby took a sip of her coffee.

'I guess it might.' The words were almost a challenge.

'It does, Nick. Pain control isn't just about making things easier for you. With an injury like this, it's important that you give your body a chance to heal. That means being able to sleep and move around gently. You need to get some of that swelling around your knee down as well.'

'I've been putting ice packs on it. The swelling's down from yesterday.'

'That's better than nothing. How much sleep did you get last night?'

Nick didn't answer. He didn't need to. The dark hollows beneath his eyes and the stiffness of his movements attested to how little he'd slept and how much he was hurting right now. Abby could strike the suspicion of him having decided to self-medicate from the list of possibilities.

'Did you take analgesics the last time you hurt your knee?' Abby could have looked that up on the hospital's computer system after he'd left, but she'd baulked at that.

He nodded. Another couple of options to strike off the list. Whatever his reason was, it must be something that had happened in the four years, since his last injury. 'Are you saying you had an adverse reaction to one of the drugs?'

'No. I'm saying that I don't want the drugs now.'

'Nick, if you don't want to tell me what the problem is, that's fine. But you wouldn't let me do my best for you last night, and I can tell you now that's not the way that I work and it's not the way the doctor I've referred you to works either.' Abby could feel the colour rising in her cheeks, and checked herself.

Something bloomed in his eyes, which looked suspiciously like respect, and Abby ignored the answering quiver in the pit of her stomach. She didn't need Nick's respect, she just needed him to see the logic of what she was trying to tell him.

'Since you put it that way...' He seemed lost in thought for a moment and then jerked his head up to face her, his stare daring her to look away. 'I'm a drug addict.'

His message was clear. Get back. Stay back. Nick knew that Abby was not stupid. She had to understand it and the only other explanation was that she was planning on ignoring it.

'Okay. What kind of drugs?' She was doing a fairly good job of staring him down. There was barely a flicker at the corner of her eye.

'Painkillers. The kind that were prescribed for me. And others that weren't.'

'But you're clean now.'

'What makes you think that?' He'd never be truly clean.

'If you were still taking opiate drugs, for whatever purpose, maybe you would have slept a little better last night.'

'Yeah. Fair enough.' It would take more than just staying off the drugs to make him whole, but Nick was done with admitting things. That was all she needed to know. He reached for his keys, which were sitting at the far end of the table where he'd dumped them last night, and showed her the small engraved disc that served as a key fob.

She leaned forward to focus on the letters, alongside a logo with a set of initials. 'IK. What's that?'

'Stands for one thousand days. In that time I haven't had as much as an aspirin or a cup of coffee.' Her gaze flicked involuntarily towards the cup of herbal tea in front of him, and Nick wondered how much of this she had already worked out for herself. 'I earned this six months ago, and I'm not giving it up for anything.'

'Your support group asks that you give up everything? Aspirin, coffee…?'

'No. That's what I require of myself.'

She sucked in a deep breath, seeming to relax slightly as she exhaled. 'I'd like to help, Nick. If you'll let me.'

She'd disarmed him completely. Maybe it was the way that sunlight from the window became entangled in her hair and couldn't break free. Maybe her steady, blue gaze, which held the promise of both cornflowers and steel. 'What do you suggest?'

Nick was expecting one, maybe two platitudes about not overstepping the mark again and a lecture on how effective ice-packs could be. Then she could do the sensible thing and wash her hands of him.

Instead, she drew a pad from her handbag, turned to a page of scribbled notes, asked questions and made some more notes. Then she produced a bundle of printed pages from the internet, selecting some for him to look at, which left Nick in little doubt that she had come pre-pared for almost every eventuality, including the one which he had just admitted to. He hadn't thought that Abby was such a force to be reckoned with.

'What do you think, then?'

Nick had no idea what he thought. He'd heard ev-erything she'd said, but the bulk of his attention had been concentrated on the soft curl of her eyelashes. On trying to resist the impulse to reach out and touch the few golden strands of hair that strayed across her cheek, aware that he could so easily become trapped. 'Sounds logical.'

She rolled her eyes, twisting her head to one side in a shimmer of liquid light, and he almost choked on his tea. 'It's obviously logical. But how do you feel about it?'

'Okay, then.' There wasn't much option other than the truth, not with Abby. 'I'd rather stick pins in my eyes.'

'Fair enough, but can you do it?'

'Stick pins in my eyes? I'd rather not.'

She gifted him with a glare that made his stomach tighten. 'Stop messing around, Nick. Will you do this?' She tapped the list she'd made with her pen.

A visit to a pain clinic, specialising in drug-free therapies, which Abby had assured him was among the best in its field. Taking the clinic's advice on non-opiate painkillers and anti-inflammatory drugs. Coming clean with the orthopaedic surgeon that Abby had al-ready arranged for Nick to see at the hospital, and hav-ing him work with the clinic to provide what she termed as 'joined-up' care.

'I can do it.' This would be harder than dealing with

the constant, throbbing pain in his knee but Nick saw the sense in it. It was his best chance of being able to get back on his feet again any time soon.

'So I'll call the pain clinic and try to get you an emergency appointment for this afternoon.'

'I'm not a child. I can make a phone call.' The thought that maybe she didn't trust him hurt more than it should have. What reason had he ever given her to trust him?

'I know. But this is supposed to be the exact opposite of what you did before. You take help. You don't self-medicate. You follow an agreed plan and you keep everyone informed and in touch with what's happening.'

She grinned persuasively at him. He'd missed her smile. 'If something was on fire, I'd be letting *you* take charge.'

'I have a box of matches in the drawer over there…' He held his hands up as she shot him a look of such ferocity that laughter bubbled up in his chest. Abby had surprised him. Under those soft curves of hers there was a backbone of pure steel. 'Okay. You win, it's a deal.'

'Yes…yes, a deal.' She was suddenly uncertain, lacing her fingers around her empty coffee cup. It seemed that she too needed something to occupy her when they were together. Something to take her mind off the heat that seemed to build when there was nothing practical to focus on.

'Would you like some more toast? That slice must be cold by now.'

'No. No, thanks.' She took a deep breath. 'Sorry to have spoiled your morning.'

'You didn't.' He tried to catch her eye but she seemed to be avoiding his gaze now. 'I treated you pretty badly,

Abby. What you did this morning says everything about you and nothing about what I deserve.'

She seemed puzzled, but the comment emboldened her. 'I'd like you to do something else, too.'

'Go on, then. What is it?'

'I want you to call me in a couple of days, just to let me know how things are going. Will you do that?'

'Of course.' It was the least he could do. 'Or I could buy you lunch.' The words slipped out before he had a chance to stop them. But it didn't really matter. They'd be wearing snowboots in hell before she accepted. Doctors might forgive, but women didn't give you the option of standing them up a second time.

She hesitated, avoiding his gaze. 'Call me on Tuesday morning. I take my lunch at one o'clock, and if I'm free maybe we can meet up.' She picked her phone up, briskly. 'I'll make that call, then.'

CHAPTER THREE

HE'D hurt her once, and she hadn't had any say in the matter then. If he hurt her again, it was going to be her own stupid fault. But this time Abby knew the score. She wasn't at his beck and call and she wouldn't be shedding any tears over him if he decided suddenly to disappear again.

It was ten minutes' walk from the hospital to the gym they both belonged to. Abby had been taking her early-morning swims at another pool for the last six months, ever since the possibility of bumping into Nick had turned from delicious excitement to self-conscious dread. But since she hadn't let her membership lapse, for fear that might be construed as running away, she could always go for a swim if he didn't turn up.

The screens and plants in the cafeteria had been designed to break up the area and give a little privacy for each table. Abby scanned the space. All of a sudden she didn't want to have to walk around and then be subjected to the ignominy of sitting down alone if he wasn't there.

'Hey, there.' His voice cut through her thoughts, like a hot knife through butter. 'Thanks for coming.'

She had been feeling shaky all morning, agitated

at the thought of seeing Nick again, and now she was concentrating so hard on not being nervous that she'd walked straight past him. He was perched on one of the stools at the juice bar, one leg propped up on the stainless-steel rail that ran around it at low level, the other foot planted firmly on the floor.

'I said I would, didn't I?' She pulled herself up onto a stool, crossing her legs so her feet didn't dangle like a child's and putting her handbag on the empty seat she had left between Nick and herself. 'What have you got there?'

'Raspberry and apple. It's nice, want to try it?' He tilted his glass towards her.

'No, thanks. I'll have the strawberry and banana shake. And one of those toasted sandwiches, I think.' She signalled to the waitress behind the bar and gave her order, looking in her handbag for her purse. Too late. Nick had already passed a note across the bar and the waitress had taken it.

'Thanks.' Arguing with him over who was going to pay made his gesture seem more important than it was. Better to leave it. 'So how are you?'

'I'm good. I've got my appointment through.'

'Good. Dr Patel's a nice guy, and the best orthopaedic surgeon in the department. You'll be fine with him.' Jay would take care of Nick better than Abby could. Better than she had any right to.

'Thanks.' He took his change and pocketed it then felt inside his casual jacket, pulling out two foil packets and proffering them. 'And I've been keeping my side of the bargain.'

'That's okay. I'll take your word for it.' She smiled

at him. 'Anyway, you could have just taken the tablets out and thrown them in the bin.'

He seemed to be considering the possibility. 'I could have. Only I would have flushed them down the sink. Always dispose of medicines safely.'

He was teasing her now and Abby felt the coiled spring that had lodged in her stomach begin to loosen slightly. The feeling wasn't altogether agreeable. 'Well, as long as you're doing something to get the swelling down.'

He nodded. 'The ice packs are helping and the people at the pain clinic gave me some good tips. I can't put any weight on the leg still, but I can get around well enough. I might try going for a swim this afternoon.'

Unwelcome images flooded Abby's brain. Nick in the pool, water streaming across his back as he swam. Pulling himself out, the muscles of his shoulders flexing. She concentrated on his knee. 'That's not a very good idea, Nick.'

'Swimming's good exercise. The water will support my leg.'

'Dr Patel will give you some exercises and he'll be able to discuss exactly what you should and shouldn't be doing. Why don't you leave it until you see him?' She could feel her irritation level rising again. What was so important about going swimming today?

'I can't.' He dismissed her with just two words and something snapped in that part of her brain that had been filtering the anger out of her responses to him.

'Yes, you can. You just won't.' Abby jumped as a plate and glass clattered down next to her, and turned to thank the waitress, who gave her a curt nod, obviously disapproving of the sound of discord at the bar.

'Let's go and sit at one of the tables. Look, there's one free over there by the window.'

'Perfect for bullying me in private.' Nick grinned.

'I do not bully people.' If he only knew, he wouldn't say such a thing. She slid down from her stool, balanced her plate and glass in one hand, grabbed her handbag with the other and walked over to the empty table. He could follow if he liked.

As she tried to manoeuvre her way into a seat, her hands full, she saw Nick's arm reach around her, pulling the chair back so she could sink down into it. Lowering himself into the chair opposite, he smiled up at the waitress as she placed his drink in front of him. 'Thanks. That's kind of you.'

The waitress nodded and shot Abby a disapproving look. As well she might. Nick was handsome, charming and, oh, so obviously in need of a little looking after at the moment. Someone to carry his drink while he dealt with his crutches. Someone to plump his pillows and stare into his molten chocolate eyes.

'If I sound as if I don't appreciate everything you've done, Abby, that's not the case.' Nick had smiled and thanked the waitress, but now his attention was all on Abby.

'But you're just used to having things your own way.'

He grinned. 'Maybe. But I value your input.'

He made it sound as if she'd made a few suggestions, which he'd decided whether to go along with or not. Abby guessed that was about right. 'So, are you up for another piece of input?'

'Go on.'

She ignored both the smile and the dimple. Particularly the dimple. 'I think you're just falling into the same way of doing things as before. Deciding what you're going to do and then just going and doing it. I think you should wait until you can speak to your doctor and get his advice.'

'What do you think Dr Patel is going to say, then?'

'I don't second-guess colleagues. Just ask him.'

'I do have a compelling reason to get back into the water.'

Abby gave in. 'All right, so what's your compelling reason? Other than the desire to prove to yourself that you're indestructible or die trying?'

The brief tilt of his head to one side told her that she'd hit on a home truth. 'A group of us from the fire station is doing an open-water swim in five weeks' time, up in the Lake District. Actually, six of them on consecutive days. I need to be fit for that.'

The audacity of the statement made Abby choke on her drink. 'Six consecutive days? How long are these swims?'

'Between two and six miles each.'

'What? Are you completely mad, Nick? I'm all for encouraging people to exercise gently, but that's gruelling enough for anyone who's fit. It's complete and utter madness with that knee.'

He shrugged. 'I have to try. I'll see what Dr Patel says, but perhaps I can strap the leg up so that it's supported in the water.'

'No. He's going to tell you exactly what I am. You're overdoing it, and asking for trouble.' Abby couldn't believe what she was hearing.

'I thought you didn't second-guess colleagues.' His gaze was making her skin prickle.

'I don't, but I'm perfectly capable of seeing the obvious. What's so important about these swims anyway? Can't you postpone them or something? I know it's late in the year, but next spring would be much more sensible.'

He shook his head. 'It's a big charity event. There are a dozen of us swimming and we have sponsorship.'

'Well, you'll just have to drop out, then.'

He gave her an amused look. 'Are you telling me what to do?'

'I'm telling you that in my considered opinion, and I do know something about this, you'll do yourself a great deal of damage if you push yourself too hard. You'll fail with the swims and you might well put yourself into a position where you'll never get fit again. Do you want that?'

He shook his head slowly, his gaze dropping to the tabletop. 'No. But I feel I have to try. I won't push it.'

Yeah, right. Since when did Nick start anything that he didn't finish? Abby swallowed the obvious answer. Their relationship was clearly an exception to that rule. 'How much sponsorship do you have?'

'It's a hundred grand in total. I'm the only one doing all six swims and so a lot of the corporate sponsorship that we've raised depends on me. If I don't swim, we lose thirty of that.' His brow furrowed in thought. 'Maybe the sponsors will allow me to do the swims over twelve days instead of six. A day's rest in between.'

'Oh, right, that'll be okay, then. You can spend twelve days on wrecking your knee instead of six.' Concern lent a biting edge to Abby's sarcasm. She buried her face in her hands so he couldn't see her confusion. She wasn't usually this aggressive with people, but Nick was pushing all the wrong buttons with her.

His voice cut through her thoughts and she lifted her head wearily. 'It's a good cause, Abby. Maybe, when Dr Patel gives my leg the once-over, it will have improved—it already feels a lot better. I don't know right now, but surely anything is worth trying?'

The look in his eyes said it all. He knew just as well as she did that this was madness but he'd made a commitment and it was killing him not to carry it through. So he was clutching at straws. Abby sighed. 'What's the charity?'

'We're doing it in conjunction with Answers Through Sport.'

'I've heard of them. I learned to swim in one of their classes when I was a kid.'

'Really?' He was on the alert suddenly and Abby bit her lip. 'I didn't think they did general classes.'

They didn't. Abby had been a beneficiary of their *Fighting Back* programme for bullied teenagers. But that was none of Nick's business. 'So how did you get involved with them?'

'They helped me when I was recovering from my addiction to drugs.' He shrugged. 'Now I'm returning the favour and doing some fundraising for them. They have match funding, so they'll get a grant for an amount equal to that which they raise for themselves.'

Abby's stomach twisted into a tight knot. 'So thirty grand becomes sixty.'

'Yeah. Do you see now why I won't give up without a fight? What would you do in my place?'

That was none of his business. She wasn't in his place and he had no right to ask, particularly since the answer would only encourage him in this scheme of his. 'Couldn't you get someone to step in and do the swims for you?'

'I thought of that, but we've already got everyone doing as much as they can. Even if we could find a volunteer, a month isn't long enough to build up the kind of fitness you need for something like this.' He ran his hand through his hair in a gesture of frustration. 'Why, do you know anyone?'

Abby's heart sank. Nick had no choice but to keep believing that he might just be able to do this. And now she had no choice.

'Yeah, I know someone. Me.'

Nick had refused point blank to even countenance the idea at first. But Abby had presented her credentials, competitive swimming as a teenager, member of a cross-Channel relay team when she'd been at medical school. And Nick knew as well as anyone that she was a strong enough swimmer, they'd raced together enough times at the gym.

The project committee cordially invited him to do the arithmetic. He did it and conceded. Not so cordially. But Abby had already secured the promise of two weeks' leave from work and stepped up her training.

'That's three miles.' His voice floated across the deserted swimming pool.

'No, it's not. I've got another two lengths to go. And I'd better do them quickly, before the advanced-swimmers session ends.'

He glanced at his watch. 'Yeah, the children's swimming classes will be starting in ten minutes. One final push, eh?' Nick was sitting at the side of the pool, wearing a T-shirt and sweat pants. Tanned, relaxed and irritating beyond measure. 'Then I'll buy you breakfast.'

She didn't want him to buy her breakfast. It had taken him over a week to contact all his sponsors personally and now that was done he'd switched his attention to her. For the last two days he'd been turning up at the pool at seven o'clock in the morning to help with her training, dispensing shouted advice and encouragement that Abby doggedly ignored.

She swam another four lengths, just to show him who was boss, and found him waiting by the pool steps, one hand gripping his elbow crutch, the other holding out a large towel. 'Here you are. Don't get chilled.'

Abby wrapped the towel around herself gratefully. Being in her swimsuit when he was fully clothed, was far more uncomfortable than she had bargained for. Much more challenging than those first easy days of their acquaintance, when the guy with heart-stoppingly broad shoulders had first beaten her by two yards to the far end of the pool then smiled in her direction and exchanged a few words with her.

'Thanks.' She looked around as a group of adults and children emerged from the changing rooms. 'Looks like I won't get much more done now.'

'You've done enough.' He reached into his pocket and consulted a stopwatch. 'An hour and twenty-five. Not bad.'

'What do you mean, not bad? What's your best time?'

'One hour ten. But you did four extra lengths.'

Even if she had, she'd still have to work a little harder if she was going to match his time. But she had another three weeks to go.

'You shouldn't push yourself.' He seemed to know

what she was thinking. 'An injury at this point would
be bad news.'

'I know. I've done this before, remember.'

He grinned, and Abby clutched the thick towel
around her tightly. 'So where do you want to go for
breakfast? As it's Saturday, we can take our time.'

Breakfast in the presence of Nick's smile sounded
fantastic, but it was forbidden fruit. On the other hand,
she needed to eat and at this rate she'd be gnawing her
own arm off before she managed to get rid of him.
'What about that place across the road? They do fresh
croissants and a latte to die for.'

'Sure. Whatever you want. I'll meet you in the
lobby...' Nick seemed to realise that he'd lost Abby's
attention and that it was now fixed on a small group of
children on the other side of the pool.

It was nothing. Just high jinks, kids mucking about.
Abby kept her eye on the group anyway.

'So I'll meet you in the lobby in ten minutes?'

'Yeah, ten minutes...' The shrill voices of the children swelled above the mounting noise in the pool and
Abby strained to see what was going on.

'What is it?' She could feel his fingers brushing her
elbow lightly, and she jerked her arm away. She had neither the time nor the inclination to stop and discuss this
with Nick. Abby marched round to the other side of the
pool and approached the group of children.

There was a little girl at the centre, red in the face
and obviously trying to hold back tears, as one of the
older girls made jokes that everyone else seemed to
think were funny. She'd been that child. Surrounded
by a ring of distorted faces, trying not to cry at their
taunts. Hoping that someone would come along and

break it up. And now Abby had the chance to do something that no one had ever bothered to do for her. She had to get this right.

'Excuse me.' Abby had to shoulder her way through the group to reach the child. 'I just wanted to ask you where you got your swimming costume? I'm looking for one for my niece, and this is so pretty.'

As she spoke, the group melted away, re-forming a few yards away behind Abby's back. She ignored them and knelt down next to the little girl, leaning in to hear her whispered reply.

'Really? I was in there the other day and I didn't see any pink ones.' Abby smiled encouragingly. 'I'll have to go back and take another look.'

She got a hesitant smile back, which felt like pure gold, and the sick feeling in her stomach began to subside a little. The child reached forward and pulled at Abby's towel. 'Does yours have flowers?'

'No, worse luck.' Abby unwrapped the towel, wrinkling her nose. 'Just plain blue. Not as pretty as yours.'

Another smile. This time bright and clear, the way a child should smile. 'Which swimming class are you in, sweetie?'

'Over there.' Abby followed the little girl's pointing finger to a group of younger children at the shallow end of the pool, supervised by two women.

'Well, why don't you go and join them? But there's something I'd like to tell you first.'

'Okay.' Half the child's attention was already on her playmates.

'If anyone ever hurts you or makes fun of you, you should tell an adult. Your mum or dad, or one of your teachers.' That hadn't worked too well for Abby, but it didn't mean it wasn't good advice in general. 'Will you remember that?'

'All right.' The child nodded solemnly and scuttled away, the jibes of the older girls seemingly forgotten. Abby sat back on her heels and took a deep breath to steady herself. The adult in her told her that banging the bullies' heads together and throwing them in the pool wasn't going to help anyone, least of all their victim. The child in her was itching to do just that.

The sound of feet scuffling on the tiles as the group behind her broke up, saved her from herself. Abby turned and saw Nick approaching and got to her feet, pulling the towel back around her.

'You're shivering.' He'd followed her to the bench at the side of the pool and lowered himself down next to her.

She wasn't shivering, she was trembling. There was a difference and Nick knew it as well as she did. 'I'm okay. I should let someone know...'

'Go and get dressed.' He indicated the children's swimming coach with a nod of his head. 'I'll let Diane know what's happened.'

He was right. She had to let go of this, pass it over to the people who were best placed to do something. It was hard, though. Abby had worked through the fear and self-loathing from her own childhood but seeing another child bullied had created a whole new set of emotions. Anger and helplessness had smacked her hard in the face, leaving her reeling.

'Go and get changed.' He had already caught Diane's eye and was pulling himself to his feet, grabbing his crutches.

There was nothing for it but to do as he said. Abby

sat for a moment, watching Nick and Diane as they talked. It was okay. Everything was going to be okay. She repeated the words over to herself as she made her way towards the entrance to the changing rooms.

Nick only had to get out of his sweatpants and canvas shoes then pull on a pair of jeans, but when he made it to the reception area he found that Abby was already there, waiting for him. 'Is she all right?' She fired the words at him almost before he had reached her.

'She's fine. Diane's talked to her and she's going to have a word with the mother. She asked me to thank you for spotting what was going on and breaking it up.'

She nodded wordlessly, her eyes fixed on the floor. It seemed that what he'd done met with her approval.

'You ready for breakfast, then?' Maybe he'd ask her. About that haunted look in her eyes and the way she'd reacted at the poolside. The way she was reacting now.

'I'm a little tired. Maybe another time.'

He supposed that 'another time' meant when he'd forgotten all about what had happened here this morning. That wasn't going to happen. 'Abby, I know that no case of bullying should be taken lightly...' he didn't know quite how to put this '...but you seem very upset.'

The look in her eyes told him that he was right. She'd chosen to see something else, something that she remembered rather than what had actually gone on here. But her lips, pressed together tightly, showed that she wasn't about to admit anything of the sort. 'I'm tired, Nick, and I didn't react appropriately. It was a mistake.'

'Our mistakes often tell us more than anything.' Nick smiled to soften the words. It wasn't a criticism. Or if it was, it was aimed primarily at himself.

'And what this one tells me is that I'm tired and I need to get home.'

'Are you sure?' He shouldn't be questioning her like this. Or rather he shouldn't care so much. If he didn't care about her answers, then asking would have been okay.

He was about to get the brush-off—he could almost see the lie forming on her lips. He caught her gaze, searching her pale blue eyes, and for a moment he saw the truth and wanted to hold Abby, protect her from every real and imagined threat.

'I'm going home, Nick.' She swung her swimming bag onto her shoulder and would have walked away from him if he'd let her.

He'd cared too much, pushed her too hard, and now she'd drawn back. Nick preferred not to think about what that mistake said about him. 'I'll drop by later in the week with the detailed itinerary.'

'Good. Thanks.'

'Keep up the good work.'

'Right.' There was no stopping her from going, this time. She turned and walked away from him, turning in the doorway to give him a wave that looked far more like *Goodbye and good riddance* than *See you later*, and then she was gone.

CHAPTER FOUR

EUSTON station was crowded, rush-hour commuters streaming from trains and making their way in a concentrated mass to the Underground escalators. Abby stood in the most open spot she could, studying the departure boards. The train for Windermere was an estimated twelve minutes late, which meant there was over half an hour to wait.

No one was here yet. No Nick at the platform entrance, where they'd said they'd meet, and the swarms of people on the station concourse were making her head swim.

Standing on her toes, Abby could see a coffee shop in one corner of the station. There was a queue of people waiting for their early morning shot, but at least she'd have somewhere to stand where her case wasn't constantly being bumped by passers-by.

She fixed her eyes on her destination and began to march determinedly towards it. She hated crowds. Rush-hour commuting was an art, and she'd got used to it, but she'd never managed to completely lose the feeling of unease at being confronted with a faceless, potentially antagonistic mass of people. And her nerves at the thought of seeing Nick again, despite the fact that they'd been in almost daily contact by email, weren't helping particularly.

There was a wait for the coffee, but as soon as she had the warm cardboard beaker in her hand she began to feel better. Now all she had to do was find a quiet corner to drink it in. She waited while another stream of people walked briskly past. Her stomach was still churning and she needed to sit down, sip her drink and get herself together.

'Oh!' Someone had collided with her case, kicked it to one side and kept walking. The plastic top flew off the beaker of coffee as Abby's fingers tightened instinctively around it, and hot liquid spilled onto her fleece jacket and dribbled onto the floor.

Nothing like looking where you're going! The words shot through her head, but she was suddenly too breathless to mutter them after the man. Her hands were full, coffee in one hand, case in the other, the straps of her handbag beginning to slip from her shoulder. As another wave of anonymous faces headed straight for her, Abby scurried towards the only form of cover she could reach, an information board at the edge of the concourse, and leaned against it for support.

'Not now. *Not now!*' She muttered the instruction to herself under her breath, so softly that even she couldn't hear the words. Her lungs were straining for air and her heart thumped in her chest as if it had decided that it wanted out and the most direct route was straight through her ribcage.

'Breathe. One…two…' Her words were louder and touched with desperation this time, but that didn't seem to make much difference. She was gulping in air too

fast and a feeling of nameless, shapeless dread was beginning to engulf her.

'Everything's okay. Just slow down.' Abby tried
again to convince her own body to respond, closing her
eyes in concentration and then snapping them back open
again as the world swam and she almost toppled over.

'Abby?' Someone was there. Someone who smelled
like Nick. Soft leather and sandalwood, gasped into
her heaving lungs and then breathed out again far too
quickly.

'Give her some space.' His voice rang out. Com-
manding enough to divert the flow of people away from
them. An arm around her shoulders pulled her into the
protection of his body and she clung to him, letting him
prise the half-empty beaker of coffee from the convul-
sive grip of her fingers.

'Slowly, Abby. Breathe slowly. On my count...
One...two...three.'

For a moment, her heaving lungs listened and com-
plied with his instructions, where they had ignored her
own. But then the noise in her ears and the banging of
her heart, craving more oxygen than was strictly good
for it, took over again. She was dimly aware of someone stopping, and that Nick had spoken to them, but
right now all she could think of was that she had to get
out of there.

'Okay, Abby. Everything's okay. Come with me.' He
tried to move her, and she clutched instinctively for the
handle of her case. 'It's all right. Someone's bringing
your bag. We're just going outside to sit down.'

Sit down. Yes. She'd like to sit down. She'd be okay
in a minute if she could just sit down. She felt the
slightly uneven sway of Nick's body against hers as

he led her through the automatic doors and out into the fresh air.

'Would you mind? Thank you. No, she just needs to sit for a moment. Thanks.' Nick had cleared a space for her on a nearby bench and Abby sank down onto it gratefully. Someone moved up and he sat down next to her, his arm around her shoulder.

Her chest was still heaving frantically. 'Anyone got a paper bag? Yeah, large one.' His voice again. 'Thanks.' Nick shook the bag out and put it into her trembling fingers. 'You know what to do, Abby. That's right.'

He helped her put the bag up to her lips and she took a breath. Then another. And another. That was better. There were a few crumbs left on the inside of the bag and she smelled the rich smell of almond paste. Must be the remains of an almond croissant.

'Better?' Nick was holding her, not tightly but close enough to let her know that he was there. That someone was there.

'Yes…thanks. Sorry.'

'Don't you worry about it.' A smartly dressed woman was bending down in front of her, and she brushed Abby's knee with well-manicured fingers. 'I get panic attacks, too. You'll be okay in a minute.'

A single tear of mortification prickled at the side of Abby's eye and she brushed it away before Nick got a chance to see it. 'Sorry to make such a fuss.'

'Hey, there. You don't need to apologise.' Nick gently slipped the straps of her handbag from her shoulder, and she realised that she had been hugging it tightly to her side. 'Let go. That's right.'

'She's all wet.' The manicured fingers brushed at her fleece, ineffectually.

'Yeah, let's get this off you, Abby.' Nick pulled at the zipper and had her out of it in a second. Obviously the result of practice. 'Your T-shirt doesn't look too bad. Just a few drops.'

She drew her arms across her body, shivering despite the warmth of the morning breeze. Nick wrapped his jacket around her shoulders and she snuggled into it, wondering if she could somehow contrive to disappear.

At least he took the task off her shoulders of thanking the concerned passers-by and sending them on their way. Finally they were alone, his arm still protectively draped across the back of the bench behind her.

'We'd better get going. We'll miss our train.' Abby made an attempt at a smile.

'We've already missed it.'

'What?' Surely it hadn't been a whole half-hour since she looked at the passenger information board. Had she blacked out or something?

'You're not getting on that train, and neither am I. I want to know what's bothering you.'

'Nothing. It's nothing, Nick.'

'In that case, you're not getting on any train.' He sat quite still, waiting for her to call his bluff. If it was a bluff. Abby doubted it somehow.

She took a breath. The feeling of dread that still clung to her receded slightly and a small, treacherous voice at the back of her head taunted her. Nick had seen her weakness now. She was vulnerable.

'What do you mean, not getting on any train?'

'Someone who gets panic attacks when nothing's wrong shouldn't be swimming in open water.' His lips quirked slightly. 'You're a health and safety hazard, Abby.'

'I'm not!'

'Then something's wrong and you're going to tell me about it.' She opened her mouth to protest and he held one finger up. 'Not here. There's a little coffee shop around the corner. You'll have a hot drink and something to eat and then you'll tell me. I'm guessing you skipped breakfast this morning.'

Abby deprived him of the satisfaction of being right by not answering. Unzipping her case, she slid a clean sweater out and pulled it over her head. Nick put his jacket back on with the hint of a grin, almost as if he was savouring the fact that she'd left a little of her scent on it, and Abby wondered whether punching him would seem ungrateful.

He was, at least, trying to put her at her ease. Avoiding the crowds. Letting her walk close to him and soak up the comfort of his bulk alongside her. Making her laugh despite herself. But Abby knew that there was no way of getting out of his questions. He was just waiting for the right time and, when it came, no amount of silence on her part was going to do for an answer.

'Feeling better now?' He'd watched while she'd downed a tall, creamy latte and a blueberry muffin, sipping his herbal tea thoughtfully.

'Yes. Thanks.' Here it came.

'So, I have this problem. There's no way in the world that I'm going to let you get on that train if the trip is stressing you out so badly that it's giving you panic attacks. Can you help me with that?'

His gaze held her fast, trapped in the most tender of bonds, and Abby gave up the struggle. 'It's nothing to do with the swimming, Nick, I'm fine with that, really.

I used to get panic attacks a lot when I was a teenager. I grew out of them.'

'Plainly. That's why you were breathing into a paper bag just now.'

'I was watching the time, trying to find the right platform, and I spilled my coffee and...there were just too many people all of a sudden.'

'I guess crowds can be pretty intimidating at times. Particularly for someone who's been bullied.' He'd obviously been thinking about this, put two and two together and come up with four.

'Yeah. I guess they probably can.'

'And that was when you learned to swim? Why you went to the charity for help?'

'You don't miss much, do you?'

He shrugged. 'Not when it comes to you, Abby.'

'I don't know what you mean.'

His dark eyes registered the lie and immediately forgave it. 'Did the swimming help?'

'Yes, it helped. It wasn't just the swimming, they held counselling sessions as well. I got to meet other kids, some of them suffering much more than I did, and I didn't feel so alone with it.'

'What about your parents?' He was unerring in picking up what should have been there but hadn't been. The things she purposely hadn't said.

She shrugged, trying to make out it was nothing. 'They played bridge with one of the ringleader's parents. Didn't want to make waves, so they pretended it wasn't happening.'

'So you did it all on your own.'

'Yeah.' All of it. She'd beaten the bullies. Won a place at medical school. Worked hard to get the letters after her name and the title of Doctor before it. 'The people at Answers Through Sport taught me how to be proud of myself. Of what I achieved.'

Abby planted her hands on the table, palms down, in a signal that this particular show-and-tell session was at an end. 'It was a long time ago, Nick. I've left that all behind me. We all have our bad days.'

He nodded an acknowledgement. 'As long as that's all it is. You talked me out of swimming because it wasn't worth sacrificing my health. I'm more than happy to return the favour if it's causing you any problems.'

'What, and lose thirty thousand pounds? Sixty, if you count the match funding.'

'That's exactly what I said to you, and look how far it got me.' He grinned. 'I can find another way of raising the money. Maybe I'll make you run for it instead.'

'I hate running. And my swimming's an answer to whatever problems I might have, not the cause. I'm looking forward to the swim and you know I can do it.'

'Of course you can. Better than I could, even without having injured my knee.'

'Now, there's an admission.' Abby managed a smile without having to force herself.

'Well, you caught me in a moment of weakness.' He grinned back at her. 'So, what is it? Whatever you want to do now is okay.'

'That thirty grand is ours, Nick. You raised the sponsorship and I'm going to collect it. And then Answers Through Sport is going to collect another thirty thousand on the back of it.'

He chuckled. 'Sounds good to me. We'll all have one hell of a party when we're done, I promise.'

They made the next train with ten minutes to spare. Abby slid into the seat opposite Nick's, waiting for him to settle himself comfortably, his leg stretched out under the small table that separated them, before she carefully tucked her feet under her own seat, not letting them touch his.

The next three hours promised to be long ones. She tried to concentrate on her book while Nick immersed himself in something on his laptop. Rubbing his temple in thought. A slow smile, when he caught her looking at him. It was like watching a commercial for men's cologne. Distracting.

Finally, she gave up and laid her book down. 'What's that you're doing? More arrangements for the swim?'

He grinned. 'No—I think that's all done.'

'That's a relief. I was wondering if you were about to email me again with another set of instructions for something.'

'No, nothing like that. Are you saying that my emails were unappreciated?'

'No. Just that you're very thorough.' Actually, Nick's emails had been great. Brief, to the point, and covering everything she needed to know about the arrangements for the swim. And she'd looked for them over the last few weeks, disappointed when they hadn't come, and there was no excuse for her to type a short reply.

'Well, this is nothing to do with swimming. It's some work I'm doing with the fire brigade up in Cumbria.' He paused. The slight curl of his lips told Abby that he was waiting for her to ask.

'In Cumbria? That's very convenient. Since we're actually on our way there now.'

'That's what I thought.' One eyelid flickered and then

he grinned. 'The guy I'm working with is my old station commander, Ted Bishop. He was promoted and came up to Cumbria a couple of years back. The idea for the swim came up when a few of us went up to visit him last year. He's been very helpful with the fun day, helping us to get a good location and all the necessary permits.'

'So this isn't just an excuse to overdo it when you're supposed to be on light duties, is it?'

'No!' He flashed her a smile. 'Anyway, there's no strain on my knee involved, I'm acting as a consultant. Ted knows that I've done some work on arson and he approached me directly. There's been a spate of attacks in the area he's responsible for, and we need to catch whoever's doing it before anyone gets hurt. Seems I may have something to add to the equation.'

Nick always had something to add to any equation. 'You mean forensics?'

He chuckled, relaxing back into his seat. 'Nothing that fashionable, I'm afraid. After I joined the fire service I did some courses in my spare time and ended up doing an MA in psychology. That led me to some work in conjunction with the university on the motivations and behaviour of fire-raisers. I've been helping Ted with some profiling.'

'Sounds interesting.' Abby was almost holding her breath. The whole time she'd known Nick he had never willingly offered any information about his past, and even these morsels were fascinating beyond their own limited worth. 'You studied psychology before you became a firefighter?'

'No. I originally studied to be a structural engineer. I volunteered for the Fire and Emergency Support

Services when I was at university and after I graduated I decided to change direction.'

'And you've never looked back?'

There was something free, clear and unbearably intimate about his short chuckle. This was more than just the idle exchange of information on a long train journey. She was finally getting to know Nick, understand some of the things that made him tick. They'd skipped that part last time, and Abby was beginning to wish they hadn't. If she'd known then what she knew now, it might have saved her a whole world of grief.

'Never. Not for a moment as far as my decision to join the fire service is concerned. Anyway, looking back is… Sometimes it's not helpful.' He caught her eye and she was lost for a moment in his gaze. Dragged across the line that she'd drawn between them, which said that anything unconnected with the swim was a no-go area. Abby shifted slightly in her seat, aware that her right leg was getting pins and needles. She reached down to rub it, thankful for the distraction.

'You okay there? I'm taking up all the space.' Nick didn't wait for an answer but reached down under the table, grasping her ankle and propping it up against his leg. 'Is that better?'

This was more than just getting comfortable on a long train journey. He'd tried to apologise to her, more than once, and Abby hadn't let him. She itemised the layers between her skin and his. His thick denim jeans. Her lighter ones. Her sock. Her trainer. There were many miles in front of them and this one, small acknowledgement that maybe they could forget the past and start again didn't seem so much to ask.

'Yes. Thanks.'

'Stretch out a bit.'

Abby stretched her cramped legs and changed the subject. 'So you'll be away working with the fire service in Cumbria while we're up there?'

'No. I'm just finishing up now. When we get to Windermere I'll be officially on holiday.'

'Unless anything else comes up.' Abby doubted that Nick would split hairs about being on leave if he was needed.

'Yeah. But I'd prefer not to admit to that, if you don't mind. Ted's already promised to call me if he needs me.' He looked up as the refreshments trolley rattled up the confined space of the aisle. 'Would you like anything?'

'No. Thanks. I might close my eyes for a little while.' Abby was tired now. This always seemed to happen after a panic attack. As soon as it was over and she was somewhere that she felt safe, she'd feel unbearably weary.

'Yeah. Try and relax. It's already been a full morning.' He grinned at her and Abby closed her eyes. Soon enough, pretending to sleep gave way to real sleep.

Sam and the rest of the group were already there when they arrived at the hotel, and Abby found herself engulfed in a group of friendly, easygoing firefighters. With a dozen other people to claim his attention, Nick's overwhelming presence seemed to dilute a little, and she began to relax. The group migrated from the lounge to the dining area then back again to the lounge, and she left them swapping stories and laughing together and made her way up to bed early.

Even if she'd woken with a start, early and in an unfamiliar bed, she'd slept well. The bright, crisp morning that awaited her when she drew back the curtains had all the promise of a warm, sunny day, and Abby showered and dressed, ready to face the morning. Today was a day to take things easy, before the swimming started tomorrow.

Drawn outside by sunshine and the promise of the lake, she wandered along a well-worn track from the hotel to the waterside. Lake Windermere, the largest of the Cumbrian lakes, was silent in the early morning. Waterbirds plunged their heads beneath the shimmering surface, diving for their food. A small boat moved across the water, going about its business against a backdrop of stunning beauty.

'Nice day.' Nick's voice interrupted her thoughts as she sat staring across the lake. This time it was the real thing and not an echo from her dreams. 'How did you sleep?'

'Well, thanks. I think it's the air up here.' Abby turned and saw Nick behind her, leaning on a walking stick. 'Hey, where's your crutch gone?'

He grinned. 'I haven't thrown it away quite yet, it's up in my room. But I've graduated onto this.' He sat down next to her on the grass. 'So, how are you feeling about the swim tomorrow?'

'Two miles. Piece of cake. Look how calm the water is.'

'Yeah. Hope it stays this way. The weather forecast's good.'

'Stop fretting. We'll do the swim in the morning, and then there's the fun day in the afternoon. I hope it's going to be good.'

'It'll be great.' He flopped back on the grass, squinting up at the sky. 'There's a couple of bands, sideshows, refreshments tent. Organised sports for the kids...'

'Bouncy castle?'

'Wouldn't be without one. Why, do you fancy trying it out? Climb right to the top and let down your golden hair.' He reached forward and tugged at the plait, which reached halfway down Abby's back.

'Not long enough.'

'Hmm. I'll bring a ladder.'

'Oh, and how are you going to get up it with that knee?'

'I'm a firefighter. We're good with ladders. It's all part of the job.'

'You miss it, don't you?' Abby leaned back on one elbow. She'd seen the way Nick's eyes had gleamed when the talk last night had turned to work.

'Yep.' His heavy lids dropped over his eyes for a moment in a brief expression of regret. 'I wish it hadn't ended this way.'

'Ended? But I thought Dr Patel had already signed you off for light duties. There's no reason you can't go back to active duty in a few months.' Abby bit her lip. She'd hoped that Nick wouldn't find out that she had been checking with Jay Patel on his progress.

'That's right. Apparently I'm a far better patient than he thought I might be.' A grin hovered around his lips. 'Probably because one of his colleagues softened me up a bit first. I'm not going back to active duty, though.'

'Is that...your decision?' Why would Nick throw a job that he loved away when he didn't need to?

'Yes. I have a new job, a promotion. Disaster planning, fire prevention. I get to run my own unit. I applied before my injury and I heard a few weeks ago that I'd got it.'

'So…that's good, isn't it?' Nick was studying the clear blue sky, and Abby couldn't make out what he was thinking.

'Yeah. Yes, it is. It's a great opportunity to make a real difference. I'll be involved with the public, with fire crews in my area. It's what I want.'

'But not so much ever since it looked like you might not have a choice? Since your injury turned everything upside down?' Abby rolled over onto her stomach, next to him.

He grinned at her. 'Yeah.'

'So what *did* you want when you applied for the job? When you did have the choice?'

Nick chuckled. 'Okay. Allow me a little irrational regret, will you?'

'As long as you know it *is* irrational.'

'I do now.' His eyes were dark in the sunlight. Tender and unbearably unsettling.

A wedge of geese flew overhead, and Abby craned her neck, following their path out across the water. 'Isn't it time for breakfast? I'm starving.' She got to her feet.

'Not yet. They don't start serving breakfast for another half-hour.' He levered himself upwards, grabbing his stick. 'Why don't we take a walk, down by the edge of the lake?'

The cool, blue water beckoned her. 'Yes, that would be nice.'

They scrambled down the steep incline that led down to the water's edge and gained a narrow path which ran beside the lake. Walking side by side meant that they had to move closer, and when Nick offered his arm

Abby did what had previously been unthinkable and took it. As soon as she was connected to his warmth, allowing it to filter into her bones, it didn't seem such a bad idea and she allowed her hand to stay curled around the crook of his elbow.

'This is a nice spot. The hotel's lovely. And this part of the lake is really quiet.' Abby turned her face up, towards the sun.

'Yeah. We chose somewhere away from the main tourist area so that we'd have a place to rest and recharge our batteries.'

'Good idea. I feel as if I've just dropped off the edge of the world for a while, it's so peaceful.'

'No more panic attacks, then?' The tension in his tone told Abby that this was the question he'd been working his way around to. Maybe even sought her out to ask.

'No. I feel as if I could take the world on today.'

'And win?'

'Of course.'

'Single-handedly, no doubt.'

'What other way is there?'

He seemed to find something funny in that. Abby fixed him with a warning stare and he shrugged. 'So we should enjoy today, then?'

'Yeah. Tomorrow will come soon enough.'

Nick didn't reply. His eyes were fixed on the cloudless sky, as if he were pondering some basic truth of the universe and the answer was up there somewhere.

He stopped suddenly. His stick fell to the ground, but Abby hardly noticed that because Nick was holding her. His heat. His scent. The bulk of his body. Protective and dangerous, all at the same time.

'Nick…what…what are you doing?'

'Wondering if you'd like some company. We could enjoy today together.' He brushed his lips against hers, his eyes half beckoning, half mesmerising. Slowly, almost as if it was beyond her control to stop it, she felt her hand move up to his cheek, saw her fingers caress the side of his face.

'Since we're on holiday…' We can do as we please. He didn't say it, but she knew that was what he meant. And what couldn't she do with Nick? His lips. His body.

Abby couldn't think. Only that she wanted him to do it. Kiss her and be done with it. It couldn't possibly be any more erotic than her imaginings. Only she'd imagined him holding her, too, and the reality of his embrace was far better. Tentatively she ran her fingers across his lips and felt them form into the shape of a kiss.

She hadn't expected anything polite or restrained from Nick. He was a man who took what he wanted, and when he kissed her he took everything and didn't stop until her head was spinning and her body was moulding itself to his of its own accord. He challenged her, invading her senses with raw passion that had a golden thread of tenderness in its weave.

When he drew back, she knew that it was only because he wanted more from her. Winding her fingers through his hair, she pulled his head down, towards hers again. For a moment he resisted, just to show her that he could, and then a teasing smile curved his lips and he gave way. Kissed her again. And again.

'Abby…' That one, broken word told her everything. His soul-crushing rejection of her hadn't been because he didn't want her. It had been something else.

'Why, Nick? What's changed in the last six months?'

'I'm not the man who can give you what you deserve, not long term. But you said it yourself that this is like taking time out of our lives. What happens here can stay here.'

She couldn't believe she was even thinking about it. Nick had already hurt her once and even though she'd forgiven him for that now, she'd not rescinded the promise she'd made to herself that he wouldn't get the opportunity to do so again. But she knew the score now. Abby understood Nick a great deal better than she had the last time, and knew he wasn't in this for keeps. She could take what she'd been craving for so many months now and then go home, before he had a chance to break her heart.

He drew back, and the breeze from the water suddenly made her shiver. Each of her senses were acute and vulnerable, as if they'd been woken from a long sleep. She wanted more. And he deliberately gave her nothing.

'Think about it.'

It was all she could think about, but that didn't stop her from still being afraid. Afraid of reaching out and finding he wasn't there. Or that he was. Abby didn't know which terrified her most. 'I'm not sure, Nick.'

He kissed her again, just a whisper on her lips but all her senses exploded. She knew now what else he could do. From now on, even his most casual touch wouldn't be the same. His dark, velvet eyes held unthinkable secrets that offered themselves to her.

'Good. Means you *are* thinking about it.'

CHAPTER FIVE

NICK didn't seem to expect an answer straight away—
in fact, he seemed intent on not having one, obviously
content to let her simmer for a while. He'd made his bid
for her, and now he was waiting for her to respond. That
was fine. If she couldn't resist him, at least she could
keep him waiting, not fall straight into his arms like the
awkward, stupid girl she felt herself to be.

Opening the door to the lobby of the hotel, he ushered her inside.

'Here they are.' Mrs Pearce, the proprietor, was sitting behind the reception desk, and she nodded her too-
bright, bronzed curls towards a young man.

'There's someone here to see you, hen.'

Nick accepted the endearment with a smiling nod
and advanced towards the young man, his right hand
held out. 'Hi. Nick Hunter.'

'Graham Edson. I'm with the local paper. Nice to
meet you.' Graham looked Nick over quickly. 'You're
doing the swim with that?' He pointed at Nick's walking stick.

'No, my injury made me drop out.' He was standing
between Abby and Graham, and his broad bulk almost

completely shielded the smaller man from Abby's view. 'A friend is swimming for me.'

Just *a friend.* No hesitation. All the way back to the hotel she'd been wondering if she might not mean a little more to Nick than that, and now he'd put her firmly back in her place. 'That'll be me.' Abby skirted around Nick and nodded at Graham. 'Abby Maitland.'

'Oh. Nice to meet you.' Graham's attention was all on her now. 'Are you a fireman, too? Firewoman, I mean. Fireperson…'

Abby saw Nick's eyes roll behind Graham's back. Louise, the newest member of Nick's crew, had been joking last night about how no one ever knew what to call her. 'It's firefighter. And, no, I'm not, I'm a doctor.'

'Ah. And you've stepped in to try and cover the swim.' Graham was looking her up and down, and the small hairs at the back of Abby's neck bristled. He was affable, unremarkable and Abby didn't much like his assumptions. Just trying wasn't an option.

'I'll be doing all six of the courses in Nick's place.'

'Hmm. I'd like to get some details about you for my paper, if that's all right. I'm doing an article.'

'Sure…' Abby reckoned that any publicity was good publicity.

'Our organiser has a press pack, giving details of the events and biographies of all the swimmers,' Nick broke in. 'If you'll give me your email address, I'll get one sent through to you this morning.'

He reached into his jacket, pulling out a notebook, and as he did so his keys jangled to the floor. Quick as a flash, Graham had pounced on them, holding them for a moment in his hand before he gave them back to Nick.

'Unusual key fob.'

Abby's stomach tightened, but Nick didn't waver. 'Yeah. What's your email address?'

Graham's eyes were on him as he reeled off the address and Nick took it down. Then he turned his attention back onto Abby. 'I just wanted to ask a few extra questions.' The journalist motioned her to one of the seats behind him and sat down next to her. 'As a doctor, I assume you're aware of the health risks of open-water swimming.'

He'd pulled a small voice recorder out of his jacket pocket and was aiming it at Abby. Fine. She could handle this.

'If you want to know our policy on health and safety, you should speak to the team's official medical spokesman.' Nick was there again. He seemed determined not to let Abby get a single word out.

'Yes, but personally...' Graham leaned closer and ignored Nick '...you must have thought about this? Weil's disease, for instance. Are you happy to take those risks?'

Nick reached around her, switching off the recorder in Graham's hand. The look on his face told Abby that he was exercising some restraint, not ripping the gizmo from the reporter's grasp and stamping on it. 'You'll have to forgive us, but we're busy right now. As I said, Pete Welsh, who is the events organiser, will email you the press pack this morning and he's available here to answer all your questions. Much better than we can, I imagine.'

He could speak for himself on that one. But the pressure of his fingers on her shoulder silenced Abby. She supposed it was better to leave it until she had Nick alone before she voiced her objections.

'Okay, fine.' Graham rose and pulled a card from his pocket, handing it to Abby. 'I've already got the press pack so I won't keep you if you're busy. I'd like to speak with you later, though.'

'I'll be here.' Abby took the card he proffered and put it into her pocket. Nick may think that kissing her gave him the right to decide who she could and couldn't speak to but he was wrong on that score. Dead wrong.

She waited while Nick walked to the main doors with Graham, virtually escorting him off the premises, and watched as the man got into his car and drove away. 'What was that all about?'

'I didn't like his questions.'

'That's obvious.' Abby blocked his path as he went to walk back into the lobby. 'I am capable of answering questions about health risks, you know. I do it every day.'

'This is different.'

'Different how? Nick, please tell me that you're not worried I'll get it wrong. I may specialise in orthopaedics but I haven't quite forgotten my general training yet.'

He stared at her, and Abby stood her ground. She wasn't moving until he gave her an answer. 'No. I don't think that. But your position, as a doctor, gives more weight to what you say.'

'So I know what I'm talking about. Doesn't that make my opinion more valid?'

'Yes, it does, that's my whole point. It's not the official one, though. You know as well as I do that, although the risk of catching Weil's disease is pretty much negligible, it can't be ruled out entirely.'

Abby threw up her hands in frustration. 'It's an acceptable level of risk. Made even less by the fact that we're wearing wetsuits, so there's no chance of infected water getting into any cuts or abrasions.'

'Right. An acceptable level of risk. Which means it's not an impossibility.' Nick let out an exasperated breath. 'What happens if you get quoted out of context, or your words get twisted to give the impression that precautions don't need to be taken with open-water swimming? If someone acted on that, it would leave you to answer for the consequences.'

'I guess that would depend on the circumstances. I'm not sure.' She was beginning to catch his meaning.

'Exactly. The press pack covers all that and it's worded very carefully. This guy's already got a copy of it and yet he wants an off-the-cuff medical opinion on a complex issue in a hotel lobby. Doesn't that tell you something?'

Now she thought about it, it did. Nick had been looking out for her. Unwilling to back down, and unable to honestly tell him that he was wrong, Abby simply stared at him.

'What are you two bickering about so early in the morning?' Pete's voice sounded by the stairs and both Nick and Abby swung round to face the retired firefighter.

'We are not...'

'Bickering.' Abby reddened as she heard Nick echo her words.

Pete chuckled. 'Well, there's something you both agree on.' He was making for the dining room and his step hardly faltered. 'Don't miss breakfast. We've got plenty to do today if we're going to be ready for Windermere tomorrow.'

Day One. Two miles. Lake Windermere.

'How did you do that?' Louise was grinning at Abby.

'What?'

'I saw you five minutes ago and you weren't wearing your wetsuit. It takes me half an hour to get into mine.'

'Didn't anyone show you the shopping-bag trick?' Abby liked Louise. She was the youngest of the fire-fighters in the group, but she gave no quarter and expected none back. Didn't trade on the fact that she was a woman, and the others obviously respected her for it.

'No. Go on, then. Show me the secret formula.'

'Here, put your foot into this plastic bag... Right, then slip your foot into the wetsuit, like so.' Abby helped Louise draw the neoprene up her right leg then pulled the bag off her foot. 'See, the wetsuit doesn't cling to your foot when you put it on. Do that with the other foot and your hands and it's easy.'

Louise wriggled into her wetsuit, and Abby zipped the back up for her. 'Yeah, that's good. Thanks.'

'Swing your arms around, make sure you've got plenty of movement at the shoulders.' Abby nodded in satisfaction. 'Yes, that's right.'

'Nick says that you've swum the Channel.' Louise was staring out over the water.

'As part of a relay team. I didn't swim the whole way.' Louise was obviously nervous and wanted some reassurance. 'Listen, you've done your training.'

'Yes. Nick's been checking up on us all. I thought he'd get off our backs a bit when he came back to work, but he's even worse now. Being on limited duties is driving him mad.'

'I imagine it would be.' Abby grinned. 'But you've swum in open water before.'

'Yep. It was part of our training schedule, we all went away for the weekend...' Louise broke off. The confident young woman that Abby had met less than two days ago was gnawing at her lower lip. 'I just don't want to let anyone down.'

'You won't.' Abby hesitated for a moment. It would have been nice to have completed this swim ahead of everyone else, if only to show Nick that she could, and she let go of the idea with a stab of regret. 'Tell you what. Why don't you swim with me? We'll do this one together.'

Louise shrugged. 'I can't keep up. The guys are much stronger swimmers than I am and, from what Nick says, so are you.'

'Then I'll slow down a bit. What do you say?'

'I think if both the women come last, we'll be in for a ribbing. I reckoned that you might be the one to keep our end up.'

'Forget that.' Abby wondered if this really was her talking. The competitive spirit who didn't let anything stand in her way once she was in the water because being the butt of that kind of joke was for losers. Maybe she'd mellowed with age. 'Listen, if they think this is all about winning, they're wrong. It's all about helping each other to complete the course and raise the money we need. That's why you decided to do it, wasn't it?'

Louise brightened. 'Yes. One of the guys at the station has a daughter who's a wheelchair user and he and his wife have to travel miles to get her to a therapy pool. I really wanted to help, but I'm not sure now that I haven't bitten off more than I can chew.'

'Like I said, you've done the training. From what I know about Nick, he wouldn't let you swim if he didn't think you could do it.'

'Right in one.' Nick's voice boomed out behind her. 'You know how to do this, Lou. Work as a team, rely on your training. And follow whatever advice you hear me shout in your direction.'

'Advice!' Louise's eyebrows shot up and Abby suppressed a chuckle. Since when did Nick give advice?

'It's orders at work. Advice here. Only I will be watching you, every step of the way, to make sure you take it.' He was good at this. His easy manner and solid dependability inspired confidence and Abby could see why all his crew held him in such high regard. 'Why don't you go and warm up now? It's about time.'

'Suppose so.' Louise gave Abby a shy smile. 'I'd like to swim with you, if that's okay.'

'Good. I'd like that too.' Abby went to follow Louise down to the water's edge, but Nick caught her arm.

'So you're not in competition with everyone, then?'

It took Abby two seconds to consider the idea. 'No. Just you.'

Nick chuckled softly and turned, making his way down to the boats, which lay moored and ready to go, while Abby and Louise walked into the water together. It was cool, but not cold. As soon as they started swimming in earnest, Abby knew that she would no longer notice the temperature of the water.

The swimmers lined up at the starting point, flanked by the boats, and on the signal to go, Abby stayed with Louise, slowing her stroke so that the younger woman could keep pace with her. Sunlight glinted on the water. That powerful, joyful feeling as she sliced through the swell and out towards the centre of the lake. The swimmers began to spread out, some ahead of them, and others behind.

Louise was trying too hard to keep up the pace, and Abby dropped back. When Louise realised that she was swimming alone, she began to relax, matching Abby's more leisurely stroke, and the two swam together. Abby found her rhythm and went on to autopilot, selecting a medium-slow song from her mental jukebox and swimming to its beat.

As they rounded the halfway buoy and started on the leg back to the shore, Abby allowed herself a glance at her watch. Thirty minutes. Louise was making good time and they should finish at just over the hour. Slower than Abby could have done, but they weren't racing. All they needed to do was finish the course. She was aware of the support boat, keeping its distance but ready to move in if there were any problems.

Suddenly Louise turned in the water, one hand shooting up. She was in difficulties. Abby stopped, treading water, her own hand up, beckoning the boat in.

'Cramp?' Abby's first reaction was to take hold of Louise and support her in the water. She might still have to do that, but unless it looked as if Louise was going under, she wanted to give her the chance to deal with this herself.

'Y-yes. Whole leg. Frozen.' Louise's eyes were wild, frightened. She was keeping it under control, but only just, and panicking was about the worst thing you could do in open water.

'Okay, steady. Flex your foot.' Abby got a mouthful of water and spat it back out again as the boat eased gently in alongside them. Hopefully, its presence would give Louise some confidence.

She could see Nick, crouched low on the deck, his questioning eyes on her. 'Cramp,' she told him.

'Okay. Louise, relax. Do you want to stop?'

Louise seemed to calm a little at the sound of his voice. 'No. Going off a bit now.'

'Great stuff. Take a few minutes. There's plenty of time.' Nick fixed a cup to the end of the pole that the boats used to pass food and drinks to the swimmers and lowered it to Louise. 'Here. Try and take a few sips.'

The warm drink wouldn't help her straight away, but it was comforting. Louise drank and bobbed up and down in the water beside the boat, easing her leg, for a few minutes. 'Okay. I think I'm good to go now.'

Abby looked up at Nick. He had been quietly assessing the situation, their distance from the shore, the weather, how Louise looked. He gave her one quick nod.

'Stay close to me, then. I'll set the pace.' Abby didn't want Louise to start racing for the shore in a panic. 'We're going to take it easy to start with.'

'Good. We'll move back a bit, but we'll stay well within reach.' Nick was searching Louise's face. The one remaining piece of the puzzle. Whether she had the heart to do it or not. 'If you start to feel any cramping, don't wait and see if it passes but put your hand up immediately. That's an order.'

Apparently 'advice' had fallen by the wayside, but Nick didn't seem to notice such distinctions. Neither did Louise for that matter, and she gave him a wordless nod, before waving the boat away.

CHAPTER SIX

FORTY minutes later, Louise and Abby climbed out of the water together and onto the jetty. The other swimmers had been watching their progress intently and Louise's crewmates surrounded her as a small round of applause rippled through the other spectators, who had walked down from the field where the fair was underway to see the finish of the swim.

The boat drew alongside the jetty, and Nick climbed off. A quick exchange of words with Louise, his hand on her shoulder in congratulation for a job well done, and he turned and made his way over to where Abby was standing.

'You were in the water too long.' His brow was creased and he almost threw the words at her. Abby wasn't sure what she had been expecting from him, but it wasn't this. She started to walk towards the camper van, where the bag with her clothes was stored, afraid to face him in case he saw her disappointment.

'We finished.'

'Yep. And you have to swim again tomorrow. I'm concerned that if you do all your swims at this pace, you'll wear yourself out.'

She turned, but only so she didn't have to shout

over her shoulder at him and run the risk that Louise would hear and take it the wrong way. 'I don't have to. Tomorrow I'll swim on my own.'

'Glad to hear it.' His tone seemed almost mocking, and Abby pushed the towel that he proffered away.

'Okay, then. Just tell me what you would have done?' If he told her that he would have just swum on ahead, leaving Louise to pace herself alone, she was going to laugh in his face.

'I never take my own advice. That's why I'm so marvellously good at giving it.' His tone softened suddenly. 'Come to the van. I'll get you a hot drink.'

He strode away from her, leaning on his stick but barely limping. Abby ignored him and stripped off her wetsuit in one easy motion, born of long practice. The day was warm and sunny but when the breeze touched her skin she began to shiver, goose-bumps rising on her arms.

'Here.' Nick was back again, a steaming mug in one hand, the towel still thrown over his shoulder. 'Take it.'

That was definitely an order. But Abby was cold now, as well as tired and upset, and she took the towel with as good a grace as she could muster, wrapping it around herself. Nick put the drink into her hands before she had a chance to even think about rejecting it, and she sipped it gratefully.

'You're shivering. Come up to the van.' Another order.

'Not if it means that you're going to lecture me.' She may not have much fight left in her at the moment, but she had enough for Nick.

He sighed. 'That was a great swim, Abby.'

'A minute ago you said it was too slow.'

'And it was. But you did it anyway to help a team-mate. Come to the van, you're shivering.'

'So I was right, then?' Abby's teeth were chattering but she wasn't moving until he admitted it.

'Yes. Yes, you were right, Abby. Will you come to the van now? Please.'

'Okay.' She couldn't help smiling at his obvious frustration. 'Since you asked nicely.'

Abby let him put his arm loosely around her shoulder and hurry her to the minibus. He opened the back doors and sat her down on the high tailgate. 'Here, let me dry your legs.' He produced another towel and rubbed hard, bringing a little warmth back into her toes, then fetched her bag from inside the vehicle and drew out a pair of warm socks, putting them onto her feet.

That was better. After the slow pace of the swim her body temperature had plummeted, but it seemed to be approaching a more normal level now. Abby wrapped her fingers around the warm mug that he had given her and drained the last of the hot chocolate.

'Right.' He took the mug from her with a grin. 'Let's get you into some warm clothes.'

He didn't give her any time to protest. He lifted her up into the camper van, following and closing the doors behind them. Producing the largest towel she'd ever seen, he wrapped her up in it, rubbing her arms and shoulders to dry her off.

'I'll hold the towel while you get your swimsuit off.' There was a trace of mischief in his voice. Just enough to make Abby's lips begin to quiver into a smile. Not enough to give her any grounds for thinking that the towel wasn't going to stay in place, covering her while she undressed.

'Okay. I'm trusting you, Nick.'

'Good. I'm a very trustworthy person. Only I do have to say that I caught a glimpse of your ankles while I was helping you on with your socks.'

'That's okay. We live in modern times.' He held the towel firmly around her while she wriggled out of her swimsuit.

'Mmm. I'm getting quite inured to the sight of a well-turned ankle. Hardly even give them a second look.' He was grinning broadly, his eyes fixed on the hem of the towel.

'My clothes, Nick.'

'Let's get you dry first.' He rubbed the towel against her back and warmth began to tingle through her. 'There, is that better?' His hands had moved to her hips and the tops of her legs. Carefully avoiding the sweet, soft places that a lover would touch.

'That's fine.' He needn't have bothered to be so solicitous. Wherever he touched her, even through the thick material of the towel, his hands trailed paths of fire.

'Here's your bag.' He lifted the bag up onto one of the padded seats, seemingly unwilling to go rummaging around in it for her underwear. Perhaps he felt it too. That craving for his skin to touch hers.

'Thanks.' She twisted one arm free of the folds of the towel and Nick awkwardly averted his eyes. Proof positive that he was feeling something. He'd seen her arm before, more times than she could count. As she reached for the bag her forearm brushed against his and he snatched it away. Proof positive times two.

Abby grabbed her underwear and Nick pulled the towel up around her while she put it on. 'Here.' Her thick, cosy sweatpants lay on the top of the pile of clothes and he caught them up and handed them to her.

'Thanks. Can you see a blue sweater in there?'

He hesitated for a moment and then carefully searched in her bag, pulling out her thick sweater and a white T-shirt. 'This what you want?'

Abby took the T-shirt and put it on, and Nick handed her the sweater, turning away to roll her soaking swimsuit in the towel. Then, seemingly at ease with going into her bag now, he pulled out her trainers. 'Sit down.'

Abby sat. In her clothes she felt more at ease. And Nick had been a complete gentleman, even if the thoughts that had been circulating in her head had been less than ladylike. Ignoring the voice at the back of her head that told her she could put her trainers on for herself perfectly well, she held out one foot.

Sitting opposite her, he perched her foot on his knee, easing her shoe on and tying the laces. Then the other. 'Don't do that to me again, Abby.'

'Don't do what?'

'Don't stand there, freezing to death, just to make a point. Next time I start acting like an idiot, feel free to kick my legs out from under me, but then you step over me and go and get yourself warm.'

'Oh, so you're taking it all back now, are you? You only said I was right to get me into the van?' She was trying so hard not to smile, but she could feel her lips twitching.

He grinned, reaching for her mug and refilling it from a Thermos flask, twisting round to sit next to her on the bench. 'Yeah, of course I said it to get you into the van. Doesn't mean I didn't think you *were* right.'

'But under normal circumstances you'd do anything

rather than admit it.' Abby took the mug from him and sipped at the smooth, thick chocolate drink.

He chuckled. 'You were right. And I'm sorry. My only defence is that I'm finding it tough, having to sit on the sidelines and worry. I'd rather be swimming.'

'Consider it a learning experience. And you're not doing too badly. I'll give you nine out of ten.' She was goading him now. Nine out of ten was never going to be enough for Nick.

He took the mug from her and set it down on the floor. Those few brief seconds, when his gaze met hers, were enough to burn what was left of Abby's resolve to a cinder.

She almost cried out when his lips brushed hers. That first gentle touch, which sought permission to touch again. And then there was no possibility of anything other than to just keep breathing somehow as he kissed her. Hard, strong and unrelenting. Unlocking the passion that she kept so tightly under control and allowing it to meet his, two fires that burned equally hot.

She could feel his hand, through layers of thick wool and cotton, inching along her ribs. Please. Please, just a little further. His fingers stopped, just short of the soft swell of her breast, and longing exploded deep inside.

'You are so beautiful.' He'd taken his lips from hers to say the words. 'I want more, Abby. I want everything you can give, and then I want to go back and take it all over again.' He left her in little doubt that when that happened it would be eleven out of ten. Or twenty-two if you counted the second time. Abby wanted that too.

'Can I trust you, Nick?'

'You can trust me. Like I said, what happens here stays here.'

That wasn't exactly what she meant. But suddenly she didn't care whether he blew her mind into a million different pieces, took her to places that she'd never been before and couldn't imagine. What he promised was exactly what she wanted.

'Will you think about it, Abby?'

There was nothing to think about, but they couldn't do anything about that here, in a van on a crowded jetty. The trick was going to be contriving to think about something—anything—else in the hours between now and when they could be alone together.

'I'll give it my most careful consideration.'

'Good.' His fingers moved in a soft caress, still just inches short of where she wanted them to be, and she gasped.

'And what about you? Are you thinking about it?' She could hardly get the words out. Hardly bear to hear his answer, in case he wasn't as consumed by this as she was.

'Night and day. I'm very thorough.'

'Hmm. Thorough. Good with ladders.' She planted a kiss on his lips and then drew back again. 'I'm beginning to like you.'

He chuckled. 'That's the plan.'

Nick started as someone banged on the closed doors of the minibus. Probably his guardian angel, saving him from himself before he forgot where he was. Or maybe Abby's. At this point he wasn't sure who needed saving most. Quickly he picked up the mug and put it back into her trembling fingers and then reached back to open the double doors.

'You finished in there?' Louise was standing outside, dressed now, her short dark hair almost dry in the sun.

'Yep. We're done.' Like hell they were. But Abby was warm and dry now, and anything else would have to wait.

'I came to thank Abby for helping me round the course.' Louise craned around him, trying to make eye contact with her new friend, and Nick stepped to one side, feeling suddenly in the way.

Abby shrugged, laughing. 'It's not a competition.'

There it was again. The way she seemed to rub along quite happily with everyone else but him. With him she was fierce, competitive, exasperating. It was driving him crazy and the only way to quell this madness was to pit his strength against hers. Find out how far they could both take things. Then he would be free to leave here and go back to his own, well-ordered, life where nothing was allowed to divert him from his chosen purpose.

'I raised five hundred pounds today.' Louise climbed up into the van and plumped herself down next to Abby. 'Only my parents threw in a hundred, so really it's only four.'

'It's great that they're supporting you like this.' She said it without even a flicker of resentment. It had to be pure generosity of spirit that allowed her to be pleased for Louise when she'd clearly had precious little parental support of her own.

'Yeah, s'pose so. They've always been good like that.'

'It means a lot.' Abby shook her head abruptly, her corn-coloured hair spilling around her shoulders. 'Come on. Let's go see what they're doing at the fun day.'

By the time they reached the field, where the fun day had already got off to a noisy start, their little group had swollen to a small crowd. Jokes rippling back and forth. Laughter. The palpable relief that the first leg of the swim had gone well and everyone had shown that the months of planning and training hadn't gone to waste. Louise professed a wish to have her fortune told and dragged a couple of her crewmates along with her into the brightly decorated tent.

'Not going to see what's in your future?' Abby had hung back, next to Nick.

'Nope. I already know.'

'Got it all planned out, have you?' Her pale blue eyes, almost translucent in the sunlight, gave the lie to that. He hadn't planned on this.

'More or less. Inasmuch as you can plan anything.'

'But things don't always go to plan.'

The fall, which had first injured his knee and marred a career that had until then been unstoppable. The drugs. Helen leaving him. Just one slip had brought the house of cards that he'd called his life, cascading down on him and plunging him into another existence, one where he'd said and done things that he could never forgive himself for.

'No, they don't. But if you don't have a plan, there's nothing to work your way back to when things go bad.'

Concern flickered in her eyes. 'Is that what you did, Nick? Worked your way back to the original plan?'

She had seen the thing that it had taken him months to divine. 'No. The thing about drugs is that getting clean is just the first step. You need to work through the issues that made you drug dependent in the first place as well.'

'I imagine that's the toughest part.'

'One of them.' He'd understood the issues and

worked through them, but that hadn't absolved him from the shame of what he'd done. 'We see a lot in our jobs, Abby, yours and mine. I couldn't deal with failure, with what I did not being enough. When I was injured, I couldn't deal with not being able to will myself better.'

She shrugged. 'Who can?'

'True. But it became everything to me. I drove myself too hard, took responsibility for things I couldn't change and in the end that broke me.' Nick's heart was thumping in his chest. He was saying too much. How could he imagine that Abby should understand?

'Saving the world's such a great idea. Just as long as you know you can't do it, and it doesn't blind you to the things you can do.' She was smiling ruefully.

'Yeah.' He shrugged. 'But things are different now. I'm the one in control.'

She looked at him thoughtfully, as if she was about to disagree with him. Nick felt the hairs on the back of his neck prickle at the thought. Disagreeing with Abby was like making love.

She opened her mouth for the first caress, and suddenly their attention was caught by the loudspeaker system. '*Dr Maitland to the Medical Tent, please.*'

'Wh—? Where's the medical tent?' She swung round, scanning the field.

'Over there.' Nick pointed to the tent in the far corner of the field and she hesitated. Catching her hand, he led her across the rough ground at the briskest trot he could manage.

Pete met them at the entrance to the tent. 'Glad you're here. We have a boy, seven years old, who seems to be having some kind of fit. The parents are here. He's awake, but he seems very drowsy and disoriented. We've called an ambulance, but it'll be a little while.'

The tent was full of people, talking quietly, waiting around to see if they could be of help. Abby was looking at them, her hands clasped together tightly. 'Thanks, Pete. I'll take it from here. I need to find the first-aid kit and get some of these people out of here.'

She'd either forgotten or was ignoring the fact that she didn't have to do this all by herself. Nick leaned over towards her. 'You concentrate on the boy. I'll deal with everything else.' He took her arm and eased through the crowd, making a space for Abby to kneel down next to a camp bed that contained the prone figure of a child. Leaving her to it, he turned.

'Can we have some room, please? Thanks, everyone, the doctor's here and she needs everyone to stand back.'

The crowd began to disperse. Out of the corner of his eye Nick could see Abby beginning to carefully examine the boy, and he grabbed the bulky medical kit, setting it down next to her.

'Thanks.' She was calm now. Steady as a rock. 'Perhaps if everyone who isn't able to help could wait outside…'

Nick began to usher the concerned onlookers out of the tent. He stationed one of the organisers next to the entrance, with instructions that only emergencies should enter, and hurried back to her side.

'So you found him lying on the ground?' She was trying to get some sense from the boy's crying mother. 'Whereabouts?'

'He'd just been playing on the bouncy castle. It was right behind there.'

'Okay.' Abby had her fingers on the boy's pulse and

swivelled round towards Nick. 'Where's the generator? Could he have got to it?'

He could see where she was headed. Pete's suddenly pale face confirmed it. What if the boy had somehow managed to get close enough to the generator to get an electric shock from it?

'It's unlikely. But we'll check.' Nick didn't have to look for Sam. He'd been his second-in-command for long enough now that each knew where the other was by instinct. 'Sam, take someone and check that the generator's still secure, will you?'

'If my kid's been injured by negligence, you'll be hearing a great deal more of this. Where's this bloody generator?' The boy's father was on his feet, face red, fists clenched by his sides.

Abby ignored him completely, but Nick could see tension in her face as she tried to concentrate on what she was doing. Quickly he drew the boy's father to one side.

'Look, I know this is difficult, but your son's conscious and he can hear what's going on around him. You need to let him know that you're here for him and that he's going to be okay.'

'Right, and while I'm doing that, you lot could be covering up whatever's happened to him. Not bloody likely.'

'There's not going to be any cover-up. We need to find out what happened so that the doctor can do the right thing for your son. You need to be with your family.' Nick almost snarled the words at the man. He could understand his anger, his helplessness. But this wasn't helping anyone.

'Fair enough. But I'm not going to let this go if it turns out that there has been some sort of negligence.'

'Neither am I.' Nick hoped to hell there hadn't been. Pete had two daughters of his own, as well as grand-children. He was always a stickler for safety and he would never forgive himself if a child had been injured through any oversight of his.

The man nodded briefly and then turned to sit by his wife's side, one arm around her shoulders and his other hand covering his son's. Abby's brief glance at Nick said it all. *Thanks. Way to go.*

'Has he been a bit off colour recently? Listless, more sleepy than normal? Maybe he's complained of head-aches or disturbance in his vision?' She turned to the mother again.

'A little drowsy maybe. He didn't want to come out this afternoon, he was holed up in his bedroom, watch-ing TV, but I didn't think anything of it.' Tears began to roll down the woman's face.

'Okay. That's fine. His breathing and heartbeat are both steady. His temperature's normal.' Abby looked down again as her young charge began to stir restlessly. 'I'm just going to sit him up.'

Gently she cradled the boy in one arm and lifted him up into a sitting position. The child was starting to retch and Abby just managed to tip the contents from a container behind her and hold it in front of him, be-fore he vomited.

'Okay. You're fine. Better out than in, eh?' She was smiling down at the boy, whose eyes were now res-olutely closed. Nick took the container from her and pushed a paper napkin into her hand, and she wiped the boy's mouth. 'Can you hear me, Ethan?'

Ethan moaned and thrashed weakly in her arms. 'I know. You don't feel well. I'm a doctor, Ethan, and I'm here to help you. Can you open your eyes for me?'

The boy's eyes fluttered open.

'Good. That's great, Ethan, well done. Look, your mum and dad are right here.'

'Hey, there, Ethan.' His mother summoned a smile from the unending reservoir that parents seemed to keep for their children. 'You had us worried for a moment there, but you look much better now.' She turned to Abby, gratitude glistening in her eyes. 'Can I give him some water?'

'Just let him rinse his mouth out for the time being.' She gave Ethan's mother an encouraging smile and Nick felt his lips twitch in response. He was proud of Abby. The only thing that held her back was that sometimes she seemed to doubt her own abilities.

He turned in response to a touch on his arm. 'Sam. What's the story?'

'The generator enclosure is secure. Jim and I checked it out thoroughly and there's no way a fly could get in there.' Nick breathed a sigh of relief and nodded quickly towards Pete. The older man got the message and seemed to breathe again.

'Find anything else out?'

'Yeah. One of the kids that was playing in that area saw him go down. He said that he seemed quite normal and then suddenly he was on the ground. They didn't see anything hit him, he just crumpled.'

'Have you left Jim there?'

'Yep. Just in case.'

'Good job. Thanks, Sam.' Nick made his way to

Abby's side, relaying the information to her quietly, and she nodded in acknowledgement.

'Okay.' She pressed her lips together in thought, looking up as a couple of ambulancemen walked into the tent. 'Will you make sure his mother keeps him sitting up in case he's sick again? I'll go and speak to these guys. Call me if he seems suddenly drowsy or disoriented, or there's anything else that worries you.'

She went to meet the ambulance crew, talking quickly to them as they made their way over. 'I'll go with you to the hospital…' She watched as the boy was lifted gently onto a stretcher and then drew his father to one side, talking to him quietly.

She turned to Nick, standing close, her voice low. 'I've just told the father that I think Ethan may have had an epileptic fit. He's given me permission to tell you, because if I'm right then there's nothing that Pete or anyone else could have done to prevent it.' Her fingers skimmed the front of Nick's shirt and he allowed himself to clasp them briefly.

'Thanks.'

'Got to go.'

'Right. Later, Abby.'

CHAPTER SEVEN

ABBY floated quietly in the hotel swimming pool. It wasn't big enough to do more than just drift and enjoy the feeling of weightlessness that being in the water gave her, but she could see the sky through the glass panels in the ceiling and she could feel herself beginning to relax. Pete had made an appearance at the hospital and when he'd heard that Ethan was doing well and that there was nothing more either of them could do had brought Abby back to the hotel. She'd eaten, spent a little while on her bed, trying to read, and then been drawn to the water while she waited for Nick to return.

'Here you are.' Nick's voice cut through her thoughts. The ones that were largely centred around him anyway.

'You're back. Been working?' He was wearing long, work-worn shorts and a T-shirt, his already tanned skin still glowing with the heat of the afternoon sun.

'Yep. The kit's all stowed and the guys will take the tents and infrastructure down tomorrow. Woe betide anyone who touches it without Pete being there.' He kicked off his deck shoes and sat down at the side of the pool, dangling his legs in the water, and Abby let herself float towards him.

'What's with the new knee support?' He wasn't

wearing the heavy brace that Abby had given him, but a lighter one, less bulky.

'Dr Patel said I could try this one out. It's a bit less cumbersome. How did things go at the hospital?'

'They agreed it was probably an epileptic fit. They'll have to do some tests.' She rolled onto her face in the water and then round onto her back again. 'I was hoping I might have been wrong.'

'You wanted to be wrong?' He raised one eyebrow. Almost a challenge, but not quite.

'Epilepsy's going to have an impact on Ethan's life. I'd rather it was something a little less serious.'

'At least it wasn't anything more serious.'

'The glass is half-full, you mean.'

'He's okay and getting the treatment he needs. I'd say it was a good deal more than half-full.' He grinned crookedly. 'You were there when he needed help.'

'Hmm. I was…' Abby had been out of her depth. Faced with a situation that was outside her speciality and beyond her experience.

'You were what?'

'Afraid.' The admission slipped out before Abby had a chance to jam the cork back into the bottle. 'I don't know how I would have handled the situation if you hadn't been there.'

'It wasn't your job to handle the situation. It was your job to give Ethan medical help.'

'Yes, but…' Nick had needed to step in and deal with the crowd of people in the medical tent and with Ethan's father. She hadn't been in control and, even though he hadn't rebuked her for it, Nick must have seen it.

'What was that piece of wisdom you offered up this morning?' He stopped for a moment in mock thought.

'About how not being able to save the world shouldn't blind you to the things you can do?'

'You were listening, then.'

'I always listen. You should try it some time.' He chuckled as Abby directed a splash of water at him. 'Seriously, though, you did what you were trained for, which was to diagnose and treat. Ethan was lucky to have you there.'

Nick's praise made her toes curl with pleasure. 'It's nice of you to say so.'

He gave a little gesture of frustration. 'This is the first time you've had to deal with serious injury outside the hospital environment?'

'Yes.' Did it really show that much?

'Give yourself a break. You did fine. You can't do everything on your own. That was one of the first things I learned when I joined the fire service.'

'Don't you ever feel afraid, though?'

'What, sending men into a burning building? Going in myself?' He shrugged. 'I'd be crazy not to. Fear can be positive as well as negative, it helps us gauge risk.'

'That's not what I meant.' The water in the pool lapped gently against the blue and white tiles that surrounded it. Fear seemed a very long way away here.

'What else do I have to be afraid of?'

'There's always something.' Like losing control. Nick had pretty much admitted to that already.

'*You* frighten me.'

'What?' Abby lunged backwards in the water, away from him.

'Yep. Gonna have to do something about that.' Mischief ignited in his dark eyes and desire stirred in the pit of her stomach. Slowly, almost as if time was obliging enough to allow her a few extra seconds to savour the action, he drew his T-shirt over his head then slipped into the pool, shorts and all, and took a few languorous strokes. Dived, swimming underneath her, and then surfaced next to her. 'Definitely going to have to do something.'

'Oh, so the great Nick Hunter can't be afraid of a woman, is that it?'

'Yeah, that's about the size of it.' He slid one arm around her waist, pulling her in, and Abby almost forgot to breathe. 'Only one thing to do when you're afraid of something.'

'Face it head on.' She was trembling now. He must feel it, her fingers fluttering uncertainly on his back and sliding across his powerful shoulders. 'Look it straight in the eye.'

He kissed her and they sank together, water closing over their heads. Small bubbles skittered to the surface and he held the kiss for long moments, before launching them both upwards again. They broke the surface together, lungs sucking in air, their bodies pressed together in the water.

'We're both adults, Abby. We can do as we please. We don't need to make any promises or have any expectations. We could just do whatever feels right.'

Whatever felt right. Was it really that easy? Right now it felt as if it might be. Maybe she should try the unexpected for once in her life. Abby was used to making a cool-headed decision about a man. Choosing someone who would fit into her routine and leave it undisturbed. Nick didn't even come close to fitting that description.

'Kiss me again.'

'Thought you'd never ask.' For once Nick did as he was told.

'You taste of chlorine.'

He grinned at her. 'So do you. Want to take a shower?'

'Yeah. Want to join me?'

Abby made to back him towards the pool steps but he stopped her. 'There's no good time to mention this. In case you were wondering how to ask, I have some condoms in my room.'

'Good.' That was a weight off her mind. Now she wouldn't have to admit that she'd bought some that afternoon. 'Thank you, Nick.' She wound her arms around his neck. 'I really appreciate that you...thought about everything.'

'Can I stop now? Thinking about everything?'

'Please do.'

By the time they'd got out of the pool, wrapped towels around themselves and Nick had hurried Abby up the back stairs to his room, she was shivering. He ushered her inside, dropping his keys onto the small occasional table by the door.

'Wow! A four-poster.' Nick's room was in the oldest part of the hotel building and unlike hers, which was bright, modern and largely unremarkable, it was charmingly old-fashioned. The large bed, complete with heavy brocade curtains, dominated the room.

'Yeah.' Nick was busy, tracing his fingers across her shoulders, and he didn't even glance at it. 'Mrs Pearce says that Henry VIII slept in that bed.'

'Really? I'm not sure I'd like to sleep in Henry VIII's bed.' Who was she trying to kid? Nick had a much more recent claim on it. And his chocolate suede eyes promised so very much.

'Actually, it's Victorian.' He reached up and thumped one of the beams above his head, his gaze still locked with hers. 'So are these, they're not structural. Mock Tudor.'

'Oh. Good.'

'Now that we have that out of the way, can I show you the shower?' He grinned wickedly, and began to back her slowly towards the bathroom.

The door slammed behind them and hot water began to cascade downwards, pushing steam into the room. The towel around his waist crumpled onto the floor, closely followed by his shorts. Abby gasped with admiration. He was beautiful. And for the moment he was all hers.

'Let me.' Her trembling fingers had moved to unfasten the towel she had wrapped firmly around herself, but his were there first. Gently pulling it from around her body. Drawing the straps of her swimming costume from her shoulders and rolling it down until it was around her waist.

She wanted to feel her skin against his, and when she clung to him a long, low sigh escaped his lips. He kissed her again, moulding her body against his until even that wasn't enough.

'Nick.'

He knew what she wanted. But he seemed to enjoy her agonies of impatience, slowly pulling her swimming costume down further until she could step out of it.

'Put your hair up.' His fingers found the elastic tie, still looped around her wrist from where she'd loosened her hair after she'd taken off her swimming cap. Abby twisted her hair onto the top of her head, securing it firmly.

A low growl of approval escaped his throat. 'I never knew that a woman fixing her hair could be so seductive.'

His words made her feel bold. He had seemed to sense that this was not something she usually did and the tremble of his limbs, so obviously wanting her but trying to go slowly, gave Abby confidence. She pulled him into the shower, picking up the soap and slowly lathering his chest.

'Two can play at that game.' He squeezed her hand, making the soap slip through her fingers, and caught it with his other hand.

The water beat down onto his back as he began to soap her body. Starting with her arms and working up to her shoulders. Slowly. Deliberately. Abby shuddered with the promise of where his hands would go next. He lingered over her breasts and she cried out. Made his way down her ribcage and Abby hung onto him for dear life.

It had to be now. He was as ready for her as she was for him. She'd never made love in a shower before. Abby's fingers found one of the grab rails and closed tightly around it.

'Steady.' His fingers were inching downwards, gently stroking, stoking the fire in her belly. 'Hang on there, sweetheart. We have a way to go yet.'

'I can't, Nick.' She was almost pleading with him. Abby didn't know how much more of this she could handle.

'Sure you can. The higher we climb, the harder we fall. But I'll be there to catch you, I promise.'

Something broke. Her will. Her resolve to stay strong. She didn't care any more if she was weak, crying in his arms. As long as he just kept hold of her. 'Don't let me go, Nick.'

'I won't.' His voice was low, almost guttural. 'I can't, not now.'

Nick wanted to hoist her up onto his arms and carry her to the bed, but he wasn't sure whether his leg would take the extra weight. The gesture would almost certainly be ruined if he fell flat on his face and crushed her into the bargain. Instead, he guided her gently, their motion almost that of a slow dance, holding her tight against his raging body. Too much more of this and he was going to black out from sheer, frustrated need. He'd sensed he should go slowly, but how much longer he could keep this up was anyone's guess.

The answer came back immediately. As long as it took. From her reaction to him, she wasn't used to a man taking his time. Maybe he could show her something different.

He guided her to the bed and lifted her onto it, lying down beside her. Unfastening her hair, he watched almost mesmerised as it spilled back down across her shoulders. Nick meant the kiss to be tender, reassuring, but somehow his hunger broke through, meeting joyfully with hers, leaving them both breathless.

She was moving against him, the delicious friction of her skin driving him crazy. Rolling her over onto her back, he parted her legs, his fingers searching for that sweet spot, hoping that she would cry out when he found it.

She did, and then again when he moved to slide one finger inside her. Almost as soon as he did so, he felt her muscles tighten and quiver, just for a moment, and her eyes widened in surprise.

He kissed her flushed cheek and moved his fingers again, making her gasp. Nick knew what to do now. Slowly, he pushed her higher, controlling the pace, until finally she broke. Her cry of disbelief turned to one of sheer pleasure as her body convulsed in time with the movement of his fingers. She was, for this moment, entirely his and more beautiful than he could ever have imagined.

He held her tightly while her body relaxed into his, stubbornly telling himself that if she wanted to curl up and sleep now, that would be okay. He could deal with it. Maybe chopping his arm off would take his mind off the urgent, almost deafening clamour that echoed through every part of his body.

'Now you,' she whispered shyly into his chest. Nick hesitated. Was his own need blinding him, making him believe that this was what she really wanted?

'I said, now you.' Her voice was steadier now, more assured, and she disentangled herself from his embrace and sat up. Ran one finger from the mid-point of his chest downwards.

'Abby...' Her name was the only thing in his head. The one word that summed up everything he wanted.

'We're not done yet.' She bent over him, whispering into his ear. Took his hand and guided it slowly across her body. Her low moan of arousal almost broke him.

Eager to do her bidding, he shifted across the bed, pulling the drawer of the bedside table open and tipping half the contents unheeded onto the floor as he groped for the packet of condoms. Nick made himself concentrate on rolling the condom down into place. No mistakes. Then he was free again, free to enjoy the way she caught her breath, eyes bright with expectation, as he rolled her over onto her back, settling his hips between her legs.

'Is this what you want?' He let her anticipate what he was about to do for a moment, before he slid inside her. Not too far. He wanted to make this last.

'Is that all you have?' The smile on her face was downright wicked and she twisted her hips, sending shivers of delight through his body. What on earth had made him think that he was in control here?

'Nope.' Another inch, and his head began to swim.

Then she did it. Raised her hips off the bed, wrapping her legs around his waist, taking him in deep. The realisation that this was the only place he needed to be hit him like a sledgehammer and when she kissed him, his control broke. He didn't just want her, he needed her. Her body joined with his. Breathing as if they were one. Each movement he made sending pleasure surging through them both.

He had no idea how long he managed to hold on. How did you measure time when each moment was everything? And however long it was, it was enough, complete and perfect. When the sweet, head-spinning convulsions of her muscles sent him over the edge he was lost, falling wildly, with only Abby to catch him.

CHAPTER EIGHT

ABBY woke, to find Nick's arms around her, his body spooning hers. Not a dream, then.

Tentatively, she moved one arm. Cleared her throat. Nick's breathing didn't falter. He must be asleep. Trying not to look at him, she eased herself away from him and got out of the bed.

'Where are you going?'

'What? I thought you were asleep.' In the soft light of a lamp glowing in the corner of the room Abby could see him propped up on one arm in the bed.

'I was watching you sleep.' He almost sounded embarrassed, as if he'd been caught taking the last chocolate from the box.

'What's the time?'

'Half past nine.'

'I suppose we've missed dinner, then.'

He chuckled. 'Yes. But Mrs P. told me the other day where the key to the kitchen is kept. I have permission to make sandwiches.'

Abby supposed that the very grin she was getting now had charmed that concession out of Mrs Pearce. 'I'll, um, go to my room and get dressed and see you down there, then.'

'Won't you stay here?' The way he was looking at her was making her tremble. She could deal with him wanting her, he could hardly want her any more than she wanted him. But the tenderness. The intimacy, which had provoked a response from deep inside her. That she wasn't used to and she hadn't banked on it happening for the first time with Nick.

He was already out of bed, pulling on jeans and a T-shirt then shooting her a grin and a wink around the closing door. Before she quite knew what she was doing, Abby grinned back and blew him a kiss.

She flipped the overhead lights on, trailing into the bathroom and squeezing out her sopping-wet swimming costume in the shower. Straightening the towels that had been flung onto the rack. Shivering slightly in the cool evening air. Smiling.

Abby couldn't think about all they'd done together. What he'd made her feel. The way she'd let go of everything, craving only his touch. Belonging to him alone and feeling things that only he could make her feel.

'Don't hold back, Nick.' She wondered whether it had sounded like the plea it had been. Whether he knew that she'd begged.

He must have known. That sudden grin, the one that made her stomach flip just to think about it. *'It's not a race, sweetheart. I'm planning on coming last.'* Despite herself, Abby found herself smiling again.

By the time he returned, balancing a tray in one hand, the tracksuit she'd left down by the pool tucked under his arm, she was back in the big bed. Knees tucked up to her chin, the covers wrapped around her like a shield. Some hope. Just seeing him again made her heart pump a little faster.

He put her tracksuit down on a chair in the corner of the room and then brought the tray over to the bed, setting it down. 'Here.' Pulling his T-shirt off, he handed it to her. 'Is this enough to coax you out of there?'

Abby slipped the T-shirt over her head, sliding out from under the covers, and he nodded his approval. 'That's better.'

She watched, as he strode over to the fireplace, finding a box of matches on the mantelpiece and lighting the candles that stood there. Flipping the lights off, he returned to the bedside.

'If we have a four-poster, we may as well enjoy it.' His eyes twinkled in the soft candlelight as he loosed the curtains and drew them around her, leaving only the side that faced the fireplace open.

'Mmm. This is nice. Like our own little hidey-hole, away from the world. Come inside.' Abby patted the space next to her on the bed.

They ate ravenously, and when Abby had collected the cups and plates back onto the tray he folded her in a lazy, satisfied embrace. Until then, Abby had always found some excuse to skip this comfortable companionability after sex. Having to leave because she'd needed to be up early in the morning. Rolling over to sleep because she'd been tired. None of that was ever going to wash with Nick. His bed wasn't just a place for sleeping and making love, it was a playground, where anything might happen.

'I don't really know that much about you.' The observation escaped her before she had time to think about it.

He chuckled, tracing his finger along her arm. 'What more do you want?'

'Oh, the usual things.' There was so much more to

Nick than she had thought when she had first met him. She wanted to know everything. Every last detail. 'You were born…?'

'Yep. Can't tell you much about that, you'd have to ask my mother. One brother, one sister. Aunts and uncles, nephews and nieces. All the usual suspects.'

'You have nephews and nieces?'

'Yep. Four in all.'

'But you never had any children yourself?' Abby didn't even know that about him. Whether there was a broken relationship in his past. A child maybe.

'No. That didn't happen. I thought it might, at one point, but…' He shook his head ruefully. 'I put paid to that.'

'How so?'

'It wasn't exactly my finest hour.' She felt his body tense against hers slightly, and he changed the subject too quickly. 'What about you?'

'Me? There's nothing very interesting about me.'

'I find you fascinating. So far I know that you were bullied as a child. There's a lot more to you than that.'

Abby smiled against his chest. 'Yes, there is. The bullying's just the bad stuff. I left that behind a long time ago.' The therapy had helped. Getting older had helped, along with the swimming. All that was left was a sense of regret that things had not been different. 'It took a while. For a long time I used to find out whatever I could about the boys who had bullied me. I think I was waiting for them to get what I considered were their just deserts.'

He curled around her protectively, his eyes flashing dark and dangerous. 'So who were they? Names and addresses will do. I'll take it from there.'

He was only half joking. Nick wouldn't do anything, but it didn't stop him from wanting to, and Abby was irrationally grateful for that. 'You will not. It took me years to get to the point of not caring about them any more, and I'm not going back there now.' She reached to brush her fingers against his lips. 'Sometimes these things are better left in the past.'

'Sometimes.' He seemed to be considering the idea. Almost tempted by it.

'So you know my darkest secrets. What about yours?' The challenge was laid gently before him, rather than being flung at his feet. If he didn't want to talk about it, that was okay.

Nick shrugged. 'Addicts can be self-absorbed, blind and cruel. I was all of those things. I was living with someone, but she left me. She was right to do so.'

Abby couldn't believe that, but Nick seemed so certain. 'How did you get involved with drugs? If you don't mind me asking.'

He reached for her, holding her close, as if for comfort. 'I don't mind.' He fell silent.

'Do you mind answering?' she cajoled gently. If Nick didn't want to answer, she knew he wouldn't, but maybe he needed to find some way of talking about it.

He sighed, pulling himself upright against the pillows that were piled at the head of the bed. 'When I first injured my knee, I tore the cartilage badly. After the operation I developed a Baker's cyst, which went unnoticed until it burst.'

Abby flinched. She wasn't in a consulting room now, and that was allowed.

'Yeah.' He grinned. 'It hurt. I was desperate to get back to work, and I thought that taking more and more painkillers would get me back on my feet sooner. I played one doctor off against another and got duplicate prescriptions. By the time I resorted to the internet, it wasn't about the pain, it was all about wanting more of the drugs.'

Abby nodded. 'And the woman you were living with?'

Nick sighed. 'I kept all of this from Helen. I started going out alone, without telling her where I was going, and even when I was at home I wasn't really there for her. She knew that something was up and thought I was seeing someone else.'

'Were you?'

'In a way I was. The drugs had become the other woman. But I let her go on believing that I was cheating on her so that she wouldn't find out what I was really doing. I let her go through all of that hurt and then walk away from me because I cared more about the drugs than I did her.'

A pulse beat at the side of his brow. If she slapped him now, Abby knew that he wouldn't flinch, that he'd simply take it as a small part of what he deserved.

'Did you ever tell her?' Perhaps Nick's insistence that their relationship was only temporary was because he had unfinished business elsewhere. The thought made Abby feel sick.

'Yes. After I got clean, I went to see her, explained everything. She didn't forgive me, but she understood. By then she had a new partner.' Nick shrugged. 'Even I could see that he made her happier than I ever did.'

'And...and you?' Abby clasped her hands together tightly to stop them from shaking.

'It's over, Abby. Helen and I were never right for each

other. It was one of those things that shouldn't have been in the first place.' He laid his hand on hers. 'Believe me.'

That was something. Abby tried not to heave a sigh of relief. 'But you still feel that you let her down?'

'I didn't treat her as I should have. It doesn't make any difference that things turned out for the best. I've been trying all my life not to be the kind of man who puts an addiction above the people he should be caring for and protecting, and I failed.'

Abby took a deep breath and went for the fifty-thousand-dollar question. 'Who was that man? The one you've been trying not to be.'

He looked at her for long moments, before dropping his gaze to where his finger slowly traced around the pattern of the bedspread. 'My father. He was an alcoholic. He left us when I was eight and that was the best thing he ever did for any of us. It was hard for my mother, alone with three kids, but not as bad as when he was around.'

'But…but you're not like that, Nick.'

'I'm just like him. He was always sorry when he lashed out at my mother. But it was never enough to make him stop.'

'But you kicked the drugs.'

He shook his head. 'Even Helen leaving wasn't enough to make me give up. I did the unforgiveable and went back to work, just on desk duties, but I still shouldn't have done it. I was planning out a training exercise and didn't bother to check everything because I was strung out, wanting to get home. Luckily someone else did and found a faulty piece of equipment that could have put lives at risk.'

'You got help then?'

'Ted Bishop was my station commander back then. I went to him, told him everything, and offered to resign. He threw it back in my face and challenged me to take the harder option. I took him up on it, took a leave of absence and got myself clean. I'll always be thankful to him for that.'

'So the fire service knows? About your history.'

'Only those who need to. Ted had to put it through channels to get me the help I needed so it's on my record, but everyone else thought that I'd re-injured my knee. I didn't have the spine to tell them any different.'

'You had the guts to do something about it. To turn your life around.' Abby hated it that Nick talked about himself like this. Spineless was the last description that anyone could apply to him. If anything, he had a bit too much spine at times.

His fingers slid across the bedspread towards hers and then stopped short of them. It was as if he no longer felt he had the right to touch her. 'I'm sorry, Abby. I shouldn't have told you about this. Not tonight.'

Abby knew why he'd told her. She'd asked. The intimacy between them had stripped him of his protective shell, and when she'd asked he'd found a way to answer. And she could feel that those answers had driven a wedge between them, reminding him of all the reasons why he believed they couldn't be together.

He swung his legs over the side of the bed, sitting up and rubbing his face. 'You should get some sleep, Abby. You're swimming tomorrow.'

'Yeah, probably.' She laid her cheek against his back, winding her arms around him. 'Will you hold me, Nick?'

'Don't you want to go back to your own room to sleep?'

'No. Why, are you trying to get rid of me?' Maybe he wasn't ready to leave his past behind yet. Another time perhaps. But she wasn't going to let him get away with thinking that he was right about himself, by allowing him to chase her away.

He turned, rolling her with him back onto the bed. 'Come here.'

Day Two. Coniston Water. Three miles.

Nick sat on the deck of the boat, watching as Abby sliced into the choppy water. He'd resisted the temptation to wake her in the night and make love to her again. And this morning he'd let her dress quickly and slip from his room, before the rest of the team stirred. Just a smile and a kiss. Nothing more, however much he wanted it.

She seemed stronger than usual, though. Her stroke was confident, economical. She'd taken the lead almost immediately and Nick had steered the support boat after her, signalling to the other boats to stay back and watch over the rest of the swimmers.

'She's a good girl.' Pete was behind him, and Nick didn't turn to acknowledge his words, keeping his eye fixed on Abby. 'She'll do the whole course in under an hour thirty if she keeps this up.'

'I just hope she doesn't tire herself.' Nick's neck began to burn. Swimming wasn't the only physical activity that Abby had been up to in the last twenty-four hours and he was the one who would be to blame if she began to flag.

'She'll be all right.' Pete seemed to have nothing to base the supposition on other than instinct, but Nick knew enough to trust Pete's gut. He'd done it enough times before Pete had retired, and it had never let him down.

'I hope so.'

Pete let out a short, barking laugh. 'Stop worrying. I hope you're not like this when you're around her.'

Nick went to deny everything, and then realised he didn't have a clue what Pete was talking about. 'Like what?'

'Jittery, mate. She won't sink if you take your eyes off her, you know.'

'I know. I'm just studying her stroke. Looking for irregularities.'

'That's what they call it these days, is it? Does she know?'

Nick turned to Pete in exasperation. 'Know what?'

'Something tells me there's something going on between you two. And you don't have much of a reputation for sticking with a relationship.' Pete's shrewd blue eyes were fixed on Nick.

'You think I'd hurt her?'

'That's up to you. If you did, I'd be sorry to see it.' Pete regarded him thoughtfully. 'I'd be sorry for you, too.'

There was no point in asking Pete what he knew or how he knew it. He'd just make some oblique comment about listening to his gut and let the matter slide. 'It's a holiday thing, Pete. We both know it. I won't make promises to her that I can't keep.'

'And why can't you keep them?'

Pete may have made a few lucky guesses, but he

didn't have all the answers. Abby had heard the worst about him from his own lips. Even if she'd had the goodness of heart not to reject him straight away, she must understand now why it was better for both of them if this was a purely temporary arrangement.

'It's a crease in time, Pete—' Nick didn't get a chance to finish. A cry from the water made him whirl round, his knee suddenly giving out. Nick stumbled, landing awkwardly on the deck.

'Watch it!' Abby was treading water by the side of the boat, grinning.

'What's the matter?'

'Nothing. Just wondered what you two were up to. I was feeling a bit neglected.' There was a playful tone to her voice, different from her usual grim determination. And she seemed entirely unaware that she had stopped and that the swimmers behind her were beginning to gain on her.

Nick resumed his position at the side of the boat. 'Just keep swimming, will you? Look, the others are catching up.'

She laughed. 'Thought this wasn't a race.' Before he could answer, she had turned, soft sheets of water streaming across her rolling body, and started swimming again, striking out strongly for the shore and the end of the course.

Nick was there for her when she got out of the water, and when she'd stripped off her wetsuit she let him wrap her in a towel. He loved doing things for her. Taking her swim hat, when she pulled it off her head, shaking her hair free. Handing her a hot drink from the van.

She was bright, almost elated. 'That was fun. I could do it again...'

'Well, your wish is granted.' He liked granting her wishes, too. 'Tomorrow...'

'Buttermere.' She regarded the sky, an inferior blue to her eyes but cloudless all the same. 'Think the weather will hold?'

'The forecast's good.'

'Well, fingers crossed. I'll just go and get changed and then watch the others come in.'

He left her to it. She seemed bright, strong. More in charge of herself than he'd ever seen her. Being here, taking part in the swimming was obviously doing her good and he should give her some space, let her enjoy it to the full. He could only weigh her down, hold her back.

When she re-emerged, dressed in warm clothes, and ran down to the water's edge, ready to cheer the other swimmers to the finish line, he didn't follow. A few hours out of the circle of delight that she seemed to carry with her wherever she went would do them both good.

CHAPTER NINE

'Where have you been?' Nick sauntered into the dining room and sat down at Abby's table as if nothing had happened. She had already decided not to wait for him any longer and was tucking into her evening meal. She'd decided not to ask him where he'd been, too.

'I...' The slight hesitation told her that he'd stayed away on purpose. 'I went to see Ted Bishop.'

Abby flashed him a brittle smile. She'd thought that yesterday afternoon might have changed things. But knowing what had made Nick into the man he was hadn't suddenly turned him into someone different. It had just cleared up a few of the questions that had been outstanding in her mind. 'About the arson attacks? I thought that you'd finished with your input on that.'

'I dropped in and took him to lunch and we had a chat about the new job I've been offered.'

'What did he say?' Abby kept eating while Nick ordered his meal. She didn't want to hear what had kept him away for the rest of the afternoon. It was probably something trivial, and then she was going to have to resent him for it.

'I did most of the talking, actually. Told him what you'd said and he just nodded sagely.'

Abby felt her shoulders relax, and she laid her knife and fork down with a clatter. Nick did this every time. Getting angry with him was a lot easier when he wasn't around than when he was sitting right next to her.

'So he's persuaded you. That it's what you really want.'

'No. You persuaded me. It was good to hear myself say it, though, and find that I really believed it.'

Pleasure leaked into her fingertips, and she flexed her hands impatiently. This was Nick all over. Charming, tantalising and cruelly honest about the fact that ultimately he didn't belong to her. It wasn't what he wanted, and Abby reminded herself that it wasn't what she wanted either. She didn't want to be the clingy girlfriend, devastated whenever he decided not to tell her where he was going or what he was doing. That wasn't what they'd both signed up for here.

'We spent some time going over the case as well.' He grinned. 'Ted can do with the help, so we broke the rules. Just for the afternoon.'

Not as trivial as she'd thought. Warmth began to permeate the protective layer that Abby had wrapped around herself for comfort. 'How's it going?'

'They're making some progress. The profile has helped, and I've suggested that there could be a grudge involved in selecting the targets. All the fires seem to be aimed at places of authority—a school, a driving test centre and so on.'

'So it's not just someone who likes to light fires then stand around and watch the damage they're doing?'

'It probably is. But where he's lighting the fires tells us something too. Ted's in contact with the police and they're working together to narrow the possibilities down, find who's doing this before he does any more harm or gets someone killed.' He shrugged. 'It's not easy, but it's all he can do.'

'You think it's a man. The fire-raiser.'

'Statistically that's the probability. This kind of fire isn't usually a woman's weapon.' He shrugged. 'But you can't rule anything out. In the end it's all just probabilities.'

He was staring at nothing. Going through those probabilities in his mind, trying to make some sense of them. Almost as far away as when he'd been with Ted for the afternoon.

'Eat. It'll get cold.' She picked up her own fork and speared a chip from his plate.

'Hey, you've got your own.'

'Yeah, but stolen chips always taste better.'

They ate in silence. Abby was hungry, and Nick had obviously worked up an appetite that afternoon as well. And even though it was still early, the hours of darkness were already beckoning her. What would he do? Would he find her again? Ask her up to his room? Every time she thought about it Abby felt a tightening in her chest, a sudden thump of her heart against her ribcage.

The waitress had brought coffee and Abby had just taken her first sip when Pete arrived, sitting down at their table without his usual *'Can I join you?'* That, and the look on his face already had Nick's full attention.

'What is it, mate?'

Pete turned to Abby. 'Could you come and take a look at Louise? She's not well.'

Abby took another sip of her coffee. 'Of course, I'll come straight up as soon as I've finished. What's the problem?'

Pete and Nick exchanged glances and Nick stood. 'We need to go now, Abby.'

Nick was right in not allowing any delay. 'I noticed that she wasn't at dinner and went to find her,' Pete explained briefly on the stairs. 'I don't like the look of her. One of the guys said that he thought she'd cut her foot but he wasn't sure whether it was when she was in the water.'

'Okay. Let me see. Maybe she's got a bug of some sort, in which case a couple of paracetamol and a good night's sleep will do the trick.' Abby hoped so. Louise hadn't said anything about a cut, and cuts sustained in the open water could go septic with frightening speed.

Pete opened the door to Louise's room without knocking and ushered Abby inside. Louise was curled up on the bed, wrapped tightly in the thick bedspread, even though the evening wasn't cold.

'Hey, Louise. I hear you're not feeling too well.' Abby sat down on the bed beside her.

'I'm okay. Go away, Abby, I just need to rest up for tomorrow.' Louise didn't even open her eyes.

She most definitely wasn't okay, but Abby wasn't about to start a wrestling match to get the bedspread away from her. 'Have you cut your foot? May I have a look at it?'

'It's okay, Abby. Leave me alone.' Louise's voice was half a plea, half a rejection.

'Come along, now, Louise.' Nick's voice was gentle but unmistakeably an order. Abby scooted along to the end of the bed as he took her place, sitting next to Louise, lifting her slightly and pulling the bedspread away from her. Almost unconsciously, Louise obeyed.

'That's it.' Nick had her cradled against his chest. 'Now, tell me where you cut yourself.'

'In the water, boss.' Louise allowed him a smile and relaxed against him.

Nick shook his head, but now wasn't the time for recriminations. 'When?'

'The day before yesterday. When we went for a practice swim.'

'Okay, well, Abby needs to look at it. Just hold still a minute.'

Louise did what she was told, extending her left leg towards Abby. A loose sock covered her foot, and as Abby stripped it off, Louise winced.

'Okay. Let's see now.' Abby really didn't need to see any more. Louise had dressed the cut with lint and plasters, but the leg was badly swollen and bright, livid red. 'I'm going to take the dressing off now.'

Nick's arms closed around Louise, holding her tightly, and she cried out as Abby pulled the plaster off. The cut was barely more than an inch long, hidden behind her ankle, but it was deep and seeping blood and pus. Nick's jaw hardened when he saw it.

Well, it might. The cut was obviously infected, and Louise's drowsy, disoriented state indicated that some of the infection was already in her bloodstream, working its way around to her heart, her lungs, her kidneys.

'Pete, can you get the car and bring it round to the front door? Nick, wrap her up in the bedspread. Leave her leg free.'

'Isn't there anything you can do here?' Pete asked her quietly.

'What she really needs is high-strength antibiotics.

The only place we can get those is the hospital. We need to go now.'

'Okay. I'll send one of the lads up to carry her down.'

Abby nodded to Pete and went into the en suite bathroom to wash her hands. Then back to Louise's side. She put her hand on her forehead. 'Not too much of a temperature. And her pulse is steady.' She gave an exclamation of frustration. 'I wish I had my medical kit here.'

'It's you she needs. Will it do any good to clean the wound?' Nick's voice was quiet, steady, and Abby's heartbeat racheted down a notch.

'We'll just be wasting time. It's not the wound itself I'm worried about, it's the poison in her bloodstream. The only way to deal with that is to get her to the hospital.'

Sam came bursting through the door at a run and Nick hoisted Louise up into his arms, passing her to Sam. Quickly the small group negotiated the stairs, and Nick and Sam put Louise into the back of the waiting car.

'Abby, you go in the back with her.' He looked at Pete. 'Okay if I take her?'

'Can you manage?'

'It's an automatic. And Louise is still part of my crew.'

Pete nodded imperceptibly and threw Nick the car keys. He slid into the driver's seat, programming the satnav, and took a look over his shoulder to make sure that Louise and Abby were settled. Then he jammed the gear lever into drive and put his foot down.

Nick had drawn up outside the A and E department of the hospital, and Abby had gone to get a wheelchair, taking Louise inside while Nick parked the car. By the time he got back, Abby was talking intently to the receptionist.

She seemed to be pressing her point, producing her own hospital ID from her purse, and the receptionist called a nurse. The nurse took one look at Louise's foot and called a doctor, and Louise was pushed quickly through the doors into the treatment area with Abby in tow, leaving Nick to sit and contemplate the wall.

He hated this. Always, whenever a member of his crew was hurt, he'd make it to the hospital as soon as humanly possible. And always he'd get stuck in some waiting room, the last to hear what was happening and unable to help or influence what was going on behind closed doors.

The doors to the treatment area shook, and caught Nick's eye. Then they opened, and Abby's head appeared, closely followed by her beckoning hand.

'What? What is it?' He made it to his feet and over to her in double-quick time.

'Nothing. It's okay. I just thought you'd like to come in and see her.'

Warmth fizzed and flickered across his chest. 'Yeah. I would. Thanks.'

She opened the doors, letting him through, and led him along the row of treatment bays, stopping outside one at the far end. 'I've spoken to the doctor who's treating her and everything's fine. I have no cause for concern.'

'What's the matter with her, Abby?' Nick matched her low tone, careful that they could not be overheard from inside the cubicle.

'Well, that cut's obviously infected, and the blood

test indicates she has a mild case of septicaemia.' She laid her hand on his chest in response to his start. 'But we caught it early. She's had a blood test and they're checking her vital organs to make sure the infection hasn't reached them, but she seems fine. You'll see a big difference in her once the antibiotics have kicked in.'

'Will they keep her here?'

'Overnight certainly. They'll probably let her go some time tomorrow or the next day, once she's seen a specialist and all the test results are through. In the meantime, they'll be putting her on a drip to get the antibiotics into her system as quickly as possible. She's getting saline as well, she's been sick and she's pretty dehydrated.'

'Good. Thanks, Abby. I wish Louise had said something about it.'

'One of the symptoms of septicaemia can be impaired judgement. People can just wander off on their own or curl up in a corner, as Louise did.'

'I should have seen that she had a cut when she went into the water yesterday. I should have checked.' Nick wanted to punch the wall but he had to make do with mentally kicking himself. The harder the better.

'It was easy to miss. I did when I helped her on with her wetsuit. Everyone knows about cuts, you've said it often enough.'

'Obviously not loudly enough.'

'If you'd said it any louder, my ears would have started to bleed. Let it go, Nick.' She gave him a little smile and turned to lead him into Louise's cubicle.

Louise looked better. Even though the saline and antibiotic drips had only just been set up and couldn't be taking effect yet, she seemed much more cheerful.

Much more together. She was biting her lip as Nick squeezed himself into a corner by her bedside, out of the way of the technician who was removing the last of the heart monitor's sticky pads from her arm.

'Sorry, Nick.'

He grinned. 'You'd better be. I'm getting too old for this. Let me digest my dinner next time before you scare me out of my wits, eh?'

A tear escaped Louise's eye and Nick took the tissue that Abby had produced out of nowhere and gave it to her. 'I should have done something about the cut straight away. But it was so small, and it seemed okay. I wanted to swim and go to the fair and I thought it would be all right.'

'Forget it. These things happen.'

'I made a mistake.' Louise seemed intent on giving herself a hard time.

'We all make mistakes. I've made a few that would make your hair stand on end.' Not Abby's. He'd told her everything and she'd hardly blinked. Had slept next to him afterwards, as well, sprawled across his chest as if he somehow had a right to be close to her.

'Really?' Louise's voice bumped him back down to earth. Appealing to her curiosity had obviously done what reassurance couldn't and she was smiling now.

'Yeah, really. One of these days maybe I'll tell you about them.' Nick manoeuvred himself into the plastic chair by the side of the bed, awkward in the tight space. 'In the meantime, your job is to get better. Is there anything you need me to do?'

'Will you call my mum and dad?'

'Of course. I'll tell them that you're on the mend, eh?'

'Yes...yes, do that.' Louise shot Abby a querying look.

'You'll be feeling much better soon. Well enough to tell them yourself.' Abby gave her an encouraging smile. 'We'll call them tonight, and let them know that you're safe and sound, and that you'll speak to them in the morning. I'll ask Pete to arrange for someone to come in and bring you a phone.'

Louise nodded. 'Thanks. You've got their number.' She turned to Nick. 'It's on the sheet I filled out.'

'I've got it.' He leaned forward, taking Louise's hand in his. 'Just concentrate on getting better, okay? Leave everything else to me.'

'Okay. Thanks, Nick.' She let out a sigh. 'I won't be able to swim tomorrow, then.'

'No, you won't.' Abby's voice was firm.

A little thrill worked through Nick's system. 'Don't worry about that. We'll get someone to swim in your place.' He didn't meet Abby's eye. Tomorrow's swim was the second short swim, only two miles. Everyone was already taking part. Everyone but him.

Louise grimaced. 'There is no one else, Nick. You know that.' She giggled suddenly. 'Unless you can fit Pete's belly into a wetsuit.'

'Nah. We don't want to frighten anyone.' Nick shrugged. 'I may do it myself.'

He could feel the force of Abby's disapproval burning into the back of his neck, but she said nothing. Nick imagined that she was waiting until they were out of Louise's earshot to make her views plain, and the thought of being on the end of her passion sent a shiver of expectation through his stomach.

'You can't...can you?' Louise looked unconvinced.

'We'll see, eh? Just let me sort that one out.'

'Okay, boss.' Louise relaxed against the pillows, looking up at the bags of saline and antibiotics above her head. 'It's not dripping very fast. Is that right?'

Nick chanced a look at Abby, who had focussed on the valve at the bottom of the bag of antibiotics, tapping it gently. 'It's okay. Little bit sluggish, maybe. Try clenching your hand and releasing it…like this.'

Louise obeyed and the drip responded, speeding up slightly.

'Yeah, that's right.' She flipped a glance at Nick. 'Give her your hand, Nick. Squeeze on his fingers, Louise. As hard as you like. That's it. Don't worry about hurting him.'

So that was how it was, was it? He was in for an ear-bashing later on, that was plain. Nick chuckled softly.

CHAPTER TEN

'So who do you have in mind for tomorrow? To swim?' They were walking across to the car park in the gathering dusk, having made sure that Louise was settled comfortably for the night. Abby decided to broach the subject gently. It was just possible that Nick had someone other than himself in mind to substitute for Louise.

He was grinning. Dammit, she'd known all along what he intended to do. 'I was thinking of doing it myself.'

Abby swallowed her concern for him, which was quickly turning to rage. 'Do you think that's a good idea?'

'I think I'm the only one who can do it.' He was still grinning.

'Nick.' Stay calm. Don't rise to the bait. 'You're recovering from a fractured patella and a torn cartilage. I know it feels better now, but you still need to take things carefully.'

'I've been doing a bit of swimming, and my leg's been fine. Dr Patel told me that it was good exercise, as long as I didn't push it.'

That's right. Throw her boss's words at her. 'And you

reckon that a two-mile, open-water swim isn't pushing it, do you?'

'I'll stop if I get into difficulties. I have a neoprene support that I wear in the water.'

'Right. Pull the other one. If you get into the water, you'll be damned rather than get out anywhere other than the finishing point.'

He shrugged. 'Dr Patel—'

'Doesn't know you the way I do.'

He chuckled. 'No. I'll give you that.'

'Oh-h!' Abby threw up her arms in frustration. 'Don't play that card with me, Nick. My concerns are strictly professional.'

'Aw. Don't you care? Just a little bit?' He advanced towards her, eyes as dark as melted chocolate, and Abby felt her resolve beginning to waver.

'Don't you dare, Nick Hunter.'

'Dare what, Abby? Dare to touch you?'

'Don't you dare try to control me.'

'Oh, so this is about control now, is it? I thought you were worried about my knee.'

'I am.' Abby was near tears. Why couldn't he see? He was trying to make everything right and the thought that he might hurt himself in the process was too much to bear. 'But it's all the same thing, Nick. You can't make a thing happen just because you will it to. If you're not fit to swim then you're not fit, and no amount of wishful thinking on your part is going to change that.'

'I'm okay. Like I said, I won't push it. If I feel that I'm doing my knee any damage, I'll stop.'

'And like I said. I don't believe you. You'll just keep going, whatever.'

'Well, we're just going to have to agree to disagree

on that one.' Nick pulled the car keys out of his pocket and thumbed the key fob to disengage the locks. 'Get into the car.'

'I'll drive.'

'Oh, and I can't drive a car now. Anything else you want to put on the list of things I'm not allowed to do on medical grounds?'

'I said I'll drive. Either that or I take the bus home.' She could at least be in charge of her own destiny, even if she couldn't persuade Nick to do what she wanted.

'Fine.' He dropped the keys into her hand. 'Have it your way. Do you even know the way back to the hotel?'

He got into the passenger seat of the car and reached for the satnav. 'Leave it, Nick. That's another thing I can manage to do without your help.'

They drove in silence. Abby concentrated on the road ahead, rather than think about Nick. How infuriating he was. How it made her heart hurt when she thought about how hard he drove himself. She slid the car into one of the parking spaces in the hotel car park and got out, waiting for him to slam the passenger door before she engaged the central locking.

'Wait.' She had stalked into the hotel ahead of him, but he caught her arm before she could make it across the reception area and to the stairs.

'What is it, Nick? You don't see things my way, and I'm not going to argue with you any more.'

They'd argued before, more times than she cared to count. But this time it had gone too far, and the corrosive silence in the car had finished the job that words had started, building an impenetrable barrier between them. His face was closed, impassive. Still unbearably handsome, and it almost killed her to pull her arm from his grasp and run up the stairs.

Okay, so I'm concerned for him. So shoot me. Someone was going to have to. Serious injury or death were about the only things right now that were going to get Nick Hunter out of her system.

Day Three. Buttermere. Two miles.

The day was idyllic, sunlight caressing the mountains and trees around the lake and shimmering across the crystal-clear water. Today had been designed as a treat for the swimmers, a manageable distance in a quiet, clean lake surrounded by spectacular scenery.

Nick slid into the water and began to swim gently up and down along the shoreline to warm up. That morning he had seen what he'd refused to acknowledge last night. That Abby's resolutely closed door and the empty space in his bed, which still bore a trace of her scent if he buried his face into her pillow, was all his fault.

He swam over to one of the escort boats, bobbing up and down in the water a few yards away. 'Pete. I thought you'd still be at the hospital.'

'They only let me stay half an hour, so I came straight back here.'

'How is Louise?'

'Fine. Looks a lot better than she did last night. She's spoken to her parents and she's got a bit of colour in her cheeks. Got stuck into the fruit that Abby sent, so she's got an appetite.'

'Abby sent fruit?'

Pete rolled his eyes. 'What, are you two not talking

now? Louise liked your flowers as well, and I've got some change for you.'

'Any news about when she'll be out?'

'Today or tomorrow. The doctor hadn't seen her yet when I was there.'

'That's great, we can go and see her after lunch.'

'That's okay. Sam's going and I think he's taking one of the others with him. They don't like more than two visitors at once, and she needs a bit of peace and quiet, not a whole gang of us around her bed.' Pete's voice was firm. 'So what's this strategy you've got that doesn't involve using your leg, then?'

'Same one I was practising in the pool with the physio before we came here. I'm still using the leg, just not putting so much pressure on it. I could do to a mile and a half without any difficulties a week ago, so two shouldn't be a problem now.' He could have mentioned that to Abby last night, but he hadn't. Instead of reassuring her, he'd chosen to goad her, pretty much daring her to walk away from him, and it was a credit to her good sense that she had.

'Is Abby in on this?'

'No.'

Pete chuckled. 'So you're reckoning on surprising her with your ability to improvise, are you?'

There might have been something of that to it. Nick wasn't sure. 'Wait and see, mate.'

'I'll look forward to it. Just remember it's that way.' Pete pointed towards the finishing point on the other side of the lake. 'If you start swimming around in circles, I'm not going to fish you out.'

'Yeah. And if the boat sinks because you had too much breakfast, you're on your own, too.'

Pete waved him away, laughing, and Nick turned and swam back to the starting line, hanging onto the rope that was stretched between two buoys. Abby was some way away, her eyes fixed on the far shore of the lake, her head never once turning in his direction. Nick cursed himself again and waited for the siren to mark the start of the swim.

The siren sounded, and Nick struck out, keeping a little behind the other swimmers. His leg was stiff, but that was just the neoprene knee support over his wetsuit. His stroke didn't have its usual power, but it wasn't bad. The test had begun. Whether he could do this swim. Whether he would give up if he couldn't. If giving up was what it took, he'd do it, for Abby's sake if not his own.

His confidence was growing, and he fell into a rhythm. Slowly he began to draw ahead of the other swimmers, striking out with more assurance as he found that he could do so without pain.

Caught up in the exhilaration of being back in the water, feeling the muscles of his shoulders stretch and bunch as he sliced through the calm, shimmering surface, he didn't notice that someone else was with him until he got almost to the centre of the lake. Nick took the luxury of a look behind him and saw that he was ahead of the pack. All but one of them.

He could see Abby's bright swim cap bobbing in the water just behind and to the left of him. He stopped, treading water, to give her time to catch up with him.

For a moment he thought she was going to swim straight past him, but with an abrupt splash she veered towards him, ending up treading water opposite him.

'Interesting style you have there. How's it going?'

'Good. Swim with me?'

She didn't answer but started to swim, a mid-paced crawl, which kept them ahead of the pack but didn't stretch either of them. Nice and easy. Just get to the finishing post. Nick adjusted his rhythm to hers, a hundred strokes. Two hundred. Three.

She had a sweet style. It was like everything she did, precise, graceful and yet with a hint of audacity. The feeling that at any moment she might break out of her rhythm, toss her head and do something wild and beautiful. The way she had when she'd made love with him. Nick took another hundred strokes to ponder that, finding that it wasn't nearly enough and that he was still thinking about it as they neared the finishing buoy.

He picked up the pace slightly, and she matched him. A little more, and she was still with him, her body sliding through the water. The urge to push her even further, see what they could do together, was growing.

Against all reason, Nick struck out as strongly as he could. It wasn't too far now, just a few hundred yards. She responded to his silent challenge, kicking out, her legs pushing her forward in the water.

They were almost equally matched. Nick's arms and shoulders were much more powerful than hers, but he was hampered by the brace on his leg and by the fact that he couldn't kick as strongly. Resisting the temptation to change back to his usual style and use his legs more, he put all of his effort into his shoulders and arms.

She was slicing through the water. He fell behind slightly and she made the most of her advantage, swimming as if there were sharks in the water behind her. Nick put his head down and concentrated hard on the finishing buoy, the raw excitement of the chase flooding his system. This had been brewing for a while now, and it felt good to get the corrosive energy of all the things left unsaid between them out of his system. From Abby's determined stroke, it looked as if she felt exactly the same.

His fingers touched the buoy and he almost crashed into it. He had no idea of whether he'd beaten her or not, until he felt her hand grab his arm and she touched home. She was breathing heavily, her eyes shining with the same thrill that he felt. Planting her hands on his shoulders, she used the weight of her body as she levered it upwards to duck his head beneath the water.

He broke the surface, laughing and shaking the water from his hair. 'What's that for?'

'Not telling me that you've invented a new stroke. What do you call it, the Crabby Fireman?'

'Suppose I deserve that.'

'You do.'

It was an unashamed come-on and Nick was nothing if not equal to a challenge. He kissed her, full on the lips, pressing his claim on her until surprise turned to passion and she wrapped her legs around his waist. It was only when he felt the wake of the boat hit them that he released her, turning to wave, while she sheltered behind his bulk.

'So who won?' Pete was up on the deck, grinning down at them.

It wasn't a straightforward question. 'I made the buoy first.' He felt her leg wind around his in the water. 'Abby won on style, though.'

In the activity surrounding the end of the swim and then lunch at the hotel, Abby had seemed to lose touch with Nick again. He was there, beside her, but there were too many people around. What she wanted to say to him didn't need an audience.

Everyone had dispersed, to their rooms or onto the patio to talk lazily in the sun. And Abby was on a mission. She tapped gently on Nick's door, knowing that he was in there.

'Hey.' His smile, and the way he stepped back from the door immediately, gave her confidence.

'I just came to collect my other swimsuit. I left it in your bathroom.'

'I was going to bring it to you. If you hadn't come.'

'Thanks.' Abby swallowed hard and made for the bathroom. If she was just here for the swimsuit, why had she bothered to go up to her room before lunch and change into the soft leather boots and the gypsy skirt she liked so much?

Her swimsuit was folded neatly on the vanity unit. She picked it up, catching sight of herself in the mirror and stopping to adjust a stray lock of hair.

'You look nice. Lovely, in fact.'

'Oh? Do I?' Abby tried to make out that she was surprised by the comment. 'It's just an old skirt.'

'Going anywhere?'

She shook her head. 'No, I've nothing planned for this afternoon.' She may as well get it over with. 'I didn't give you a chance to explain last night. I should have trusted you.'

'I don't see why. It's not as if I'm a stranger to unrealistic expectations. I should have told you.' He sat down on the bed. 'I owe you an apology, Abby.'

'I think that's my line.'

'What, you owe yourself an apology? What for?' The deliberate misinterpretation and his wayward grin told her that nothing more was needed. They both knew what they'd done and now it was behind them.

'Does this mean I'm redundant now?'

'What?' His surprise was genuine. 'No, Abby. Why, did you think I was going to try and take over from you?'

'The thought crossed my mind. You took all the precautions and you're fit to swim.' She wouldn't have blamed anyone in Nick's place for taking over the final swims, just out of spite. But spite wasn't really Nick's style.

He shook his head. 'I was fit to swim two miles. On one day. I'd be asking for trouble if I tried to do any more. Anyway, this is your project now. Don't you want to finish it?'

Abby breathed a sigh of relief. 'Of course I do. I just thought...'

'I wouldn't take the swim over from you, even if I was fit. It wouldn't be fair on either of us. I'm happy to have done as much as I could and now I'm going to quit.' He stood, taking a couple of steps towards her. 'Come here.'

There was nothing more to say. She closed the gap between them, letting him take her in his arms. Losing herself in the hunger of his kiss, the sweetness of his desire. Somehow managing to twist the buttons of his shirt open so that when she ran her hands across his shoulders there was nothing to stop her from feeling the smooth ripple beneath his skin.

'Stay with me this afternoon, Abby.'

'Yes.'

He kissed her again, moulding her body against his.

'Got to warn you. If you don't take your clothes off in the next ten seconds, I'm going to do it for you.'

The raw power of his frame, the strength of his desire only lent a greater edge to his tenderness. Her allotted ten seconds were just enough to slip her boots off, and then he took over, undoing a couple of buttons on her blouse before losing patience and pulling it over her head.

Scattering their clothes on the floor, drinking in her kisses like a man possessed, he backed her towards the solid, old-fashioned sideboard, reaching for the condoms on the way. There was barely time for him to catch up a pillow from the bed to cushion her from the wooden surface, before he lifted her up, perching her in front of him.

'Abby...' His voice was deep, urgent.

'I know. I know. Me too.' She wrapped her legs around his waist, leaning back, her arms supporting her. There was no possibility of prolonging the moment this time. It had to be now.

'Look at me.' His words cut through the haze of wanting. 'Look at me, Abby.' She looked at him. Stared into his eyes as he slid inside her, watching the pupils dilate even further, every movement of their bodies reflected in his face.

She was gasping for breath, almost whimpering with pleasure. She was caught in his gaze, knew that he must be able to see everything she was feeling, and she didn't care. Nick dominated her completely, and she had never felt so free. Nothing had ever felt this right.

One hand left her leg, and brushed against her breast, sending new jolts of sensation through her. Swiftly, tenderly, mercilessly he took her to the very edge, keeping her there for agonised moments until she felt her body respond to his caress once more, shaking uncontrollably as he moved inside her, drawing out her pleasure until there was nothing more to feel.

The balance tipped. As her own body began to relax, his tightened. He coiled one arm around her, supporting her back, planting his other hand behind her on the sideboard.

'Abby. Please...' He was trembling now, pressing her to his chest.

'It's okay, Nick.' She soothed him gently. Here in the sunlight, face to face and unable to hide anything from each other, the intimacy would have been terrifying if she didn't want it so much. Tightening her legs around his waist, she rolled her hips and he roared out his release.

For long moments neither of them moved, still shaken by the enormity of what had happened between them. Then he kissed her, his lips tender on hers.

'Come to bed, Nick.'

He wrapped his arms around her, hugging her tight, seemingly unwilling to move. 'I'm not so sure I can walk just yet.'

She giggled, straightening up and clasping her hands behind his neck. 'I'll throw you over my shoulder, then.' She almost felt that she could. She felt she could do anything right now.

'Oh, yeah? Like to see you try it.'

CHAPTER ELEVEN

NICK groaned as he pulled himself back from the velvet darkness of sleep. Abby was lying on her back next to him, her head propped up on his chest, her fingers locked with his. All he could feel was pure, sated happiness.

'You awake, sweetheart?' He knew she was. Even though he couldn't see her face, he could see her eyelashes, fluttering gently against the profile of her cheek.

'Yes.'

That was all that needed to be said. For the next few minutes anyway. She'd done it again. Ripped him apart, claimed each piece of him for her own and then effortlessly put him back together again. Nick wondered if her name was now stamped right through him, like on a stick of rock.

'What's the time?'

He looked at his watch. 'Half-past six. Plenty of time before dinner.'

'Good.' She shifted, rolling over onto her side and tucked her shoulder under his arm, snuggling in close. 'I'm too comfortable to move.'

'Me too.' Nick allowed himself to run his fingers across her shoulder. The softest, most velvet skin on her body. Or perhaps that was her belly. Or her breasts. He'd have to run through the options again before he made a decision.

'We could always miss dinner. Get something sent up.'

'Oh, no.' He twisted his head around so he could catch her eye. 'You need to keep your calorie intake up. No skipping meals.'

'Right.' She gave a mock salute. 'Boss.'

Nick felt the chuckle, coming up from somewhere deep inside his soul and rumbling through his chest. 'So long as you know it.' She aimed a play punch at his shoulder and he twisted away, wincing as he felt the muscles pull. 'Steady on with the shoulder. It's already taken a bit of a beating today.'

'You should have said. I could have massaged it for you.'

'I think you did, didn't you?' After that first, earth-shattering embrace, they'd taken their time. Spent hours, touching, massaging, learning each other's bodies. A long, slow burn when Abby had finally let go of the last vestiges of her self-sufficiency and laid claim on her pleasure. Their pleasure. She'd driven him half-mad from sheer sensual overload by the time she'd finished with him.

'That was different. Therapeutic massage can hurt a little when you ease the knots out.'

'Definitely not therapeutic, then. I was hurting much more than a little.'

She chuckled. 'That was your own fault. I seem to remember you were the one calling the shots at that point.'

'I loved every minute of it.' Every second. Every

move she made and each one of her soft sighs. Nick wondered whether he should tell her that and decided against it. They sounded too much like the words of a man who was falling in love.

'Me too.' She rolled away from him, stretching luxuriantly.

'I was thinking of driving over to see Ted Bishop tomorrow afternoon.'

'Again?' She grinned at him. 'I thought you weren't involved with the case any more. That you'd done your bit and you were on holiday now.'

'That's absolutely true. I could give you the excuse that Ted's a friend. I don't get to see him much when I'm down in London.'

'You could. I'll reserve the right to take that with a handful of salt. Any wounds anywhere I could rub it into?'

'All over the place. I can't guarantee that the conversation won't touch on the arson case. But if you're not too tired after the swimming, would you like to come with me?'

'So you're not going to sneak off this time without telling anyone.'

'Not without telling you.'

'Do I get to see a fire engine up close?'

'Yeah, if you want to. I can call him and we'll meet up at one of the fire stations. The guys there will undoubtedly tell you more than you ever wanted to know about a fire engine if you express even the mildest interest.'

She chuckled. 'In that case, you've definitely got a date.'

Day Four. Derwent Water. Four miles.

Four miles, and Nick was with her all the way. The stiff breeze, which whipped the water into white peaks, was not enough to stop Abby from making the distance within the planned time, and the group arrived back at the hotel to find that Louise was back and confined to her room.

'Thought you were going to have lunch upstairs with Louise?' Nick grinned at her as Abby sat down opposite him in the dining room.

'I was, but she got a better offer. Sam's up there with her.'

'Really?'

'Yes. Keep it quiet.'

'Why?' Nick looked puzzled.

Abby rolled her eyes. 'I thought you didn't miss anything. Louise thinks that Sam's really cute.'

'Sam? Cute?' The combination of the two words had obviously not occurred to Nick before. 'I've heard him called a few things, but cute's never been one of them. What have they been giving her in that hospital?'

'Don't be like that. Sam's really sweet. And he's obviously got a soft spot for Louise as well.'

Nick shrugged. 'Well you're obviously privy to some insider information here so I'll take your word for it.' He leaned across the table towards her, his words almost drowned in the hubbub of conversation around them. 'So what about me, then? Am I cute?'

'Not a chance.' Abby laughed at Nick's injured expression. 'You're *very cute*.'

He made a gesture of mock horror, but the grin didn't leave his face for the duration of the meal and he was still smiling when he collected Pete's car keys from him and ushered her out of the hotel.

'You look nice.' His hand strayed to the small of her back and stayed there and he leaned close as they walked. 'Extremely cute.'

'Thank you.' Abby felt her cheeks flush. She'd hoped that the time she'd taken with her appearance this afternoon wouldn't show.

'Sweet as well. You always look sweet.' His thumb moved against her spine. 'I like your hair loose. And that reddish colour suits you.'

'It's raspberry.' She reckoned her face was about the same shade as her woollen jacket at the moment.

'Hmm.' He took advantage of the fact that the car park was screened from view from the hotel by a stand of trees and twisted her round against the car, pressing his lips against hers. 'Not strawberry?'

'I don't think so.' She pulled him against her.

'Maybe I should make completely sure.' He kissed her again. Tender enough to melt her heart. Demanding enough to set it clamouring for more.

'Ow. What's that?' Something was digging into her ribs and Abby slid her fingers inside his fleece jacket and pulled a rolled-up newspaper from the deep inside pocket.

He chuckled quietly. 'Local newspaper. Mrs Pearce says that there's an article about us on page four.'

'Oh, well, let's have a look, then.' Abby unrolled the newspaper and spread it out on the roof of the car, turning the pages. 'Here it is.' She scanned the article carefully.

Nick was reading too, over her shoulder. Suddenly, abruptly, she felt him tense and then turn away.

'What? What's the matter, Nick?'

He wasn't looking at her. He didn't seem to be looking at anything in particular, just a point in the middle distance that didn't exist. Abby turned back to the newspaper, scanning the pages, and then she saw it. It took a moment for the words to sink in, and she reread them with growing horror as it became plain that her eyes were not deceiving her.

'What on earth....? Who wrote this? It's all lies!'

'No, Abby, it's not.' He leaned against the car next to her. 'There has been a spate of arson attacks in this area. I'm consulting with the local fire authorities. And I am an ex-junkie.' His eyes were dull. Dead.

She wanted to shake him. Or kick him. Anything to make him fight. 'It's not true, Nick. They're making it sound as if drug taking is the only thing you've ever done. Here...' she stabbed at the paper with her finger '...it says "*a drug user, currently suspended from active duty*".'

'I am.'

'You're someone who had a problem with drugs, overcame it years ago, and is now off sick with an unrelated injury, sustained in the course of duty. That's entirely different.' Abby grabbed his arm, digging her fingers into his biceps. 'Nick, stop this.'

'Yeah.' His grin barely made it to the sides of his lips, let alone up to his eyes. 'Nothing I can do about it. Best thing to do is just ignore it and get on with the job in hand.'

'Yes. Unless I see that creep of a reporter again.' Abby had noticed the name at the head of the article. 'How did this Graham Edson guy get all of this? We hardly spoke to him.'

Nick shrugged. 'Maybe Ted wanted to give me some good press and mentioned my name. Maybe Edson recognised my key fob when he picked my keys up and put two and two together. Rings up HR, gets chatting to someone and then slips in how good it is that I've been clean for a while. All it takes is for someone to agree, in all innocence, and he's got his confirmation.'

Abby felt sick. It was that easy to take a man's career and trash it in the papers. At least this was just a local paper. She swept the newspaper off the roof of the car, screwing it up into a tight ball, and stalked over to the wastepaper bin. She would have completed the gesture and set fire to it, only she knew that Nick's first instinct would be to put it out again.

He was still leaning against the car, watching her quietly. She couldn't bear this. The way he accepted it as if it was his due. Grabbing the front of his jacket, she pulled him close. 'We can deal with this.'

'Yeah.' His eyes had softened, but he kept his hands in his pockets. 'Look, what do you say we give this afternoon a miss?'

'Why? What else do you want to do?'

'I'll go and see Ted. I was just thinking that it would be better if you stayed here.'

She didn't need to ask. Abby knew exactly why Nick wanted her to stay behind. 'I don't think so.' If he thought that she was ashamed to be seen with him just because of a stupid newspaper article, he didn't know her very well.

'I may be taking a little flak because of this. Not from Ted, not from the guys here. But I don't want you to get mixed up with it, Abby.'

'You think I can't deal with whatever anyone dishes out?'

His shoulders relaxed a little. 'No. Will you be able to handle me not being able to deal with it?'

Abby grinned at him. 'Piece of cake. I can handle you any day of the week, Nick Hunter. Get into the car.'

Abby stuck to him like glue, sliding her fingers around the crook of his arm when they walked into the fire station together and practically needing to be prised away from him by the young firefighter who had volunteered to show her around while he talked business with Ted. Nick watched, a faint stab of resentment catching him as someone else's hands guided her up into the driver's seat of the fire truck, and then turned back to Ted.

'It's my fault. I should never have said anything about it.'

It was bad enough having to think about this latest humiliation, let alone talk about it, but Ted had obviously been beating himself up about it. 'I'm not in hiding, Ted, there's nothing wrong with mentioning my name. This might not be my choice, but it's not the end of the world. I always said that if it came out, it came out.'

Ted grunted, unconvinced. 'You never said anything of the sort.'

'If you say so. I always thought it, though.'

'Just thinking things doesn't get you anywhere.' Ted was looking at Abby, pointedly.

'Leave her out of it, Ted.'

'Is that what you're doing?'

'I'm trying.' Nick frowned. 'Without much success at the moment.'

Ted chuckled. 'That figures. Most women have a protective streak a mile wide.'

Abby wasn't most women. And Nick had been secretly loving the way she'd stuck by him so fiercely, like a mother bear with her cub. Ready to cuff him if he stepped out of line but reserving her full fury for anyone who dared to confront him. He didn't need her to defend him, but the idea that she wanted to gave him a reason to hold his head up and face the world.

'She doesn't need to protect me, Ted, and neither do you. I'm okay. I'm not in any trouble over this.'

'As long as you know where to come if you are.'

'Of course I do. Thanks, mate.'

He dragged his gaze from where Abby was inspecting the inside of the fire-engine cabin, questioning her guide closely on something. Even at this distance she seemed to shine. As if there was a light source behind her pale blue eyes that threw everything around her into shadow. Nick wondered how much he could do with his life, what things he could achieve, with her smile to guide him, and shelved the thought. It wasn't going to happen.

He turned, indicating the pile of papers under Ted's arm. They promised to be a great deal simpler to deal with. 'So. Are those just for show, or have you got something for me?'

CHAPTER TWELVE

Day Five. Ullswater. Two miles.

Two easy miles, in preparation for the big one tomorrow. Eleven swimmers set off and eleven made the finish, Abby way ahead of them as usual, and as usual was escorted home by Nick on the support boat.

He looked tired. Not surprising after last night. When they returned from the fire station his mood of smiling optimism had seemed to dissolve and he'd gone to his room, on the excuse that he had to do some work for Ted.

When she'd tapped on his door late in the evening, he'd received her with a smile and asked her to stay, but he'd sat up most of the night in a small pool of light in the corner of the room, his laptop open in front of him.

He disappeared again after lunch, leaving Abby to spend the afternoon with Louise, who slept most of the time. By dinnertime she was bored with her book and frustrated with Nick.

'You're back.' She hardly raised her eyes from the pages when he knocked on Louise's door and quietly entered the room.

'I haven't been anywhere. She's asleep?'

'Yes.' Was that all he could say? He hadn't left the hotel but he'd been somewhere all right. With his father, maybe, telling him yet again to get out of his life and stay out. The ghost of a man that Abby didn't even know hung in the air between them, clamouring to be heard in the silence. Nick's brow furrowed and he beckoned her out of the room.

'What's up? Is she okay?'

'Yes, she's fine. She's had a major infection, it's taken it out of her.'

'Yes. Of course.' He sighed, running his hand back through his hair. 'As long as that's all it is.'

Abby shot him a glare. 'This is not about Louise. I'm more concerned about you.'

'Me?' He started guiltily. That slide of his eyes to one side, the way he couldn't quite face her told Abby that he had some inkling of what she was getting at.

Grabbing his hand, she marched him along the corridor and down the stairs to his room, closing the door firmly behind them. 'Why do I always have to prise everything out of you, Nick? I know when something's going on because you disappear on me. Can't you just talk to me?'

'I've got nothing to say, Abby. If you have, you'd better say it.'

The atmosphere in the room began to sizzle, like a pan heated up to boiling point, the lid rattling ominously. It felt good. At least Abby knew that Nick was there, not far away, in some place of his own that she couldn't reach.

'Fair enough. Some idiot writes something in a newspaper about you and suddenly you're hiding yourself away up in your room, pretending to work. Not sleeping. What do you think's going to happen? Do you truly believe that anyone who knows you is going to care?'

'I'm not *pretending* to work. And, yes, since you ask, I wouldn't blame anyone for thinking it makes a difference. I do.'

'Right. I know you do. If you want to think less of yourself because of what your father did and because something you did bore some faint resemblance to that, that's your prerogative. But don't expect me or Sam or Pete to just fall into line and think the worst of you because that's not what friends do. Have a little respect for us.'

'That's not fair, Abby. I respect you. I respect Sam and Pete.' He turned away from her and started to pace. Not a good sign. Pacing generally didn't augur well for any kind of amicable ending. Abby felt her shoulders slump and pulled herself upright to disguise her misery.

'Fine way you have of showing it.' She threw the words at him with an effort. If he was going to turn away from her again, she may as well get what she wanted to say off her chest.

His dark eyes blazed with defiance. 'Dammit, Abby, you don't know…'

'Then tell me. Show me. Don't just hide behind the mistakes you've made. Have the guts to come out and make some more.' Her chin was tilted aggressively towards him, and he took a step closer to her.

He took hold of her shoulders and the hairs on the back of her neck suddenly stood to attention. 'So what do you suggest I do?'

'Go downstairs and talk to them, Nick. It won't be the first time you've gone into a tough situation, knowing that they have your back.'

'This is different.'

'It's not. Trust me, Nick, it's not different.'

He pulled her towards him, wrapping his arms around her shoulders. Abby could hear his heart pumping, feel the kiss that he dropped on the top of her head. 'I…I do trust you, Abby.' The admission was obviously a difficult one for him to make, but it was a good one to hear, and Abby snuggled in closer to him.

'Let's go downstairs, then.'

'No. Not yet.' His hand slid down her back, turning the last dregs of anger into desire. 'Once again, we have unfinished business.'

Plenty of it. The energy that had been buzzing between them was sparking, crackling, looking for some kind of outlet. She reached up, finding the spot at the corner of his jaw that always made him shiver. 'So finish it, then.'

Nick had been as good as his word. It hadn't been easy for him, but he'd spread the newspaper on the table, in the lounge, made his confession and let Pete and Sam question him. It had been okay. Difficult, but okay. Just as she'd known it would be. And from the way Nick had squeezed her hand when he'd thought no one had been looking, it seemed that it was a relief to him as well.

They both lay on their backs on Nick's bed, staring at the canopy over their heads, talking. Both were fully clothed, and Abby wondered whether getting undressed and seducing him again would quell her night-before nerves. She guessed so, but Nick was having none of it, adamant that she needed to get a good night's sleep before swimming in the morning.

'What's the time?'

'Ten-thirty. You sleepy?' Nick raised himself up on one elbow.

'Yes. Kind of.'

'You think you might sleep if we went to bed?'

'Probably not.' Abby stretched and yawned. 'Perhaps in a while.'

'Okay. Come here.' He rolled her over on her side and curled up behind her. That felt so good. Leaning against his body, completely safe. Totally secure. Abby began to drift.

Quite what it was that woke her up, Abby wasn't sure. Maybe the crash of breaking glass. Maybe Nick, on the alert and rolling off the bed, dragging her with him. Whatever it was, Abby's eyes were open and she was wide awake before a sheet of flame began to engulf the curtains.

She was running before she could even think, Nick behind her, pushing her forwards towards the door. As soon as he made the corridor, he slammed the door closed behind him.

'What was that?' She asked the question to thin air. Nick was already halfway down the hallway, punching the alarm point on the wall, and bells echoed through the building. Pulling one of the two fire extinguishers that were fixed to the wall by the fire doors that led to the stairs, he lifted the heavy cylinder effortlessly.

He was going to go back in there. Abby wanted to scream at him, stop him somehow, but she swallowed her words. *This is his job. He knows what he's doing.*

Sam appeared from a nearby door, fully dressed, and gravitated to Nick's side. 'What's going on?'

'Something just came through my window. Looks like a petrol bomb. Check all the rooms in case there's

anything else and get everyone together in the downstairs hallway. Get a couple of men outside, checking
the grounds, and you find Louise and make sure she
gets downstairs safely.'

'Okay, boss.' Other members of the team were ap-
pearing in the hallway, some dressed and others hastily pulling on their clothes, having already gone to bed.
Sam quickly deployed the men and made for the stairs
in the direction of Louise's room.

Abby flattened herself against the wall, acrid smoke
entering her lungs. This wasn't good. She should get
out but she couldn't leave Nick. She couldn't help him
but she wouldn't leave him.

'Downstairs, Abby. With the others.' It was a point-
blank command. Nick beckoned to one of the men, and
the two of them gingerly opened the door, Nick going
in first with the fire extinguisher.

Abby got halfway down the hallway. Far enough to
be out of the way but close enough that she'd be there
for Nick if he needed her. He seemed to have everything
under control, but this was a volatile situation. People
got hurt in volatile situations.

Nick had said it was a petrol bomb. Was this the
work of the fire-raiser? She supposed it must be. Why
here, though? She tried to go through all of the possibilities in her head, but she couldn't think. All she
needed to know, right now, was that the fire was out
and Nick was safe.

It seemed like an age, but finally he reappeared, his
face and arms streaked with smoke and sweat. 'Abby…'
There was a warning note to his voice.

'I heard. Is it out?'

'Yeah. We need to keep an eye on it, in case it reignites, but we got to it quickly.' He shook his head slightly, as if he knew that he'd been diverted from his original purpose. 'What are you doing still here?'

'Looking out for you two.'

'I told you...'

'Yes I know what you told me.'

He rolled his eyes, but he was grinning. 'Fire is *my* job.'

'And potential casualties are mine.'

He shrugged, as if he knew that he wasn't going to get any further on this one. He was learning. 'Would you like to go downstairs and see if you can find any casualties down there, then? I'm afraid we're a bit short on any here.' He lifted his head as Sam hurried through the fire doors. 'Status?'

'There was another minor one in the dining room. All under control, no one hurt. We've called the police and the local fire service.' Sam grinned. 'Thought we'd better let them know we've been putting fires out on their patch.'

'Right. Where is everyone?'

'In the hallway. Louise is down there too.'

'Okay, we'll keep them there for the time being. It'll be easier to keep everyone safe if they're not wandering around outside. Everyone's got their eyes open?'

'Yep. I've got the guys checking outside and inside in twos.'

'Good. Nice job, Sam.'

Sam nodded. Nick's praise went unremarked on, but it was clearly not unheard. 'Do you think this is all there's going to be?'

'I don't know.' Nick was obviously worried. 'Will

you stay here until you're sure that this one's safe? Got your phone?'

'Yes. Where's yours, though?'

Nick grinned. 'Let's see. It might be toast.'

Abby followed them into Nick's room. There were dark stains on the ceiling, the curtains were hanging in tatters, flapping in the breeze from the broken window. The smell of smoke and petrol. Abby didn't look at the black, charred section of carpet, just a few feet from the end of the bed, where whatever had been thrown through the window had rolled across the floor.

Nick picked up his phone from the bedside cabinet, checking it quickly. 'Looks okay.' A tone sounded from Sam's pocket. 'Yeah. Call me with anything.'

He caught Abby's hand and made for the door. 'We're off downstairs to find some casualties for the lady.'

'She can start with me. Louise bit me when I tried to carry her down the stairs. I might have blood poisoning.' Sam's voice floated after them.

'Serves you right,' Nick called back over his shoulder, without stopping.

CHAPTER THIRTEEN

HE HUSTLED her downstairs, where Pete was supervising while Mrs Pearce bellowed names from the hotel register, liberally dispensing her displeasure when people failed to answer promptly. Nick shot Pete a querying glance and Pete nodded. All okay down here.

Nick didn't let go of Abby's hand, and she followed him into the dining room. Partners, maybe? Or perhaps he just wanted to keep her close so he could keep an eye on her. He bent to inspect the charred carpet, wincing as he did so. In the heat of the moment Abby had forgotten all about his knee and Nick obviously had too.

'This one doesn't look as big as the other. Look.' He indicated the broken window. 'It came through there, but luckily the curtains were drawn back so they didn't catch. This is the seat of the fire, and it's definitely not as big as the one in my room.'

'So…' Abby couldn't see where he was going with this.

'So I reckon this one was the first. Then whoever it was moved past the front door, down that way.' He pointed towards the side of the building where his room was situated.

'What is this, Nick? Is it something to do with the arson cases that you're working on?'

'Looks like it. I imagine that he's been following his own press.'

Fear clutched at Abby's heart. 'You mean…he's after you?'

'I'm the one who got his name in the paper. And with all the publicity for the swimming, it wouldn't be too difficult to track me down.' His lips compressed into a thin line. 'I'm sorry, Abby, I've got you mixed up in this.'

'No, you haven't.' She dismissed the idea with a wave of her hand. 'So what do you think he's going to do next? Might he still be here?'

'That's my immediate concern. We need to know that everyone's safe and that there are no more petrol bombs about to come through any of the windows.' His face had a look of sheer, unstoppable determination. 'And catching him would be good.'

'Where do you think he might go next?'

'Probably kept going in the same direction then around the side of the building. There's plenty of cover around there from trees and bushes, and you can see what's happening at the front.' He seemed to come to some decision and he was on the move, halfway to the door. 'Come along.'

He led her upstairs and through the maze of corridors in the sprawling building, stopping opposite the door of Louise's room. 'We can see most of the side area from here.'

Flipping off the hall light, he took her hand and opened the door. Abby followed him into the darkened room, watching as he gingerly parted the curtains. 'Okay, stay low. Have a look around and see what you can see.'

She strained against the darkness outside, rough shapes emerging as her eyes began to acclimatise. 'Nick! Look, there's someone there.'

His hand was on her arm, steadying her. Or maybe stopping her from doing anything that he hadn't approved first. 'I see him.' Flame showed briefly behind a cupped hand, illuminating the face of a young man. Nick cursed quietly. 'The idiot's lighting a cigarette.'

Nick obviously wasn't worried about his lungs at the moment. Fire safety for arsonists. It would have been funny if the situation wasn't so serious.

Something flared and arced through the air. Nick almost threw her across the room towards the door, rugby-tackling her to the floor in the hallway. A whooshing sound reached her ears and she fought for breath.

'Get off me.' His weight was pinning her to the floor. Warm. Protective. And she couldn't breathe. He looked around quickly and then rolled away from her.

No flames or smoke. Nick was on his feet again, loping to the end of the hallway and opening the fire-escape door, and as she followed him Abby could see why. A petrol bomb had lodged in the branches of a tree, which was beginning to burn fiercely.

The sound of sirens came in the distance, suddenly swelling as flashing lights rounded the corner and a fire engine came to a stop outside, closely followed by a couple of police cars. Men were running towards the side of the building, and the dark shape below broke cover.

'Don't...' Nick roared into the darkness, and half slid, half ran down the fire-escape steps. His quarry had obviously decided that there was time for one last assault, and flame flared in his hand. This time, though, there was no uplifted arm, swinging the deadly missile towards them.

Fire shot across the grass at his feet, and the figure jumped back and started to run. Flames were flickering around his arm, where he had spilled some of the petrol, and she heard Nick's cry of frustration as his leg finally gave way and he fell to the ground.

'Get down.' He was shouting now, scrambling towards the figure. 'Roll on the ground.'

The fleeing shape ignored him. Whether from panic, or pain, or determination not to be caught by the police, who were closing in fast, Abby couldn't tell. She ran down the fire-escape steps, following Nick across the uneven ground.

Their quarry took the low fence to the road in one bound. Unable to slow his momentum, or maybe unable to see the danger, he threw himself right into the path of an oncoming car.

Nick let out a roar of agony. The young man's body catapulted upwards, as if suspended by invisible wires, which then snapped and dumped him back onto the roadway in a tangle of limbs.

He reached the motionless body a moment before one of the policemen, who stripped off his jacket and helped Nick douse what was left of the flames. By some instinct he seemed to know that Abby was right behind him, and he turned, yelling at the converging policemen, 'Let her through. She's a doctor.'

She knelt down in the middle of the road, police officers standing on both sides of her to stop any oncoming traffic. Somewhere in the back of her head, from the direction of the car, which had slewed wildly across the road, a woman's wails registered.

'We've got you, mate. Lie still and let the doctor look at you. Hang on.' Nick's voice. Trying to get through to a wounded man, give him some comfort.

She heard him call to a police officer to fetch a first-aid kit from one of the police cars. Unzipping the man's jacket, she quickly inspected the damage. The thick padding of his jacket had protected him from the fire, and his arm was pretty much untouched. It was the collision with the car that had done all the damage.

'What do you need, Abby?'

Her brain clicked into autopilot. 'Gloves…' She snapped on the surgical gloves and cleared the man's mouth. 'His breathing's shallow. Get someone to apply pressure to that leg to stop the bleeding.'

Nick passed another pair of gloves and padding from the first-aid kit to one of the policemen who had come shouldering his way through the group that had formed around them and reported as a first-aider.

She was dimly aware of the fact that Nick was holding the man's hand, and she could hear him talking to him. Trying to find a way to get through to him, tell him that someone was here for him and that he should live, not die here on the road.

'See if you can find a pulse.' Abby searched for some glimmer of hope and found it, beating threadily under her fingers and then slowing to a stop.

'CPR.' She braced herself over the man's chest and started to count. What she wouldn't do for a defibrillator right now. Adrenaline. Anything that might help save her patient. The sound of her own voice, counting, seemed unnaturally strident over the murmur of activity around them.

'Paramedic's here.'

'Right. Take over the chest compressions, will you, Nick, while we set up the defibrillator and the ventilation?'

She knew what needed to be done, but Abby also knew that she probably didn't have as much hands-on experience of this kind of thing as a paramedic. A man's life depended on her making the right decisions now.

'He's in asystole.'

Abby assessed the reading from the defibrillator carefully. It was her call, but she wanted the paramedic's view as well. 'I don't see any sign of VF.'

'Agreed.'

'He's not shockable, then. We'll give him adrenaline and continue CPR.'

They worked together for twenty minutes. Twenty minutes when there was little hope of even the slightest glimmer of life, but Abby wouldn't give up until they'd done everything according to the book. Finally she sat back on her heels.

It was her responsibility to declare the man dead, and she went through all the checks, waiting for the paramedic's agreement at each step. She took a deep breath. This was the first time she'd done this. 'I'm pronouncing him dead,' and followed it with the time.

She stripped off her surgical gloves, throwing them into the bucket that someone had provided for waste disposal. It seemed too heartless to just stand up and walk away, leave the man lying here on the road, the cannula and all the other paraphernalia that had been used to save him still in place. She knew they had to stay for the coroner's examination, but it seemed wrong somehow.

Nick laid the man's hand down on his chest, and Abby realised that somehow he had managed to keep hold of it the whole time, without getting in the way of the work that she and the paramedic had been doing. At least there was that. Whenever the fragile spark of life had left that broken body, the man hadn't been completely alone.

Through the numbness she could feel Nick pulling her gently to her feet and guiding her away from the body. 'You're done here, Abby.'

She wouldn't cling to him now. Wouldn't cry either. She was surrounded by men who had seen this all before and she shouldn't let them know it was her first time. She'd seen death before, but she'd never been the one that everyone had looked to for those final words.

Nick did her the courtesy of not saying anything. There was nothing he could have said, he must know that. Just being here was good enough. The paramedic, on the other hand, seemed anxious to speak to her.

'Where are you from?'

'London. I work down in London.'

The man held out his hand. 'Steven Bell. Pleasure to meet you.'

Abby took his hand with trembling fingers, conscious that those few words were praise indeed from a man like this. The stoical, seen-it-all guys who spent their days on one of the sharpest ends of a tough profession. 'Thank you. Um…me too.'

She wasn't sure what she was meant to do next. Was she supposed to stay here? Sign something? Nick would know, he had to have seen this kind of thing before, but she didn't like to ask him in front of everyone. Abby was contemplating her next move when Nick made it for her, turning to Steven. 'The police will handle things from here on in?'

'Yes. I just need to get my paperwork straight and then I'll be off. This is my last call for this shift.'

Nick nodded. 'Cup of tea?'

'Yes. Thanks.'

She knew the exchange was all for her benefit, but she didn't care. Nick put his arm round Abby's shoulder and she followed his lead as he turned away from the little knot of people around the body.

It was two in the morning before Nick contrived to slip away with Abby to her room. He had insisted that she give her statement here and not at the police station, and tried to hurry things up, but there had beern procedures to go through. A man had died.

Abby had been keeping it all together, helping Mrs Pearce with tea and sandwiches for everyone, calmly recounting the events of the evening when questioned. She wasn't the sort to break down under pressure, and he respected her for it, but he hoped that now the pressure was off, she would start to let go.

She sat down on the bed, seeming weary suddenly, as if someone had tied lead weights to her limbs. Maybe she would talk about it now they were alone. Maybe not.

'Let's get you into the shower, eh?'

She sighed. 'You go first. I just want to sit here for a moment.'

He didn't want to leave her alone, but this wasn't about what he wanted—it was about what she needed. 'Okay. I'll be right here. Just call if you want me.'

'Yes. Thanks.'

When he emerged from the bathroom, pulling on a clean T-shirt that he'd borrowed from Sam, she was in exactly the same place that he had left her, still staring at her hands. He sat down beside her, careful not to touch her arm with his, and she hardly registered his presence.

'Some people…some people you just can't save. You know that as well as I do.'

'Yeah. I just feel so…' She shrugged. 'You know.'

'Yeah. I know.' That sickening feeling of loss, of helplessness, when things went horribly wrong and someone died. The first time was always the worst, but it didn't get much better after that. 'But you did everything that could have been done, Abby. Everything.'

'You think so? I just keep thinking…'

If anyone was to blame, it was him. He'd tried to reach the guy, put out the flames that had been licking around his sleeve, and he'd run. Maybe if he hadn't chased after him. Or if his knee had been stronger and he'd been able to catch him before he reached the road…

Now wasn't the time for those thoughts. He needed to focus on Abby, who seemed to be trying her damnedest to accept the blame that ought to be apportioned to him. 'I think that there was nothing more you could have done.'

She nodded. 'Why did he do it, Nick? I don't understand.'

'Fire-raising isn't the most logical of pursuits.' Nick wished he had a better answer for her. There was a time for thinking about motives and the sheer bloody waste of it all, and in his experience two o'clock in the morning wasn't it. 'Come along. You need to shower now, sweetheart.'

She looked up at him, gratitude in her eyes. 'Thanks for looking out for me, Nick.'

He shrugged. 'Forget it.' His own words seemed to stab at him, right between the ribs where his heart beat. 'No, on second thoughts, don't forget it.' He took her hands between his. 'I want you to remember, Abby, that you don't have to deal with everything alone. That there are people out there for you.'

She seemed just as much taken aback by what he'd said as he was at saying it. Nick gave them both a moment to digest it and then got to his feet. She took the hint and followed him to the bathroom.

'What about the woman who was driving the car? I thought I saw the police breathalysing her.'

Her mind was obviously still worrying at the loose ends from the evening, and if the truth was told there were plenty of them. 'Yep. They took her down to the police station. One of the guys told me that the breathalyser reading was positive.'

Abby slumped down into the chair in front of the mirror, staring at herself, as if the answers were there, written on her face. 'It all just seems so…so sad.'

'Yes. It is.' He made an effort to smile and even the watery result seemed to cheer her a little. 'But you said it yourself. We can't do everything, but we do our best. That has to be good enough.'

A tear rolled down her cheek. Nick watched it, realising that this was the first time he'd ever seen her cry. All she'd been through, and she'd saved the tears that might have been shed for herself to spend on a man who had tried to do her harm. Before he could do anything to comfort her, she had brushed it away.

'I don't suppose you noticed whether there was any hot chocolate left in the kitchen?'

Nick wasn't sure whether she really wanted hot chocolate, or whether she wanted to get rid of him. Or maybe she was just responding to his need to do something, anything, for her right now. Whatever. 'I'll go and see.'

When he returned, the sound of the shower running was filtering out from the bathroom. He put the Thermos mug down on the cabinet by the side of the bed, and then he heard it. The quiet sound of her weeping.

Abby wasn't sure why she had sent Nick away. Force of habit, she guessed. As she scrubbed at her body, cleaning away the blood that had soaked through the fabric of her jeans and the grime that streaked her arms and face, she half wished that he had ignored her and stayed.

You don't have to deal with everything alone. Nick had been there for her tonight. He'd known when to take charge and when to stand back and let her get on with what she had to do. Even then, she'd felt his strength.

The thought that it wasn't always going to be this way drove her to her knees, one hand over her mouth to silence the sounds of her tears. When she cried, she cried alone, always. And yet this time she wanted Nick to hold her.

She didn't hear the bathroom door open and she had no time to compose herself when he opened the shower door. There was no time to protest when he stepped inside, shutting off the flow of the water and lifting her to her feet and into his arms.

'It's okay, sweetheart.'

'It isn't, Nick. A man died.'

'That's not what I mean.' He caught a towel up, wrapping it around her shoulders, still keeping her body pressed safe against his. 'It's okay to feel afraid. To feel the pain when the odds are just too much against us, and we fail.'

Suddenly the dam broke. Abby reached for him, and hung on as tightly as she would have gripped a lifebelt thrown into stormy seas. Sobbing into his chest until she was breathless and gasping for air, then crying some more.

'That's it, sweetheart.' He seemed to understand that she wasn't just crying for tonight. That she was crying for all the other nights when she'd had no one to hold onto.

Finally the sobs subsided and embarrassment began to set in. 'Sorry.'

'Don't you dare.' He tilted her face up towards his, brushing her cheek with his thumb. 'We all cry, Abby. The best of us do it with a friend.'

She couldn't help a smile. Just a small one. 'You're all wet.'

'Mmm. So are you.' He wrapped the towel around her more firmly. 'We'll dry off, get into bed, and I'll hold you. Keep the wolves at bay.'

'Yours too?'

'Yep. Mine too. Tomorrow's a big day.'

'Today.' The thought of curling up with Nick soothed her. Maybe she would be able to sleep a little after all. 'It's today already.'

CHAPTER FOURTEEN

Day Six. Lake Windermere. Six long miles.

THE sky was an unbroken sheet of grey cloud, and the water was choppy in the stiff breeze. Today, of all days, the weather had decided to turn.

Her back ached. Her shoulders hurt from the efforts of last night out on the road, trying to save someone who could not be saved. Abby tried not to think about it. She could no longer help him, but there were other people she could help, if she did this swim.

Wading into the cold water, she swam for a while, up and down, getting used to the temperature and easing the aches in her body. She was swimming alone today. The small group of swimmers was on the jetty, ready to cheer her off and then drive to the finishing point. But Nick would be there. As he always was, on the boat, which was bobbing up and down by the starting point, ready to accompany her around the course.

'Okay, Abby?' She could see him waving and his voice drifted across the water. She struck out for the starting buoy.

* * *

Two miles. Already she was beginning to feel tired, and her shoulders were aching. It had been agreed that she would take feeds from the boat every two miles to help her keep her energy levels up, and Abby slowed, treading water as the boat closed in.

They were losing time, but it didn't matter. All that mattered was making the finish and she needed some nourishment today. Something to lift her spirits. Every time she'd started to get into a rhythm, the dull beat of a heart, which slowed and stopped, had echoed in her head.

Nick appeared at the side of the boat, leaning over so far that his shoulder was almost in the water. 'Here.' He handed her a warm drink and she took it from him, the brief almost-touch of his fingers more welcome than the drink.

'That's better.' She drank it down and threw the cup back onto the deck, behind him.

'Are your shoulders okay?' He was there again, this time handing her half a banana.

She hadn't said anything about her aches and pains, afraid that Nick wouldn't let her swim. He must have seen her easing her back and shoulders, though, before she'd got into the water. Noticed her erratic stroke.

'Yeah, fine. Just a little stiff.' She was feeling better already, although whether that was from the food and drink or the heat of his smile, she wasn't sure.

'Can you get a rhythm going?' He seemed to know exactly what the problem was.

'I'll try.' It was all she could promise.

'You have great rhythm.' His grin and the quick wink, which were just for her, were unmistakeable in their meaning. Abby flipped a few droplets of water to-wards him, and he laughed. 'Go for it, honey.'

She turned in the water, striking out away from the boat. Nick stayed by the side of the craft, his weight making it list slightly, signalling to Pete to stay in as close as possible. She could hear his voice, although it seemed miles away, calling out the beat of her strokes, and she focussed on that, trying to follow his lead.

Four miles. She was starting to flag again, and this time she reached a deeper pit than the last. The finish point looked about a hundred miles away and fatigue was thundering through her body, demanding that she give up. It had started to rain, and she could see almost nothing through her goggles, but she could feel the in-creasing choppiness of the water.

Nick again. Handing her a warm drink. Hazily she noticed that he was wearing a wetsuit, and wondered when he had put that on.

'Status, Abby.' His voice was warm, cajoling.

'My status is…shit.' Suddenly she couldn't go on. She wanted to be up in the boat. It wasn't the lake that had conquered her, it was everything else that had hap-pened over the past few days.

'Sure it is.' She felt rather than saw his bulk sliding over the side of the boat and into the water. 'But you'll keep going.'

Damn him! She didn't want to keep going. She wanted to go back to the hotel and curl up somewhere warm and comfortable. But he was waving the boat away, and there was still a spark of something, deep down, that told her that she wasn't finished yet.

He started swimming and she followed him. Stroke

for stroke. They swam together, Nick breathing to the right and Abby to the left so that they could see each other. One. Two. Then she saw his face in the water beside her. She kept going for that, ignoring the pain in her shoulders and back, living just to see his face one more time.

No words. No signals or glances. He was just there, swimming next to her. That meant more than anything. In a haze of determination and fatigue, her muscles screaming for respite, she just kept going, forgetting about anything other than the fact that he was there.

'Couple of hundred yards. Keep going.' His voice again. Was she really nearly there? Abby focussed in the direction she knew the finishing buoy must be, and saw it. Bobbing up and down in the water, and suddenly more beautiful than a buoy had any right to be.

She struck out for it, and then her fingers touched it. As they did so, she felt his arm around her in the water, supporting her. She held one aching arm up as a signal she'd touched home, and a cheer floated out across the water from the spectators lined up along the shoreline.

Exhilaration flooded through her. The boat was closing in, ready to pick them up, and she waved it away. 'I want to swim in.'

'That's my girl.' Nick was grinning broadly. Abby struck out for the shore and he followed, swimming with her until they were close enough in for their feet to touch the bottom.

He didn't touch her. Didn't help or support her as she struggled out of the water. She knew why. It had been her swim. He wasn't going to spoil that at the last minute. And even if she'd done six miles, and more, on plenty of occasions before, this one was different. She'd overcome so much more this time.

She fell to her hands and knees on the slippery pebbles and he bent towards her. 'Stand up, Abby. You walk out, you don't crawl.'

His words jerked her to her feet. Just another couple of steps and she was clear of the water, and he had his arm around her waist, supporting her as her frozen, jelly-like legs made out that they were walking up the shingle. Letting her accept the wild delight of her welcoming committee for a few moments, he hustled her up to the windbreak that the team had erected by the side of a steep incline and guided her into its cover.

Numbly, she registered that he had her out of her wetsuit and costume and wrapped in a towel. Woolly hat, woollen socks and gloves to warm her frozen fingers. Warm trousers and a sweater then a jacket. It occurred to Abby that Nick had a talent for this. He'd got her out of her wetsuit and then raised her body temperature faster than seemed humanly possible.

'Thanks, Sam.' He acknowledged the mug that had suddenly appeared around the edge of the windbreak, the hand disappearing again in deference to the chance that one square inch of Abby's flesh might be exposed. 'What's so funny?'

'You.' She took the mug gratefully and took a sip. 'You're not as good at dressing me as undressing me. My jumper's on back to front.'

'Not so much practice. Or enthusiasm for the job.' He stripped off his wetsuit and grabbed the towel, winding it around his waist. 'I've got a change of clothes in the van.'

He'd come prepared. Known that she would be struggling this morning and had quietly gone about his own arrangements to support her, if she needed it. Gratitude warmed Abby's shivering limbs. Being there for her hadn't just been chance—he'd made sure of it, right from the start.

She followed him out of the cover of the windbreak, watching while he limped across the stony ground to the van. This had taken its toll on him as well.

A wolf whistle cut the air, making Abby jump. She'd turned her back on Nick and gone to accept the hugs and congratulations of the others while he opened the back of the van and got dressed. Abby imagined that no one was under any illusions about the nature of their relationship, but she didn't want to make it obvious by leering at him. She could look all she wanted later.

'What are you doing here, Lou?' His laughing voice was directed towards Sam's car, where Louise sat, wearing even more layers of clothing than Abby was.

'Enjoying the view, boss.' Louise wound down the window and leaned out. 'Wanna go through those moves again?'

Everyone laughed. Nick shook his head, buttoning his jeans and pulling a sweater over his head. After shave, again. Man runs out of water. Towels himself dry. Pulls sweater over perfectly muscled torso. Slowly. Nick was a real loss to the advertising industry.

Abby pushed those thoughts to the back of her head. Everyone else seemed to be taking the joke in good part, including Nick, who laughed at the barrage of comments from the crew, and disappeared into the back of the van, looking for his shoes. Limping back over towards her, he joined the group.

'Are you going to wait while we clear up and get the buoys in?' Sam turned to Abby. 'Or I can run you back to the hotel? I'm dropping Lou back there now. I just brought her out for half an hour to see the finish.'

'I'll stay.' Abby wanted to be with the team. Part of the jocular, no-holds-barred banter that they batted back and forth between them. Close to Nick, who was often the butt of their jokes but never seemed to retaliate beyond a slow shake of the head and a shrugging laugh. He was in charge, but never needed to show it. Teasing and jibes didn't seem so bad in this atmosphere.

Sam nodded and began to trudge across the shingle towards the car, leaving Abby to cajole Nick into sitting down with her in the shelter of the van. 'Where's your knee support?' She'd noticed that Nick had been moving gingerly across the rough ground.

'On the boat. The one I use for swimming is wet.' He grinned at her. 'It's okay.'

'Doesn't look it. Does it hurt?'

'Not really. I'm just tired. It gets weaker when I get tired. Perhaps you'll take a look at it when we get back to the hotel.'

He must be tired. But Abby knew he wouldn't leave, any more than she would, until everything was packed up. She took the excuse of keeping warm and snuggled against him, watching as the boat drew up at the jetty and a couple of the men jumped aboard so they could help Pete haul the buoys in and bring them back to shore.

'I've been meaning to ask you.' Nick broke the silence.

'Ask away, then.'

She felt his chest heave as he took a breath. 'I know you were going to go home tomorrow. But the rest of us are staying here for another four days.'

'Yes?' Louise had already asked if she would stay over the weekend and Abby had already said yes. But she wanted Nick to ask. More than she had thought it was possible to want anything. Abby held her breath.

'So it would be great for Lou if you stayed. You could keep an eye on her.'

Disappointment curled around Abby's heart. 'Louise doesn't need me here.'

'No.'

'Right, then.' Maybe she would go home tomorrow after all.

'I do.'

She wanted to take the admission in her stride. Pretend that it didn't mean everything to her. It was just four days and then they'd go back to London and she would lose Nick again, for good. But it was four days of rest, relaxation and, if Abby had any say in the matter, more of that mind-blowing sex. Surely no one who could make love that way could be entirely unreachable. She was grasping at straws, and she knew it.

'Okay.'

'Yeah?' His grin said it all. The mind-blowing sex was a done deal.

'Yeah.' She smiled up at him. 'You only had to ask.'

The group of swimmers stayed together as a long, late lunch morphed into celebratory drinks at the bar and then into dinner. Abby made the effort to stay awake, but after dinner her fatigue began to overtake her again and she went to her room. Nick would join her later. The exchanged glance, his smile and the answering excitement in the pit of her stomach told her so.

She was dimly aware of him having been there during the night, but he hadn't woken her. Abby woke late, stretching her stiff limbs gingerly, to find that she was alone.

Nick must be up and around already. A stab of disappointment marred the dawning of what otherwise seemed to be a perfect day. Maybe he'd gone to get breakfast. Breakfast in bed would be nice.

As if responding to a cue, the doorhandle twisted silently and the door opened. Nick appeared, accompanied by the smell of coffee.

'Mmm. Just what I need this morning.'

'Thought you might.' He smiled at her and Abby's heart froze. He'd put the coffee down on the small writing desk in the corner of the room and sat upright on the hard-backed chair. His smile was nothing like the one he usually wore in the mornings.

'What's up?'

'Have some coffee.' He poured her a coffee and handed it to her, leaving the other cup and the plate of croissants on the tray untouched.

'What's going on, Nick?'

'I have to leave.' He looked at his watch. 'In about fifteen minutes.'

'Why?' All Abby could think about were four words, playing and replaying in the back of head. *He said he'd stay.*

He planted his elbows on his knees, hands clasped tightly together. 'When I checked my emails first thing this morning there was one from yesterday, from the fire authority down in London. I've just called them, and they want to see me as soon as possible.'

'What about?' The look on his face told Abby that this couldn't be good.

'About the job offer they've made me. Seems that they were contacted yesterday by a national paper for a comment on the story that appeared in the newspaper here the other day.'

'What? But, Nick, I thought they already knew about your addiction. What on earth's going on?'

'They did...do...know. I was completely upfront with them. But this is a very public-facing job and it's a newly created post. Putting someone in who's just been disgraced in the papers might not be such a good idea. Politically speaking.'

Abby stared at him. 'So they're going to withdraw the job offer just because someone tells lies about you in the paper? That's not fair. I'm not entirely sure it's even legal.'

He shook his head abruptly. 'No, that's not the way it is, Abby. They just want to talk to me, about a little damage limitation. But if it's clear to me that taking up that job is going to hurt the service in any way, I'll be the first to pass on it. It's not just the story in the news-papers now. A man was killed the other night as well.'

'That wasn't your fault either. Nick, I know that this looks bad, but we can fight it. We can answer every single one of their questions and show them that you're not to blame for any of this.' Abby was pleading with him. Willing him to refocus. See things with the clar-ity with which she could see them.

A glimmer of gratitude showed in his eyes and it al-most made Abby break down. Nick shouldn't need to be grateful for the truth. He was the most honourable man she knew, and this wasn't fair. 'We'll see.'

'Well, we have to tell them.' Abby put her cup and saucer down, and stood up. 'I'll be ready in ten minutes.'

He caught her arm. '*I* am going to tell them.'

'I was there, Nick. I saw what happened. Look, we don't have time to argue about this.'

'No, we don't.' He held her arm firmly. 'I'm going down to London to answer their questions. That's all it is, questions. No one's made a decision on anything yet.'

The look on his face made Abby shiver. 'What about you? Have you made a decision?'

'I won't be the one who brings the work of the fire service into disrepute. If I'm not going to be able to represent them properly, I'll step aside.'

'No. No, Nick, you can't do that. I won't let you. Surely the fire service won't let you.'

'They won't have any say in the matter. Neither do you.' His words were chilling enough. The look of grim determination on his face was even worse.

'Don't, Nick. Please don't...' Abby wondered whether tears would sway him. Probably not. They'd just make him feel worse about what he was going to do. She couldn't cry to order anyway.

His face softened. Maybe he knew that her heart was sobbing, screaming in pain. 'Abby, you can't stop me. Please, don't make this any more difficult than it already is. I have to go. Alone.'

'But... No, Nick, I'll go with you.'

'I said no.' The grim, lifeless look had recaptured his features. 'Abby, we were clear about this, right from the start. We were never going to keep things going between us when we got back to London. I sorry, but I have to go back now.' Abby knew what he was thinking. He'd been here once before, his job in jeopardy, the future uncertain. Nick was in damage-control mode. If they didn't have a relationship, then he couldn't ruin it.

He didn't wait for her answer. Abruptly he let go of her arm and he was out of the door before she could gather her wits, the scrape of a key sounding in the lock.

'Nick!' She beat against the door with her fists. 'Don't you dare...'

'Pete will come and let you out in half an hour when he gets back from the station. In the meantime, just simmer down, will you?'

Simmer down! She'd give him simmer down. Abby kicked the door hard, yelping as her bare toes impacted on the wood.

'Stop that. Just stay put and drink your coffee. This is for the best.'

'Okay. Okay, I'm calm now. There's no need to lock the door, I won't follow you.' Like hell she wouldn't. But raging wasn't going to make Nick open the door and she had to find a different tactic.

'Good. Sit tight, Abby.' A quiet bump on the other side of the door, the way the wood moved slightly against her cheek, told Abby that he was leaning against the door. Her fingers moved to where his cheek would be. Somehow she knew that it would be there, pressed against the door, just like hers was.

'Nick. I...' If she said it, she'd only scare him away. If she didn't, she wouldn't get another chance.

'Me too, Abby. But it's time for us to wake up now. Go back to where we came from.' There was a sound, a movement on the other side of the door, and then silence. Abby listened for the sound of his footsteps, anything that meant she still had something left of him, but the carpet in the hallway robbed her of even that.

CHAPTER FIFTEEN

SHE contemplated sliding down to the floor, curling up in a ball and crying. Or screaming, beating her fists uselessly against the wood. She wanted to do both, but neither of those options was going to do any good. Abby took a deep breath and grabbed her phone.

'Louise, I need your help.' Abby cut short the lazy acknowledgement of her call, and explained quickly what had happened. She left out the bit about Nick having just walked away from everything that they had together and concentrating on the fact that he needed help and seemed determined not to take any.

'Okay. Are you dressed yet?'

'No, give me ten minutes, though, and I'll be ready.'

'Fine. You grab a shower and get dressed and I'll find Sam. Wait there for us.'

There wasn't much choice about that one, and Louise had already cut the call anyway. Abby made for the bathroom, moving at speed.

Ten minutes later, almost to the second, there was a knock at the door. Abby lunged for the doorhandle, twisting it roughly.

'We can't find any spare keys in Reception, and Mrs P.'s disappeared off somewhere. But it's okay, Sam's coming for you. Can you open the window? Watch out for the ladder, and be careful you don't knock him off.'

Abby whirled round as a scraping sound at the window indicated that the ladder was being put into position. Muffled voices sounded outside, and she ran to the window, checked that Sam wasn't outside yet, and flung it open.

Sam was halfway up the ladder, a couple of his crewmates at the bottom holding it steady. It seemed that Nick had an all-out mutiny on his hands.

'Sam.' Right now she could have kissed him. 'Thank you.'

'Can you climb down?' Sam looked ready to throw her over his shoulder.

'Of course I can.'

'Right-oh.' Abby stumbled backwards as Sam levered his bulk through the window. 'Is your handbag and laptop all you need to bring?'

'Yes. I don't have time to pack. Can I give you a ring later about my things?'

'Sure thing. You climb down first, and I'll follow.' He gave a wave to the men below, and helped Abby out of the window, making sure her hands and feet were securely on the ladder. 'Don't rush, there's plenty of time. Move one hand or one foot at a time.'

Abby grinned at him and began to climb down. The ladder was rock steady, held both at the bottom and by Sam at the top. She made the ground, and Sam followed quickly, her bags thrown over his shoulder.

Louise appeared, walking briskly around the corner of the building, bundled up in a fleecy jacket. 'Let's get a move on, then.' She was obviously in charge of this particular operation. 'Come on, Sam, we don't have any time to waste.'

Nick walked into the steel and glass reception area. It was almost deserted, apart from the receptionist, who was talking intently to a young woman who had her back to him. A blonde, corn-coloured plait, which fell down her back made his stomach lurch uncomfortably. Today everyone looked like Abby.

He'd done the right thing. It had almost ripped his heart from his chest to leave Abby behind like that, but this wasn't her battle. And somehow he'd managed to overcome the almost unstoppable urge to let her help him fight it. It was enough to know that she'd wanted to. He needed to let her go now, while he was still strong enough to do so. Before he descended into the chaos that now seemed to await him.

The woman at the reception desk turned and he almost dropped his briefcase. She was dressed in a fitted red jacket, with a black skirt and high heels. Carrying a leather notecase under her arm. Looking more alluring than any woman had a right to look. Abby.

Abby. How had she got here? She'd been locked in her room. Pete had been instructed not to let her out until he got back from the station, and then only if she promised not to leave the premises. There was only one other train that could have got her here in time, the one that had left an hour after the one he had taken.

It was impossible. Just as the red of her lips was impossible. The silky sheen of her stockings and the way that the light glinted in her fair hair. She was business-like, sexy and completely gorgeous, all at the same time. No man in his right mind could resist her.

'What the hell are you doing here?' He took her by the elbow and muttered the words into her ear.

'Ah, here he is.' Abby turned to the receptionist with a smile.

The receptionist nodded. 'I'll call and let them know you're here, Mr Hunter. It'll be a few minutes as you're early, so please take a seat.'

'Thank you.' Nick managed a smile and almost frog-marched Abby over to the group of chairs furthest from the reception desk. He waited for her to sit down and pulled one of the leather chairs up close to her seat. 'I repeat, Abby, what the hell are you doing here?'

'I came to give you something.' She was as brittle as a dry stick, holding herself tense and straight. He wanted to hold her, have her melt into his arms. He wanted to get her out of here, so that he could do what he had to do.

'What?'

'This.' She opened the briefcase and drew out a folder, laying it front of him. Nick stared at it. 'This is my account of what happened the night before last. I wrote it on the train on the way down from Cumbria. There are accounts from all of the crew, as well as statements about their confidence in you. They emailed them through to me and I printed them out when I got home.' She gave a little smile. 'While I was changing into my battle gear.' She knew how good she looked. She'd done it deliberately, so that no one would question her right to be here. So that he wouldn't send her away.

'Abby.' He longed to pick the folder up, take hold of what he was offering him. With an effort of will he kept his hands still, fingers gripping the arms of his chair. 'It doesn't make any difference. It's not a matter of the way things are, it's how they look. The people I'm meeting know what happened. They don't need to see this.'

'Well, that's fine, because it's not for them. It's for you.'

'I can't do this, Abby. I can't put my own interests above those of the fire service.'

'No one's asking you to. If you believed in yourself as much as the people who work for you do, you'd know that staying and fighting was the best thing for you and the service. That you've got far too much to give to just turn and walk away.' She reached forward and twitched at the cover of the folder and it fell open. 'Read any page, Nick. They all say the same.'

'Don't, Abby.' She was picking away at the whole fabric of his being. Everything that he believed in. He didn't have time for this now, he'd already made his decision about how he was going to handle this meeting.

'It's done, Nick. I'm here. This folder's here. You can turn your back on all of it if you like, but you'll be doing a gross disservice to the fire service and to yourself.' Her lip was quivering.

'Mr Hunter…Nick Hunter.' The receptionist's voice drifted across the cavernous space. 'You can go up now.'

'Can you give me one minute, please?' The receptionist nodded and Nick turned back to face Abby.

'Just take it, Nick. Put it in your briefcase.' She pushed the folder towards him with shaking fingers. 'You don't need to read it. It's enough to know what's there, inside it.'

Maybe it was. If only he had more time. Half an

hour, fifteen minutes even. Nick picked up the folder
and stowed it safely away in his case. 'Abby...I...'

'Go, Nick.' She summoned a smile. 'Good luck.
Make the right decision.'

He couldn't bear to look at her any more. Couldn't
stand to even think about what she was offering him. It
would kill him if he started to believe that he could be
the man he wanted to be, and then had those illusions
shattered. Better stay with what he knew. He nodded in
her direction, hardly even looking at her, then turned
and walked away.

Abby had accepted coffee from the young woman at
the reception desk. She'd read the leaflets stacked in
the display rack and done a mental fire-safety audit on
her flat. Twenty questions, eighteen of which she could
answer satisfactorily. If nothing else came out of today,
at least she would make sure to test her smoke alarms
regularly in future.

She'd done what she'd come to do, but she couldn't
leave. Maybe Nick would need someone to speak up
for him in the meeting. Someone who had been there,
and who could refute any of the claims that the papers
might be making.

'They won't be long now.' The receptionist gave her
a smile. She could hardly have missed Abby's agita-
tion, the way that she had been hard put to sit still for
the last hour and a half. 'You'll be able to see when
they come out.'

'Where?' Abby scanned the large, double-storey reception space. A maze of glass and steel, which gave
the impression that the building was transparent, without it actually being so.

'Up there.' The receptionist pointed to a mirror set above the entrance doors. 'You can see the entrance to the conference room.' The mirror was angled so that the area next to the lifts was clearly visible from the reception desk. 'It's handy for me to keep an eye on what's going on down here and up there at the same time, without getting whiplash.'

Abby grinned, staring up at the mirror. As if in response to the intensity of her gaze, the conference-room door opened. 'Look. Is that them?'

'Yeah. Looks as if it's gone well.'

It did. Nick was standing with three other uniformed officers, and all four were talking. Laughing. Nick seemed taller somehow, his body language quite different from when he had walked away from her. As if a weight had been lifted from his shoulders.

'Do you think so?' Abby needed a second opinion. This was too important to believe the evidence of her own eyes.

'Commander Evans is staying to talk. That's always a sign that he's happy with the way things have gone. Your friend should be too.' The receptionist gave her an encouraging nod and it occurred to Abby that she probably knew exactly what this meeting was about, along with everything else that went on in the building. Abby looked upwards again and saw Nick shaking hands warmly with what seemed to be the senior man. This was no polite *sorry it didn't work out* handshake.

'He'll be down in a minute.' The receptionist was looking at her intently, and Abby realised that she had tears in her eyes.

'Yes. Look, I have to go. Will you tell him…tell him I said good luck.'

'But he won't be a moment.'

'Yes. Yes, I know. Will you tell him, please?' Abby knew all she needed to know. Nick had taken the step. He'd believed in himself, and he'd fought for his future. Louise would let her know the details, all in good time. For now this was everything. And she wasn't going to spoil it by hearing Nick's goodbye. She'd heard that once today and it had broken her heart. She knew just how much she was capable of, and what was coming next was way beyond that.

'Sure.' The receptionist shrugged.

'It's important.'

'I'll tell him. No one gets in or out of this building without me knowing about it.'

'Thanks. I appreciate it. Really appreciate it.' Abby turned and almost ran out of the building, her high heels echoing on the granite floor. Harsh. Lonely. She was going to have to get used to that.

CHAPTER SIXTEEN

ABBY smoothed her hair and took a final twirl in front of the mirror. She looked fine. A little gaunt maybe, but she hadn't been eating. She hadn't been sleeping much either, but twenty minutes in front of the mirror had taken care of the dark circles under her eyes.

Her first instinct had been to rip up the crisp, white card that had arrived in the post, begging the pleasure of her company on Saturday evening at a party to be held in celebration of the success of the swim. She didn't want to see Nick again. He'd turned out to be the one man that she'd been looking for. The one she could trust. The one she could love. She'd been so afraid that he might break her heart, but Abby had gone ahead and done that all on her own, by wanting things that Nick had told her he couldn't give.

But Louise had called, begging her to come, then Pete and then finally Sam, who sounded as if he was reading from a prepared script and who awkwardly used all the entreaties that Louise had already fired at her, and in addition just happened to mention that Nick wouldn't be there, because he was out of town on a trip in connection with his new job. Abby had put him out of his embarrassed misery and accepted. It would be good to see everyone again.

The doorbell went at exactly six-thirty. Opening the living-room window, Abby saw Louise at the main door to her block of flats and waved down to her, before picking up her handbag and the soft woollen wrap she'd chosen in case the evening became chilly and going downstairs.

'Hey, you look nice! Give me a twirl!' Louise squealed her approval as Abby spun round, the red, filmy skirt of her dress floating out around her legs.

'You look lovely, too.' If the last three weeks had taken their toll on Abby, they'd obviously been kind to Louise. She'd lost the deep hollows under her eyes and was healthy and beaming. 'Are you sure we're not a bit overdressed for the fire station?'

'No, I said to wear something nice. And it's not exactly the fire station. There's some land at the back, adjoining the park. We use it to park the truck on when we have open days.'

'Oh.' That didn't sound much like somewhere you'd dress up for either, but Louise seemed to know what she was doing, and Abby obediently got into the car when Sam jumped out to open the door for her.

Everything became clear when Sam drew up outside the fire station, letting the women out and driving away to find a parking place. Louise led Abby along an alleyway to the side of the main buildings, which opened up into a large courtyard at the back, walls on three sides to separate it completely from the working area, the fourth side open to the empty parkland beyond and cordoned off with ropes. There was a marquee, and the trees that surrounded it were decorated with lights, which were just beginning to sparkle as dusk approached.

'See. Looks pretty, doesn't it.'

'It's beautiful. I never would have imagined that this was here. Who did all this?'

'Oh, some of the guys.' Louise was walking briskly, almost dragging Abby behind her. She slowed when she got near the marquee, opening the flap and motioning Abby inside.

The tent was ablaze with light, a temporary floor laid on the uneven ground, tables along one side for food and drink and soft music coming from speakers slung in the canopy. And it was completely empty. Abby whirled around to find Louise, only to see that she had disappeared.

'Hey, Abby.'

Light suddenly dawned. Abby took a deep breath to steady herself, and turned round slowly to face Nick.

He looked fantastic. A crisp, white shirt, open at the neck, with a dark suit. It didn't take much to make Nick look delicious. In fact, it didn't take anything at all.

'I think I've been set up.' She took one cautious step towards him. Another self was screaming at her to turn and run, get out of there, but she ignored it. Her heart was already shattered into little pieces. What more could he do to her?

'Yes, you have.' His body language was tense, like a coiled spring, but his dark eyes were full of tenderness and he was smiling. He seemed happy to see her.

'So there's no party?'

'It starts at eight.' He shrugged. 'And I am, as you can see, here. I have to be really, it's my party. Something to say thank you to everyone.'

'You did all this?'

'Yes.'

They'd run out of things to say already. Suddenly Abby didn't want any more of this. She turned away from him, but he was at her side in one swift movement, his hand laid gently on her arm. 'Don't go, Abby. Please.' A pulse beat at the side of his jaw.

'There's nothing more to say.' She was close to tears. 'I don't know why you went to such lengths to get me here, Nick. Nothing's changed. We said that we wouldn't carry on with things after we got back to London, and we haven't.'

'I have something to say. And since you won't take my calls, I had to resort to subterfuge. Did you listen to any of my messages?'

'No.'

'Didn't think so.' Her admission had hurt him, however much he seemed to have expected it. She could see her own anguish reflected in his eyes.

'What's the point, Nick?' Abby was trying to be angry with him but she couldn't. All she felt was grief, tearing at her.

'I just want a minute of your time, Abby. Just one minute, to say what I want to say, and then you can do whatever you want. I'll take you home if you want to go, or you can stay here until the party starts.' His gaze left her face, slipping downwards to the floor between them. 'If you want me to beg, that's fine. I can do that for you, Abby.'

She took pity on him. 'One minute. And then I'll ask Sam to take me home.'

'Yeah. If that's what you want I'll go and fetch him. In a minute.'

'That's what I want.' Why couldn't he have left things alone? 'What is it you have to say?'

'I've been thinking hard about this, Abby.' He hesitated. 'Won't you come and sit down with me?'

'No. It's okay, go on.' Sitting down was unnecessary. And he'd already wasted five seconds of the time she'd promised him.

'I'm not afraid any more, Abby. I can have a cup of coffee in the morning or go for a beer after work, without feeling that it's the first step on a slippery slope that's going to lead to addiction. I'm not my father and I never will be.'

'I know that, Nick. You proved it, when you believed in yourself and fought to keep your job.'

Some of the tension left his face, and the suspicion of a grin threatened the corners of his mouth. 'You believed in me, Abby. You gave me the chance to be the man that I want to be. With you by my side I could have faced anything—a shattered knee, a broken career— and still not given up. I know I've made mistakes in the past, and that I don't deserve you, but I do love you and I want more than anything to make you happy.'

'What?' Abby caught her breath so quickly that she started to choke. His arm shot around her waist and he led her to a chair, sitting her down and fetching her a glass of water.

'Here. Are you all right?'

Abby flapped her hand impatiently at him. 'No. Not really.' She took a few sips of the water.

'Heimlich?'

'Don't you dare.'

'Tissue?' He reached for his pocket.

'No, thanks.' She didn't care about the tears that were streaming down her face. 'Nick, are you quite mad?'

'Don't think so. Although you're the medic, so I guess you'd be better placed to make a call on that than me.'

'But you said…you said you didn't want…'

'I know. I was a fool.' He pulled a chair over and sat down opposite her, leaning forward, his elbows on his knees. 'You're the best thing that ever happened to me, Abby. And we're good together, can't you feel that?'

She felt it. Abby reached out, letting her fingertips graze his cheek. How she'd longed to touch him again. A shiver ran through his frame, and he grasped her hand, holding it for one more precious moment against his skin. 'I'm afraid, Nick.'

'That's okay, Abby. It's okay to be afraid but please trust me. You were there when I needed you, let me be here for you now.'

'I do trust you, Nick.' Maybe, just maybe he could achieve the impossible and make this right.

'I won't ruin this chance by leaving you in any doubt about how I feel. I love you. I want to marry you. I want us to live together and have children. I want you to never stop telling me when you think I'm in the wrong, because I trust your judgement better than I do my own.' He pursed his lips. 'Mostly.'

'Mostly!'

'Well, no one's right one hundred per cent of the time. But you were right about me. You saw me for what I was, made me change, and the man you changed me into fell in love with you. Then you left.'

'I thought…'

'I know what you thought, Abby. You thought that I

was strong enough to stick to what I said about splitting up with you when we left Cumbria. You overestimated me there.'

'Maybe I underestimated you. Maybe I underestimated myself. I didn't think that either of us could change.' She smiled at him and he caught his breath, his face reflecting her own hope.

'But we could. We did. Giving in to you, Abby, was the best thing I ever did.'

'You put up a fight, though.'

'So did you. I loved every moment of it. We're both fighters, Abby, but there's no malice there, we fight because we care. Then we make up.' He leaned forward and kissed her forehead lightly. 'I particularly love that part of it.'

'Yes. Me too.' That sweet surrender. His and hers, together. 'I…I suppose we could buy a house. Or live in yours. My flat's not really big enough.' Tentatively she began to allow her imagination to explore everything he'd offered her. All the delights.

'We'll find somewhere that we both fall in love with. Somewhere that's big enough for the family we'll make together.'

His face was alive with possibilities. Dreams that Abby thought she'd dreamt alone. 'I'd like that, Nick. A family. You'd make a great father.'

'We can get started on that just as soon as you'd like.' A hint of mischief glinted in his eyes. 'I'll always love you, Abby. And I'll always do my best to protect you and make you happy.'

It was all or nothing now. She was going to try for it all. 'I'll always love you too, Nick. You've already made me happy.'

He fell suddenly to one knee in front of her, taking her hands in his. 'Will you marry me, Abby?'

'Yes, I will.' She answered the question as swiftly as it was asked. Why delay? She didn't need to think about it, she knew it was what she wanted, and she couldn't wait a moment longer.

They were both grinning like children, hardly ready to believe what they'd just done. Finally Nick seemed to remember something and felt in his pocket. 'I've got a ring. If you don't like it…'

'I don't think there's much chance of that.' If he tied a piece of string around her finger it would be the most precious thing in the world to her. Abby held out her hand, noticing that it was trembling, almost as if it didn't belong to her.

'We'll see. Close your eyes.' She felt his hands on hers and a little thrill of anticipation coursed through her as his lips brushed her cheek. Then she felt him slip the ring onto her finger.

'It's beautiful, Nick.'

'You haven't opened your eyes yet.'

'Yes, I know. It's beautiful.'

He laughed and then he kissed her. Soft, tender, with that delicious edge of longing that told her that there was more. That there would always be more. She clung to him, and he held her tight.

'Open your eyes, sweetheart. Please. Make it real.'

Abby opened her eyes, staring up at his face. Then she looked at the ring on her finger. A gold band, with a fire opal flanked by two diamonds.

She caught her breath. 'It's…it's the most precious thing I've ever owned, Nick.'

'I wanted to have something to give you if you said yes. But if it's not what you want, we can change it…'

'I love it. It's beautiful.' She wrapped her right hand protectively over the fingers of her left, hugging them to her chest. 'Don't you dare try and take it back.'

He chuckled, all assurance again. 'I won't take it back.' He took her hands in his, kissing her fingers. 'Would you like to dance? Or I have a crate of champagne stowed under the table if you'd like something to drink.'

'Yeah? Pretty sure of yourself, weren't you?'

He laughed. 'Not really. I was going to save it for the next try if you said no.'

'There was going to be a next try?'

'You don't imagine I was going to give up, do you?'

Abby laughed. 'Now you come to mention it, no, I don't. Thanks.'

'What for?'

'Not giving up on me.'

'I'll never give up on you, sweetheart. Dance with me.'

It was five to eight and Louise and Sam had drunk more than enough tea with the crew on duty in the ready room. Nick still hadn't phoned, as agreed, to let Louise know the coast was clear.

'Perhaps she's killed him.'

'Nah. Nick knows when to duck.' Sam grimaced.

'We'd better go and see. Before everyone else starts to arrive.' Timekeeping was a habit. The tent would start filling up at the stroke of eight.

Louise hurried downstairs and across the uneven ground to the marquee, Sam in tow, along with Pete and his wife, whom they'd met on the way. Carefully twitching at the tent flap and peering inside, she flung it open, laughing delightedly. Nick and Abby were together, on the dance floor, swaying in perfect time to the slow beat of the music, as if they were the only two people in the world.

Nick looked up, his face shining. 'What are you waiting for? Help yourself to champagne. I'm—'

'Engaged.' Abby was glowing too. 'We're both engaged right now.'

* * * * *

So you think you can write?

It's your turn!

Mills & Boon® and Harlequin® have joined forces in a global search for new authors and now it's time for YOU to vote on the best stories.

It is our biggest contest ever—the prize is to be published by the world's leader in romance fiction.

And the most important judge of what makes a great new story?

YOU—our reader.

Read first chapters and story synopses for all our entries at
www.soyouthinkyoucanwrite.com

**Vote now at
www.soyouthinkyoucanwrite.com!**

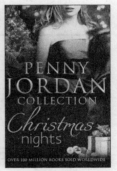

The World of Mills & Boon®

There's a Mills & Boon® series that's perfect for you. We publish ten series and, with new titles every month, you never have to wait long for your favourite to come along.

Blaze

Scorching hot, sexy reads
4 new stories every month

By Request

Relive the romance with the best of the best
9 new stories every month

Cherish™

Romance to melt the heart every time
12 new stories every month

Desire™

Passionate and dramatic love stories
8 new stories every month